Kreka—Barbarian Queen

Joan Silva

Library of Congress Catalogue Card Number 99-091454

Silva, Joan
Kreka—Barbarian Queen

1. Attila the Hun   2. Barbarian Conquests   3. Turko-Mongol People
4. Hungarian History   5. Rome and the Barbarians

ISBN 0-9675169-0-0

Copyright © 1999 by Joan Silva
All rights reserved. No part of this publication may
be reproduced or transmitted in any form or by any means
electronic or mechanical, including photocopy, recording, or otherwise,
or stored in any information storage and retrieval system,
without prior permission in writing from the publisher.
First published in 1999 in a hardbound edition by
Black Scarab Press, Oak Ridge, Tennessee, USA.

Cover and Illustrations by Carol Minarick
Design and typography by Marilyn Schuette

Printed by Black Scarab Press, USA

Printed and manufactured in the United States of America

First Edition, 1999

Kreka—Barbarian Queen

Joan Silva

Acknowledgements ... iv
Author's Note ... v
Historical Persons ... xi
Glossary ... xiii
Introduction ... xv
Prologue: Before Our Story Begins ... xvii

Part I: The Great Khan ... 1

Part II: The Great Wars ... 143

Epilogue: After Our Story Ends ... 323

Acknowledgements

I am thankful for the generosity of many manuscript readers. My grateful thanks especially to: Herr Doctor Heinrich Benedikt, Professor of Austrian History, University of Vienna, deceased; Dr. Robert Peters, Professor of Victorian Literature, Emeritus, U. Cal., Riverside; Sylvia LeMoyne, retired Art Editor, The Idaho Statesman; David Chorlton, poet and artist; Sonya Eichler, artist; Dr. Thomas Carlson, Corporate Research Fellow, Emeritus, Oak Rige National Laboratory, Oak Ridge, TN; and Professor J.K. Anderson, Department of Classics, U. Cal., Berkeley; for their technical, historical, and writerly advice. My thanks also go to Carol Minarick, an artist in Oak Ridge, TN, for her thoughtful and beautifully crafted illustrations that appear on the cover, endpapers, and part titles; and to Marilyn Schuette, Oak Ridge, TN, for the layout, design, and typography of this book.

I thank my second husband, Ralph, for his unending patience, understanding, and support. And, lastly, my thanks to the late Otto Maenchen-Helfen, without whose monumental scholarship in art, language, and archeology, this book could not have been written.

I am forever grateful for the time, interest, and help so many people have given me in completing this project.

Author's Note

Kreka was queen, and partner, to her husband, Attila, the Hun. Theirs is a story of hardship and war in a time not unlike our own. It was a world of tumult and upheaval. It was, however, no more fearful than our own. Chemical, and biological, warfare, the 'ethnic cleansings' and massacres of our century, are ample evidence that our world is neither secure, nor humane. The potential blessings of our time can turn on us with the press of a computer button. In the personal, and human, sense, the violent and turbulent time of the Huns holds a certain attraction compared with the 20th Century.

Certain aspects of Hun culture surprise us. The role of women is one surprise. Like their counterparts among the Mongols, Hun women were free, productive members of their group. Though scarcely Amazons, they were skilled horsewomen, fighters, and hunters. They grew up handling hunting bows, and bringing down game. Wellborn Hun women owned property, bequeathed it to whomever they wished, presided over their own flocks and wagons, and lived in their own yurts. Women ordered, and managed, their lives independent of men. If they were inclined, they took an active role in the community. In placing wellborn Hun women beside other women in history, we might think of Eleanor of Aquitaine, or the Empress Dowager of China, and not come too far off the mark. They were free agents, capable of rule. It is in this context that we encounter Kreka, Queen of the Huns, and Attila, King of the Huns.

Certain events in the story of humankind bring sweeping changes. One such watershed was the battle of Adrianople in 478 A.D. In this battle the Goths annihilated two-thirds of the Roman army. The Huns had been pushing the Goths from the north. This had placed the Goths in the way of the Roman army. The importance of the Huns in the north, and what this portended, the Romans had not bothered to ascertain. Even separating Huns from Scythians was too much to ask of a people bent on demonizing barbarians. The barbaricum being everything beyond the borders of that far-flung, strained fabrication called Empire.

The fact that political borders are meaningless to mounted armies capable of driving more than fifty miles a day under physical conditions so adverse we can scarcely conceive them was ignored by the Romans. Politics, religion, and the natural desire of cultures to cohere, conspired to make Pagan and Christian worlds opposing forces. Christianized accounts of the fifth century were not overly concerned with truth. What could not be used as theological or political propaganda was cursorily consigned to the bin of falsehood. Since Huns had no written language until the time of Ghengis Khan they had no defense against spurious accounts of their lives. In their zeal to win the public relations war Roman apologists for Empire became shameless liars.

In 441 A.D. Attila, with his brother, Bleda, crossed the Danube from the east and captured the small market town of Margus on the west bank. The greedy Bishop of Margus, not content with looting Roman tombs, had made the mistake of going after Hun tombs. Terrified by Attila's troops thundering at the gate, he bartered the city for his life.

Margus was the opening shot: Attila, and Bleda, invaded the interior, driving as far as Constantinople. The Romans sued for peace, and in August of 443 the Emperor Theodosius' set his annual tribute to the Huns at 2,100 pounds of gold. Here, the known history of Attila, warlord of the Black Huns, properly begins.

The mysterious Black Huns appeared as dramatically as a meteor. They were headquartered between the Carpathians and the Urals, in what became Eastern Hungary and Southern Rumania. This was Attila's heartland. Here, more than fifteen hundred years ago, his main ordu (warcamp) flourished, and disappeared as suddenly as it had come. There are yawning holes in the history of the time that archeology has not been able to fill, but a fortunate windfall covers the years between 441 and Attila's death in 453.

We know that in the summer of 445 Attila, for reasons best known to himself, had his brother, Bleda, assassinated. He then reigned alone, being given, among many lurid names, the Roman title dominus talius mundi, God Over All The Earth. His territory reached west to east, from Southern Germany to the Volga and Ural Rivers; north to south, from the Baltic, to the Danube, the Black Sea and the Caucasus. A glance at an atlas shows this to be a vast, contiguous land empire. His rule is a tiny blip on the screen of history, but he ushered in a final period of barbarian onslaughts against the Late Roman Empire. He made a significant contribution to the demise of Rome as imperial and colonial superpower of the ancient civilized world. It's been speculated that had Attila won a decisive victory at the battle of Châlons in 451 the Christian religion, along with Rome, might have gone the way of the dinosaur. This could well have led to Asian domination of Europe.

Attila, the Scourge of God, as he was called, was a plain man. The Romans, inveterate lovers of pomp, gave him fearful titles, but he gave himself no great airs, contenting himself with the title KhaKhan, Khan of Khans; King, King of Kings. To the practical warlord of a practical people this was enough. He left it to others to apply their own names to him.

He was a man driven by private passions, beset by visible warts of personality (his drinking bouts were legendary), and under continual pressure from his people for gold. There was an innate common sense about him. He wore no crown, dressed and ate as a common person, was loyal to his friends, and decimated his enemies. In short, he was all too human, and though his personal tastes were simple, he was not a simple man. Attila was as sophisticated as any ruler forced to juggle the psychologies and tactics of armies, and the needs of a fractious people in a tough world. He sensed, as did Ghengis Khan after him, that there was an insidious danger in horse cultures attempting to fit themselves into the ways of the sedentary peoples with whom they came in contact.

So long as they had open land at their backs steppe warriors were able to appear and disappear at will. Space was a safety net vital to hit-and-run tactics of hunter-horsemen, and land loomed large in their psychic security system. Much that has perplexed history about Attilanic Huns and other transhumanic peoples is explained by their mystical reverence for a heartland. Cultures such as Rome's, habituated to the practice of empire building as a response to military victories, have puzzled over this reverence. When they might have reached out and consolidated an empire the Huns retreated to the far plains, snatching defeat from victory. This was the Roman view. The Hun view of such retreats differed from that of Roman historians who wrote their story.

If we look at Attila minus the overlay of hatred and scorn synonymous with his name, we see that Rome used a time-honored tactic to blacken him. They imbedded tales of bizarre cruelties within a basis of fact. Fantastic tales were told of the Hun armies. They were savages, crazed killing machines. We must discount these tales. We must not paint Attila with the same brush that tars truly aberrant personalities. Unspeakable epithets belong legitimately to Adolph Hitler, but not to Attila. He was an ordinary warlord who, more than most of his kind, was successful in what he set out to do. He was a man of his time and his people. He ruled and fought as warlords do, and as such men go he was notably levelheaded.

Before Attila's time, during the millennia of great migrations across High Asia, precursor Turko-Mongol peoples, whose origins are still in dispute, moved slowly westward over an area spanning longitude and latitude, not miles. They lived as closely, as indigenously, with the land as human beings have ever managed to do. They had no equal as hunter-warriors until the coming of Ghenghis Khan 800 years later. Ghenghis, however, secured his "empire" by embracing debatable philosophies of Empire. This, Attila never did.

Following the murky period of migrations Hun culture barely changed for fifteen-hundred years. But, during the 20th century the old culture was essentially erased. Now, only tiny pockets, such as the area around the Tuva Basin, inside the borders of what was once the

Soviet Union, remain. Very little about these people is certain, but no less an authority than the late Professor Otto Maenchen-Helfen believed the Attilanic Huns were a strain of Turko-Mongol people connected to the Mongol hordes of Ghengis Khan. I agree with his view. I see the two as distant cousins existing together on the branches of a family tree stretched wide in time as well as space.

At the beginning of the fifth century the Attilanic Huns were the opposite of an imperial culture. They were a semi-nomadic, raiding band people. In this, they were akin to Native American cultures. Like Native Americans they saw plunder as part livelihood, part excitement. Loot was for their own use, for their own clans. If the Huns were to tap into the riches of Empire, a force fit for the task had to be carved from a chaos of competing tribal needs. For this, a talented, charismatic leader was necessary. Such a warlord was Attila. Rome, of course, had a vested interest in promoting a picture of him as the Antichrist. His armies were the armies of judgment day. They were Gog and Magog, storming down out of the barbaricum. Romans concocted a picture of brigands without tactics, lacking in sophistication and military expertise. Huns were simply a bunch of dirty, undisciplined bandits. It suited Rome's purpose to top off tales of insane orgies and bloodletting with visions of whirlwinds and fiery thunderbolts. Such a debased, and terrifying, picture of Huns during the time of Attila was as false as the glorified picture Rome painted of herself. Against a barrage of self-serving Roman reportage the true story of Attila and his people was buried. If few facts were known about the land, and the people, of the Scourge of God, everything could be imagined—and was.

This is an historical novel, not a historical record. Much that was taking place at the time is ignored, or does not pertain. It is, nonetheless, an attempt to correct the Roman record. Along with accounts of Attila's military exploits (the only context in which most ever hear of him) this is a more down-to-earth view of the Huns and their lives. Insofar as modern scholarship, and meager archeological evidence, allow, I would direct our imaginations into more fruitful channels than barbarian-hating historians of their time, or latter-day interpreters,* have had any desire to do.

Noting the egregious lies, and the errors, in our own recent history books, we would do well to refine our notions of war in the Dark, and not so dark, Ages. In our century the grisly truth of war has been made clear. We have been forced to let go of romantic scenarios we once imagined. We can no longer speak of grand armies marching forth to grand wars without getting a laugh. This reality check must be doubly applied to a past that saw common warlords knocking heads with empires. In picturing Attila, and his time, we look through a tunnel clouded with the dust of war and decimation. And, we remind ourselves, that the 20th Century is a time not so dissimilar.

How will the future see us? The smallest shifts bring daily changes in our views. We have only recently emerged from a time when all predators were placed under the label "bad actor," condemned as so much prehistoric ooze. With growing understanding of the principles of ecology, we now allow animal hunters to take their place in the common hierarchies of life. The same view can be taken of Attila's time. He was a natural-born predator, and plunder was his game. If neither pure, nor simple, he was fitting to his time. He was an integral player in his ecosystem. From a vantage point, fifteen-hundred years down the road, we can see a man who lived, fought, and died, much as every man.

The world of the Huns has come to us by way of dark innuendo, and legends unsupported by fact. To correct the story we need only follow the trail of evidence, and reap the benefits of intelligent hindsight.

---

* The late Professor Maenchen-Helfen being an exception.

Historical Persons

Attila: Khan, King of the Black Huns; a charismatic warlord.

Kreka: Khatun, Queen of the Black Huns; Attila's first wife, his advisor, partner, lover.

Ernac: Youngest son of Kreka and Attila; heir to Attila's kingdom.

Onegesius: Attila's Prime Minister; loyal advisor to the Khan.

Edecon: Renowned Hun warrior, tutor to Ernac, loyal friend to the Khan.

Berichus: Attila's Chief Lieutenant in the field.

Aëtius: Roman General; one-time guest/hostage of the Huns, Attila's archrival.

Dengezic: Kreka and Attila's second son; a natural warrior, plotting to gain his own army.

Ellac: First son of Attila and Kreka; an inept soldier, weak leader.

Ebnedzar: Attila's son by a second wife; half-brother to Ellac, Ernac, and Dengezic.

Uzindur: Attila's son by a second wife; brother of Ebnedzar, half-brother to Ellac, Ernac, and Dengezic.

Priscus: Roman historian; visitor to Attila's encampment.

Adamis: Kreka's chief steward; in love with his Queen.

Anatolius: Roman ambassador to the Huns; an able negotiator.

Eskam: A holy man, mystic, astronomer, and shaman; loyal to Kreka.

Eskayar: Daughter of Eskam, one of Attila's many wives.

Pope Leo I: Leader of the Christian Church at Rome; later St. Leo.

Valentinian III: Western Emperor of Rome.

Honoria: Sister of Valentinian III.

Ildico: Burgundian Princess; Attila's last wife.

Glossary

Anda: a friendship bound by a blood oath.

Bisman Tngri: spirit who bestows bodily (warrior) strength.

Buqas: a bull calf; name of Attila's grandson.

Etugen Eke: Great Earth-Mother.

Eyase: a young hawk removed from its nest for training.

Great Tngri: all-encompassing heavenly being.

Managan Tngri: spirit of the hunt and of animal life.

ongghi: free-floating spirits who wander the earth looking for vulnerable targets. These spirits visit disaster, illness, and death on their victims.

Optimate: a close associate; personally chosen guard or confidante.

Ordu: main camp of a group of Huns; especially a main war camp.

Passager: a young hawk able to hunt on its own (falconing term).

Qara buden: the common people; those not wellborn.

Quiriltai: a gathering of Hun clans for the specific purpose of selecting a leader of all the clans; *i.e.*, a Khan.

Qumys: fermented mare's milk.

Solidi: gold coins used by Romans during the Byzantine period (singular, *solidus*).

Strava: mourning ceremonies on the death of a leader. Characterized by slashing of cheeks and wild riding, death is celebrated by lamentations mixing grief with joy.

Tamga: a personal brand, used for identifying the owner of horses, goats, and cattle.

Touman: for many centuries, the basic military unit of steppe armies. Organized by the decimal system in units of 10, 100. 1,000, and 10,000 warriors, was the major fighting unit.

Yurt: tent dwelling used by Turko-Mongol peoples throughout central Asia; a wood lattice covered with skins and thick, pounded felt.

Introduction

In 445 A.D., Attila had his brother, Bleda, killed and became Khagan, Great King, sole ruler of the so-called Black Huns. In the short eight years following Bleda's death Attila's military machine invaded Roman territories both East and West. He rocked the Empire, and his war against Rome culminated in the infamous Battle of Châlon at the Catalaunian Plains.

On that frightful day at Châlon Attila led a formidable force, an army of more than 250,000 Huns and Germanic tribesmen, against equal numbers of Romans and Visigoths. Châlon was one of the bloodiest, certainly one of the costliest, battles Roman forces ever fought. The armies engaged in mid-afternoon and the fighting continued into the night. Groin deep in gore vast armies stood locked in combat, quitting only when exhaustion made it impossible to continue. Through the night the groans and screams of the wounded resounded; the next morning bare tatters of grand armies stood facing one another across a plain stacked high with corpses. None had the strength to go on. At Châlon in one afternoon and evening more than 100,000 men died, the outcome of the crucible at Châlon was indecisive — but crucial historically. Had Attila prevailed the course of history could might well have changed, the spread of Christianity been checked, and the Western world, our world, been just one more casualty of the day's grim harvest. This singular confrontation remains one of a handful of battles considered critical in military history. Attila, The Scourge of God, very nearly transformed the direction the civilized world would take, and more than fifteen-hundred years later the disquieting presence of this remarkable barbarian king haunts our imaginations.

Before Our Story Begins

"What have you heard this morning, Ku?" Kreka said.

She turned on her couch and cast a sleepy look at the early light. Attila's first wife watched Ku spooning broth into the hungry mouth of the girl-child, Bahka Beki.

"Ruga Khan's steward summoned Bleda and Attila to his pavilion long before dawn," Ku answered.

"Ruga is truly dying, then," said Kreka. She flung back her quilts and sat upright.

"I fear so, mistress. He cannot last. His breath barely flutters in his chest."

Ku abruptly set the child on the floor of the yurt. The baby set up an indignant, earsplitting wail.

"Hush, child," Ku scolded, "I've no time for your tears today."

Kreka smiled and reached to take the toddler in her arms. She mouthed ageless soothing sounds, crooning into Bahka Beki's ear and stroking her plump, teary cheeks until she was quiet.

Ku hitched up her outer furs with a flourish. Scooping quilts and carpets up in her sinewy arms she stripped Kreka's sleeping couch and hauled the bundles outside. She gave the large quilts several hearty shakes and attacked the small carpets, stick flailing until a fierce cloud of dust came up around the entrance to the yurt.

"Ku! Enough!" Kreka admonished, waving the stinging fog away.

"Sorry, mistress," Ku said shortly, "but this must be done and it must be done now. The brothers will return to their yurts soon. They'll be in no mood for any nonsense to do with turning out carpets."

"You're right," Kreka said.

Attila's wife lowered the sleeping child onto the carpet and turned to her dress. She began plaiting her waist-long sable hair, deft fingers winding smooth loops onto her head. As she worked her hair into place she reviewed the coming days.

Had she truly seen the mourning ceremonies for a dead leader as a youngster? Or were the pictures that flashed in front of her built from the vivid tales of old women? Kreka wasn't absolutely sure, but the images didn't seem a mere fantasy.

When Ruga's spirit passes into the land of eternal seasons, she thought, there will be *strava*, paradoxical mix of weeping and merrymaking, untrammeled grief and wild celebration. She asked herself if she had been part of this ritual of mourning. She knew she had witnessed it; it would be impossible to imagine. And it would be the same for a Khan as for a simple warrior. It would be more intense, but it would be the same.

At the death of Ruga Khan warriors would ride out shrieking, hacking off their hair knots and howling their lamentations. Blades would score their cheeks until blood poured. When the hours of lamentation and bloodletting were done Ruga Khan would rest in his finest battle gear. The lines of mourners would file past the body as it lay on its dais. The Khan would lie serene in the center of his silken tent while hundreds of mounted warriors circled the open pavilion. Hour upon hour the men would ride chanting, reciting funeral dirges, honoring the black standard of the Khan.

The warriors would recall his exploits, tell and retell the stories of Ruga's life. Women would wail, their voices mounting in thin crescendo over the chanting of the men. Hearing their mothers, the children, too, would take up the keening. Memory flooded back to her. Kreka's mother had carried her to the burial rites for common warriors when she was only a baby, and she remembered weeping with exuberant abandon. The camps of the northern tribes did not mourn silently, nor did the camps of the Huns.

There would be detailed preparations. The Khan's body would be bound inside three coffins; first iron, then silver, then gold. Gold and jeweled weapons would be strewn over his coffins, swords and bows from the trappings and ornaments he had plundered and used during his lifetime.

The chief shaman would do his divining. He would read the haruspice; the scarrings on the burnt shoulder bones of a sheep. From his reading of the bones a burial site would be chosen for the tomb of his warlord. The body of Ruga Khan would be carried in darkness to his grave. He would be buried in a place of desolation, his coffins rooted in the hollow beneath a cairn of unmarked stones.

In this hidden place death would come to those who accompanied the body. After their lord was safely in his tomb a rain of arrows would cut them down. His servants and his favorite horses would sleep with Ruga Khan. Advisors and friends would join Ruga in death. Men and horses would ride with him and common people, the *qara buden*, would serve him. The living would provide even their lives to the dead Khan. Food, drink, and companions would be on hand to greet Ruga in the land of eternal seasons. The chief shaman would offer himself up voluntarily so that the Khan did not face his new life without spiritual solace.

The ceremony of sacrifice was a lesson as well as a mystical connection, a reminder that it was taboo to disturb a grave, or to rob it of its treasures. The fate of these unfortunates would be the fate of anyone who desecrated the spot.

Bleda came suddenly to Kreka's mind. After the dust from Ruga's burial rites has blown away, Attila's brother will be full of himself, Kreka thought. The very image of Bleda was distasteful. He would be everyplace at once. He would be loud, silly, obnoxious.

Attila would sequester himself, speaking little and planning much. Through the time of bereavement negotiations critical to the future of their camps would go forward, and Attila would be at the heart of these negotiations.

Much meat and *qumys*, much food and drink, will be needed for the ceremonies in Ruga's camp, Kreka thought. No, she corrected herself quickly, this will no longer be Ruga's camp. It will be the camp of Bleda Khan, and of Attila Khan. And she was first wife of one of these Khans.

Her head was still heavy from sleep and Kreka had difficulty winding her heavy plaits and tugging them into place. She anchored the hair with combs of silver and turquoise, and surveyed herself in the polished copper.

The face that stared back at her was not delicate. Kreka's bones were large, her jaw definite. Strong, catlike eyes gazed at her from the mirror. As the years passed her features would become heavy, but today they were clear and fresh. She was quite beautiful enough to greet her reflection with pleasure.

"I'm going to check my herds, see that the grooms have kept the foaling mares separate from the stallions," Kreka announced.

She gave one last raspy cough, jumped to her feet, and bolted the thick, suffocating air of the tent. The granules Ku had set flying left Kreka scarcely able to breathe. Taking the excuse she fled the camp and strode toward the field where her favorite gelding stood grazing.

Among thirty or more horses was the large white horse called Lotar. He was from breeding stock out of the northern clans, Kreka's father's clans. Attila had given Lotar to his wife as a gift the spring their first son, Ellac, was born. Lotar would soon be seeing his fourteenth summer. He had become a magnificent specimen and Kreka made certain he had special care. Because he called to mind her first days with Attila, Lotar was precious to her.

Kreka recalled perfectly the events of the day Attila had swept into the northern village with the force of a dark, southern whirlwind and carried her from her father's tents. It seemed impossible to her that fifteen seasons of fat horses lay between that day and this.

The day he came for her she had been bursting with romantic longings. He had entered her father's yurt with a brief command; she should ride out with him at once. When she heard his voice all the conventional fears that beset young brides fell on her head. She wanted the adventure, and the freedom, of marriage, yet she was fearful. Kreka was afraid of finding herself committed to a man who was not her equal. What if Attila wasn't the outstanding man she imagined him to be?

But he had been that man. He had been that and more. She found him more than a leader to be reckoned with. He was a partner with appetites to match her own. As his phallus pierced her body on their wedding night, plunging to the mouth of her womb, love pierced her heart. Kreka had been ready for him, oiled and eager, on the marital couch. With a strength and erotic creativeness that took him aback Kreka gathered Attila inside her. Her lust was not easily slaked, and she led him through a fragrant, carnal dream. Kreka was mistress of every lascivious artifice, striking wanton poses Attila could not have imagined on his own.

"Kreka, my wife," he had whispered to her.

His body welded itself within the twists and arches of female spasm and he ached with the impact of this lovemaking. By morning his member was tender, wilting when he would have had it respond yet again. When he had called her "wife" for the first time, he'd said, "The promise in your eyes was no lie. You are a leopard of a woman, Kreka, a witch-woman."

"Am I?" she said, lightly. "Well, you can count yourself fortunate that it isn't my grandmother who shares your marriage bed. I come from a line of women who make boast that they can put the strongest man in his grave. Until the day she died my grandmother was a mare with a good appetite. She loved nothing more than the thrust of a man inside her secret folds."

"You're not altogether your grandmother," he said slyly. "Your buttocks are ample as a mare's rump, but your heart is that of a leopard."

She laughed.

"Don't laugh," he'd said. "Your eyes blaze red in the firelight, and flecks of blood dance in their darkness. The shaman has told me that the fires of love are dangerous for me."

On their wedding couch Attila had spoken truth to Kreka. He had taken as his first wife an unusual animal, a woman of vigor and independence whose imprint would stay with him for life. And he had foretold the circumstances of his death with uncanny accuracy.

"Your imprint is on me, Kreka," he told her. He was embarrassed to say it, that this intense connection had been forged between them in one short night.

"You've branded me with your *tamga*," he said. "Kreka's mark is seared into my flesh."

In their early days together he gave his wife astonishing passion, but his was outstripped by her own. It was physical alchemy that first bonded Kreka to her husband, though later she found other reasons for her affection. When the hypnotic magnetism of a hot, young male had faded, she found Attila to be a man of honor and good sense. These traits she respected. Attila, the man, she accepted without reservation from the beginning, but Attila, the warrior, she could not fully accept. She had set herself against his powerful military ambition, and this lay like a heavy stone on her spirit. She loved this man, and she feared for him daily.

Kreka threw her shabrack on Lotar's back and rode clear of the herd. It was impossible to concentrate on Ruga's death. Her mind went to Attila, and to the coming days.

There were questions. Would there be a *quiriltai*? Would the clans gather? Would one of the brothers be chosen Khan over all? Would Bleda, fool that he was, try to take the title by force. Attila had only recently come back to their camps for good. His time as hostage among the Romans was over, and the Roman, Aëtius, had left his place among the Huns to return to the west. Would Bleda now be witless enough to fight Attila for the kingdom? Did he imagine himself capable of ruling alone as King of the Huns? Would Ruga divide the territories between the brothers, or would he name one of them outright?

If Ruga did not choose between them, a wasteful time of jostling one another for the top would ensue. Bleda was oldest, that dictated a certain protocol. But the future turned on what action the sinking warlord took in his final hours.

These were but a few of the questions that rode with the first wife of Attila as she cantered along through the greeny morning haze. This was the Hun homeland, and in the early summer of 434 A.D. the lush plains northeast of the Danube seethed with Hunnic life. The grasslands were alive with women, children, warriors, and the thousands of animals that were their lifeblood.

While Ruga Khan, uncle of Attila and Bleda, lay dying in his silken pavilion, the war to the west slogged dispiritedly on. The campaign was mired down for want of leadership. It lacked the zeal the Romans had come to expect of Hun warriors. It had been thought the Khan would prevail easily but an unexpected reversal halted the army, and on the heels of the stalemate that followed, the Khan's heart and liver failed him.

Today Ruga's legs were but swollen lumps. His abdomen was painful to see. It fell pale and distended, in a sagging pouch. His belly was that of a pregnant ewe on the eve of giving birth to twins.

Two soldiers entered Ruga's tent. The Khan's first wife brushed past them. As she left Ruga's side she turned her face away to hide cheeks streaked by tears.

Bleda and Attila were ushered in by the chief steward. He signaled them to silence. The motionless figure resting on its deeply carpeted couch stirred and a serving woman touched Ruga's hand. She offered him a bowl of drugged wine. He refused it. A fresh convulsion attacked him and he retched uncontrollably. The company that gathered around him stood in polite stillness.

When his choking subsided the Khan saw his nephews standing inside the doorway. He motioned them to come to him. They approached the couch and knelt, one on each side of his bloated frame. They extended their hands to his.

He took Attila's hand, grasping it in his calloused fingers, and then reached for Bleda's. Years of working the rough hide reins had turned the skin of their hands hard as horn, and the palms scraped one against the another.

Ruga looked at Bleda. He muttered feverishly, and Bleda heard the words he had waited to hear.

"You will take the large territories to the north," said Ruga slowly. "This is the birthright of the eldest son of Mundzucus. Rule the Goths and Gepids strictly. Make use of them. Get the Acatiri under control. Finish this war with the Romans."

To Attila he said, "You, youngest son of Mundzucus, will take your birthright here in the homeland."

Bleda and Attila bent to kiss his hands. Ruga made a sign to his steward and the man moved to Bleda's side. He whispered, and Bleda rose. Triumph flashed across his face, a malicious grin aimed in Attila's direction.

Bleda turned to leave and Attila rose to follow, but Ruga's fingers gripped his nephew's hand urgently.

Stay," he said, his breath rasping.

Attila knelt obediently.

"Listen, Attila," the dying man wheezed. "No matter who sits on the throne in Rome, Aëtius rules. Watch out for him. I trusted him too far. I was too soft. Don't make my mistake. Leave nothing for the enemy to use against you. Burn the earth behind you. One final thing. Bleda has nothing in his belly. Yet he must have his birthright, to deny him would breed more ugliness in him."

Attila nodded.

"You, Attila," Ruga whispered, "have the wolf in your belly. This has been seen in the signs, and in your unbending will. The exchange of hostages is complete. You learned from your time among the Romans. Aëtius also learned in his time with us. Take care. Wrest the northern rule from Bleda as soon as you are able. When you see a vision of his death in the omens — act!"

Ruga turned his eyes onto Attila's and held them there.

"Your father, Mundzucus, was your grandfather's favorite. If he had lived, Khan Balamber would have named your father Khan. Mundzucus should be saying this to you, Attila. Instead, I am here to say it. What I say was your father's wish. It was Khan Balamber's wish. You are the chosen."

Again Attila nodded.

"The clans are yours," Ruga murmured.

The sufferer let a weary moan. His mouth worked and he fought for breath, trying to master his failing body.

"The gods gave you a soul of iron," he said, finally. "Your path is clear. The mark of the warlord is yours, use your power wisely."

Death rales started in Ruga's chest. The rub of sodden pleura radiated through the *yurt*, resonating hollowly. His chest heaved, his grunts deepened. Ruga's formidable struggle was ending and the stench of suffering surged around his couch.

Attila neither spoke nor moved.

He sat beside Ruga patiently. As Attila sat watching Ruga's face the sun fell. He lifted his eyes to see the monstrous clot of burning matter drop through saffron and scarlet waves at the far horizon. The afterglow spread slowly until a sallow reflection on Ruga Khan's lifeless face was the only light in the pavilion.

Attila reached to touch Ruga's cheek and closed the blind eyes.

"Life ends," the young Khan said. He stood looking down at his uncle.

"Had you been able," he said to his uncle's body, "you would have prevented my coming to power. You would not have chosen me to rule, but it was Bleda or me. You had no choice, Ruga, and you obliged me after all. I do not resent your ill-will. Toward the dead my heart is forgiving."

"May your bones rest undisturbed, brother of my father," he said.

Attila, grandson of Balamber, son of Mundzucus, left the tent. Ruga's dying was something he would not forget.

The Great Khan

1

This morning I helped the cart boys take down the supports of my yurt as we loaded wagons for the move to summer pastures. The sun was uncomfortably warm and memories of Attila came rushing at me. I recalled another day when the sun had been unseasonably warm.

I thought of Attila, of how he loved this rolling earth. His joy in being alive was unrestrained. Fine weather, or foul, Attila loved life in all its parts. Even in his worst tempers there was an energy about his presence that made one want to be with him.

I dropped the willow stave I was holding, stopped to look at the earth, and saw tiny shoots of green were pushing through the thaw at my feet. The time of lean horses has passed. The season of growing pastures is here, and the days of high grass and fat horses will go too quickly. They always do. Now that my life is given up to duty there is small time for pleasure, or freedom for unplanned moments. I am more independent than I was before Attila died, and much more independent than before Ernac became the Khan's official heir. But there are ever fresh problems to resolve, and I'm expected to answer to the people's needs.

I do not complain by saying this. My life is one of privilege, a life many would envy. My steward handles my affairs, and there are servants and hangers-on. I have more help than anyone needs. It's not right that Ernac's wife be engaged at menial chores, but I often feel useless. I enjoy a job like this. Putting my back into familiar work, pulling poles and loading them on the wagons is satisfying, and common satisfactions have become a luxury for me.

My thoughts wandered on unfocused until a passerby grabbed my attention. An old soldier noticed the long jagged scar on my forearm and he stopped to remark on the welt.

"What happened there? Such an odd scar," he said, obviously curious as to how I had come by it.

I smiled at him, glad to have the chance to tell my story. It was as if no time had gone by. I could see myself as I was the day it happened. I saw my hands on my reins, felt the movement of my gelding under me. As clear as the face of the man in front of me I could see that day.

"It was a Hun arrow did it," I said. "I got this the summer Attila was named Great Khan."

The man nodded, encouraging me to go on.

"It was the summer of the war against the Acatiri," I said, "the summer Attila's brother, Bleda, was killed. Remember how the Acatiri pestered our camps until Attila rode against them?"

"I do," the man said eagerly. "I remember when Bleda was killed. I fought in that war against the Acatiri myself, and the Khan was a soldier formed of thunder and fire. He was magnificent. I'll never forget the warrior he was then."

"You know how it was that summer," I said. "Tell me what you remember about the Khan, of how he was then?"

But the man would say no more. If he had any critical thought about Attila he didn't voice it. He turned away on some errand of his own and disappeared toward the center of camp.

Twenty-five battle seasons have come and gone since then but I can still smell that earth, see the waving grass, and hear the voices from that day. I marked it as the day my life truly began.

Attila was not yet Great Khan. I was yet a child, though I thought myself grown. I knew nothing, but thought that I was wise. The wound I suffered that afternoon, and the night of fever that followed, cut through the protective web covering the mind of a child. The crisis brought me awake and forced the woman in me to open her eyes. That day is fixed in my mind. I feel the texture of it, see the expressions on every face, just as I see the new, green shoots coming up from the ground in front of me.

Kreka had sent me out to dig roots. I had only a sharpened stone and I was wishing for a metal digger. The stone was cumbersome, and prying out the thick roots took more muscle than a young girl has to call on. I'd gone off in a hurry that morning and now I was stuck with the awkward tool.

The sun was overhead before my sack was full, and I made up my mind the next time Kreka sent me out to gather something for her medicines I would have a metal digger. The root I was after that day is called valerian. Kreka makes good use of it, I will say that. Valerian brings healing sleep to the wounded, and it relaxes men unable to rest from muscles overtaxed by pulling the bow.

Except for the frustration of using the stone digger the morning passed pleasantly, and I enjoyed being out away from camp. But I was already becoming muscle-sore, and as soon as my sack felt heavy I was more than ready to quit.

I jumped eagerly onto Red Atagha's back. The ride was my reward for a morning of hard work. I love to ride dozing under a bright sun, moving with my horse across clean, open land. It was early in the season of fat horses and the new grass brushed my legs in soft strokes. The air was uncommonly still. There was no whining of wind, only the shrill call of a distant hawk and the singing of nearby larks. The snuffle and roll of my gelding was a sedative for my tired limbs, and I quickly nodded off.

As it turned out I was too comfortable for my own safety. How long I'd been sitting in my shabrack asleep I don't know, but a sound startled me to my senses and for a few moments I didn't know where I was. I pulled to a stop, my heart jumping. Raucous shouts were coming from behind the hill in front of me. I froze. And then, very near, came an explosion of voices. I was certain I'd slept myself into an early death.

I prayed my head would clear. An arrow abruptly sailed past me, and I ducked down behind my gelding's neck to listen, trying to grasp what was going on. As soon as I could make out a few words I knew I'd wandered into a skirmish between Attila's men and a stray band of Acatiri. Just over the brow of the hill I could hear the warriors yelling challenges to one another. The whang and whistle of bow and arrow rose over their cries. The men were dangerously close.

How these Acatiri had penetrated so near our camps I'd no idea, but one thing I knew, they wouldn't get away. Attila's men had ridden out looking for Acatiri more than two days ago after a scout reported activity in the area and he has found them. Bad luck for them. He's cut off their escape. And bad luck for me coming upon them at the height of the fighting.

I was afraid I would be trapped, unable to move, and even more that I might be seen. I looked around me for an escape and saw a narrow gap between the rocks ahead. I thought to circle wide and slide through. Though the hill was teeming with men if I made it through the rocks I had a clear ride to camp.

I lashed Red Atagha to a froth and made it through the defile, but not before a stray arrow caught me in the forearm. I paid no attention at first, intent as I was on getting myself to safety. Then I saw the blood gushing. I was still several miles from camp and knew I had to keep riding, but a terrible weakness came over me. The arrow had gone deep and I was losing blood in a stream. I slid from Red Atagha's back to rest for a moment. He waited, sensible horse that he is, until I managed to get back on. By then my head was so foggy that I left it to my gelding to take me home. The next thing I heard was my own voice wailing above Kreka's angry pronouncement.

"One of our own arrows," Kreka was saying to Ku.

Then, "Hush your bellowing, Beki," she exclaimed harshly. "Your screams will attract the soldiers."

Beneath the exasperation in her voice there was concern.

"Soldiers," Ku muttered. "They don't know what they're doing."

"Kreka," I whimpered, "my arm hurts. I can't stand up."

"Hush, child." Kreka's hand came down over my mouth, pushing me down into layers of felt and carpet. "Suck in your breath, girl. Suck hard. Clamp your mouth on this leather and don't scream."

I tried to do as she said, though I was frozen with fear. My teeth stretched over the leather ball Kreka had stuffed in my mouth and I couldn't breathe. Beneath the piles of dusty wool I was blind and half-deaf. Still, I felt the surge coming up around us, a confused welter of human voices and the screams of horses. The din made a cruel thunder, a pounding in my head.

The fighting had entered the camp. Arrows were whining and swords chopping at the air. I could hear the crunching when metal found bone, and I flinched each time I heard a blow. Such a grunting and thrashing of men and horses was whirling about the yurt that it was impossible to say where the battle was going.

Kreka will save us, I thought. I blessed her, put myself in her hands, and lost consciousness.

"Eieyiee! Nothing but war, nothing but war," my adopted mother was grumbling as I came to myself.

"There will be no fresh meat today and the pot holds nothing but three-day-old mutton," Kreka muttered.

Knocking her meat hook viciously against the copper cauldron, Ku, and Kreka with her, cursed the men. They loosed a storm of curses against the shaman, Teb-Ogatai, against Bleda, and most of all against Attila, who had blessed Kreka with another son to bury during the middle of the last cold season.

"No use for them in this world. No use. Sour mare's milk, the lot of them. Vulture bait," Kreka said.

Then she snorted out Teb-Ogatai's name. No doubt she was conjuring a pain-filled, private vision of the shaman. Far out in the eastern desert her imagination was staking him spread-eagled in the sun. She saw him, helpless, watching for the first black wings to darken the sky of the Gobi over his naked body.

"Oooh — poor Teb-Ogatai," I thought. I could imagine the revenge Kreka would have on the shaman for his part in this day.

I remembered what she'd said only the day before. "Stupid little men playing at their stupid little games," she'd said. She was unaware that a sharp-eared young vixen was listening.

Kreka believes these present skirmishes are ill-advised. She maintains they're not for territory, not even for gold. She believes they stem from the hatred Attila harbors for his brother, Bleda. Attila has bad feelings for his elder brother that push him to gain the upper hand. But Kreka also blames the shaman, Teb-Ogatai, for inflaming Attila. He encourages him by foretelling good fortune for these raids. Teb-Ogatai tells Attila he is invulnerable.

And, then, she blames Bleda himself. She says he is weak, listens to fools, and allows himself be used. Bleda knows Attila will do nothing to him directly. He would never strike his brother with his own hand. The bond between Attila and Bleda is sacred. They are blood *anda*, and to kill him would be a sacrilege. Attila will have one of his lieutenants strike the blow. No one would ever accuse Attila of being cowardly. It is loyalty to tradition that holds his arm, a loyalty stronger than his desire to settle with Bleda personally.

I kept trying to breathe slowly. Kreka is nearby, I thought, I can rely on her sharp wit. If I should survive to womanhood I will be like her. Tender in love, Kreka is toughness itself in hate.

She has been my wet-nurse, teacher, protector and companion. She took me into her yurt on the day my mother was taken in a raid by tribesmen from the western regions. My mother was rumored to be Kreka's half-sister, a rumor she denies. When she took me in she had two lambs to nurse, Ernac and myself. The Khan's youngest son and an orphan girl were suckled with the same milk. When I was weaned Kreka rolled fresh dough in balls and dipped them in meat juice to tempt my nipple-hungry mouth. It was she who swept out of nowhere to carry my flailing arms and legs from the path of Attila's troops when he and Bleda were still fighting as one army.

In those days, more than six seasons past, Attila was in Kreka's yurt at every dusk. When he was not at war or hunting he could be found in her *yurt*. How they whispered, and how they laughed, slapping at one another over the sleeping rugs.

They met when they were very young. At that time Attila was out raiding with his father, Mundzucus, and Kreka was still in the tents of her father, a chieftain in the north. Mundzucus bested Kreka's father, and after his defeat her father would hear no talk of a marriage between his favorite daughter and the young son of Mundzucus. Kreka has said her father was a man poisoned by grief over the untimely death of her mother in childbirth. He was a man who lived only for war and for revenge on his enemies.

When Mundzucus and Attila came to her father's tents to settle on terms for peace between them Kreka's eyes found Attila's. A flame blew up between them. They didn't forget the pledge they made in their exchange of glances. Two battle seasons later Attila and five of his picked men took her from the tents of her father. This mock kidnapping was what Kreka had been praying for. Truly, they are well-suited, and though Attila has many wives she is his first, and still his favorite.

Their first son, Ellac, is now a general in the north, and their second, Dengezic, rides at Attila's side. Ernac, the youngest living son, is too young to ride with the men, but he is the son chosen to succeed Attila. As the youngest he is called Keeper of The Camp and Hearth. He will inherit the homeland. More importantly, it's foretold Ernac will save the kingdom of the Khan after Attila is gone.

Today the welfare of this camp depends heavily on Kreka and her sons. Because she has borne sons, and because of the influence she has with Attila, Kreka is greatly favored. She has the pick of the herds, the most promising geldings. She has the strongest young men to pull her wagons and tend her flocks. She has three sons who have grown to manhood, and other sons who were buried as babies, and she has never lowered her eyes to her husband. She is a proper Hun woman. For this Attila respects her.

Kreka came out of the tradition of northern tribes beyond the Great Sea where the women are as fierce as the men. She has drawn the blood of more than one man in battle. The southern women are weak and lazy in Kreka's eyes. They don't know how to choose fresh pastures, or rear orphan lambs. Of course, she exaggerates, for among our people only the toughest men and animals survive. I've heard that settled people, the city-dwellers, look down on the rough life we lead. If this is true, they do not understand our ways. We know what a good life is, and where it is. True, we are tough, but is the soft life of a city better than ours?

Attila spits on the filth of the towns. He sees the press of so many bodies so close together as loathsome. Being forced inside a city — Attila calls it the small death — is like being in a prison. It is a world of narrow streets and dank rooms where sun never penetrates, a world without warmth, with no felts or carpets to comfort weary bones. Trapped in such a place a Hun will fall ill with the wasting sickness.

Air…I needed air…was the noise of battle fading or was I near to losing awareness again?

I felt Kreka's touch on my arm.

"Bahka Beki. You can come out. The fighting has passed to the west of us."

I looked on Mother Kreka's face out of my puffy eyes and once more I was safe.

She smeared my wound with the heavy salve that heals all wounds except those that are poisoned. She bound my arm and fed me broth and bread. Ku offered me meat but I wanted none of it. I was weak from bleeding, and now I was safe I wanted to sleep once more.

I listened drowsily to the women moving about the yurt, and heard Kreka remove her heavy outer skins and busy herself with dressing her hair. She dismissed Ku and I knew she expected Attila to come to her. When I heard the felts lift in front of the door I closed my eyes and feigned sleep.

"How is it, Kreka?" he asked.

"Shhhh," she admonished him. "Beki has been wounded by one of your careless bowmen. It wasn't a treated arrow that caught her but the child was terrified, convinced she was bleeding to death."

He growled and stepped over to look down at me.

"A sorry little creature," he said. "But you will make her into a worthwhile woman. She could be first wife to Ernac. What do you say, Kreka? Would that please you?"

His hand brushed my cheek and I breathed in the savor of horse and clean male sweat. The smell of him was that of a man who'd come from a leisurely morning ride instead of from battle.

"Don't try to distract me," she said.

He grunted indifferently.

"You love war too much, Attila," she went on. "War, wine, beautiful women, and nursing old grudges, these are your weaknesses. Between them they will finish you. What lunatic need do you have that even now you must plan another campaign, conquer another kingdom? Tribute from the Eastern Emperor is in the thousands of pounds each year. You ride and raid where you wish. What do you want, Attila, that you don't have?"

He turned away from me to look at her and I opened one eye. Kreka's face is never more beautiful than when she speaks with strong feeling, and it was lovely now.

"Bleda is dead," he said.

She didn't drop her eyes, but stared straight back at him with a look I didn't comprehend.

"Ssss-sss, ...," Kreka's tongue curled itself against her teeth.

"Now there is only you," she said. "There will be a *quiriltai* and the vote of the Assembly will be for you. Now Attila is KhaKhan, King of the many clans. The iron of his sword will rattle the Dome of Great Blue Heaven. The very earth will shake beneath us and the fires of battle will rise up to the skies. But take care, Attila, don't challenge the old gods as the Romans have done. The Gods are fickle, they might desert us, never to return."

He didn't answer and she turned away. She filled a steaming wooden bowl with pungent mutton and watched him settle himself on the quilts. She handed it over and waited until he filled his belly before she spoke again. Sitting cross-legged in front of him she watched him eat. His fingers lifted juicy chunks two at a time and stuffed them in his mouth. The yurt was filled with great gulping noises until his bowl was empty. Belching, he held it out for more.

No word passed between them. They have a fine sympathy of spirit, each knows what the other feels and thinks. Attila knows Kreka doesn't approve of what he's planning, and he knows she's angry that the skirmish flowed into our camp today. Also, she knows what happened to Bleda. Without a word of explanation from Attila, she knows. I'll ask her what happened, and she'll tell me when she's ready to speak of it.

"Listen, Attila." Kreka took away his second empty bowl and seated herself once more in front of him.

"Your precious Teb-Ogatai;" she began, "that false shaman and foreteller of mighty victories, that holder of sacred secrets, has secrets of his own. He thinks more of his own power than of your welfare. I don't trust him. He is no real shaman. He's full of bluster and blow, and lately he's been fawning on Ernac as if he were the boy's mentor."

Kreka's eyes examined Attila's face.

"You are a Khan, now to be Khan of Khans," she said softly. "It is up to you to say who will influence and who will not. My spies tell me Teb-Ogatai was seen near the far northern borders when he knew you were off in the west. You should find out what he was up to there."

"Serious talk, Kreki. But I'll look into it."

"Yes, you will," she said, "because I am ever one with you. I speak openly because our fate is one. Since we were first together the haruspices have shown it."

"You are too wise, Kreka, and I am only a foolish warrior," he said. He chuckled and grabbed for her waist.

"I will think about this," he said. "Now let's enjoy one another. No need to make your face so dark. Your cheeks should bloom as the sun over morning grass. Your eyes are too beautiful to darken them with scowling."

Kreka can't resist Attila when he flatters her, and when I heard her laughing along with him I knew there would be no more serious talk tonight.

In lovemaking how does Kreka take care of herself, I thought briefly. How does she do what she says women must when they want to stop a baby from starting in their belly? I must remember to ask her about this. She's always lecturing me on how important it is to know women's lore. Since I will one day bear babies I must give more thought to these things. At that moment, however, the rugs were warm and my eyes were heavy.

I knew no more until a thin line of light hit my face and my eyes flew open. Had I slept the night through? I must have, I thought, for Kreka was up and humming, folding the sleeping quilts.

I moved my arm to test it and was overjoyed to find I had no pain. I was exultant. What I heard Attila say about marriage plans for myself and Ernac had cured me overnight.

Attila would be amazed to hear how Ernac and I talk to each other when we're alone. We are very close, and have decided on our own that when we have our own tents I will be his first wife. I'm well-fitted to be a partner to Attila's heir. I have more than twelve seasons of experience in the camp, and I ride and hunt as well as Ernac. Game falls to my arrows as easily as to the arrows of any boy my age.

I'm skilled with camp animals, and proud to say I saved a pair of orphaned lambs last winter. I warmed them with my body until I was able to run down two ewes who had lost their own sucklings. Kreka showed me how to make a ewe take an orphan by rubbing the scent of her dead one's bloody skin on it. Once the live lamb begins nursing her it's as if she has no memory of the dead carcass.

These weeks of growing pastures and growing herds are the best of the season. The skirmish with the Acatiri yesterday meant nothing. Kreka is right, yesterday's conflict was a silly squabble. What bad luck it would have been for me to die in that minor clash.

Minor as it was, there will be consequences for yesterday's fighting. I know what Ernac will say. He'll say his brother, Ellac, should be disciplined for bad governing. Attila's oldest son is responsible for the tribes in the north. Ellac acts as his general there and the Acatiri general, Kuridach, had the best of him yesterday. The Khan's son shouldn't have let the fighting come this far to the south.

The Acatiri are always pestering Attila. Ernac says they're like ants crawling over the ears of a raging leopard. Their forays hone Attila's warriors and give them practice that keeps them sharp. Weak neighbors are good training for the important wars in the west.

Now awake, I felt no weakness, none of the trembling that had overcome me the night before. I told myself that recovering so easily was a sign that I should forget about yesterday and ride out on Red

Atagha. And I will if I can get away from camp, and from Kreka. She clucks at me when she sees me sneaking off for a ride.

"Always out on your gelding," she says. "You really must spend more time in the yurts with the women. Before you can have your own tents you have to learn to weave and sew sleeping quilts," she scolds me.

But I come back at her. I can't see that there's much to learn, I say. I can do what's necessary. I can cut meat for the cauldrons. I can turn stiff hide to soft leather. Working the hides is as tedious as digging roots, but I'm strong and capable. As for weaving and embroidery, all that's needed is patience. The rugs and quilts Kreka values so highly are for comfort and pleasure, not for need. I have more than enough time to learn these things.

There will always be another battle, time enough for handwork when the wagons are on the move. Between battles we play. These are the times of idling and taking pleasure. Between battles we eat, drink, and listen to stories of adventures beyond the Great Sea. We play crazy jokes on one another, jokes only Huns can appreciate. And we give thanks to the gods.

I mean to take advantage of these days. Now Bleda is out of the way, Attila will do exactly as he pleases, and war pleases him. There's no power that can influence him to change. When he makes up his mind to something no one can sway him. I've seen this in the way he handles his wives and sons.

Ellac confers with Attila, and Dengezic rides at his side, but they wait on his words. Neither his sons, nor his many women, have found the key to unlock Attila. Only Kreka knows him. She has some magical way with him. Sometimes it seems Kreka herself is a shaman. She has great knowledge of herbs and great healing powers, and she seems to know what Attila is up to before he acts. I tease her and call her a shaman. She doesn't answer, but she doesn't deny my words.

Attila's own generals don't know him as Kreka does. When Attila learned that Aëtius, now a general for the Western Romans, had left the home he had with us, no one except Kreka dared approach him. No one mentioned Aëtius name in his presence. It's true Aëtius came to our people as a hostage, but he was treated with respect. His *yurts* were placed next to the tents of the wellborn. He was given every freedom and every comfort and treated as one of us, as if he was born a Hun.

After his term as hostage was over Aëtius turned on us and went over to the Romans. He now fights against Attila. When Attila learned of this betrayal he hunted alone for many days. He came only to Kreka's yurt for comfort, and that only once in two moons. I heard Ellac tell Dengezic that Attila hates Aëtius more than he hated Bleda. But Bleda was never a match for Attila, and Aëtius is clever as well as brave. There's been no battle between these two, but it will come, of that I'm certain.

"Bahka Beki. You lazy girl. The sun is far up."

Kreka's words meant the end of my thought-wanderings. Letting me lie abed for pity of my wound was a kindness, but now she has inspected my wound and seen there is no poison in it I will get no more special treatment.

And that suits me well enough. I can hear Ernac outside yelling for me, urging me out to my shabrack and my horse.

On such a day, with my energy fast returning, I have no desire to do otherwise.

2

    Bisman Tngri was smiling on me and the strength of eagles lifted my limbs.

    I jumped on Red Atagha's back. I named him for the god of the horses and his name has given him good fortune. From birth Atagha has been a warrior. He has never faltered from weakness, never startled in fear. He comes of wellborn stock out of Attila's personal herds and he is truly worthy of a great lord. Attila's war-horse, Bahgatur, is from the same stock. Red Atagha can best even Ernac's gelding in a race. The god of the horse has found a home in my three-year-old.

    I was in such high spirits that I cried out jubilantly as we cantered off. Ernac gave me a black look. My dear friend is serious-minded. He never fails to let me know that he disapproves of my mad outbursts. I don't let Ernac dampen my enthusiasms. I indulge my nature and let my head go where it will.

    Thoughts of Attila often fill my head. There is a memory from a morning two seasons past that is especially dear to me. I'd been spying out the steppe eagle and the peregrine at their nesting that spring. I knew just where the nests were and which birds had laid their eggs. I was pleased to be able to tell my foster-father where to find them and I hoped he would ask me to show him where the fledglings were hidden. Attila is an avid falconer. I knew what pleasure it would give him to see the nests.

    Near the nests the falconers wild-catch young birds as soon as they can fly. They never touch the *eyases* who cannot yet make the air. *Eyases* are for novices, but we watch where the nestlings huddle from season to season, for here we find the small game needed for training birds with the lure.

I didn't have to wait long. Attila was ahead of me. He had already spotted several likely nests, and one morning just as early birdsong hit the air he appeared at Kreka's yurt.

I heard Attila and his groom and I ran out to them before they could dismount. I babbled at them, prattling on about what a promising day it was. Attila, of course, knew what I was hoping.

"Well, shining yellow eyes," he said, "it is time for us to ride out to the nesting sites."

His own eyes glowed with anticipation. Attila loves falconry almost as dearly as he loves war. His trainers had been out to prepare the blinds, and we rode on ahead. The trainers had covered a fresh kill under a large bow net, and there we settled to watch for a *passager* to return to claim her kill.

Soon a plump peregrine fell into the net. She came so fast my eyes didn't catch so much as a shadow above us before she dropped. With a flick of his wrist Attila pulled the waiting cord and the bird was his.

She was a lovely creature. Her pale, speckled breast glistened, her dark eyes glittered, as she tore savagely at the net. Her powerful wings struggled mightily to gain the air. Attila was delighted with her, and he had good reason to be. She was a vigorous specimen. It turned out that Attila and this falcon shared many wonderful hours together. He named her Aruvqan, the pure princess, and for several years she was his favorite hunting companion.

All was going well, and then I ruined the morning. I lunged forward impulsively to touch the marvelous bird through the net, but before my hand could reach her Attila's arm struck mine. He knocked me onto my haunches. Attila's hunting knife came down on the neck of a blunt-nosed viper coiled close to the net. It was over in a flash. The spring sun had brought the viper out to sniff the kill and I had failed to see it coiled there motionless.

"What a find!" cried Attila. Laughter billowed cheerfully from his vast chest.

"Here," he roared, "here, little one, take the head as a gift for Kreka. Maybe she won't scold us for idling away the morning."

He picked up the severed head and shoved it in my face.

"Kreka will make use of the venom in her healing arts. Here, I give it to you," Attila said, pushing the dripping head at me. I was trembling. I couldn't take the thing in my fumbling fingers. Attila must have seen that I was frightened for he quickly withdrew the seeping stump and stuffed it in his game bag.

"A successful morning, eh, Beki?" he said. "The sun is high. It's time we were back in camp."

He nodded at the trainers who had followed us and signaled them to bring the falcon. He tied my horse behind his, swung me up in front of him and we rode silently. He was whistling, while I was trying to control my shaking. When I overcame my panic and found the voice to speak I tapped Attila's chest and turned to look into his face.

"You saved my worthless life," I croaked. "From this moment I swear my loyalty on the head of Mother Kreka. If you are in danger I'll come through fire to save you."

Attila looked down at me. How he managed not to laugh I don't know. He must have been bursting with merriment at the seriousness of my pledge, but when he answered his words were respectful.

"You are young to be swearing an *anda* oath of loyalty, but it is pleasing to me that you wish to swear the oath," he said. "Your heart has told you it is right and you have offered your pledge. I accept your pledge. Consider me your blood *anda*."

He drew an arm around me and whipped his horse to a run. His face was alight. I could scarcely believe it at the time, but now I feel it was more than approval that made his face bright. I'm sure that at that moment he felt a father's love for me.

Enough of my recalling. I'm far too fond of experiences that I've shared with the Khan and I tend to dwell overmuch on the memory of them.

When Ernac and I rode out the morning after my arrow wound we had the urge to fly — and fly we did. The feather grasses swept up our legs past our horses' flanks. The air snatched at our lungs and we soared, racing all out, whooping until we were breathless as our mounts. We pulled in at the top of watchtower rocks winded and laughing. That race was enough even for Red Atagha.

We rested at the top of the rocks and looked out across the countryside. This high escarpment boasts a wide, flattened platform at the top, and from it you can see the grassland for many miles around. It's a perfect place for a quick nap, but we knew better than to dismount. The rocks are too exposed. Also we didn't want to seem irresponsible children off at play, so we began scanning for signs of game. If we can bring back a marmot or a couple of grouse, I thought, we may not be questioned the next time we ride out.

Ernac took off in a great burst, his leg-skins flapping. He wanted to bring first blood so he could brag over me, but I'd made out something he'd missed. In his eagerness to get the first kill he failed to spot a big-nosed antelope near at hand. The creature was standing still as a stone less than fifty yards from me. If I moved slowly and carefully I could pull an arrow and have a shot away before it bolted.

I asked the help of Manaqan Tngri to steady my hand. The bow sang along my arm, springing out in a perfect arc. It was a solid hit and I ran quickly to claim the carcass. Big-nosed antelope aren't all that large but I couldn't have carried the whole of it by myself. I determined that Ernac would carry the gutted hind quarter while I took the head and shoulder home in triumph.

Stooping to dismember the beast I talked to myself, repeating the words I've heard since I was a baby.

"We of the Far Country are blessed," I chanted. "We are rich in grass and game. No land can match this. How secure we lie. Protected bowl of forested mountains to the north, Great Sea to the east, pastures to hold back the deserts to the south. Every abundance is ours, every generous gift Etugen Eke, our Earth-Mother, can give is here."

I was just warming to my subject when Ernac's yell broke through my voice.

"Whooeee. Whooeee, Beki," he yelled, rushing on me. "Here you are," he shrieked.

As soon as he saw me separating the joints of my antelope his happy look faded. He had two birds behind his horse-pillow and he was sure he'd made a good kill until he saw my prize.

"Well, friend Ernac, where have you been?" I said. "I was afraid I'd have to leave part of this fresh meat for the buzzards."

I made out not to notice his disappointed sighs and went on cutting my meat. He would pout until we reached the yurts, then he would get over it.

"Here, take this. It's yours for helping me," I said.

I lifted a leg joint up to him, then we put our backs to the work. We tied the slippery joints in back of our horse-pillows with sinew. They were too large and awkward for our game bags and I could imagine Kreka's eyes when she saw what Red Atagha carried on his back.

Suddenly Ernac's head jerked up.

"Beki!" was the only word he said. He took one breath, and the blood drained from his face.

His sharp ears had picked up horsemen. I stood listening for hooves, and could make out two riders. They came into sight on the horizon and we followed their line of travel. It was clear we'd been seen. It was too late to do us any good, but now we understood how careless we'd been. We were so absorbed in getting the meat on our horses we'd forgotten the basic rules of safety. Had we been alert, as we should have been, we would have been halfway back to the yurts before they spotted us.

As it was, the riders were closing on us swiftly and we could see they were warriors. Ernac nudged me and we fell silently into the tall grass. Either these men were known to us, or we were dead. My hunting bow would be of no help, and Ernac's, though stronger, couldn't have pierced the leather armor these men were wearing. With tight throats and beating hearts we waited. They rode within hailing distance, and as they neared they moved more slowly, seeking the exact spot where they'd seen us go down. They probed the high grass with their whips. Bending down, they peered into the thick patches of green, motioning back and forth to one another. We both held our breath and prayed.

"Please, Etugen Eke," I prayed, "please let them miss us, after all."

We waited, motionless, and intent on the riders' every movement. It was an endless agony. Visions of iron coming at us from above filled our heads. We knew what we could expect if we survived the first thrusts of their swords. The men spoke softly, examining the grass around us. They were tracking us like game. My heart was overtaken by such fear that I felt it would stop beating.

The warriors were not going to miss us. The hooves of their horses came into view through the grass next to us, so close we could hear their uneven breathing.

We gripped each other's hands and gave ourselves up for lost, when, "Ho there, Ernac!" a deep voice demanded. "What are you doing lying here in the grass like a wounded bird?"

Two bronzed, grinning faces leaned over us.

"Surely you're not that tired from your hunting. And Beki? Your skin is pale as a Roman's. Come, come, up on your feet. We cannot have the son of the Khan and his friend lying terror-stricken before us. What would we be accused of if Attila saw you prostrate at our feet?"

This is a familiar voice, I thought.

Emnedzar! Of course! I should have known! Emnedzar and Uzindur are always together. Our faces were afire with shame as we stood to greet Ernac's two elder half-brothers.

We'd had a harmless reminder of the importance of keeping childhood lessons and we knew our good fortune was undeserved. The keen taste of fear in our mouths would fade, and considering our carelessness we should have been lying dead at the foot of the rocks.

We had been taught better. Attila will be angry, I thought. What will he think when he hears of this? He could have lost his youngest son in one unguarded moment.

"Mount up, you two," Uzindur ordered brusquely. "You're wanted in camp. This is a happy day. Attila needs his sons at his side. The *quiriltai*, the council of clans, has been called. Warriors will flow over the mountains and across the steppes. They will choose a new Khan. Such feasting you have never seen and may never see again. A Great Khan is not proclaimed every day!"

Uzindur's arms were pumping up and down and he was flushed with the importance of his news.

I turned immediately to Emnedzar, whom I trusted for his calm strength, and blurted out a question. "Is this true, Emnedzar? Is Attila to be proclaimed Great Khan?"

My heart was beating with something more than fear. I always speak of Attila with the respect a chieftain commands but I can't see him as others do. He is the one who comes to Kreka's yurt and bends over me in the nest of my sleeping quilts. His hands tied me onto my first horse and watched over me when I took my first falls. When I was too big for Kreka to carry he lifted me in his own arms, swinging me up on his massive shoulders so I could witness the crowds at the Feast of Midsummer.

Such precious times are over, I thought. The only father I've known now belongs to the people and the important wars, and I will soon be forgotten. I was ashamed of my selfishness, but I couldn't help the stab of jealousy that shot through me.

Emnedzar must have seen something of my feelings for he looked down kindly at my stricken face.

"Yes, little yellow eyes," he said, "it's true. Word has gone out. Within a few days the generals and their troops will be in sight. Every chieftain from the four corners will be here, and every woman fortunate enough to be wife of a chieftain will come behind them in the wagons.

"Yurts will spring up across the plain," he said, his arm sweeping across the horizon in an all-embracing gesture, "like a forest of young trees. Countless thousands will be here to see it happen, and it will be as Uzindur says. Your eyes will witness what none here have yet beheld. A great king will be chosen, the king of many peoples. And that one will be Attila. Only the sands of the desert are more than the numbers of warriors he will command. He will rule the clans."

I caught the distant look that came over Emnedzar's face and I knew he was seeing into a future I couldn't imagine.

Ernac seized his brother's reins, staring avidly into his face. "Will there be new conquests in the west?" he asked. "Will I be allowed to ride with the troops?"

Ebnedzar answered curtly. "Yes, to your first question. No, to your second."

Seeing Ernac's mouth fall, he lightened his words. "Perhaps you will go to the north with Ellac. The gods themselves can testify to your need of training. A tutor should be found for you. Ellac will see you get to go on the raids and hunts, but for you the battle campaigns must wait. Hurry, both of you, we're expected in camp."

With this the brothers wheeled away. Uzindur gave a fearsome scream as they raced back the way they had come.

Suddenly I realized I'd been so inward-looking I hadn't given a thought to what Ernac's reactions might be. I was sure he was disappointed in Ebnedzar's words and I spoke to him, hoping to comfort him. We trotted, trailing far behind his brothers, while I chattered at him.

"Soon you'll be at the head of your own private guard, Ernac. When you've passed your twelfth season Attila will give you your own guard. Even now your groomsmen do your bidding without question. You deal fairly with the men and you live by your word. The men know you would not betray their loyalty. You see — already you have learned the rules for governing men. Attila knows this. You bear heat and cold as well as a seasoned warrior. True, you haven't been tested in battle but you have the ways of a leader. I'm sure these things haven't gone unnoticed."

Ernac didn't answer and I didn't expect he would. He kept his face forward, gazing at his horse's mane. I could only hope he'd heard my words and would remember them as he watched his brothers riding off without him. Then, still wrestling with my selfishness, I, too, sank into silence. We rode, glumly, separated by our own concerns.

How small those concerns were. Had I foreseen the changes that were on the way I would have covered my eyes before them. But Ernac and I were children, and full of childish confidence. We had the confidence of innocence and welcomed excitement. We could see great victories before us and great defeats did not worry us. We gave no thought to the consequences of the wars that would wipe out life as we knew it. Our lives, after this summer, would not be carefree. We saw none of it. We questioned nothing.

Ernac and I were poised between one uncertain time and another, yet we saw the future as a brighter version of the past, a soft open plain rolling out in front of us. We hadn't experienced the sting of sobering defeat and no prospect appeared daunting. We had courage, and more than enough energy, to handle what fate meted out. What the future brought, we would conquer. Or so we thought then.

3

The incident at watchtower rocks went unnoticed. News that the *quiriltai* which would name a new Khan had been called spread like a grass fire and preparations took on a frantic urgency. I didn't see Ernac for many days. Meanwhile the gathering of clans was building along the horizon like a bank of thunderheads on a sizzling day. I was kept at a steady run, fetching and carrying for Kreka. My eyes rolled in my head. I was dizzy with orders.

"Ho! Bahka Beki, take these prime skins to Attila's personal groomsman", "Ho! Bahka Beki, take this linen cloth to the yurt of your aunt", "Ho! Bahka Beki, find the man who has promised ten fresh killed goats for tomorrow". On and on it went until I thought I would drop where I stood.

Each day more yurts appeared along the outer edges of the encampment, each day more horses were added to the spreading herds grazing in the near distance, and each day I spotted more strange faces among familiar ones.

One morning I stepped out of the yurt and paused to check the growing herds across the plain. Squinting into the low sun, I saw animals and yurts stretching away in every direction. Farther than my eyes could see tents flowed across the land. We were surrounded by an unending ocean of men and animals. I had a moment of panic. I was accustomed to an uncluttered expanse with only our private herds strewn lightly over the grasslands. The sights and sounds of such a huge, milling throng felt threatening to me.

This weight of life, the constant hum as of teeming anthills, will smother us, I thought. The morning breeze buzzed with human voices and voices of animals. This was my first experience of the clans close by. We move with the seasons and we travel far, but we go with those of our own camp. Up until now other camps had been only hearsay to me.

Now, seeing the land abustle with the life of other clans, the many-layered tribes of our people became reality. Our own camp is large, but when wagons and supplies are not following after the soldiers, it is Kreka's camp. There are periods when she alone is in charge. Then, everything is filtered through her and her servants. When the men are off at war every piece of gossip and every opinion comes through my foster-mother.

Looking across the city of tents it came to me how sheltered I've been, raised in the den of a powerful woman, a woman who keeps the world at bay. My foster-mother is wellborn, a woman of property, first wife of Attila. She protects her own. Our home camp is Kreka's world, I thought, but she, too, now moves in a world of larger responsibility. The change this brings will not be all good, at least not in my eyes. After Attila has taken the title of Great Khan I will play a lesser role in his life, and in Kreka's.

I stood there lamenting my loss, seeing my childhood disappear. And, I observed, here comes another sign of change.

A small group of men came bearing down on our yurt. They had Zercon, the Moor, in tow. With much bowing and saluting, Zercon was twisting his already deformed body into monstrous shapes. Raising one shoulder, he exaggerated the hump in his back, all the while babbling nonsense words and making obscene gestures. Zercon was a laughable sight, but I didn't find him funny.

When Bleda was alive, Zercon, the freak, was his favorite. He took him everywhere, even into battle. In Bleda's eyes Zercon could do no wrong. Attila's brother relished the frivolous, and certainly no creature is sillier than Zercon. Bleda kept the cripple by him like a pet dog, coaxing him to play the fool. Attila's elder brother was never a serious man. He wasted his life in aimless pursuits. He, and his group of like-minded companions, lived for gambling and witless pastimes. Zercon was Bleda's jester, and he enjoyed the favors that come to those who hover around a powerful warlord. I took note, however, that Attila and those around him did not find the Moor amusing.

What will happen to Zercon now Bleda no longer lives, I wondered? He may be given as a gift to the king of another court, for I doubt Attila wants to keep him, and Kreka cannot bear the sight of him. The ways of fools do not sit well with her. She may pity him, but she doesn't trust him. I've often heard her say there is much guile in acting the part of the fool.

I turned away from the group hoping they would pass on by. I saw they were headed straight for Kreka's yurt and guessed they were here to plead Zercon's case with my foster-mother.

"Greetings to the yurt of Khatun Kreka," the shaman, Teb-Ogatai called out.

He smiled broadly at me.

"What a magnificent morning we have, sweet child. We are greatly blessed. The God of Great Blue Heaven smiles on this *quiriltai*. In two suns the choice will be made. Attila will be king of all the clans gathered here. And how does your esteemed mother today?" he asked. "Is she within?"

Fawning and scraping, the shaman placed himself in front of me in a posture of exaggerated subservience. I smiled back politely, and hid my satisfaction. If Teb-Ogatai speaks to Kreka on behalf of the Moor his support will do the jester no good. I turned to lift the skirted felts at the doorway, and as I did so Kreka appeared. She motioned the shaman inside and shooed me away, reminding me of the task she had given me.

"Off with you, Beki," she said. "You have things to attend to."

I wanted to hear what Teb-Ogatai would say but knew Kreka was right to remind me of my responsibility. Keeping to business is hard for me. I'm unable to get to work without dallying. Turning a thing over and over in my head is one of my worst faults. Still, even Kreka concedes the fault may be useful when I become first-wife to Ernac.

The job I have today is an honor. How it came about that I was given this responsibility I don't understand. It should have gone to someone older and more experienced.

I have been given the task of picking the garments Attila will wear when he takes the sacred baton into his hands and is declared Khan of Khans.

Ornate fabrics will be laid out for me to examine. There will be tunics heavy with silver and gold, coats and trousers sewn with jeweled embroidery. I am determined to keep to Attila's tastes. He dresses simply, wears no fancy garments, no embroidered cloth or silken tunics. Gold and adornments are not his habit. Even his boots are without ornament. I've never known him to indulge in display and I don't expect him to now.

I began organizing my choices in my head. First, a tunic of pale linen with light tan breeches to go under fur leggings. Then, the darkest of sables for his outer garment. A fur dark as his beard will give him a dignified and stately air, the look befitting a Great Khan. Attila needs little help to appear impressive. His shoulders are vast, his arms thick as tree trunks, and, though he's no taller than any other man, when seated he seems a giant. On this occasion, however, he will be standing, and his dress should add to his stature.

He will wear an embroidered hat with fur edging. This will be replaced during the ceremonies with his war helmet, to be placed on his head by the Khatun. He will choose his own boots, his girdle will be the Khatun's choice, and finally, he will be given the gold and silver buckle of authority for his waist. The buckle will surely be his only concession to fancywork. It will combine Attila's personal insignia with clan insignia. His personal symbol will not be chosen until he has an auspicious sign to show him what the symbol should be. When the portent appears Attila will make his symbol known and the gods will bless it.

I was afraid I would make a mistake in my choices, but I knew Kreka would inspect everything. She will not let me go wrong, I thought. Then it came to me why I'd been given this honor. The Khatun was giving me a chance to appear capable in Attila's eyes. No matter what I chose she would make it appear correct. Kreka would oversee my efforts. My first reaction, as I realized what she had done, was that she was treating me like a child. Still, she knows how important it is to me to seem grown-up, and she knows how I long to look good in Attila's eyes. Well, then, I thought, I will do my best to make the experience useful.

I hurried on, intent on my mission, and the felts of the tent lowered behind me.

"Be seated, Teb-Ogatai," Kreka said. "Will you share my morning broth?"

She motioned the shaman to a seat on freshly beaten carpets. He arranged himself with undo ceremony, gathering the folds of his coat around his legs in elaborate swooping gestures designed to impress large audiences. This shaman is in love with himself, he takes every opportunity to show himself off as a dramatic figure, thought Kreka in disgust.

Shaking his head at her offer of food, Teb-Ogatai put on a severe face. "My thanks, esteemed wife of the Great and Blessed, — heaven's luck to him — but my mission is pressing and delicate, and I have little time. I've had my poor morning portion. As you know I do not eat overly much. My appetites are as simple as I am."

Unmoved, Kreka surveyed the face of the man who meant to damage her husband, the charlatan who would undermine Attila's rule. He has no scruple, she was thinking, and there is no straightness in him. I must find a way to turn him aside, else he will use Zercon to influence Ernac. My son could very well be taken in by his flourishes and fine words. But I must be careful, for Attila doesn't see the shaman for the snake he is.

Aloud, she said, "My dear friend, how can I help you with your delicate task?"

"It's come to my attention, Khatun, that in preparing for the Great Assembly, Attila's youngest son, Ernac, has been left without a role to play. I know you and Attila have your minds full. I offer my humble person as stand-in for you. I propose to take responsibility for your precious son. Attila's power is absolute, of course, but jealous souls will be among the guests. Jealousies lead to unfortunate accidents, especially since it's well known what has been foretold regarding the boy's future."

Teb-Ogatai made his words into a warning.

"The Khan's heir shouldn't be left alone during the coming days," the shaman said. He paused, giving Kreka a chance to respond, but she said nothing. Her silence gave a melodramatic twist to his next words.

"I propose," he went on, "that I be given the privilege of taking Ernac under my wing. I will guard him and guide him in your stead. There is much for you to do, and time is short. It would be a singular honor for me to have Ernac sit with my retinue during the pledging. The chieftains are long-winded and Zercon amuses the boy. His presence will be a pleasant diversion and the time will pass painlessly. Long ceremonies are boring to a child, and you, respected Khatun, must have your mind free as you sit at the side of the one and only."

The shaman's eyes widened in exaggerated appreciation of the ceremonies that would make Attila the Great Khan. "Protocols are a tedious business, are they not, except to those directly involved?" he said.

Teb-Ogatai fell silent, his eyebrows raised. His expression was fixed, anticipating Kreka's reaction.

Reclining on her pillows in front of him she watched the shaman patiently. Her face revealed nothing.

"How very kind of you, dear friend," she said, "to offer yourself in the service of such a trivial task. And how wise of you to divine the delicacy of the situation. I will think about your proposal. You may expect an answer before the day is out. My woman, Ku, will come to you with my greetings. I'm in your debt, Teb-Ogatai."

Kreka stood and the discussion was ended. Both of them were smiling as the shaman left her. But as soon as he was gone she let her anger roll.

"Worthless rabbit dung hiding in the form of a man," she spat. "I'll see to it there's a role for Ernac, a role this rotten misbegotten viper can't challenge. He'll not get his way. I'll not give him a chance to perfect one of his dirty schemes, not with Attila as his target."

Yanking on her outer furs Kreka strode from the tent in the direction of Eskam's yurt, her mind working furiously. "Teb-Ogatai has made a fatal mistake. He has placed himself in my hands," she whispered.

And she laughed.

4

The *quiriltai* spoke, and then the council spoke. They spoke with one voice, and they set the date of the Khan's investiture.

The day of ordaining arrived with only restless animals responding to the sun's first probing rays. On the previous night the camp had been caught up in riotous celebration and the revelers were gone in drunken sleep. Eating, drinking, and frenzied dancing had left the camp a shambles. When the sky paled peace descended, but men and women slept heavily, uneasy even in their sleep. Indiscretions and half-formed purposes had been foolishly revealed as the ewers of *qumys* were filled and emptied. Drinking contests can raise demons in men, demons that speak imprudent words. The words stick like arrows in overheated brains and become thorns, thorns become stinging nettles imbedding themselves in drunken minds. Devil thoughts, remembrance of wrongs not righted, pledges betrayed, and secret hatreds grown fat with festering become monsters burrowed deep in troubled brains.

Light cuts through darkness, the poison seeps away, and the unhealthy ogres dissolve in the air of the day.

"Stand still child! How can I plait your hair with you squirming and squeaking like a trapped vole?" scolded Ku. "Be still. These jeweled ornaments are a special gift from Attila and they must be securely fastened. He cannot be embarrassed by the flutterings of a nervous young girl. Remember, you are wellborn, a member of his family. His household must make him proud on this day."

"But, Ku, I'll be late. Kreka went on long ago. It's so long since she left," I wailed.

"Nonsense. It's only been a short while."

Refusing to be hurried, Ku knotted the end of my thick plait deliberately. She wove the ornaments into my hair so that the red of coral and the blue of turquoise were seen from the front. The large silver knobs stood purposefully out from the sides of my round head. Turning me to face her, Ku placed both hands on her hips and inspected her work.

"Yes," she announced, "you will do."

"Walk slowly, keep the dignity of your station. And don't forget to stand with your hands folded in front of you," she called to my back.

I was already on my way, racing toward the pavilion and the center of activity.

In the summer camp Attila's house sits on a hill surrounded by rows of wooden palisades, for no house, not even Kreka's, is allowed to sit higher than that of the Khan. His is a grand sight, the floor formed of close fitted wood planks, slick and beautiful to look on. When Attila leaves on a hunt Ernac and I sometimes sneak in and go sliding over the smooth wood. I've had more than one sliver stuck in my buttocks from this mischief, but I wouldn't dare complain of a sore behind for fear of being found out. Today the floors are laid with wool and silken carpets and the side felts are rolled up so the people can view the Khan and his family as they receive their honors and gifts.

Servants from Onegesius' house intercepted me and took me with them. I will be standing with the family of Attila's Prime Minister, and Ernac will stand with his brothers. I had imagined he would be too young for such an honor, but Kreka says his presence next to his brothers will bring luck to the day. Scarrings on the bones of a recent foretelling have shown Ernac will save the kingdom after the death of his father. Three nights ago a sheep was killed and the shoulder bones stripped and burned in the fire. When the haruspice was read Ernac's status had changed, and he is now to be watched over by servants of the Khan's own house.

For this haruspice the reading of the bones was done by Eskam, a shaman who came to us from the Acatiri people. Eskam was given to Kreka as a captive two winters ago. This makes Teb-Ogatai furious. He seethes with anger at the presence of a rival in our camp. But as Eskam was a gift to Kreka from Attila he can do nothing about it.

Eskam is fanatically loyal to the Khatun. He is convinced her influence saved his life. Recently he reported a vision regarding evil *ongghi* spirits to the Khatun. These spirits, he says, are threatening to the safety of Ernac and Attila. I know nothing of the history of these spirits except that they are harmful.

Those of us who walked with Onegesius approached the edge of the crowd and the people parted to make way. In front of the *qara budun*, the common people, are prominent men and women like ourselves. Onegesius, his household, and other nobles, are counted among the privileged. Not so privileged as those of Kreka's household, of course. Other nobles can give no order outside their own household without the consent of the Khan, but Kreka can order anyone in our camp — except Attila — to do her bidding.

We walked with heads high through the path opened for us by lines of young women in fancy embroidered linen dresses. Their arms arched above our heads forming a canopy of long colorful scarves. Beneath this canopy we made our way to the pavilion where Attila and Kreka will sit to be displayed before the people.

Were Attila simply receiving ambassadors, or tribute, Onegesius would sit at his right hand, and one or two of his sons or advisors at his left. This is no ordinary occasion and not even his sons will sit with him today. Our party will be standing down and to the right facing the pavilion. Ellac, Dengezic, and Ernac, will stand next to us, and next to them the half-brothers, Uzindur and Ebnedzar. Other wellborn people will be gathered on our left according to their family place.

When everyone is in place the baton of authority will be handed to Attila and he will raise the sacred sword to the crowd. His five sons will mount their horses to start the circle of warriors moving around him, and other horsemen will follow, chanting their praises, and giving thanks for the gift of a Great Khan.

I was grateful to be part of the ceremonies, but I was trembling for fear I should be called on. If I am singled out in any way, I thought, I will surely shame myself. My hands were damp and sweaty. When I'm excited my hands give me away. Embarrassed by my loss of nerve, I tried to hide my wet palms in my skirts.

We crowded close to the front of the pavilion. I couldn't see above the throng, and there was no Attila to hoist me up on his shoulders. A choking dust rose up as the groomsmen began to bring the horses around. I strained my neck upwards, determined not to miss anything. Onegesius stepped forward to receive the sacred baton from Teb-Ogatai. All eyes were on the Prime Minister, who will be presenting the baton of authority to the Khan. From each clan a leader will rise to speak, each will give his oath of loyalty and drink from a bowl of wine and fresh horse blood.

Each man will swear to defend the Khan with his life. This pledge, and the *anda* pledge of brotherhood, are unbreakable. Should a man break an *anda* oath he will be dishonored, and his kin with him. If such a man doesn't lose his possessions and his life it's only because the one he wronged has a soft heart and pleads forgiveness for him. Such a man usually is tortured, he may be impaled or crucified. Often his sons and heirs are executed with him.

I worked my way to the front where I could see each man's face as he rose to speak. Each one declared his allegiance freely, and each gave a lengthy pledge of loyalty. Attila's picked men were mounting their horses, and I saw Ellac was up, followed by Dengezic, and then Ernac. When I saw Ernac would be riding with his brothers I had a stab of envy, in spite of the pride I have in him.

The horsemen started slowly but they soon turned into a surging throng. The lines on foot snaked toward Kreka and Attila ever more slowly, a rope of people stretched far into the distance. Every important personage here must give personal tribute. Dignitaries carried silver and gold vessels, mounds of embroidered silks and carpets, and coffers of jewels from the southern lands. There were foodstuffs; the hard, red-hot peppers Attila loves, and a myriad of fruits. There were goats, sheep, horses, and piles of pelts. There was slick sable, fluffy fox, and harsh-haired wolf.

The crowds, pressing toward the pavilion, thinned in front of me as more and more horsemen jumped into the widening circle. At last I could see Attila, his powerful trunk and shoulders looming squarely above the crowd. He was quite the handsomest of men. My face grew hot with a confusion of pride and love when I saw that he wore the sables I'd chosen for him, and that the mountain leopard furs I had grabbed impulsively were thrown across his shoulders.

I caught sight of Kreka who was receiving a heavy jeweled girdle from the hands of a prosperous looking trader from the south. He asked her to honor him by placing the girdle around her waist. Kreka turned to look at Attila. He smiled broadly and nodded. She stood, hooked the jeweled belt around her, and the crowd roared its approval. This tribute to her was well-deserved, and it pleased me to see my foster-mother greeted with affection and respect.

Attila rose, waiting for the baton of authority to join the invulnerable sword in his hands. The sword was lost to us for generations and given back to us by the guiding hand of the God of War. The very summer Bleda was killed an ordinary shepherd was led to the spot where the blade lay buried. Only the hilt was visible. The shepherd dug it up and carried it to Attila. The moment he touched the sword the people knew Attila had been chosen to lead them. From the hour of his birth the omens have favored him. The Great Tngri has set him apart, and the sacred sword is proof that his leadership is ordained by the gods.

I saw the familiar, enigmatic smile playing over Attila's mouth, and once again I felt the force in him. I caught my breath. I looked on the face of my father and found my eyes were stinging with the salt of my tears. Attila stood gazing out ahead of him. He alone appeared unmoved. The Khan stood before us as a mighty stone beneath whose power the people bent their heads like windswept grass.

Onegesius stepped out, the baton of authority in his hands, his head lowered. There came a hush. Attila took the baton into his left hand and Onegesius fell, prostrating himself. Attila raised the sacred sword in his right hand, stretched up his arm, and offered the services of the sword to his people. As the surface of the weapon turned its magnificent cold face glittered in the sun. The Khan called out, beseeching the blessings of the crowd on this symbol of good fortune and invincibility. Then, he invited the people to take their share in whatever the fortune of the sword brought to us.

As the crowd caught the flash of the sacred weapon a mighty wave of thunder broke over the pavilion. The songs of the horsemen rose up, the warrior's chants becoming a chorus of thousands. The clans gave voice in praise of the Khan of Khans.

"Here is the son of Mundzucus, brother to our Khan, Ruga.

Here is the man who caused the gates of the city, Margus, to open, the Great One who takes tribute from the Emperor of Constantinople, the one who brought his people two-thousand pounds of gold, two-thousand pounds of gold from the Emperor.

Here is the ruler of the many tribes, the Great Khan. Here is our leader.

Here is the one blessed by the ninety-nine Tngri. Here is the one blessed by Koke Mongke Tngri, blessed by the forty-four Tngri of the eastern side, blessed by the fifty-five Tngri of the western side.

Here at last is the chieftain to fill our hearts.
We are here to salute him, the Great KhaKhan.
Attila, the Khan.
Here is the Khan of Khans.
Attila, — Great is his Name!"

This final invoking of the Khan's name echoed over our heads, giving rise to guttural howls from the men standing around me. The common soldiers could not bear to be on the ground while Attila's sons and his picked men circled around them. Men still on foot dashed for their mounts, racing to vault on the back of any horse they could reach. A general crush followed, everyone rushed to join the riders. Battle cries rose and fell. The fever was catching and a fierceness swept over me. My skin tingled, and the hair rose straight up from my neck.

The thousands here today are but a small part of the armies of the Khan. Still, they are the soul of the warriors he commands, and I could see the heavenly plains mirrored in their eyes. In them I saw the vast and silent land they spring from. I saw them rise up screaming from dark, low hills. Bows whining, arrows singing, I saw them ride straight into the eyes of their enemies. There, they circled, yelling over the bodies of the fallen. Then they melted soundlessly into the earth.

These are my people, I thought. I prayed that the Great Tngri should ride with them, that the force of the sacred sword would empower them, and that each man would strike it home.

I went down on my knees. I gave my private prayer for the Khan, and I vowed to keep this moment fresh in my heart.

Seers and tellers of stories will speak of this day, and I, too, will hand it on. I will tell my children I saw Attila take the baton of office into his hands, saw him lift the sacred sword out to the people, and heard them roar their approval.

I will tell my children that on the day Attila was invested with the authority of a Great Khan their mother heard the warriors shout his name. They called him Attila, Khan of Khans.

And I will tell my children that day cannot be too well remembered.

5

It has happened as Edecon said it would. I, the youngest son of the Great Khan, am training to be a warrior.

I will start with weapons. This morning I go to the workshop of a famous bow maker, and, Edecon tells me, I'll be going to the north with Ellac at the end of the season. Changes are coming quickly. The shaman, Eskam, has altered my life. The reading of one haruspice has made my father look on me with new eyes.

I wakened this morning in the yurt of Edecon, who is now entrusted with my education. As soon as I finished my broth I was taken into the presence of my father. Edecon immediately retired and I was alone with the Khan. I was not at all certain how to act. I confess that I've always been afraid of my father. His eyes are hard as the iron of his great sword and his rages are frightful. Today, however, he didn't appear so dreadful. Perhaps being Great Khan has brought a change in him. He put me at my ease, motioned me to sit on the pillows beside him, and spoke to me as men speak to one another.

"So, Ernac, — what do you think of your new quarters? Is there anything wanting, anything you need you don't find there?" my father asked courteously.

I shook my head, and lowered my eyes before him as I've seen Edecon and his counselors do. He waved a hand in front of me. "There's no need for formality, Ernac," he said. "You are my son, not my servant. Listen now, and try to remember what I say."

His eyes were heavy on me, waiting for a response. It was difficult, but I raised my eyes to his and kept my head up.

"Understand, Ernac, all lessons, lessons in the use of weapons, lessons in tactics, are learning the ways of governing. I will give you your first lesson," my father said. "It is this. You must not show subservience. This is not out of vanity, it is from necessity. A commander is proud, not for personal glory, but for the glory of his armies. A warlord must have the trust and respect of his warriors, and one does not avail without the other. Having trust and respect for their leader, men will vie with one another for the privilege of serving him. They will have pride in serving him. Do you understand me, boy?"

I nodded dumbly. I heard his words but their meaning was vague. In fear of my father's gaze, I waited for his next words, my mouth hanging open.

"If you are to command," he went on agreeably, "your men must look to you in the smallest things. You must be in their minds at all times. They must wait on your reactions and discount the views of other men. When men speak of you around their fires they will relish telling of your unspeakable courage, of the countless camps and cities you have destroyed, the mountains of plunder you have taken, the thousands you have killed and swept from their homes."

My father's eyes were fixed on my face, and my skin crawled with embarrassment. Even those closest to Attila are intimidated by the energy and intelligence in him. It makes men quiet in his presence. I could find no words.

"You have no questions? Is there nothing you wish to ask me?" he said.

I couldn't answer him. Exasperated, my father took hold of my arm.

"Does a jackal have you by the throat, boy? Do you understand what I say?" he said.

Suddenly, he began shouting at me. I startled and drew back, trying to escape his hands, certain I was about to get a beating for my idiotic silence.

Instead, the Khan let go of my arm and pulled at his ear. I could see the veins in his neck stand out, bulging with angry blood.

Anything that comes into my head is better than sitting mute, I thought. Then, an idea came to my rescue, a question I had always wanted to ask.

"Well, sir," I said, feigning a boldness I didn't feel, "do you care about your soldiers. Do you care when they are killed?"

His eyebrows drew together. "That is an impertinent question, Ernac."

My head fell. "Yes, sir", I answered quickly. "My question was stupid. I don't know what made me ask it. I'm sorry."

"No," he growled, "it was not a stupid question. It was impertinent. I said the words I meant. It was an honest statement of curiosity, a question worthy of the son of the Khan."

He scowled deeply, and I shook, afraid he might be losing his temper again.

When he spoke, however, it was not in anger.

"I will not answer this question," he said. "Instead I will tell you something you may find useful. If you remember little else I say today, remember this, Ernac. Life hands a warrior nothing he has not the courage to take. Never commit yourself to a course you are unable to see to the finish. If you commit yourself you must see it through, no matter the cost."

"You mean like an order for a fire-storm that can't be called back after it's given?" I said.

"That's what I mean," he said, and he stopped.

I waited but he did not go on. I felt I had to fill the terrible pit of silence around me. I swallowed, and said in a small voice, "But if your order was unwise, what then?"

"Then you must find a way to turn your order into a wise course without abandoning your purpose."

I sat blinking nervously and finally ventured another question.

"Do you hate your enemies, father?" I asked.

"An enemy is useful. You will learn from your enemies," he answered carefully. "My enemy gives me opportunity, through my enemies I test myself. Hate saps power, Ernac. Hate places needless obstacles in a warlord's path and makes fools of wise men. Only a fool hates his enemy."

I sat, hoping my father would add a few particulars to help me understand his lesson. He didn't and I returned to my first question.

"Why will you not answer my first question, Khan?"

A smile passed over his mouth. At least he isn't angry, I thought.

"Because, Ernac," he said, "this question is one each man must answer for himself. When the time comes for you to answer you will have learned to judge this for yourself."

Another painful silence followed, a silence in which I searched for words. I couldn't bear the tension. My control broke and I acted the simpleton once more, speaking when I didn't mean to.

"But how will I learn to judge, sir? I will need a teacher," I cried in a high, cracked voice.

My father threw his head back and laughed. How his face changes when he laughs. The fierce, frightful Khan becomes for these moments a mortal man.

"Watch me, Ernac. Watch me. You will need no other teacher," he said, and clapping me on the back he yelled for Edecon.

When he entered Attila smiled. To me, he said, "We will talk again, Ernac. Until then do not forget what I have said today."

To Edecon he said, "Mind the lad well, worthy counselor. He is precious to me."

Bowing, Edecon replied, "I will attend him with the greatest of pleasure, Attila. I treat his life as my own."

Then we left my father's yurt to seek out the famous bowyer.

We came upon the man at his work outside the main campsite. On the ground around his yurt were piles of wood, horn, and bone, laid out in different sizes. A stench of glue and sinew hung over the old bowyer. On the ground in front of him was an unusual slab of poplar. Poplar seldom grows so large and the slab must have come from a venerable tree.

He was squatting over the slab. Hunched close, he measured with his hands, forming the outline he wanted the wood to take. I knew he wouldn't cut into the piece until he was sure what the shape should be and how to achieve it. Cutting the wood is an art that comes from caressing many war bows, and from many prayers offered up to the mounted war-god, Dayicin Tngri.

The dried up figure in front of us was Uldach, the bowyer who has fashioned every war bow Attila has carried with him into battle. Uldach is the most experienced bowyer of our camp — perhaps, of any camp. Edecon tells me it takes a lifetime to learn the art to perfection. We give great honor to the masters of weapon-making, for the work is painstaking. A man must apprentice ten seasons or more before he is given the freedom of making a bow on his own.

Gesturing me to silence, Edecon approached Uldach and waited until he had done measuring. He reached down to stroke the wood. His gesture brought a nod of appreciation from the bowyer.

"Lovely, is it not?" Uldach said. "It was given me by a friend who obtained it from a trader. He was told it came from the area of Han Tngri, in the Tien Shan far to the east. I can believe it was nourished near such peaks. It is noble wood, tough and resilient. I would say it is worthy of a Great Khan."

Uldach's calloused fingers ran along the grain, smoothing the wood lovingly as if it was burnished gold.

"You are right, Uldach," Edecon said. "It could be worthy of a Great Khan."

He pushed me forward into Uldach's line of vision, saying, "This is Ernac, youngest son of the Khan. He has recently been placed in my charge. The first thing Attila asked that I do was bring him to Uldach for instruction. Make your greetings, my boy."

"I am honored to meet you, sir," I said, bowing to the gnarled figure. "My father has told me you are the only man he would entrust with making a bow he carried into battle."

"Is that so?" Uldach stood up, peering narrowly into my face.

"Would you like to know why a warriors bow is the keeper of his soul, boy?" he asked.

I nodded energetically.

"Then, I will tell you. In the sinew and bone of his bow is the beginning and the end of a warrior's life on this earth. If a man cannot trust his bow he's better off riding in the wagons with the women and children. The day a warrior's bow breaks in battle is a day of ill-omen. He must purge himself before he can use another. For one full moon he must fast and pray to his personal Tngri. Until a new bow has been blessed for him he cannot go again into battle."

Uldach watched me carefully. His eyes were covered by a milky film, yet I had the feeling they saw through my body and into my spirit. I would be afraid to lie to him.

"Do you wish to learn, son of the Khan?" he asked.

"I do wish to learn," I said. "I respectfully submit myself to your teaching, Master Uldach."

Not satisfied with my answer, he continued to question me,

"Do you have patience?"

"I do, sir. Or I think I do. But what exactly do you mean, Master Uldach?"

"You ask, and I will tell you. In making a bow correct materials are essential, but that is the least of what is required. You must learn how to choose and gather materials, how to master the art of cutting and molding. It takes more than eight suns just to put a bow together. Before this you must know how, and when, to glue the wood, the bone and sinew, next to one another, so their strength becomes a hundred times the strength of each alone. After a bow is assembled there will be many moons of adjustment. And after that comes the time of drying and curing. Ten battle seasons, maybe, until a bow is ready. Ten battle seasons for one bow!"

Uldach shook a bony finger at me.

"You see, boy, no other people have mastered the methods needed to make war bows of this quality. Before a bow goes to war it becomes part of the fiber of a man. The maker lives with it, concentrating on that bow for almost as long as you have lived on this earth. This is what it takes to fashion a war bow, son of the Khan."

More impressed than I was willing to show, I nodded sagely. I had no idea how it would feel to work so long and so carefully on anything, but I put on as if I did. I didn't want to seem a callow youth in front of this Master of Weapons.

"You are a quiet youngster," Uldach said. "Quieter, perhaps, than you should be. However, the blood of Khans runs in your veins. I can see you have a sober bent. You think before you speak. There is something in you to be developed."

He turned his milky eyes on Edecon.

"I will instruct him, counselor. Bring him to me two suns from now and we will proceed."

With that Uldach hobbled away and went scratching through his piles for bone and horn to fit to the poplar. I noticed how terribly lame and bent he is. He must have more than sixty seasons, and that is more than most men live.

"My thanks, Uldach, for your courtesy. And the thanks of our Khan," Edecon called after him.

I was not happy with myself as we walked away. I've been too much in the yurts of women, I thought, too much in the company of Bahka Beki. I find myself uncomfortable in the presence of men who know more than I do. I have so much to learn from these men who have experienced war, but how else can I hope to lead the thousands upon thousands a Khan must command?

On the first day of my new life I had become aware how inadequate my knowledge was.

"Do you think that slab of poplar wood could turn into a war bow, Ernac? Might it be a fit weapon for the heir to the Khan's kingdom?" Edecon broke in on my thoughts.

"I don't know," I replied miserably. "I'm afraid I don't learn these lessons easily. My attempts to grasp these things are feeble. It seems to me I'm not fit for the role I was born to take."

"Nonsense. You are perfectly capable, my boy," Edecon corrected me firmly. "You are not Attila, of course, but who is? Your father is a rare natural leader, Ernac. No man can compare with him. The first time I went into battle with Attila I was stunned. I, and others like myself, know how fortunate we are. We who follow him serve him humbly. Attila is the ultimate warrior, and a treasure to his people. I will serve him gladly until I die. If you, or any of your brothers, were one quarter the man your father is you would be great. Following behind such a man makes you seem small, I know that. Remember, too, that you've had no other lads your age to test yourself against. That will change. Your mettle will be gauged in the coming months, and you will find yourself more capable than you imagine."

As we reached Edecon's yurt, now my home as well, he halted. He placed his shaking hand, which is always unsteady because of his nervous disease, on my shoulder and looked into my eyes.

"Remember who you are, Ernac. You are the son of a strong and powerful warlord, nephew, and grandson, of other Khans before him. Your name, Ernac, means Great Hero. A hero must overcome obstacles. Every warlord starts life as you are starting. You haven't proved yourself, but you will, you will. Apply yourself diligently. You will prevail."

"I hope you are right, dear Edecon," I said.

To myself, I thought, Edecon shakes outwardly, I shake inwardly. He can't know how little I understand of what I have seen and heard today.

"I leave you now to report to the Khan," Edecon said. He bowed and moved in the direction of Attila's house.

As he left he threw me some unsettling words.

"It could be that piece of poplar wood we saw today will become the first war bow of Ernac, saviour of the Empire of the Great Khan. What would you think of that? The bow should be ready for battle in about eight seasons."

My mentor couldn't have known the fear his words brought me.

Waving in his unsteady, offhand manner Edecon turned and was gone, leaving me to wallow in uncertainties about myself and my future. Perhaps I am learning. At least I can see that while the glory of battle and the lure of plunder are exciting, they are a small part of being a leader. Successful strategies in war, and providing necessities for your people, require more than the desire for glory.

Leading a single raid would be challenge enough, but the art of successful campaigns, like crafting a war bow, calls for the seasoned mind of a warrior. A daunting prospect, but somehow I must acquire that confidence. Within myself I must build a man who would dare to be Khan.

I can't imagine how it would feel to be a veteran warlord, a man of such heavy responsibilities. Until today I didn't think that much about it. I can't envision myself taking on such a life. Perhaps a day will come when I am comfortable with such burdens. However that may be, I doubt I will ever fit into the skin of a warlord as neatly as my father does.

6

"Yes, my lord, there is peace on the Danube, but it won't last. Like other times of peace along these borders this will be short-lived," said Onegesius. He spoke as if picking up on a conversation from long ago.

The Khan and his Prime Minister sat their horses in the midst of the rolling prairie grasses. They seemed content to enjoy the sun on their faces, to let the wind work its way through the tangle of mane and tail on their horses.

"We can't mount a campaign against Aëtius in the west with these stinging wasps forever at our backs." The Prime Minister's voice was anxious.

Attila pursed his lips and stared distractedly into the distance.

"We must subdue these Acatiri once and for all," Onegesius continued earnestly. "Their war chief, Kuridach, is with you. My spies are the best, and they assure me their information is correct. Turn the Roman sympathizers in Kuridach's camp to your purpose. Show them what you can do for them, Attila, and the Acatiri are yours. Then the Persians, even the Gauls, will fall into your camps. Your oldest son cannot do this in your place. You must lead the men in person. Ellac is true of heart but easily taken in by oily words. He is not a leader. It's up to you."

"Theodosius is behind in his tribute," Attila said.

It appeared he had not heard what Onegesius said. "I don't like it. He has given nothing in this last year. Now he's repairing the garrisons along the Danube we destroyed only two seasons past. Next time I'll mount a force that will do more than knock at the gates of Constantinople."

"It's imperative we get Kuridach and his people behind you, Attila. These little wars are sapping your strength."

"It's imperative my own troops are behind me," snapped the Khan. "They see that the promised tribute hasn't come. They see the plunder they expected slipping away from them. Aëtius will thwart me."

Onegesius smiled. "Thwart you, Great Khan?" he said.

"He has set himself against me." Attila's face was grim. "He betrayed me. That cannot go unpunished."

"You are not so forgiving of Aëtius as was your Uncle Ruga in his time, true, but Aëtius is a Roman General. He is, after all, a soldier doing his duty. The fact that one man betrayed your trust needn't sour you on other men, my lord. Not every man who serves you will betray you. There are trustworthy lieutenants ready to act on your behalf publicly, as well as those who act for you quietly. "

"Mmm-mm. You mean your brother, Scottas, Onegesius?"

"I mean no disrespect, my lord, but your brother Bleda was an easy target," Onegesius answered.

"Yes, Bleda was an easy target. Even so Ellac was no help to Scottas," Attila observed wryly.

"Even as I said,— not everyone is a leader of men." Onegesius said, shifting heavily in his saddle.

"Within the yurts of the Acatiri," the Prime Minister said evenly, "it is told Bleda foolishly walked into an ambush designed to embarrass you. They say his death was planned by Kuridach, and that Scottas and Ellac came too late to save him from the assassin's sword."

"That is the truth as I've heard it," Attila said. For a fleeting second his face showed anger, then it became as a dark rock in muddy water.

"No more will be said of this," the Khan said with finality.

"Then we are in agreement," Onegeius said eagerly. "We move this summer against the Acatiri. One of my own lieutenants will be sent to inform Kuridach. I'll take care his captains do not get wind of it before we are ready. Kuridach has only been waiting for your move, Attila. He'll welcome it so long as your power appears overwhelming to his men."

"We are agreed."

"Good," said Onegesius. Relief enlivened his voice. "I'll call the offensive. Your personal guard will ride to claim hereditary privilege and the ranks will shout your praises. They will give you victory."

Attila motioned to his falconer waiting nearby. At the Khan's signal, the man pulled off the tiny leather hood and released the jesses, freeing Aruvqan, the pure princess. The falcon took wing, screeing in raucous joy. The men followed her with appreciative eyes, watching as she ringed upward, riding the wind high into the clear sky.

"Is she not beautiful, Onegesius?" Attila yelled.

He took off, following the flight of the falcon. The wind sucked his words into silence. The Khan rode hard after Aruvqan, but when he reached the fat pigeon she had hit in mid-stoop, the falcon was already ringing high again. She was so fast, her strike so violent, that the pigeon's head barely clung to its body. When Attila picked up the dead bird the head fell, hitting the ground with a plop.

Aruvqan's kill and the thrill of the chase lifted the spirits of Attila and his Prime Minister. Onegesius raised his quirt in salute to the falcon as she turned to come back for her kill. Her trainer moved in quickly, dropping a hunk of fresh killed lamb in place of the pigeon, and readied himself for her dive. The three men sat gazing upward, tracking Aruvqan's wheeling arc through blank blue sky, entranced by her flight.

"Aruvqan is as beautiful as Eskam's daughter, Eskayar," Onegesius said admiringly. "The shaman would not be unhappy if you should decide to take another wife, my Khan. It would cement good feelings between you."

"Eskam is a wise man." Attila nodded approval of the idea. "His foretellings are accurate more often than not and he's recently divined well for me. Now my son Ernac begins serious training for his future. Eskam has seen the wisdom in this, and more. He warns me of evil *ongghi* spirits that come to walk among us."

"Shall I send the Khatun Kreka to speak with Eskam about arrangements for this marriage?" Onegesius asked.

"Thank you for the kind offer, my friend, but I will approach Kreka," Attila countered with dry humor. "That is a matter best left to the two of us."

"I understand," Onegesius said, straight-faced. "Decisions in a family must be united."

The two men relaxed their reins, savoring the mild weather and the rare moments of companionship.

"Speaking of shamans, my lord, I have found both good and bad in them," mused Onegesius. "One cannot be too careful with them. They are cunning in promoting their own power. Stories come to me from my men of strange western priests who believe only in one Tngri, priests who make sinister beings of our Tngri. They say we worship demons and fiends. What do you say of such priests, Khan?"

Attila snorted contemptuously.

"I have not forgotten the Bishop of Margus," he said. "That notorious old robber of tombs was a disgrace. His hands were polluted by the ashes of the dead. When he had looted the graves of his own people he crossed the Danube and stripped our tombs. That he should not have done. When we stormed the city gates he ran and opened them to us himself, so eager was he to save his own skin. With priests such as that how well can one think of shamans who worship one Tngri?"

"I remember that so-called bishop. You speak the truth about him," said Onegeius. "But it's not only the priests who lie about us. The Roman people have taken up malicious beliefs about us, and about our practices in war. They abhor us. I've heard Roman mothers frighten their children with tales of our brutishness. They say we boil babies, eat their flesh, and drink the blood of women. It's as if they do not know we have children and wives of our own."

Attila grimaced in distaste. "Romans are a sorry lot, corruption has rotted them to the core. They've become weak. They are cheats and panderers, clutching the cloak of law around them as if it could cover their decadence. The truth is Roman law has worn too thin for useful cover. Law must serve the needs of a whole people, else it breeds rot. Rule must spring from the root to touch the topmost branch."

With that the Khan lashed at his horse and tore ahead of his Prime Minister. But the Khan's fury, ever ready to ignite when Romans were mentioned, was brief. Attila slowed to a canter and Onegesius caught up with him.

The Khan said to his friend, "Let the Romans tell what they will of us. Such talk makes us the more terrible. Our reputation advances before us and wins half our battles. So we are monsters, let the gossip rest there. Talk doesn't hurt us."

"That's true," Onegesius said. Taking his cue from Attila, he shrugged lightly. "Talk doesn't hurt us," he said. He looked sideways at his lord and there was mischief in his glance. "The Romans call you the Scourge of God, Great Khan. Children chant your name in the streets and frighten one another with your dreadfulness."

"I've heard what they say of me, but what of themselves, Onegesius?" Attila said. "I've seen Romans massacre whole towns, and they didn't spare suckling babes or their mothers. I've seen the bodies of villagers who got in their way stacked like stones for building walls. I've seen cities turned to ash under the savagery of their troops. The Romans are not gentle in war, and we do nothing they do not. We are quicker and more thorough, that's all."

"Indeed," said Attila's Prime Minister, "we've seen what Romans can do when they're roused. For myself, I couldn't say who is more brutish in battle. War is not a place for niceties, is it, my Khan?"

"War is a lesson in survival, Onegesius. For every man killed there are twenty witnesses, men who will live to lie about what happened." Attila laughed. "Everyone remembers himself as brave and recalls other men as base cowards, — this is the wisdom of survivors."

"And what of the killers? What do they learn? I sometimes wonder, Attila, what I have learned from the deaths I have brought about. When the battle madness is on me I don't think of it but afterward I wonder."

"Onegesius."

"My Lord?"

"You are an unswerving man, a worthy man. After my own family it is you I trust. You must never change, never turn against me. I have many *anda* brothers, some blood kin and some pledged to me by oath, but it is you I trust."

"I know that, my Lord," said Onegesius.

The two men rode on in sympathetic silence.

7

Teb-Ogatai rubbed his palms and blew on his blue fingers. His soft, pulpy body shivered in the sharp evening cold.

"Baldin, ..." he hissed. "Over here. By these stones."

"Here you are, holy one. I couldn't see you in this moonless night," Baldin answered.

"Be quick, give me your report. There will be little time before I'm missed."

And," Baldin sniggered, "you don't care for the cold of the evening."

"Cease your prattle, son of a viper. Tell me what you know."

"Bad news from the north, holy one. You are betrayed. Attila acted before your spies could warn Bleda. Attila's brother is truly dead, dead and rotting beneath unmarked stones in Acatiri country," Baldin whispered.

An involuntary gasp rose from Teb-Ogatai's chest. "Kuridach assured me the report of Bleda's death was false," he breathed. "He's betrayed me. I'll be found out."

"I fear so, my lord shaman. Now Bleda is dead the General of the Acatiri sees the omens unfolding before him. The eastern Romans have no real influence with the Acatiri soldiers, Teb-Ogatai. The common fighting men have no respect for the Romans, but they respect Attila."

"What you say makes certain what I must do. I am forced to act. Suspicious and cunning as Attila is, I dare not delay."

"What can you do, Teb-Ogatai? You have no real power," Baldin whined. "The Khan is fully in command. His control is unchallenged now that Bleda no longer shares the rule. This is not an auspicious time to try to check Attila. I can't see why you are so determined to pit yourself against him. What can be of such vital consequence? What's so urgent that you would knowingly cross the new Khan? Such a terrible gamble to take. What folly!"

"I have my reasons, "the shaman said obdurately. "Popular warlords do not benefit men of religion. I learned this among the priests of the gigantic snow mountains. The monks of the high peaks south of the Tien Shan are very powerful. There, warlord and priest are one and the same. They advise that when a priest can't offer gold or jeweled swords he must cultivate fear. The people must fear me more than they fear Attila."

"The people do fear you, Teb-Ogatai. I still don't see what you gain by crossing Attila. What do you mean to accomplish?" Baldin said dubiously.

"I mean to ruin Attila's influence with the common people, and I do not quibble at the method. What you tell me, little fox, makes my aim more difficult. But I can still make life uncomfortable for this Khan. I had thought I might sway Kuridach through Bleda's influence, then let the Romans and the Acatiri carry out the mischief for me. That plan falls with Bleda's death. I had the ear of Attila's brother. Had Bleda lived Attila might have been brought down without the world being wise as to the source. The gods have decreed otherwise. I can't use the Khan's brother in my design. That's unfortunate, but there are other ways. Attila is superstitious, especially where it concerns his favorite son, Ernac. There's the weakness I can use."

"How can you use it?" said Baldin.

"I'll publicly challenge that groveling cur of Kreka's," Teb-Ogatai pronounced. "I'll goad Eskam into a foretelling that can be worked to my advantage."

"That's very uncertain, Teb-Ogatai," Baldin said unhappily.

"Not if I use my advantage swiftly. Ernac must be killed promptly and my advantage turned to gain, Baldin. If you do as I say we will succeed."

"Not I, venerated one, I can't be involved. I value my poor hide!" Baldin said, horrified at Teb-Ogatai's suggestion.

"You are already compromised," the shaman said. "You will do as I say."

"But there can be no certain outcome," Baldin pleaded. "I can guarantee nothing, Teb-Ogatai, and I live in fear of the Khan's eunuchs. Plotting against Attila is suicide, you know that. You are an artful shaman, there are multitudes of tricks in your bags, but you cannot make a miracle. I can't be part of something that would bring the wrath of the Khan down on me. I cannot bear pain. Since a child I've always flinched at the smallest twinge, and the tools of the official torturers are enough to turn anyone's stomach. The means they employ, the obscene instruments with which they ply their trade, are too awful. Stories of the touch of their implements turn me faint. Only last week I heard of a man who..." Baldin shuddered.

He couldn't finish. The unfortunate Acatiri who had been caught spying for Aëtius had been crucified, very slowly and very publicly, in this very camp. "Please, I beg you, holy one, do not make me take part in this!" Baldin pleaded.

Baldin's flesh was icy, not with the cold, but with fear. He could already feel the exquisite pain he would suffer at the hands of the Khan's eunuchs.

But the shaman showed no sign of yielding to his terrified henchman. Instead Teb-Ogatai grasped Baldin's tunic, pulled him close, and breathed the rot of his hatred into his face.

"There will be no disaster," he said, "and I need no miracle. Listen well, little fox."

Their voices faded into the darkness as Teb-Ogatai hurried his horror-stricken henchman back toward the warmth of his yurt.

8

"Ah, Eskam, how good to see you. And you, Eskayar."

Kreka inclined her body in greeting to the wiry shaman and his blooming daughter.

"Esteemed Khatun, hello," Eskayar exclaimed. "You are looking very beautiful!"

"You are too kind, girl." Peering into the pouches Eskayar was carrying through the marketplace, Kreka raised her eyebrows with approval.

"You must be a great help to your father," she said loudly, meaning that Eskam and those walking in the market should hear her. "I see you've found some lovely, hard-red peppers, the sort the Khan is partial to. You must take good care of your household, Eskayar."

"Please, take them for the Khan's pot, Khatun." Beaming, Eskayar held out three bright specimens to Kreka.

"No, no, little one," Kreka declined. "Ku has more than enough for us in her pouch. I wished only to compliment you on choosing them."

Eskam, following the two women closely, spoke up with pride. "Eskayar has taken care of the provisioning and cooking in our tent for two full seasons. Her embroidery is as fine today as that of any woman. Her handwork wouldn't shame your own house, Khatun."

"You are a fortunate man to have such a daughter." Smiling on the pair, Attila's wife gave every sign of cordiality and good will.

Eskayar dropped her eyes to her feet, giving herself a few moments to recover the polite reserve she'd been taught. Her composure returned, but Eskayar's high color and bursting energy couldn't be hidden.

"I'm glad I chanced on you today, Eskam," Kreka went on. "There's something I wish to say to you. You don't mind, do you, Eskayar, if your father and I have a short walk alone?"

"She doesn't mind," Eskam answered for his daughter. "Go on with your selections, child, while the Khatun and I talk together."

Kreka gazed thoughtfully after Eskayar as she wandered off to disappear inside the yurt of a cloth merchant.

"She is a delightful girl, Eskam," the Khatun remarked.

"Yes, Khatun," he said, "she's the light of my eyes."

"You have reared her with care," Kreka praised the shaman. "Eskayar has about her an air of the wellborn, the attitude that comes from being with the right kind of companions."

"I rejoice in your words, Khatun. I hope I've given her the correct upbringing. It's not easy for a father to raise a child alone," he replied, "but she's grown into a good-natured girl and she's devoted to me."

Strolling through the wide avenues between tents Kreka and the shaman conversed in voices that were meant to be overheard. Ku followed behind them, picking wares from vendors for Kreka's approval.

The Khatun and the shaman smiled at the passersby. Seemingly, they had nothing more serious on their minds than pleasantries and shopping. Their errands might have been as inconsequential as seeking out delicacies for entertaining dignitaries, and, in fact, that was what those who saw them assumed. All the camp knew a delegation from the Emperor Theodosius was only a few days away, and that the hospitality of the Khan's houses was being readied for their arrival.

"It's my pleasant duty, Eskam," Kreka said, "to inquire into Eskayar's welfare, and to ask the favor of a meeting with you regarding your daughter's future."

"I am honored by your request, and touched by your concern, dear Khatun," Eskam said, bowing formally.

"Then you will come?" she said.

"You have only to name the day. I shall be there, whenever you summon me," the shaman answered simply. "You know my affection for you is boundless. There is nothing I would not do to please you — and, of course, to please the Khan," he hurried to add.

"You'll have me blushing like Eskayar if you continue to ply me with such extravagant compliments."

Kreka laughed, linked her arm with the shaman's and bent her head close to his. Lowering her voice, she said, "Now I have more serious words to impart, Eskam. Attend me, then think on what I say in private. Teb-Ogatai has given away his intent. He thinks me ignorant of his design but my agents have found him out. He plans to lure you into a public contest of divining, then use it to discredit you. With this subterfuge he hopes to gain the ear of Attila, and to influence him regarding Ernac's future. He means to make use of you to do it."

Eskam sucked in his breath anxiously.

"Have no fear, my friend, he will not succeed," Kreka pronounced, her mouth a hard line. "But we must be careful. When Teb-Ogatai approaches you with his challenge come to me with the details. You must be very shrewd in what you choose to predict. We will prevent this odious shaman from getting his way."

Loosing her arm from Eskam's, Kreka raised her voice for the benefit of onlookers. "My sincere compliments to Eskayar, honored shaman. The Khan and I extend our best wishes to you. We shall look forward to your visit, and we count on a felicitous result in the matter we spoke of."

"My respects to the Great Khan, blessed Khatun. I await your pleasure."

Eskam bowed and they parted company as casually as they had met.

After her evening bowl of broth Kreka was restless. She walked into the countryside calling out to a herd boy here, checking a gall on her favorite mare there, or clucking a greeting to one of her geldings. No one else was about. With the darkness a muted quiet had settled over the camp, but the Khatun was not in tune with the stillness. She paced through the herd, her long legs moving in agitated strides. She turned back and forth, forth and back. Realizing with a start that she shouldn't be seen in this state, Kreka checked her feet. She collected herself and strolled deliberately back into camp.

Inside her tent she forced herself to sit. She wanted to relax, she needed to focus her thoughts, but concentration was difficult. Thoughts of the shaman and his dark intentions were getting in the way.

She reminded herself there were preparations to be taken care of. Hospitality for the delegation from the Eastern Emperor had to be in order. When that was done she would be free to deal with Teb-Ogatai. Naked flesh whispered over soft skins as Kreka slipped under her sleeping quilts. She smiled at the wicked things that filled her head. There were so many ways she could torment this shaman.

No, she admonished herself severely, this was not the time for caprice. The dog of a shaman must be disposed of quickly. Since Attila became the Great One the days were disappearing like fast-running water. A major campaign was in the planning. Petty concerns must be dealt with before they took up the yurts and loaded the wagons.

She had only Ernac's rearing to complete. Now he was in the hands of Attila's men she should be able to give her energies to advising her husband. He, who sorely needed a level head and a strong support he could trust, had only her.

Even the best of advisors had a habit of letting their own interests get the upper hand. She trusted Onegesius as far as she trusted any of Attila's counselors, but he too had children and wives vying for influence. She knew his first wife, Herekan, had known her too well, and too long. The woman was a lover of position and show more than a friend to her husband.

Who does a husband have in the end, Kreka thought, if he hasn't a loyal wife to stand beside him? His sons will murder him in his bed, tear the seals of power off his body, and sink his coffin deep in its tomb. Just so, she thought — and then these same sons of her womb would plot to kill each other for the privilege of calling themselves Khan. This she knew. She loved them with a mother's ancient cord of attachment, but she did not always like them. She was incredibly weary of their whining and their big expectations. Why must they insist she speak on their behalf in everything? Men should speak for themselves.

Already Ellac had demonstrated he couldn't be trusted to handle the Acatiri. Because he was inept, Attila felt he must travel north and do the job himself. Now Dengezic had come to her complaining he hadn't been given his own territory to control. To placate him land must be ceded, troops given for him to play with. Then, he too, would be fomenting conflict.

And Uzindur and Ebnedzar, though not sons of a wellborn woman, would not be content waiting in the *ordu* for long. As soon as a plan was announced for the western campaign they too would demand their own warriors. Each new command meant one more strain on a rope stretched to its limits. Attila's sons asked the impossible; they asked that the Khan should turn over half his armies to them while he was at the peak of his power.

Kreka sighed. She acknowledged that she was worn out with the squabblings of Attila's sons and heirs. She yearned for one final battle that would secure the Khan's control. He could do it, she thought. The people had a pent-up hunger to ride behind a strong leader, and Attila was a leader of men like no other. There was a magnetism in him, the power to rouse men and inspire their devotion. She wanted him to take the people to a defining victory. Then, perhaps, there would be a time of rest for both of them.

"I swear," she lamented aloud, "Ku is the only one who understands how I feel in this."

The Khatun lifted her head to the breeze. Rising from her couch she stood in the doorway staring at a plump moon.

"Attila has his faults," she said to the moon, "as what man born to woman does not."

Not for the first time, she felt irritation at her husband's short temper and his excesses. But, she reminded herself, her husband was more than a man among men. He was also a person of charm and sweetness. Attila had been the companion of her youth, and her lover in womanhood. He was the one with whom she had shared her growing up. That time was irreplaceable. They divined one another now as if they had once inhabited a single skin.

"My sons! Phaahh! I will say it," she spat. "At times they sicken me."

Even Ernac gave her grief. This affair with Teb-Ogatai was a repulsive business. She defended Ernac's interests only because they were Attila's. She had no appetite for queenship, not the ambition of many noble wives. She had no impulse to manipulate her sons' careers, or gain power through them. She cared less than a rotting boot for power and succession in the kingdom.

Her most fervent wish was to see Attila give up his unending need for war. Surely they had had enough of war in providing for the needs of their people. There should be no war except to get what the people must have. Empires created obsessions that destroy a people. Look at Rome, their leaders were unbalanced by their overstretched ambitions. She would like the man she cared for to have a time of rest before he became one with the Great Tngri.

She wished he did not hold to old wounds, old betrayals, grudges that ate at his peace of mind. Even she had to admit he'd been tempted by Roman wealth. But who would not be? Visions of easy living, of untold wealth and power, were inviting. But Attila was a Hun, Kreka comforted herself. He was a man of the open country, Hun to his bones.

Of course, he had a father's natural desire for sons to succeed him. But the sons were not the father. If they deserved to be Khan — any of them — they must win power without his help. They must take their places as Attila did after Ruga's death.

As for Bleda, he must, indeed, have been the son of that pallid hostage who served in their mother's yurt.

"What a weakling!" she exclaimed. "I can't believe he and Attila were children of the same seed. Bleda was no more fit to rule than a worm. Attila was right about him."

These thoughts, and more, passed through the mind of the Khatun as she lay back on her couch to toss uneasily through the remaining hours of the night.

9

"Come along, Ernac. I want you to accompany me," my father ordered. I walked obediently, and silently, behind him as he set about dealing with the tasks that go with leadership.

Five hundred pounds of gold ingot were carried to outlying houses surrounding the palisades of the Khan.

Attila walked out, inspected the gold, and walked straight back to his pavilion. He ordered the wine bowls to be filled. Inside, the company, Roman and Hun alike, awaited his pleasure. No one would dare to drink before the Khan. When Attila raised his wine bowl to the Roman ambassadors seated below him they watched him, waiting to lift their bowls until they saw him drink.

Attila didn't drain his bowl. He took several swallows, placed the bowl deliberately at his feet, and pointed to the remaining wine, remarking offhandedly, "This bowl is still more than one third full."

No one answered.

The Khan raised his head. Legs crossed in front of him, hands on his knees, elbows akimbo, Attila looked out over the assembly. His chin jutted out arrogantly.

Still, no one spoke.

Suddenly, Attila shouted over the heads of the Romans. "Five hundred pounds of gold is not seven hundred. Your Emperor promised me seven hundred pounds. And that is nothing. The Emperor is already fifteen hundred pounds behind in his yearly tribute. He owes me two thousand pounds for this year alone. Two hundred pounds does not begin to pay off his debt. However, I am a fair man. I will drain my bowl when the remaining two hundred pounds promised by this delegation has been brought to me."

The Khan cast a glittering eye over the group of envoys. The delegation looked at one another and none would meet Attila's eyes. After a lengthy silence, the leader of the group, a certain Anatolius, spoke.

"Great Khan, the Emperor Theodosius means no disrespect. Five hundred pounds was the load for one pack-train only. The remaining gold will arrive in a second caravan. It will be here within the week."

Attila stared at him. "This tribute is not enough," he said flatly, and he swept the bowl of wine from the carpet in front of him.

Berichus, seated at Attila's left, stared heavily at the Romans.

"Where are the fugitives Theodosius promised to return to us?" he said to Anatolius.

No one among the Romans answered him, and Berichus went on. "Many Roman slaves have escaped, they have not been returned. The Khan has waited patiently for the Emperor to give them back. Many of our own countrymen were also taken hostage and have not been returned. When we give our word, we consider it law. Theodosius swore to return the hostages to us. How, then, should we deal with an Emperor who does not keep his word?"

The Khan shook his head, blinking and frowning as if to clear an unwanted sight from in front of him.

Anatolius then attempted to calm my father's mounting temper. He stated, very firmly, that the hostages would be returned within the next moon, but the hand that held his bowl trembled. I was seated below Berichus, between Dengezic and Ellac, where the flow of talk was hottest, and I could see my father's anger blowing up like a bank of gale-driven clouds.

"You know me from past negotiations, Great Khan," Anatolius said in tones of supplication. "We've met before, and we have made agreements. Granted, that was only a small peace, a small agreement, but we respected one another. I know you expected Senator to come as chief envoy for these meetings. The fact that I am here in his place may be cause for suspicion, but, believe me, Senator and his entourage tried to reach you. He was afraid he couldn't make the journey overland, and he attempted to sail by way of the Great Sea."

Anatolius halted and gestured helplessly.

"Senator's ships were destroyed by an unseasonable storm," he said. "His party had bad luck. Don't think ill of us for our bad luck, Lord Attila. It is not easy to reach your camps. I have been truthful with you, and you have not found me a liar on other missions to you. My Emperor means to fulfill his promises, but it takes time. There is much territory to cover between Constantinople and your camps."

Attila listened carefully to the explanations. He looked long into the face of Anatolius, Master of the Troops.

"You have had enough time," the Khan said, finally.

He raised an arm to summon the serving people. The slaves came in, their silver platters heaped with meats and breads. They threaded their way between the stools and offered a selection to the guests. But the Romans' stomachs were not up to feasting. They were so uneasy about the Khan's state that their gullets opened only to the wine. They drank too much and ate hardly a thing.

The first round of food was taken away and another awkward moment came upon the house. This time Onegesius shattered the spell.

"This delegation from the Eastern Emperor lacks sincerity," he pronounced. Leaning far over he looked into the eyes of Anatolius. "Why should we believe your words? We are not fools. You may be hiding your intent. How do we know your intentions? We must have proof."

The envoys whispered among themselves. After their consultation Anatolius spoke. "I will remain as Attila's prisoner until the entourage arrives," he said.

At his words the Khan began yelling. "What kind of man do you think I am?" he screamed. "Am I a man who would dishonor the name of the ambassador Theodosius sent to me? Am I a man who would imprison a nobleman, a commander of the Romans? I want the tribute due me. I want the hostages held by the Eastern Emperor. I want no hostage from the ranks of this delegation. What good would it do me to have Anatolius as a hostage," he roared.

"See this boy," he cried scornfully, indicating the spot where I sat between my brothers. "This boy is my son, Ernac. He has yet to see twelve summers pass. This boy has more honor in him than ambassadors from the Empire. He has been taught well. He knows what truth is, and he knows a lie. I should ask him if you tell me the truth."

I was aghast, thinking my father might actually ask me to speak. Instead he passed over me and turned his attention to one of his large hunting dogs. He pointed to the dog, thumping its tail at his feet.

"Or, maybe I should ask this dog? Maybe Romans are the sons of dogs, not of men. Maybe this dog will answer for you. If you are sons of curs, give me a dog's answer!"

He went on berating them until the veins in his forehead swelled with anger. He lashed out at the Romans ferociously, in a way that made it impossible for them to respond. By this time I didn't know myself how much of his bluster was real, and how much for show.

Then, without warning, my father motioned to one of his personal guards. The man seized on one of the slaves, a Roman hostage who had been serving Anatolius. In front of the startled guests the poor man was dragged before Attila. The guard pushed him flat on his face, ordering him to show proper respect before the Great Khan.

Berichus and my father were laughing loudly, and my father said to the guard, "Tell this slave to stand up running if he hopes to keep his head."

Hearing my father's words, the man jumped to his feet and turned toward Anatolius to plead for mercy. Anatolius' mouth dropped, and the terrified slave moved to bolt. A single stroke to the back of his neck from the short sword of the guard cut him down. Then, the legs of the headless body moved as if to run, taking a step or two toward the envoys before the bloodied form collapsed, spraying a red stream over the robes of the Romans.

The slave's blood spurted from his headless neck and his limbs jerked, the movements alarmingly lifelike. It was a dismaying sight, and it brought gusts of laughter from the Huns, and a raw joke from Berichus. The Romans were silent, their skin the color of raw *qumys*. Many of the men had drunk too much wine and two of them lost the contents of their stomachs on the carpets. Even Anatolius paled.

My father's guard wiped his sword clean and ordered three slaves to pull the headless corpse from the pavilion, while others threw sand over the curdling remains. The head of the slave was promptly impaled on a staff, raised up before the crowd, and turned to face the Romans. The eyes were wide open as if aware, the mouth slack as if about to speak. The Romans glanced at one another. Except for my father's laughter the pavilion had become ominously still.

Onegesius leaned over and placed his hand on the Khan's arm. He said something into his ear, something only Attila could hear.

"My Prime Minister wishes to speak," the Khan said, suddenly calm. "He has my permission."

"I have a proof you might offer to show your sincerity," said my father's chief counselor. "Anatolius is no use to us as a prisoner, but his head on a lance would be an example to others. Lord, Attila, unconquerable Khan of the Huns, will not be deceived without exacting retribution. I propose we wait seven suns. If your train does not arrive within that time with the remaining tribute and the hostages, Anatolius will offer up his head."

A startled ripple passed through the Roman delegation. There were gasps and angry murmurs.

"No, no, — we cannot allow such a pledge. Such an insult to the Emperor cannot be considered," came from the envoys accompanying Anatolius. Anatolius himself, however, nodded agreeably. "It is a fair proposal," he said. "My fate is in your hands, Great Khan."

He cast his head down on the carpet and held it there as a sign of submission. Attila stroked his beard in that way he has when he is thinking. Then, he placed his chin in his hand and smiled. His eyes fell approvingly on the bowed head of the Roman envoy. "Very well, Anatolius," he said, "I accept your pledge. I take it as a good faith offer."

Anatolius raised his head and a cupbearer approached to pour fresh wine for the Khan. My father lifted his bowl, toasted Anatolius, and a second cupbearer appeared to pour for the Roman, the fellow trusting his head would not follow in the path of the slave before him. Anatolius drank, giving a fervent prayer to Attila's good health. More wine followed, and another round of fruits and sweetmeats arrived, this time on gold dishes.

The dispute seemed to have been smoothed over, but I was unsure who had had the best of the exchange. Between Attila, his counselors, and the envoys from Rome, the negotiations had ended in a puzzling way. I studied my father's face and decided he had come out on top. Though there is some risk in the proposal, I suspect this Master of the Troops believes the risk to himself is small. Anatolius, by pledging his head, especially after the beheading of the slave in front of his eyes, has made the Khan appear terrible in negotiation.

I'm only guessing, of course, and I only imagine that what occurred is what the Khan and his advisors wanted. In negotiations with my father it's impossible to know what's planned and what is a whimsy that comes to him in the heat of the moment. This is another lesson I must master. How do I learn to dissemble successfully?

After the agreement was reached I was excused from the company. The men will drink and tell tales until they fall over on their pillows. It will go on until sunup. No one leaves the presence of the Khan until they are dismissed, and my father is the most prodigious drinker in the kingdom.

Before I left, however, a tale worthy of repeating was offered by a renowned teller of histories. I have heard this story many times but I still find it instructive.

"Long ago," the storyteller began, "we were in want. Meat was scarce and men went out seeking game near a swamp near the Great Sea called Lake Maeotis. There they saw a stag run into the swamps along the lake and they followed it. This deer was acting strangely, now stopping to wait for the hunters, now running as if to lead them on.

"The men were in awe of the stag, for they saw it was a blessed Tngri, and imagined it had been sent to guide them. They were quaking with fear. They dismounted and went on foot through the swamps, following where the deer led. The stag took them deep into marshes that are known to end in an impassable sea. But the deer took them by way of a strip of firm ground that led beyond the swamp. It led them to the land called Scythia. The Tngri of the deer showed us a verdant pasture. Since that time we have had success hunting in the country beyond the swamp," the storyteller finished.

His story illustrates the value of respect for the Tngri of the animals who watch over us and provide us with sustenance. Their lives are hard, as our own are hard, and we give thanks for their friendship.

Night came on quickly. Pine torches were lighted, the wine began to flow in earnest, and I was allowed to return to the tents of Edecon alone. I was glad to be free of the merrymaking, and to think on the changes of these past days.

There is much that's unsettling, much I don't understand. Ordering the slave beheaded, for instance, seems an unnecessarily brutal act to me. Such cruelties may serve a purpose I can't see. My father's actions don't always make sense to me, and though no one questions them, I think he often allows his violent impulses to get the better of him. I have a difficult task in sorting out my father's reasons for acting as he does.

10

Today the Romans left our camps. I was helping Ku turn out the carpets when I saw Zercon, the Moor, riding off with them. He was escorted by two of Attila's own guards. The Moor was leering, and stroking his male organs in the same ridiculous way he always does. Ku made me look away, saying it wasn't fitting that a member the Khan's household should stare at his antics.

Teb-Ogatai's intervention didn't help the Moor and I'm glad of it. Now, it seems, the Khan is sending him back to Aëtius as a gift. Attila doesn't want to look on Zercon, but I also imagine he means to send an unkind message to the Roman general by giving him the fool as a gift. Attila does very little without motive.

Theodosius didn't send back our hostages, but he sent more than the two hundred pounds of gold he had pledged. He sent seven hundred pounds, five hundred more than the Khan expected. This was an attempt, says Ku, to make up for the tribute Theodosius hasn't given us thus far this year. The Romans, therefore, were sent away with the Khan's temporary good wishes, and yet one more demand for the return of our hostages.

It's now ten suns since the first Roman envoys arrived. I was watching from the door of our tent as the second caravan approached three suns ago, and I watched today as they left us. Anatolius rode in the lead and his head was firmly in place. Gossip has it he was never concerned that he would lose it. He must have been certain the second caravan would arrive. The breath of Attila's sword on his neck didn't shake his nerve. I give him credit for coolness. There's never complete surety in such things. An attack from a band of brigands can wipe out a caravan, or simply delay it. In spite of his outward unconcern, Anatolius must have been relieved when the gold arrived.

I've seen Ernac only once to speak to in these ten days, and he said the Romans were passing their time in gambling and in little else. I didn't bother to find out more than that. I'm glad to be rid of them, with their wild, heavy beards, their eyes staring out of milk-white skin. The faces of Roman soldiers have a ghostly cast to them.

The days go quickly, and suddenly it's very warm. Now, in the fifth moon of the year, the sunlight lengthens and long hours are spent keeping track of hundreds of foals and calves. Along with routine tasks, I am kept busy with the animals, busy enough not to miss Ernac's company.

He, of course, is at the workplace of the bowyer. He spends every waking hour there under the watchful eyes of Edecon. And when he is not with Edecon, Kreka's steward, Adamis, is with him. Kreka worries increasingly over Ernac's safety. Apparently there is some dread malediction hovering over him. The shamans differ in their predictions, but both declare there are unlucky demons, evil *ongghi* spirits, influencing his fate.

Eskam insists another divination must be done. Protective spirits must be invoked to contravene the negative spirits. Teb-Ogatai has spread it about that on a certain day (which he hasn't named) the Khan's son will be struck down by an evil force. According to him, Ernac will fall victim to the Demons of the Wandering Lights who visit earth in the guise of horrifying illness and death. These demons touch a person with their light and the victim perishes from their malignant touch.

Kreka spends her days as usual but she is distracted and distant. I'm left to work and pass my time alone without friend or companion. Ernac has been maddeningly preoccupied. He's so absorbed in his new life, so protected by his mentor and by Adamis, that our former easy friendship is impossible. Already the carefree mornings when I would wake to hear him calling my name outside the yurt seem far away.

The Khan and his retainers have been at falconry since the Romans left. Their business was completed quickly, with relief on both sides, and the camp is quiet on the surface. Beneath there is more than a little apprehension. No one knows what Teb-Ogatai may reveal in this public exhibition of his, which is only one sun away. The Khan would never deign to watch the display in person but he'll hear of the shaman's revelations. His spies will be about, of that we may be sure. They miss no smallest detail of what goes on here.

I remain Bahka Beki, the curious one. I've made up my mind to see this public demonstration for myself. Teb-Ogatai has noised his performance abroad with confidence. He must be very sure of himself. He intends to conjure forces that will reveal where and when the *ongghi* spirits intend to fall on Ernac. He will ask the spirits for a sign telling him what Ernac's fate is to be. Then, it's said, Teb-Ogatai will invite Eskam to prove his prediction wrong.

Answering him will be a great challenge for Eskam.

When the day of Teb-Ogatai's divining arrived I was forced to sneak out from under the back of the yurt. Kreka refused me permission to witness the event. As a member of the Great One's household, she says it wouldn't be seemly for me to be there. That may be, but I'm determined to see what marvels this shaman can produce.

Ku disappeared before it was light and hasn't returned. No doubt Kreka sent her to watch the proceedings. What Ku knows Kreka will know as soon as Ku's fat legs can get her back to the tent.

Kreka is right to send her, I thought. The shaman should be watched, no one knows what he may do. As I hurried toward the edge of camp, I was glad to know Ernac had been taken out of the way. He is safe, hunting in the company of Edecon and Adamis until the commotion is over.

I smelled the excitement before I came on the open area where the camp was gathered. People surrounded the shaman, but they kept a respectful distance. They were swaying with the rhythm of Teb-Ogatai's drum. The shaman started his drumming before dawn, soon he will approach the ground of the spirits. When he steps onto spirit ground he will stand with them, and there the evil ones will invade his body. The spirits will take over his limbs and make him dance. They will take over his mind and his voice. Finally, they will talk through him, and his words will be the words of the spirits.

There was an opening among the close-packed bodies and I could see Teb-Ogatai whirling and stamping. I squeezed in. The people were pressed so close the bodies moved as one person. They were hypnotized by the rhythm of the drumming. Fast, faster and faster, the beating sounded. Each crack of Teb-Ogatai's staff on his drum shook the feathered horns of his headdress. Sparkling lights flew from the polished metal ornaments that bedizened the shaman's apron, and the lights scattered over the heads of the people.

His chanting filled our ears. Teb-Ogatai was calling up the forces of thunder and lightning. A gleaming copper mask covered his face; slender curving teeth grew down from the mouth of the mask, and the eyes that jutted from his forehead protruded, rolling in their sockets. Teb-Ogatai was a demon, an evil *ongghi* spirit come to life in front of us. We listened as his chant began to take form. The words of the gods began spewing through the shaman's mouth, words as dreadful as his looks. The pictures they painted threw terror into our hearts.

Whirling, chanting, and beating his drum with increasing fever, the shaman spoke, and the curses of the gods came pouring out. I can recall only a small part of what he said.

> "I have seen him, the White Old Man.
> He has come to me, the White Old Man.
> In a vision he has come to me,
> Lord of the Earth and of the Waters,
> Lord of the Wandering Lights.
>
> Thus he spoke to me,
> Through fire he spoke, saying,
> 'I will let loose an hundred kind
> Of Devils. Like rain upon evildoers,
> I will loose wounds, evil dreams,
> And illnesses.

The evildoers they will be betrayed.
Disaster and misfortune — this will I
Give to them.
I rule as lord over life and death.
This I will give to them.'"

I couldn't have heard my own voice over the exclamations of the crowd, but I heard the shaman's final incantation. He called up the clouds and wind, and they came over us. The wind rose threateningly and clouds blew overhead.

In the interval of gathering cloud and wind the shaman's voice ceased, and the wind died with his voice. Teb-Ogatai lifted one forefinger, fanning it back and forth slowly. The sinister finger came to rest pointing at a piece of wormwood sage no more than twenty-five paces in front of him.

The crowd looked on pop-eyed as the clump of sage burst into flame. It wouldn't have surprised me had everyone there fallen to the ground, and indeed, a few did fall, screaming in fright. Others ran as if to escape some invisible doom.

I tried to draw back from the throng. The spectacle seemed too real and I wanted nothing more than to escape from the frenzy the performance had unloosed. My knees were weak and shaking as I fought my way toward the edge. Somehow I managed to get myself outside the circle where I fell to the ground and sat, catching my breath.

When my head had cleared I understood the shaman's demonstration was a trumpery spectacle. I knew how Attila would have laughed at me, thinking to use his word trumpery. The Khan is fond of this odd word, which he claims to have gotten from Orestes, his Roman scribe. No one knows for certain, though, for sometimes Attila makes things up to suit himself. One thing I know, the practical Khan would have reacted to today's display with disdain. This knowledge makes me more confident in my own reading of the shaman's performance.

Teb-Ogatai outdid himself, I thought, and it was nothing but trickery. The burning wormwood caused a sensation, but it wasn't the spirits who set it afire. The shaman's words seemed to link Ernac's fate with the fate of known evildoers, but what terrible thing could Ernac have done to bring such curses down on himself? Too much is hidden in the shaman's performance.

Nevertheless, it will be up to Eskam to put on an equally impressive display. I pray he can do it.

In the meantime I will take care not to give this shaman too much credence. Yet, there was power in Teb-Ogatai today. He can bend the winds and the clouds to his will, and if he can see what the future holds for Ernac, my forebodings may not be so foolish.

Teb-Ogatai's vision saw Ernac struck down with a fatal illness. This, so the shaman says, will happen at the next full moon. He won't name the exact day and I know why. He wants to force Eskam into trying to confound his prediction and naming the day would make it too easy for him.

According to Teb-Ogatai, nothing can change Ernac's fate. In truth, how can anyone be protected against their fate? That, of course, is the difficulty. A foretelling of doom can be vague, yet too fearsome to ignore. Who knows the consequences if a foretelling is confounded? The shaman has constructed a black, unspeakable nightmare from which it seems Ernac cannot escape. The shaman is free to tell the people what he will, and until the fateful day arrives we will not know whether he is right or wrong.

Teb-Ogatai's words faded and the wormwood became a smoking skeleton. The mood of the crowd was turning ugly. I should have fled the place as I had intended, but I made the mistake of pausing to hear what the crowd was saying. There were mutterings of Ernac and his ill-fortune. The words made me hesitate and I was pulled back into the madness. I became frantic. My need to get free became a craziness in me. I had to get to Kreka. My only thought was to hear her views. I plunged clumsily through the crush of bodies, unable to break from the surging feet. In the center of the mob I choked and stumbled over a man who, in his own madness, landed a powerful blow to my back. He shoved me to the ground where I rolled, gasping for air. I clutched the legs of someone standing next to my hands. I grabbed the legs and two strong hands met mine, hauling me upright.

I was staring into Ku's eyes. She had seen me go down and rushed in toward the spot, she was fumbling for me when my hands found her. The two of us broke free of the rabble and sank onto bare ground away from the seething mass of bodies.

"Ku. Thank you," I gasped.

"Are you hurt, little Beki?"

"No. You reached for me just in time. I'm in your debt."

"Can you get back to the tent without help? I was off on an errand for Kreka. It was only luck I was here," she said.

"I'll be fine, Ku. I just need to catch my breath. Go on. Your errand waits."

"It was a narrow escape, little Beki. I'm thankful I was here. Take care. There are unfortunate goings-on right now. I think you…"

Ku broke off, hugging me to her. Then she scuttled off in a direction that would take her away from camp. She has lied to me and I don't know why, I thought. Kreka sent her to observe this demonstration, her presence here owes no more to luck than my own.

Still dizzy and unsteady on my feet I dusted myself off and went to find Kreka. I reached our tent and was about to lift the door flaps when I heard voices from inside. I hesitated when I heard Attila speaking.

The Khan was inside with Kreka, and I'm ashamed to say I stood still, listening. There was no question they were alone, and from the hardness in their voices I guessed they were angry with one another.

The outcome might have been different had they known someone was listening. Still, it might not have changed anything. Perhaps this confrontation between them was meant to take place.

11

"He is my son," I heard Attila say.

"He is your son," she said, "but you can't keep him from every threat. You can't keep him penned like a sick horse. His fate will be his own. Would you quarrel with fate?"

Attila didn't answer.

"I have never questioned your devotion to duty, Attila. No more would I question your devotion to your own kin." Kreka went on as if he had answered her. "I want what is best for your son. He is my son as well, and I have a say in this. It's best that he stay in camp to face what comes. His safety is of great concern, but no one can escape their fate."

"I'll not let him be cut down," Attila countered. "Ernac is the future. I dream of the battles that will test him, the triumphs he will preside over. I dream of his future."

"If that's your only dream you are only half a man, Attila."

At this I held my breath. He will reach out and strike her to the ground, I thought. Instead, he was silent.

"Teb-Ogatai would get inside your head," Kreka went on, her voice rising. "He wants to twist your mind, and he knows your weakness. He's playing with you. If you think only of the future, only of the predictions regarding Ernac, you will miss what's going on under your nose. You are the present, Attila. You must not let this shaman sway you. He mustn't influence you with his tricks and wild predictions. He fears you. Rightly so. As your power grows his influence wanes. Can you not see it?"

The Khan was stung by Kreka's words. I could hear frustration in his voice, but he didn't lash out. He allowed Kreka to speak to him as if he was not the Khan of a Thousand Clans. She was dressing him down as if he were a young boy being disciplined by his mother.

I couldn't help myself. I stooped to find a crack where I could place an eye, and I peered inside. She reached to touch his hand, and he jerked away from her.

"What is it you mean, half a man?" he said.

"I mean life is not a broken bow. The past and the future are not separate issues," she said more quietly.

Kreka's words were measured, her eyes probed softly for something she didn't find in Attila's face. She might have been speaking only to herself, her voice was so intimate.

"We know the past; we see the present; both make the future, Attila," she said. "The future is formed action by action. Life pushes us along, until there is but one direction to go. Still, I agree that we must keep our wits about us. I say protect the boy, but only as far as common sense can. If you remove him entirely from our camps it will send a message of weakness to the shaman. Wait until Eskam does his haruspice. After that, if we see it's necessary, we will hide Ernac. Act wisely in this, my love."

"I do act wisely," Attila said.

He folded his arms across his chest. As only he can do, Attila made himself the Great Khan, the man in him hidden behind the mask of a warlord.

Seeing him harden, Kreka also hardened. She flung her arms at him in wild fury.

"All right, have it the way you want. You always get what you want. Why did you have Bleda killed?" she hissed into her husband's face.

"He was in the way of a settlement with the Acatiri," the Khan said, surprised by her challenge.

"Why do you question me in this now, Kreka?" he said. "You know I must have the Acatiri behind me. Their loyalty is necessary. I must fight this war, though I don't especially want to do it. I must give the people what they wish. I do what is necessary," he said. "I do what is necessary."

"I looked into your eyes the day you told me of Bleda's death," she said.

"What are you telling me?"

The Khan's mouth became a flat slit, and suddenly they were both dangerous people. It wouldn't have been safe to stand between them.

"What's done is done, Attila," Kreka said, her voice taut. "But the act lives on in you. I can see it. Having Bleda killed was necessary. True. Exactly so. But there is more. Your hatred did not die with your brother."

"You try my good nature," he said, puffing up in rage.

"And you try mine," she retorted. She had become lost in her anger. Truly, they were both far gone in anger.

"Your hatred didn't die with Bleda," she said, her eyes challenging him, "because you lied to yourself about your reasons for having him killed. You excused yourself even as you planned it, by telling yourself it was necessary."

Attila's face went crimson, his lips purpled. He will fly at her with one more word, I thought. I was thoroughly alarmed at the escalating of these attacks on one another, but she pressed him further.

"You despised Bleda. You couldn't bear his foolishness, couldn't bear to share the rule. You couldn't bear his very existence. You would have taken any excuse to kill him, whatever the cost. There's the raw truth of it," she yelled. Her face was unrecognizable, her eyes pure fury.

"Yes," she screamed, "you had to be rid of him. He was a wart, a blemish on your image of a perfect warlord. You must have control, even over your image. Nothing less satisfies you. Blind, stubborn, seeing nothing, admitting nothing; even in front of me you continue to pretend. Hatred killed Bleda, simple hatred. Do you know so little about yourself, Attila? Can't you see yourself, you simpleton?"

Kreka threw out epithets like poisoned arrows. She was a frothing sea, heaving and tossing in uncontrolled tides. This was a pot that had simmered too long. A lifetime of not saying what was uppermost in her head bubbled in Kreka and she overflowed in front of my poor watering eyes. I was afraid to blink lest I miss something.

The two of them snorted and panted, as dangerous as rutting stallions. Attila raised an arm, ready to kill. He meant to knock her across the yurt and smash her head to bits. He was intent on wiping the anger off her face and his fist crashed viciously into her shoulder. The very energy of his anger ruined his aim. The blow glanced off, knocking her to one side and taking her off her feet. She scrambled up, gathering her arms in front of her as if she would hit back at him.

He lifted his other arm, aiming again at her head, but something stopped the blow. His love for her, perhaps, or, perhaps, the peculiar authority of the woman who stood her ground in front of him. What else would have prevented him I don't know, for she made no slightest move to dodge him. She stood inviting him to carry out what it was in him to do.

He stared into her eyes and his arm collapsed. Consternation took the place of the killing rage that had filled his face, and the tempest faded.

After a bit he spoke. "Why do you do this, Kreka?" he said. "What is it?"

A breath of reason touched her mouth and the glare of her eyes dimmed.

Then, "Fear," she said. "What I have ever felt for you. My love, and my fear for you, has made me a crazy woman."

She collapsed onto the carpets with a baleful sigh. "Nothing less could bring me to the point of losing my senses. I lied, Attila," she said. "Neither Ernac nor the future, concern me overly. Only you can make me crazy. You are the curse of my life, my own. I do not draw breath without thinking of your welfare."

"In other ways I am a sane woman," she said, and she laughed at her own words. "Not my children, no other being, touches me as you do. You are a complex man, difficult to deal with. No one knows that better than I. At times I wish…" She broke off, reached as if to touch his face, but checked herself and drew back her hand.

"…ahh-hh, well," she finished, "we are caught, aren't we. Life gives each of us a special problem to solve. You are the problem life gave me."

Attila shook his head. "I can't grasp what you mean," he said. "I've never understood you, Kreka. The workings of your heart and mind are a puzzle I haven't yet solved. You know me well, better, I sometimes think, than I know myself."

His breath came in an exhausted rush, and he dropped his arms to his sides, deflated.

"Your loyalty and support have helped me," he said. "Over the years your counsel has proven valuable, too valuable for me to ignore."

Absently, he began to finger the wisps of his beard. "Tell me what is it you fear in the matter of Ernac and the shaman?" he said.

"That you will become a partner in bringing about the fate Teb-Ogatai predicts for our son," she said. "If that should happen it will be you who suffers most."

She laid out the words with such conviction they seemed undeniable fact.

"How could that be?" he asked, shaking his head.

She reached out to him. This time she took his hand in hers to pull him down beside her. "It's not easy to keep a person from their fate when the omens are strong, my love, but it can be done."

Her hands rested on his shoulders. Her will probed his eyes.

"If you take Ernac from camp," she said, "you fall into a trap. This shaman wants to flush you like a bird. He knows your heart. He knows your plans for Ernac and he thinks to frighten you into moves that will make you look weak before the people, exaggerated reactions that will allow him to make sport of you."

"Exaggerated reactions," Attila repeated.

"Attempts to insure what no man can insure. We can't guarantee Ernac's safety, Attila. There *is* no safe place. Not in our camp, nor in the countryside with your own picked men, is there a spot of perfect security. If there is risk, take it here where I can watch Ernac myself. Eskam is a holy man. Teb-Ogatai is but a schemer. I choose to trust in Eskam's power and my own watchfulness. If I fail the consequences will fall on me."

"I can't see why you would allow Ernac the freedom of the camp now? If you're wrong we lose too much," he argued. "I can't countenance what you ask me to do. I have other sons, but Ernac is the future. I won't risk losing him."

"There is no perfect choice, Attila," she said impatiently. "Take this small risk now or an enormous risk later. In your arrogance you haven't taken this shaman seriously. I speak of your welfare when I tell you to take him seriously. Teb-Ogatai will not leave off his plotting, and if he's not stopped he'll undermine you here in your own camp. He is dangerous. His intent is clear as a mountain stream, but it must become public. Let him place his own head beneath the sword."

"Teb-Ogatai is too crafty to fall into a trap, even a well-laid trap," Attila replied.

"He is clever," she said, "but not as clever as he believes. His scheming can be brought into the open. Let it come out. No one has denied him his public demonstration, and many will take his predictions to heart. Now you must lure him into revealing how he works against you. It's you he means to undo, my own, not the boy. How can I make you understand?"

Kreka made an odd, ill-coordinated gesture, and turned in my direction as she did so. Her face had sagged, grown tired and thin. Hastily I removed my eye from the crack. I heard her body move away from him, and then I heard Attila approach her.

"Your efforts are not in vain," I heard him say thickly. "I see what you're telling me. We will find a compromise in this. It's not easy for me when we differ, Kreki. You strip to essences, and you are too often right. I fear you can see my future. I know you can make me doubt my own opinions. You may be right about this shaman. I hope you are wrong. You know what Ernac means to me."

His voice trailed off.

I'm sure more passed between them but I didn't hear it. I hid in the shadow of a nearby tent thinking Attila might come out. He didn't appear, and, finally, I scurried off.

There is much I don't understand about this, but what I saw and heard reminds me of what Ernac tells me about negotiations between statesmen. It was violent, but in some way this was like a diplomatic maneuver, like meetings between the Roman envoys and the Khan. It was certainly confusing. I wouldn't have dreamed Kreka would speak to Attila the way she did. The clash between them showed a side of their relationship I had never suspected.

I've always felt I understood them. I lived in Kreka's tent, was privileged to see the private world of Attila and Kreka. It appears I missed more than I caught. Whatever the nature of their bond, and I know it is deep, all is not smooth between them.

They love one another, yet the conflict between them is no simple thing. This formidable collision between them shook me to my bones, and I don't know why that should be. There is more than I can grasp going on between these two, but then I've little experience in such matters.

The more I understand the more puzzled I am.

12

"The sky was blue-black. Scarcely a beginning hum of bird sound could be heard when the man rose from the bed of grasses he'd been lying in. He had been there through the night watching the constellation of the Great Bear revolve in velvet space, and praying to the Golden Nail, the star that does not move. He had been repeating a single supplication.

"Golden Nail, stay; Golden Nail, stay," he prayed.

Tracking the gods of the skies, the man repeated his prayer and passed the night. The path of the moon rode confidently among the stars, and true to his oath, he continued invoking the gods that live in the Great Bear.

Without stopping to taste broth or chew a mouthful of meat, Eskam mounted the horse that stood grazing nearby. Together they swung silently away over the damp prairie dawn. As the first rays of sun broke above the rim of morning cloud he turned his horse sharply to the right, riding for a low edging of hills just visible to the south. His horse moved evenly and the man fell asleep, his face set in worry lines. Not hurrying, not lagging, the lone horse and rider moved steadily upward toward the high point of the hills. When the sun stood directly overhead the man reached the place he was seeking.

Rousing himself, Eskam dismounted and hurried to his chosen spot as if he was in some danger of being late. He squatted on his haunches and stared at the ground in front of him. An eccentric pattern of marks had been scratched into the earth here. His mouth moved, again repeating his prayer. He reached into a fold of his outer fur, took out a round metal object and placed it carefully in the center of a circle etched in the earth. Then, pulling a thin rod from inside his coat, he drew lines that made an even crisscross pattern extending outward from the object. The pattern was as perfect as the spokes of a wheel.

He lifted his eyes from the ground for the blink of an eye and brought a handful of unnaturally straight twigs from a leather pouch hanging about his neck. He stuck them upright, placing them along the lines he had drawn. More than an hour passed while Eskam continued to examine the earth before him. He traced and retraced the lines with his forefinger. The pattern followed the shadows that were creeping along the ground.

Finally, the wiry figure was satisfied. He jumped to his feet. Eskam had been squatting long, and his legs should have been numbed through, but he sprinted for his animal. The ground fell away beneath them like a snow-fed river and disappeared behind the horse's rump in a vanishing ribbon. Before the sun grazed the evening horizon they were within hailing distance of the yurts.

Far enough out to be protected from curious eyes Eskam reined in abruptly. He slid from the sweat-drenched flanks and slapped his wind-broken horse into a thick forest of green furze at the edge of camp. He stopped to catch his breath, and as soon as he could move without wheezing he slipped unnoticed into his tent. Once inside, he fell, sinking gratefully onto the carpets.

Watching the movements of stars, charting them in their pathways, brought the shaman peace. When he did this he disappeared into a beautiful and secret place. He could remove himself from those around him, and this was one of the things that marked him as a shaman. From early childhood Eskam had sought the visions that were given to him through signs he found in the heavens. The signs were too difficult in obtaining to explain to others and they had formed in him a man apart. This was the man he wished to be. To some these visions might have been unsettling, but to Eskam they brought serenity. His mind-journeys into the skies brought him a comfort and calm he could find nowhere else.

Eskam's mind drifted.

"Can I prefigure the sun's darkening?" he asked himself. "The moon is one thing. But the sun…? I must be accurate. Great Tngri give me your help … let me figure correctly. If I can do it the Khatun will be grateful. It would give me great happiness to be of service to her."

Eskam smiled at this bright prospect, but his body toppled forward onto the rugs. He slid into slumber, while images of beauty continued to swirl inside his head. This day and night had shown Eskam more than patterns of sun, moon, and stars.

He descended the slippery byways into sleep thinking of the plains, so lovely in early summer. His images of the plains in spring fashioned further prayers in his head. Eskam fell asleep repeating them.

"Shoots from every bulb and plant emerge, grass flows long and lush, horses and goats grow fat, riverside groves of fern and moss, oak and hornbeam, show their color. The glistening film of spring graces the earth.

"Tender birch and alder rustle in the fens, leaf and bloom murmur. Ease your burdens, children, incline your ears to harmony. Indulge in laughter and sympathetic gesture, open to hope of radiant new life and freshening earth.

"Blessed Etugen Eke, our Earth-Mother," Eskam prayed, "thank you for the blanket of spring you have woven and laid over our land.

"We are covered in her light," was Eskam's last phrase as he fell into dreams of spring. He saw the bright greens of sprouting earth, the generous pastures, the mare's milk flowing. He tasted the ewers of *qumys*, offered and taken with a pleasure due the gift. He touched the softening air, and smelled the season of welcome that Earth-Mother dedicates to beneficence. In this time the soul of the people and the soul of the land are one, the earth bursts with love and young foals are at play with their dams.

Through one revolution of sun Eskam slept where he had fallen. So absolute was his exhaustion that he did not come to himself until late the next day.

13

Just as Eskam's spirit was reluctantly joining his body a single rider appeared in camp. The rider was not challenged and he slid from his horse heavily, the signs of a long journey and little food evident in his movements. Weather and hardship had scored his cheeks, and the creases told the story of a veteran soldier.

Two groomsmen hurried to take charge of his mount, a powerful bay gelding. One of the grooms hung back. Leaning close, he spoke into the rider's ear. The soldier gave him a few words and the groom hurried off.

Squatting, the soldier drew a few strips of dried meat from his pouch and wolfed them down. A slender youth brought him drink and left it in front of him. It went untouched. The man didn't appear aware of his surroundings. He seemed to be waiting, as if resting between calls to battle. He rolled drowsily on his heels.

In spite of his apparent disinterest in what was going on, the man responded to a half-grown girl who approached and squatted next to him. There was an exchange of greetings and a one-sided conversation. The soldier asked the questions and the girl answered, gesturing excitedly from time to time. When he fell silent she continued to sit in front of him, large-eyed and inquisitive. It was clear she had questions of her own to ask, but the man shook his head and waved her away. Seeing no more was to be had from him she rose and scampered away.

Alone, the soldier muttered unhappily, his head rolling in the warm sun.

"Gone too long, been too far," he grumbled. "Need my own tent, sleep next to my own wife."

He was sick with fatigue, and a welter of soundless complaint moved in the confused recesses of his mind. He shook his head trying clear the fog, but his eyes soon drooped and his head fell onto his chest.

"No rest yet," he mumbled. "Not until I report to the Khan. I don't relish this, the news isn't good. There is only unrest in the north. Kuridach and Ellac have been unable to quell the Acatiri."

He lifted his head, looking to find something of interest, something to keep him awake. There were changes since he had ridden out one moon past. The child, Beki, had certainly been eager to tell him of Teb-Ogatai's strange performance. Indeed, his antics must have struck terror into those who watched. His tricks smacked of secret purpose, of issues vital to the future of the camp. Dengezic would have the latest gossip on this before he spoke of it. He was eyes and ears for Attila, and he needed reliable information before he offered an opinion to the Khan.

At that moment a tall, lean man walked directly up to Dengezic, seated himself in front of him, and asked, "What do you require, my lord? I came as soon as I had your groom's message."

"Information, Kursik. I need information," Dengezic replied. "I await the Khan's summons. I need to know what's happening."

"What do you wish to know, son of the Khan?" asked the spy, Kursik.

"Everything of interest to my father. I want to hear everything, even the smallest detail. I pay you in good gold, give me everything."

"Of course, my lord, I won't omit the most insignificant detail!" Kursik exclaimed.

"Well, then, speak up," the soldier demanded, and Kursik launched into a brisk recital.

"There is much to tell, Lord Dengezic. First, the marriage of Attila to Eskayar, daughter of Eskam. There is much enthusiasm for this marriage. Eskam met with Kreka and the Khan and the exchange was auspicious on both sides. I know Eskam, my lord. He's trustworthy, a sincere and honorable man, and a true believer. He's also sensible, which endears him to Attila. Sensible men appeal to the Khan's practical nature.

"Also," Dengezic's informant proceeded, "the shaman acted wisely in the matter of the marriage. He didn't ask too large a bride price. Of course, the Lord of Lords can pay, his coffers are full. But Eskam's reasonable request made the Khan's feelings for him more brotherly. My wife, Uma, may she live in perfect health for many seasons, cost me dearly in herds and flocks. I expected to pay dearly, of course."

Kursik chuckled. "She was my first wife and a wellborn woman, anything less would have been an insult."

"So,...," said Dengezic, "announcement of the Khan's marriage has been made?"

"Yes, my lord, given by Adamis, chief steward of the Khatun's household. Eskayar is not, strictly speaking, of noble family, and the negotiations needed a delicate touch. The wedding is set for the day after the next full moon, a date fixed by Eskam himself. Teb-Ogatai's curse will be lifted from your youngest brother at the full moon. If Ernac has not been struck down by then the pall of this malediction will cease to have power over him. Only black forces of witchcraft could act the day after the full moon. So says Eskam," Kursik pronounced, and rolled his eyes heavenward to placate evil *ongghi* spirits who might be listening.

"What are the black forces Teb-Ogatai predicts? And what witchcraft?" Dengezic said. He appeared confused by Kursik's words.

"He hasn't told everything," said Kursik, "but Eskam knows much. He has powerful amulets that can foil evil spirits who might touch Ernac. He had a vision in which the nature of the evil was revealed to him."

Kursik went on, "Eskam says the day chosen for the Khan's wedding is lucky. As soon as he said this there was a shift in the mood of the camp. There is still foreboding, but it's possible Teb-Ogatai's predictions may be averted. Some speak openly of witchcraft on Teb-Ogatai's part. I've had word of this from my chief groom."

"And you believe these whisperings, Kursik?"

"I believe there could be truth in them," Dengezic's spy ventured cautiously.

"And you are suspicious?" Dengezic said.

His source shrugged. "Let us say we should be alert. I will say this, Lord Dengezic, if you wish to keep your place in the heart of the Khan, distinguish yourself in the coming campaign. Attila wants a quick solution to the northern question."

"And?"

"Be watchful of too much success too quickly. This advice I give for nothing," Kursik said archly.

"What are you saying?" Dengezic frowned. "Speak plainly."

"I speak as plainly as I can. Forces wait to challenge the swift rise of any man. As the old saying is — strong winds fell tall trees."

"I see," said Dengezic, nodding. "You give wise counsel, my friend."

The two exchanged glances.

"What else did Eskam's vision reveal?" Dengezic went on.

"Ahhh, here is the heart of it. He says there is soon to be a fateful day when the sun hides from us. If this is true we must pray he will not keep his face from us for long. Eskam is versed in the ways of the gods that live in the skies. He will labor to drive darkness from the face of the sun. Eskam is a wise shaman, he usually predicts accurately. The day he names is that of the next full moon. This means a mixed prediction; bad on the day before the Khan's wedding, good on the day itself. There is a lightening of spirits in camp, but gloom still hangs about the edges."

"You're correct, Kursik, there is uneasiness in camp. I could feel it when I rode in. But if the sun hides from us we will pray. We will sound drums and blow horns until the Great Light is pleased to show himself once more."

Kursik shook his head sadly. "No foretelling of the sun hiding himself is auspicious, my lord," he said.

"But," he went on, "let us look on the other side. We will rejoice when the sun returns to us. Then we will celebrate the wedding of the Khan."

"If Ernac is not struck down before that," Dengezic replied grimly.

"We will pray that does not happen, my lord," said Kursik in gentle reproof.

Dengezic looked at the ground. "Mother Kreka? She is well?" he said.

"She is. Indeed, she is very well. She is pleased with preparations for the wedding. Your mother is no lover of state occasions but she enjoys family observances. What pleases her pleases our Lord Khan as well," Kursik said.

"That is the truth," Dengezic said. He said this with conviction, and with some sarcasm.

Why does Attila seek Mother Kreka's views, he was thinking? Why does he consult her? His mother wouldn't allow him to have troops of his own. He'd have no favorable word from the Khatun. Too much power was attached to her word. He honored her as a proper son; nonetheless, the Khan's affection for Mother Kreka was a weakness in him.

Kursik rattled on, unaware Dengezic no longer listened.

"It's well the Khatun approves of this wedding," said his informant. "She will see to it the occasion is splendid. The camp is looking forward to having your uncle, Oebarsius, with us. His presence indicates the eastern clans will be with the Khan when he goes against the Acatiri."

"My uncle Oebarsius will be coming? Good," said Dengezic genially. "I'll enjoy seeing him. He has a talent for friendship, and he's been a loyal support for the Khan and the Khatun."

"Yes," said Kursik, "he's been steadfast. Oebarsius supported your mother and father in dark days when others did not. I know only what I've heard, of course. Have you heard tales of those dark days, son of the Khan?"

"I've heard you are king of the gossips, Kursik," Dengezic said. "And," he added, "that is why I pay you so handsomely."

Kursik showed his teeth.

"I don't know this tale, tell me of it, Kursik," the soldier said. "I'm eager to hear stories of my father."

"Well," said Kursik, wading into his favorite pastime with relish, "there is a story that sticks in my head. I've often thought the seeds of Attila's hatred and distrust of Aëtius lie here.

"You know that Aëtius was a trusted ally of the Khan. He was an *anda* brother when they were young, untried warriors. Then came disaster. Aëtius marched into Italy with more than ten thousand of our people behind him in answer to the call of a certain usurper named John. He engaged the Eastern forces, and hundreds were brutally slain on both sides. It was a short, bloody campaign, and in the aftermath, Aëtius was reconciled with the Empress Mother, Galla Placidia.

"It was then," Kursik related, "that Aëtius' treachery revealed itself. He planned to turn on our troops from the rear, and with the troops of this John at the fore, destroy our army. John was caught and executed before the battle began, and Aëtius' plan went awry. He turned to the Empress for protection and fled to Gaul in her service. Soon after the Romans attacked us. They took provinces and fortifications long held by our people, even reaching the Danube. We had no strong leaders."

Kursik wanted to settled in for an afternoon of tale-mongering, but Dengezic was impatient

"Attila doesn't forget a betrayal, anyone knows that, Kursik. Certainly, he knows the Romans are rabid dogs who must be constantly watched lest they bite the master who feeds them. The Khan loves no Roman. There's nothing new in this."

"True, Lord Dengezic, but our own countrymen to the East and North didn't answer the Khan's call for help against Rome. Of all the clans who might have sent aid, only Oebarsius did so. The Khan remembers who has helped him."

Kursik was not easily diverted. His mouth never stopped moving. But since an occasional pearl dropped from it Dengezic gave up on stemming the flood of words.

Kursik waxed flowery as he warmed to the sound of his own voice. "Such betrayals have taught Attila the value of loyalty. You know this to be true, second son of the Highest," Kursik parroted.

There was more praise to be sung to the King of the Huns.

"Your father's heart is stout, his courage faultless," Kursik recited. "When the camp is hungry every man eats before the Khan, when there is thirst every man drinks before him. In battle he's the first to ride out and the last to leave the field. I've seen him put his own life in peril to come to the aid of a fellow warrior. His need for comfort is small. He despises show and luxury. His ways are the ways of a Great Lord."

"When did you see the Khan in battle, Kursik? Which battles do you speak of? I don't seem to recall them," said Dengezic.

"Oh, this was long ago, before you were old enough to ride, Lord Dengezic," Kursik lied.

"Before I was able to ride? That was long ago, indeed."

"Ah, yes, long ago. But that's another story for another day. This day is for speaking of the Khan."

"Please, no more!" Dengezic said pleadingly. But he was grateful to Kursik for keeping him awake.

"The Khan's exploits are worthy of repeating, my Lord. I know the tales of his cruelties and deceptions by heart, I've heard them so many times," Kursik ran on. "But those who tell of his cruelties don't tell of his generosity, or his mercy."

Dengezic couldn't help himself, he laughed aloud. He had seen his father in battle and his acts made a mockery of Kursik's flattering portrayal.

"What a bootlicker you are, Kursik," he said.

"I don't say your father is better than other men," Kursik responded. "I say only that he is not unnecessarily cruel. Do you recall the two green, young nobles who were brought in as captives? They had ridden in the vanguard of a battle against him and they were crucified, horribly tortured and executed in this very camp.

"This the Khan allowed. He didn't intercede on their behalf," Kursik went on, "and some blamed him for it. But in this he could not have shown mercy if he'd wished. It would have been perceived as weakness. He presides over executions, but he is judicious. Except for the heat of battle Attila doesn't act with excessive ferocity."

"You know this to be a fact, Kursik?" Dengezic said. Despite his weariness Dengezic found the spy's prattle entertaining. The flow of self-serving babble was spread so thick it became an amusement.

"Yes, oh, yes, it's true." Kursik's waved his arms in an excess of enthusiasm. "It would be beneath the Khan to personally engage in tortures like the Persians kings. Or to act as the Romans do, putting on executions in the spirit of entertainment. Yet, he must satisfy the dictates of order. That is the responsibility of a leader. Beheadings and impalings have strategic purpose. Attila is a warrior, he partakes of the bloody ways of war. I admire his firmness. He is an example for his people."

Finally, Kursik's interminable recounting of his father's godlike characteristics began to pass over Dengezic's exhausted head. He was yawning uncontrollably and his mind drifted, to fasten on his youngest brother.

Ernac, the simple little toad, thought Dengezic, understands nothing of war or politics, not even as much as Kursik. To him war is a game to learn in the yurt of the bowyer; politics, a lesson to learn sitting at the feet of his teacher, Edecon. Ernac would never be fit to lead men, he hadn't the temperament. He'd been too gently dealt with. He was soft. Why the Khan bothered himself with his brother's fate as a warrior Dengezic didn't understand.

Dengezic's head fell forward on his chest. Kursik waited a few moments and saw his audience had escaped him.

"Will there be anything else, my lord?" he asked reproachfully.

Dengezic's head jerked up. "No," he said. "You have told me much. How much of it is useful we will see. Go, but keep your eyes and ears in good health. There is more gold to oil them should they turn dry."

Dismissed, Kursik stood to leave, then paused for a parting message.

"A word of warning, Dengezic," he said. "Adamis, — he may not be what he seems. He is a man who bears watching."

Dengezic peered after his informant. That was one warning he would remember. Kursik was not the first to warn him against Mother Kreka's steward. Adamis would be watched.

Alone, the soldier smiled contentedly. "I know things about many people," he said to himself, "but these things I do not say. Around the fires in the evening men call out to me, 'Ho, Dengezic, what think you of this one or that one?' or 'You ride with the Khan, always at his side. What do you say of today's fighting, Son of the Khan?'

"I do not answer. I laugh and go on drinking. I say nothing of what fills my mind. I am the only son of the Khan who is a real soldier. I am proud to live the life of a warrior," Dengezic declared to the empty air.

His declaration was interrupted by a servant of the Khan's tent. Standing stiffly, Dengezic answered the summons.

There were brief formal greetings, Attila wasted no polite words on his second son. Dengezic's exhaustion was no shield against the sharp exchange that followed. Attila's mind was made up.

As he left the Khan's tent Dengezic reeled with fatigue, and a black depression settled over him. In his father's eyes he was no more than a common bowman. Attila would not move against the Acatiri until Ernac's future had been resolved.

Blast his brother's childish hide, and blast his father's protective instincts. "We should be off to the north as soon as the wedding takes place," he told himself.

Still, there might be more to this wrangling between shamans than it seemed. Onegesius was being sent to prepare for the northern campaign and the Khan's spies were active. Until he heard what they had to report he would put aside his impatience, join in the activities of the camp, and learn what he could.

"When the Acatiri are beaten it will be my turn. With the Acatiri safely in the Khan's camps I will have my own land. I am set on that," he muttered.

With this stubborn resolve burning in his head, Dengezic, second son of the Khan, sought his own tent, his wife and a well-earned rest.

14

"Don't you know where you are, Ernac? Wake up, lad, you're going to fall off. Do you hear me?"

Ernac straightened in his shabrack when Adamis poked his whip handle peevishly into the small of his back. All three riders were irritable. They were weary of enforced isolation and idleness, and they passed their ill-feeling back and forth between one another. Several yards behind Adamis and Ernac, Edecon rode, dozing fitfully.

Too many days of aimless riding, making lonely bivouac and rising to the prospect of one more purposeless day of drifting had sapped their vitality. The days were slack, they ate and slept fitfully, waiting for the signal that would lift them out of their torpor. Within two days ride of the yurts of the Khan the three circled, waiting for the message that would bring them in.

Adamis' lanky legs hung loose, his square suntanned features an expressionless mask. Women found Adamis attractive, even handsome. What Kreka's steward thought was hidden in a perfectly shaped head that had never known the pressure of a deforming loop. His butter-smooth skin gave the impression that a milksop lurked beneath his well-formed muscles, but one glance into Adamis' yellow-green eyes wiped out any misapprehensions regarding his character.

In spite of his physical good fortune Adamis was not vain. No one had given him cause to be. He had the ways of a beautiful person who is unconscious of his gifts and he made few enemies at the court of the Khan. Certainly, he made no gratuitous enemies. He carried himself with dignity and gave his attention to the duties the Khatun placed upon him. He paid small notice to other people and none could say what was in his heart. People noted he was a perfect steward and thought no more about him. Adamis inspired a confidence barely tinged with envy.

Edecon's slight frame, in contrast, and his nervous movements, coming one upon the other in waves, gave off unsure quivers of alarm. Ever ready with a diplomatic word or a shallow quip, he, nevertheless, left behind him a wake of uneasiness. He was unaware of this, as Adamis was unaware of his physical attractions. Where Edecon was concerned, one had a feeling, not exactly of distrust, but of small misgivings.

Yet Attila had given Edecon his seal of trust. The veteran warrior passed with absolute freedom back and forth between the boundaries of the Khan's territories and the outside world. In his youth he'd enjoyed a reputation for impeccable bravery, and his exploits had been preached by many a mother dreaming of glory for a beloved son. Edecon was the stuff of legend in his own way. His comings and goings were highly visible, but none could say what he held in his mind any more than they could of Adamis. Neither was given to handing out confidences within the camp.

The group of three had been riding in silence. As afternoon shadows grew across the plain they saw a pair of riders moving in their direction. The horsemen were not in a hurry and it was evening before they found their way to the fire where meat and drink awaited them.

The two riders greeted the three men waiting by the fire and sat down. None of them felt obliged to state their business or ask questions before they shared food. Their horses grazed nearby and the men slurped their broth with audible grunts of satisfaction.

"What word?" asked Edecon finally.

"You are to return. We ride tomorrow," Ebnedzar answered.

"The Khan is satisfied, then, regarding the boy?" Adamis said, probing Ebnedzar's expression. His gaze rested heavily on the Khan's middle son. Clearly, he would not accept a glib reply.

Ebnedzar met the eyes of Kreka's steward unflinchingly, but he rose and stretched without answering. Uzindur didn't look up. He had busied himself over his meal.

Ebnedzar smiled and turned to Ernac. "Are you tired of the wandering life, little brother? Well you might be. In your place I'd be grinding my teeth. Your studies have missed you, and there is work to be done in the yurts of the Khan. Have patience, we'll be there in two days. Four days after that, if all goes well, the marriage of the shaman's daughter, Eskayar, and the Great Khan, will be proclaimed. Then the celebrating begins."

Ernac's deep-set eyes searched the face of his elder brother. He didn't find what he looked for and he turned away, biting his lips in frustration. He didn't want the tears building behind his forehead to be seen.

Darting away from the firelight, Ernac pulled his sleeping furs onto the ground, placing them well apart from the men. These last days had been difficult for him. Whatever seeds of manliness might have been sprouting in Attila's youngest son had wilted. He felt totally inept and helpless.

Misgivings were eating away at Ernac's vision of himself as a potential leader of men. He needed reassurance, needed the confidence of meeting a challenge well. Ernac was desperate to master an obstacle, any obstacle, but nothing likely appeared on the horizon.

He wondered if grown men, men like his brothers, knew when they had crossed the line into manhood. Ernac didn't know where the line was much less whether he might have passed over it. Other men knew things, but he, Ernac, knew nothing. Furthermore, no one would tell him anything. If they were trying to shield him from the malediction that hung over him they hadn't succeeded. He knew better than anyone the curse Teb-Ogatai had decreed. It was the reason for the curse he didn't understand.

"Are you asleep, lad?" Ebnedzar squatted in front of Ernac's unhappy face. His eyes were wide open. He preferred not to talk but he could hardly pretend to be asleep.

"Not quite," he said gloomily. "I was thinking of the coming days. I couldn't put my mind to rest."

Ebnedzar scratched his nose uneasily.

"You worry too much, Ernac," he said. "You are under the care of the Great Khan. You must trust that. You haven't the right to question. Now sleep. The stars roll in their proper path and the Khan looks out for you. These next days will pass and you will see better times."

He reached and touched his brother's hair, then stood up yawning. Ebnedzar was fond of the boy in a remote, protective way. Ernac evoked protective instincts. There was something both pathetic and endearing in his eagerness to become a man, and in his intense desire to please Attila.

The men were soon asleep. Under stars that rolled in their proper path, as Ebnedzar had observed, they were at peace. But the boy, who had not yet seen battle, who had neither killed nor seen men killed in war, did not sleep. His heart was not as tranquil as the hearts of the seasoned soldiers.

Back in the bustle of the camp there was no free moment to give to personal worries. Attila's uncle, Oebarsius, arrived to represent the eastern clans at the wedding festivities and set up his tents near the palisades of the Khan. He made himself visible, walking about in a high humor. Oebarsius was a man who never stopped at one joke when two were possible. He took obvious delight in the company of Kreka and Ernac, and they took delight in his. The Khan's uncle was a man of energy and optimism, and in his presence Ernac lost his look of pinched distress.

Preparations for feasting and drinking occupied the camp. Tributes of wine, fruit and sweetmeats, came streaming in from outlying bands of traders. Untold numbers of sheep, goats, cattle, and birds were slaughtered and roasted, or boiled in salted water. Countless leather bags were filled to overflowing with the *qumys* that had been fermented and beaten to a froth by the servants.

Ernac had been back in the main encampment for barely three suns when Eskam's predicted eclipse took place. Just as morning camp routines were beginning a mist began to move across the sun. The shadow spread slowly, as Eskam had said it would. The sun lost power and morning light receded. Though the day was without cloud the sky turned to slate as the chill, colorless membrane grew. The ominous pall spun outward from the sun until earth and rock alike were coated in a dull, yellow film. The very atmosphere was muffled, morning bird sound ceased.

Then the lamentations started; raucous clanging, ringing and beating, pleading and wailing, belligerent screams and yells mixed with ceremonial chanting that came from Eskam. Beneath the human din and cry swelled the bewildered howling of dogs who huddled next to the doors of the yurts for comfort.

The actual eclipse wasn't witnessed. The camp had no impulse to disobey the proscriptions surrounding this awesome hour. People stayed covered in their tents and waited for day to overcome the false night.

Inside Edecon's yurt Adamis and Edecon waited nervously. They were armed against a visitation of the curse laid on Ernac. They stood with drawn swords, their eyes circling the bottom edges of the felt, then turning to the smokehole at the top where the White Old Man could enter to strike at the son of the Khan. Long minutes passed, and the tension in their faces deepened into scowling lines of strain.

In the center of the yurt, quaking under a pile of rugs and quilts, crouched the object of their concern. And directly in front of the tent that held the Khan's precious son, sat Eskam, swaying to the rhythms of his chants. His sacred staff sliced indecipherable patterns through the air in front of him. From the spot where Eskam was practicing his rituals of safeguarding there issued a malodorous smoke that invaded the nose, clinging in the nostrils.

The dark hour continued, the air was filled with banging, wailing, chanting, and the smells of peculiar potions. There was a sense that the eclipse would never be over. The people felt condemned, cast into an unearthly half-light.

They had almost given up hope when the sun decided to come back to them. With godlike fingers, the life-giving radiance sent a golden shower flowing over the land. The light touched a lone figure squatting outside the yurt. Eskam sat praying steadfastly, speaking to the gods he found in everything.

Miraculously, then, the smells of fear and scrofulous potions melted into the sunshine. The people saw their deliverance as Eskam's doing. It was his triumph. They spoke of the shaman's astonishing powers, and he was given credit for the sun's return. It became common lore that Eskam had given the sun back to the people and saved the Khan's heir from a malefic destiny.

15

A cheerful sun shone on the wedding guests, and with the sun came a welcome lifting of mood. Even the sober-natured, the rare individuals who lacked the cheerful Hun temperament, were in a mood to celebrate.

At midday brief wedding rites were held. Pledges of loyalty were exchanged between the families and the bride-price was bestowed on Eskam. Horses, including several of the Khan's white geldings, adornments and furnishings, were given to the shaman.

Custom demanded that the new husband ride to the bride's family yurt and take her by force. The Khan, well-rehearsed in his part, arrived at the yurt in a swirl of dust and a flourish of white mane and tail. The excited crowd stamped and clapped, urging him on. He leaped from his mount and peered inside the open doorway. Eskayar screamed, running and dodging in mock terror. Attila, in his turn, gave a convincing show. He moved his sword as if to strike Eskayar's friends and relatives, and they allowed him to overpower them. He grabbed Eskayar, hauled her outside, and threw her on his horse, slapping her buttocks with a satisfying thwack.

The Khan leapt up behind her, flashed a ready grin, and squeezed Eskayar to him. Much to the delight of onlookers he placed a meaty hand firmly around one of her breasts, raised an arm in triumphal acclaim and let go with a great bellow as he dashed off with Eskayar in front of him. The bride and groom had performed in approved fashion and they disappeared amid high-spirited shouts of approval and blessings from the multitudes of well-wishers.

The tableau went without incident and after the couple were gone a wild spirit swept through the camp. Everyone felt free to celebrate in earnest and the effects of wine and *qumys* were soon evident in the lively moves of the dancers. Their feet shook the ground, and their faces glistened with sweat.

"Ha!" cried the musicians. They were carried along on the thrumming beat of the single-stringed lute and the drum. The rhythm led the dancers into dizzy, ever tightening circles until they fell breathless.

"Ha! Ha! Ha! ... Ha! Ha! Ha!", their voices sounded above the music. The chanting and clapping brought the dancers to a state of exaltation, then down to collapse. As the hours passed few figures remained upright. Only the hardiest, or the most foolish, continued until they fell and couldn't rise. This was, after all, only the first day of a feast that would go on for days.

Members of the Khan's household walked out among the *qara buden*, drinking and dancing for a short while. They then retired to an expansive, decorated pavilion built for the occasion. Here, the nobles enjoyed their own, less strenuous, brand of celebration.

Here the Khatun held court, presiding graciously over retainers, friends and relatives, and wellborn families who had her favor. She and Oebarsius lounged on pillowed carpets in the center. Others, according to rank, surrounded the outer edges of the pavilion. Serving people wove in and out of the crowd offering up heaping, pungent platters of food. There was bread and fruit, more wine and *qumys* than anyone should consume, and course after course of meat. The crowd soon reached an agreeable state of drunkenness.

Four of the Khan's sons sat below their mother and their uncle, Oebarsius. Only Ellac was missing from the family gathering. Onegesius' need for him in the north took priority over this purely family occasion. Preparations for Attila's upcoming campaign were going forward in outlying districts and Ellac's presence in the north was required there. The Khan meant to see that confidence in his resolve remained high with the Acatiri.

The rest of the family relaxed, enjoying the scene. Dengezic, Ebnedzar, Uzindur, their first wives, and Ernac, lifted their wine bowls often. Dengezic, who held his liquor well, was drinking mightily without apparent ill effects, but Uzindur was already leaning on Ebnedzar's shoulder.

Ernac's head was beginning to buzz. He didn't know exactly what to expect from the wine, but it didn't seem to him he had been blessed with the vaunted capacity of Huns for spirits. Each time the serving girl filled his wine bowl Ernac returned her smile, but his stomach didn't follow suit. His last cup of wine had tasted bitter. It had a strong aftertaste that left his mouth dry.

Mother Kreka caught his eye. She raised her bowl and drained it in a toast to her youngest son. Ernac felt obliged to answer her and drank deeply, raising his bowl in salute to his mother. Kreka was wearing the jeweled girdle that had been given to her at the ceremonies proclaiming the Great Khan. Ernac had never seen the Khatun looking so vibrant. She seemed alight with an internal fire.

"My mother is lovely," Ernac murmured drunkenly, "a match for any woman half her age."

He was a lucky man, he thought. He acknowledged his good fortune in having been whelped in the tents of the Khan and the Khatun. Then he giggled, realizing this was the first time he had consciously thought of himself as a man.

No more happy observations came to his lips. His head was now swimming in sickening waves. He could scarcely keep a grip on the roll and swell of his stomach, and the feasting seemed to go on interminably. Finally, most of the revelers fell over on the carpets snoring, and Ernac was able to ease his way out of the pavilion without being noticed.

Staggering and lurching he found his way to Edecon's yurt. Retching, but unable to vomit, he dropped onto his sleeping couch in a stupor. Ernac knew nothing more until he was wakened by an urgent need to relieve the powerful spasms in his stomach and bowels. He roused himself, and this time there was no difficulty in emptying himself. He drained himself of more liquid than he imagined one body could hold and lay back down in the yurt shaking. Under the quilts he found Edecon, who had also wandered back to his tent drunk.

Ernac called out to him in a thin, reedy voice. Weakness and nausea produced the querulous voice of an old man.

"I don't know what's happened to me, Edecon," he said. "The wine didn't agree with me. I've never felt like this. I can't see. I have a hard time forming words."

Ernac made a supreme effort to extract this much from his failing senses before he collapsed, floating in an eerie half-world. Edecon himself was numb from drink, and didn't hear the tremulous voice beside him. It was several hours later that Edecon became conscious of the moaning and threshing next to him.

Then, he remembered the voice calling to him. Edecon lifted himself on one elbow, peering through the tent for the source of the sound. He threw back the quilts to reveal the tortured limbs of Ernac tangled between layers of furs. He touched the boy lightly. A raging fire was coursing through Ernac, and Edecon drew back his fingers in reflexive shock.

A chill shot through him. He bolted the tent, panic clutching his aching head.

16

I heard Ku's voice outside, and what a marvel it was.

"The Khatun," she proclaimed, "needs help. She's lost a runaway mare and her yearling."

I knew the yearling she spoke of. I remember keeping him in the yurt as a weanling during a cold spell in his first winter.

Ku's news breathed life into me. I had felt I couldn't face another day inside the yurt. I had no desire even to rise from my quilts. I relished Ku speaking sharply to Adamis, for she has a way about her that doesn't allow argument.

"You, and Bahka Beki, are wanted in the Khatun's tent," she announced.

I couldn't have hoped to escape the yurt with my most pathetic pleadings, but Ku's order rescued me. Adamis and I started just after sunup, and with hard riding we found the mare's spoor a little past midday. We allowed ourselves a short stop, pulling up near a bunch of scrub next to a mound of burial rocks. We were hungry and thirsty, and the sun was fierce, but I had no complaint. My energy was high, and Red Atagha was beside himself with joy. He had been languishing for many days to no purpose in the near pastures, as I had in the tents of Onegesius.

"Ho, Beki," Adamis shouted. "We stop here. The track is fresh, we'll catch them by sunset." Dismounting, he squatted near the burial rocks and began to gnaw at a joint of mutton.

I hobbled Red Atagha and settled myself to satisfy my own stomach. When my gut was full I was eager for news from Kreka's tents. I couldn't resist putting a question to Adamis.

"Is the danger truly past, Adamis?" I asked. Kreka's steward is not known for talking overmuch and I was surprised at his ready answer.

"Truly, it is. Mother Kreka walks about with Oebarsius and her face is free of dread." He nodded gratefully to himself.

Your own face, Adamis, I thought, reflects relief.

"Ernac," he went on, "is eating well. His flesh is coming back. His bones no longer stick out like knives under his blankets. The flush of fever comes on him in late afternoon but less so each day. He asks for you, Beki. I think he's well enough to have a visitor."

Adamis' mouth cracked in a rare smile. He actually looked pleased. So, taking advantage of his mood, I pressed my luck.

"And what of Edecon?" I said. "Has the Khan forgiven him for failing to protect Ernac?"

Adamis' face darkened and I knew I had pushed too far.

"Best not to talk of Edecon right now, little Beki. The Khan has much fury to vent. He blames everyone except the Khatun and Eskam. As for Edecon, he wisely stays out of Attila's sight. Even you would do well to be careful for now."

My heart fell. I didn't wish to hear what Adamis said. I'd been hoping to speak to Attila. A daughter's heart leans toward comforting her father. But, I reminded myself, he is the Khan, I can't gain entrance to him as I have in the past. During these last weeks, in the space between spring and summer, Attila has gone beyond my reach. He has become a remote figure.

"We've rested long enough." Adamis stood and caught his horse's reins. "After the execution of this false shaman the Khan's outlook will improve, Beki. After the campaign in the north begins he'll have problems more to his liking to occupy his attention."

Adamis turned to his mount, and his face took back its taciturn mask as we tracked the wayward horses through the afternoon. I was occupied with what Kreka's steward had said. If what Adamis says is true, I thought, this awful period is over. I do have lingering doubts about the aftermath of Ernac's illness, but, at least, I can now begin to plan for our future. I pray Adamis knows what he's talking about for Ernac's illness has given me the worst scare of my life.

At first word of his sickness I was sent from Kreka's yurt, and a safe, comfortable spot was made for Ernac in my place. When he was stricken there seemed little hope for his survival and the world stopped moving in our camp. No attention was given to ordinary matters, only the daily reports of Ernac's condition mattered. Soon it became clear he'd been the victim of a poisoning. There was no doubt this had been a deliberate attack on the life of the Khan's heir and Attila's fury rolled like an earthquake.

The unfortunate who placed the poison in Ernac's cup was caught and put to the torture. Still Attila's rage boiled. More than one hundred men have died, and many more will die, before his need for revenge is satisfied. The people closely allied with Teb-Ogatai, even those whose names were barely connected with him, were herded into the central compound and impaled or beheaded. In the middle of the compound stand many tall stakes sporting bloody moon-shaped heads at the top. The heads hang like a small army of round banners as we pass through the compound. Their numbers are still growing.

Today I had rather strange news from Ku. It's said the Khatun has interceded on behalf of the poisoner. Declaring further torture would yield nothing more from Baldin, Kreka has ordered the painful ministrations of the eunuchs ended. Baldin's agony was protracted and unusually refined. He will never have normal use of his legs, and his hands are fingerless blobs that will never be able to serve himself or any other.

It appears, however, that he told the truth as far as he knows it. It's an odd twist, but what is left of him will now be given into the service of the one he tried to kill. The Great Khan would not hear of sparing Baldin's life until Mother Kreka pointed out his maimed body can be a living warning to any who would dare touch someone under Attila's protection. It is the Khatun's wish that Baldin's eyes and ears now stand guard over Ernac. And he may need them. I would not breathe my doubts to a living soul, but I fear Ernac will never be the same as before his illness.

Those who were with him in the first days were convinced he would die. I was allowed to see him only once in the ten days after he was stricken, and that only because I am his betrothed. Witnessing physical agony is considered bad luck, and I admit the force of his seizures was frightening.

Kreka never left his side. Day and night she massaged his pain-racked limbs and bathed his fiery, delirium-ridden head. Kreka recognized the symptoms of the poison in Ernac's wine as an extract of the wormwood sage Teb-Ogatai burned in his public demonstration. Medicine concocted from wormwood is often used, especially in spring. Properly mixed it can rid a child of a winter's bellyful of worms, but the Khatun well knows that too strong a dose can be deadly. Therefore, she mixed a potion to counter the poison wormwood. She and Ku forced it down Ernac's throat time and again and held his head while he vomited it up.

What brash impulse caused the shaman to risk poisoning Ernac on the very day the curse was lifted from him I cannot imagine. That is only one of the puzzling aspects of the attempt on Ernac's life. That he survived the poison can be seen as a miracle, but I believe Mother Kreka's knowledge of herbs and healing arts really saved him.

When Teb-Ogatai's evil act became open gossip his life was in jeopardy, and when whispers of his nefarious act began to circulate among the *qara budun,* he was lost. Rumors of the shaman's duplicity came first from well-known informers in the Khan's household. Agents operate everywhere on behalf of the Khan, but many in this camp are loyal only to the Khatun. Ku, for instance, informs for Kreka only. Attila certainly doesn't need the Khatun's spies, for his own are the best. They, too, have been busy gathering proofs of Teb-Ogatai's guilt. Now, the people say this shaman was a practitioner of witchcraft, never a shaman in the true sense. So witchcraft is charged against him, as well as the attempt on Ernac's life.

Wedding festivities for Eskayar and the Khan were ruined by the attempt on Ernac's life, but Eskayar willingly helped Kreka nurse him. From the moment Eskam learned of the tragedy he has prayed tirelessly to the Great Tngri for Ernac's recovery. Attila has given Eskam the highest honor in thanks for his prayers. He will now be head shaman, and personal advisor, to Attila. The Khan's show of appreciation to

Kreka for her skill and dedication in saving Ernac is boundless. It's very gratifying to me to see Attila search for ways to show the Khatun how grateful he is.

As the days pass, my fears for the life of my future husband have been replaced with worry about the aftermath of his peculiar illness. Ernac is very weak. He suffers long periods of confusion, even fits of unconsciousness. On top of this, the arm and leg on his left side don't always answer the commands of his mind. The Khatun is comforting. She tells me recovery will take time and rest, but she constantly assures me he will come back to himself. I only hope she's right. I shall certainly do everything in my power to make that happy day a reality.

There are many problems facing us, and it's a small matter, still, I would like to know what Edecon's fate will be. Adamis, ever close with his thoughts, was not forthcoming when I questioned him on this. The future of Ernac's mentor is precarious. We won't know what the Khan's thoughts are until events show themselves more fully. Edecon could be called to the northern campaign, for example, and not return. Such a vague ending is not unusual for one who falls out of favor with Attila. The Khan doesn't much care for killing except in battle, when angry over a betrayal, or for important political purpose. Attila is ruthless when there is reason to be, otherwise, he's mild-tempered.

It's said Teb-Ogatai's fate will soon be announced. I shudder to imagine it. His execution will be a public affair, and whatever the method used to carry it out his death will be terrible. This is one public performance in which Teb-Ogatai won't be swaggering and waving to the crowds as he loves to do. I never liked or trusted him, and he did an awful thing, yet I can't help feeling sympathy. The official torturers are ingenious in their devisings. The eunuchs are as devoted to cruelties as they are to hatching complicated plots.

After Teb-Ogatai is executed I'm sure the camp will settle back into its normal routine. The Khan's worst fears for Ernac nearly came to pass, but since a kind fate acted to save him, Attila will turn his mind once more to battle. The Great Khan is eager to be away to the north. He itches for the business with the Acatiri to be finished so he can start his assault on Aëtius in the west.

There are more than enough secrets in this camp, but it's no secret that Aëtius is the man upon whom Attila seeks to avenge himself.

17

"I will be more relieved to have this finished than Attila will," the Khatun said to herself.

Today Kreka wanted to be especially attractive. She struggled to plait her heavy hair evenly. Winding the dark loops onto her head, she secured them with silver and gold pins. She was in control of herself, but she was cranky and impatient. The effort to make herself appear young and beautiful was tedious. She was aware that she looked every minute of her age. Jerking her polished copper mirror down from the tent pole the Khatun surveyed her wavering reflection.

She winced at what she saw.

"Ahhh, ahhh," she moaned. "The flesh of my cheeks has fallen away. I must remedy that. I look like a haunted woman. Attila must not suspect there's more in the smudges under my eyes than nights of sleep lost tending Ernac."

Patting her face gently, Kreka tried to coax a bit of color into her skin, a little pink to soften the sooty pouches beneath her eyes. She heard a soft rustle of hide and fur, and she let her mirror drop. Rising to greet her husband she extended her hands.

He covered them with his.

"You are prepared, Kreka?" he asked.

His question lacked irony. He knew his wife was capable of performing the ceremony she'd been chosen to enact. He would not have thought to question her resolve. His words were an expression of concern, a recognition of the strain she'd been under.

Attila paused and looked at her, waiting for her answer. She glanced at him obliquely, and her heart moved. The face of Attila, the combination of power and sensitivity, never failed to touch her. His pale eyes created a curious affect. One green, one gray, they stood out like smooth, cool agates against his swarthy skin. They transmitted self-containment and strength. This is the look of a conqueror, she thought. Yet he seems indifferent, unaware of presenting himself to the world as a hard gem of arrogance.

Kreka returned Attila's warm look. Her eyes were alive with affection. How she valued this man. What would she not do for him? What had she not already done for him, risked for him? She had even offered up her youngest child as a protective shield for her husband. Sudden resentment flared in Kreka's heart, but the feeling clashed with the task she must now perform. She quelled her stab of anger, aware that she had no energy for a fight.

"Is it time, then?" she said resolutely.

Attila nodded slightly, comprehending her mood.

The Khatun's eyes focused mechanically. She saw in front of her the body of her enemy and her pupils slicked with anticipation.

"I am ready," she pronounced. Her smile was flat.

"I've had a long rest. I'm much revived. Are the others in their places? Is the jackal conscious?"

"My eunuchs are not bunglers, Kreki," the Khan said. "The wretch is conscious and wishing he was not. Teb-Ogatai's birds of death have been hovering for hours. Everyone is assembled. Ernac is there as well."

Attila frowned. "I hope he is well enough for this. He's seated on his cushions in the place of honor. He'll signal when he wishes you to deliver the blow."

The Khan put his hand to the doorflap, raised it, and motioned Kreka to step out. Together they emerged from the doorway of the Khatun's yurt. Side by side, they walked down the slight, fifty-yard incline to the spot where a hushed crowd waited for them. There was not a murmur from those gathered to watch the final moments of the shaman, Teb-Ogatai.

This would not be a gladsome performance, but a performance it surely was. Today the Great Khan, warlord of a thousand clans, would witness the execution of a man who had plotted against one of his heirs, a man who had thought to kill Attila's favorite under his very nose. In the Khan's own encampment a viper had been hatched, a viper who dared to imagine sinking his teeth into Attila, Lord of the Huns. The importance of the occasion needed no explanation.

The sad apparition around which this orderly crowd had gathered made no sound. For hours no moan, or scream, had issued from the nude figure that hung crucifixion-fashion from a center post. The shaman's head rolled, and his eyes drifted open and shut without focus. Dried spittle encrusted his mouth and chin, but there was little blood to be seen. The shaman had more than enough in him for Kreka's sword to unleash.

Very skilled were the hands of the Khan's torturers. The shaman's body, impaled at wrists and ankles, skin a sheet of sweat, told only a small part of his torment. His travail had proceeded in full view of the camp. The post from which his body dangled was low. A man of normal height standing in front of him could have reached over the top of his head.

Today a single eunuch hovered, splashing water over the shaman's face, hoping to keep him conscious. Two others had been relieved of their duties and had promptly deserted the scene. For almost four days three eunuchs had assiduously balanced doses of pain with doses of revival. They could have continued for at least as many days again for the delectation of onlookers. A few complained the man's shrieks and moans disturbed camp routine, but the eunuchs persevered. For another full sun they continued poking at his tender orifices with wooden instruments, scraped at bone, and dug at flesh with thin metal knives.

The reason for this extra day of attention from the official torturers was Ernac. The Khan's son must be far enough recovered to carry out his part in the ceremonies. Law must be adhered to, rules must be observed, and the man who plotted to kill him must die at Ernac's command.

The Khan, and the Khatun, seated themselves on the pillowed stools provided for them. Their faces were expressionless twin moons.

When she was very young — terribly long ago it seemed to Kreka — she had witnessed a similar scene in the camp of Ruga Khan, Attila's uncle. One of the Khan's trusted advisors had been caught secretly leaving the tent of Ruga's chief wife. It had crossed Kreka's mind then, and why she remembered it now she couldn't say, that the man was mad to risk his life for one casual night with his lord's wife. If, indeed, the assignation had been casual he had been rash beyond belief. Kreka had never learned the details of the incident. She remembered only that Ruga had had his advisor executed, but had taken no revenge on his wife.

Whatever the truth of that long ago day, this day was in no way similar. This was the opposite of accidental. This was a day for which Kreka had planned well. Teb-Ogatai's death was her doing, and it belonged to her. This, the Khatun knew. It was no more than fitting that hers should be the hand that dealt the mortal wound. If Ernac hadn't been so weak it would have been his hand. As it was, the honor became hers. Her hand would be the hand of her son. Rightly so, she thought with satisfaction.

The Khatun remembered, too, in regard to that long ago day in Ruga's camp, that she had been unable to understand how Ruga Khan could lift his arm with such elegant ease, position the sword, and with one skillful thrust, end his advisor's life. But in middle-age Kreka had traveled beyond childish borders, where the responsibilities of life and death are unimaginable. Now, it was she who sat in the seat of the executioner. Lords, and common folk, alike, face the same fate, she thought dispassionately. For most the gods decide. In this instance Kreka had taken the decision into her own hands, and she had been lucky.

The means to carry out her plan had simply come to her. Perhaps it had come from the great Etugen-Eke, her Earth-Mother. The Khatun had sought cunning, and she had found it. It passed her mind that Attila might suspect there was more involved here than Teb-Ogatai's traitorous scheming. No matter, she thought. It was time, and she would finish it.

She turned her eyes to Ernac. Waiting rigidly for his cue, hardly able to keep his emaciated body upright on his cushions, her son accepted the motion of Kreka's head with his eyes. Mindful of his image before the people, Ernac thrust his thin hand straight forward, brought it across to the post where the shaman was hanging and dropped it. The effort was nauseating. He ground his teeth to keep from retching.

Adamis, seated next to him, supported the boy with his body. All the while he studied the face of the Khatun. Her steward's eyes bored through the space between them, his heart reaching out to her.

The Khatun acknowledged her son's gesture with a nod. Rising from her stool, she moved to stand in front of the Khan. In order that she would not be raised higher than himself in front of the *qara budun*, he rose with her. Pulling his body sword from its sheath, Attila laid the blade flat across his palms and thrust it out to the Khatun. She inclined her head to him, and for a moment their eyes locked. Then, with smooth inevitability, as oiled bodies slide against one another in the night, the blade slipped from his hands into hers.

Kreka spun on her heels, her incomparable stride carrying her to Teb-Ogatai in a half-dozen steps. She snapped her head up to look at his face. She craved a certain recognition from him, and she indicated her wish for a dash of cold water. The official torturer obliged with a vengeance. The full contents of a bucket was drained over the shaman. His head lifted for an instant.

To the onlookers the startled twitch on the shaman's face meant nothing, but to Kreka it was a moment of unspeakable consummation. This was the admission she had sought from her enemy before his accursed spirit departed the earth. With one eloquent flick of his eyes Teb-Ogatai gave her what she wanted. His look told the Khatun that Teb-Ogatai knew who had brought him to this end.

She gathered the awareness inside her, clasping it lovingly. Her broad-spaced eyes fastened on the shaman's and she raised the sword, hilt gripped with both hands. Fixing the blade chest high in front of her Kreka drove the iron in and up. Without touching bone the sword pierced the main chamber of his heart. The hilt hung sagging from the shaman's diaphragm for a bare moment, then his blood came pouring onto the ground in a scarlet waterfall that descended directly at the feet of the Khatun.

Kreka stepped back quickly, her head lowered to hide the triumph that whipped across her face.

18

In one fluid motion the Khatun carried herself from the bloody, consecrated spot back to her stool. She didn't look at the body of the man who had taken so much precious time and energy from her. For more than four years his evil intent had dogged her life. He had ruined her days, and denied her restful dreams. He had not even been a worthy adversary, only a determined one.

She'd understood he must be eliminated, but the planning had taxed her. This was not the kind of game she cared to play. In order to dispose of this bothersome shaman the Khatun had been forced to risk the life of one of her sons, and to jeopardize the respect and esteem she enjoyed in her own camp. She resented being forced to do this. That some unworthy son of a cur had forced the Khatun to play this dangerous game was intolerable.

What if I'd been wrong about him, Kreka thought?

Ah, but there,… it's over, she thought gratefully. It was over, she was not wrong, and they were free of his dark presence. She prayed not to meet another like him in her lifetime.

Kreka placed her hand over Attila's and gave him her most dazzling smile. Her smile said all is well, the world is good, let us go forth to meet the day.

The two of them made their way through the solemn crowd to Attila's pavilion. They halted briefly to speak to a man here, to touch the head of a child there, but they didn't linger. There were private words to be spoken between them.

As they neared the edge of the central compound Kreka turned and caught sight of Adamis' golden arms lifting Ernac from his seat.

She watched him settle her son back onto his litter. Her steward had been a rock of reliability. When Attila left for the north she would find a proper reward for him. She would repay Adamis in full for his loyalty. He deserved a special boon.

Inside the tent Attila motioned his wife to the raised sleeping platform, thick with carpets and silk coverings. Kreka took his invitation and reclined, hoping to relax. She knew she must rid herself of recent pressures. She tried turning her mind to the business of the coming war but was unable to shake off the residue of ill-feeling. It wasn't easy to forget, to set aside the sufferings of her son, and her own worry.

What a black star Teb-Ogatai has been, she thought. Too much had slipped away in her preoccupation with the odious shaman. Now she admonished herself to shed all thought of the shaman. That time was finished, and she must be free of it. She must give her full attention to Attila in the coming months.

Again she turned a dazzling smile on her husband.

"You're exhausted, my love," she said. "I know how these days have weighed on you. Come, sit beside me. You need to discuss your campaign in the north. Tell me everything I need to be aware of while you're gone. And how is your new bride? I haven't seen her recently. Is she well?"

Kreka threw her hands in the air. "I'm dismayed at myself," she said. "I've been lax in my duties to Eskayar. Forgive me. I'll make it up to her. With so many new responsibilities, and no one to advise her, I know she's been ill-at-ease. After you're gone I'll tutor her well, you may count on it."

The Khan's face brightened at his wife's brisk tone and he, too, sat down. Attila had feared the Khatun would be inclined to dwell on the execution of Teb-Ogatai, on his infamous plots and unforgivable acts. There was much he wished to say, and he wanted these last weeks forgotten. Attila preferred not to dwell on his personal failings. He still rued the day he and Kreka had almost forgotten themselves and done one another awful harm.

He deeply regretted this loss of control in himself, and also, he'd been embarrassed to discover Kreka's informants more alert than his own. After he had left her tent that day he had set his spies to work. When they told him Kreka's information was accurate he'd been too contrite to admit it to her. He would talk of that later, he said to himself, after the hurt had faded.

There was another small matter Attila didn't care to reveal, not now or ever. Kreka had done him a favor by pursuing a course that lent itself so beautifully to the destruction of the shaman. The Khan had allowed her to endanger Ernac's life, though he knew the risk. His spies had been lazy but they had told him enough. He would be freed of much uneasiness in the north because his wife had chosen to act on her own. She had been right to act, but she had been wrong in one thing. Attila had not trusted the shaman. Yet, he'd had no overt reason to move on Teb-Ogatai and his followers. Attila was grateful to his wife. He'd been able to use the dramatic gamble designed by the Khatun. He admired her creativeness. The crisis she'd contrived had given him the opportunity to appear strong in revenge, as well as magnanimous in the matter of the pathetic, cowardly Baldin.

As it turned out, Ernac's illness had brought the encampment together in sympathy for the Khan. The mere fact the boy didn't die quieted mutterings of evil omen planted by Teb-Ogatai. The rule of the Khan of Khans had met its first big test of internal power and had come out on top.

Attila was superstitious to a degree, but superstition never prevented him from using the fears of others. No matter how close the shaman had been to the gods, or how far from them, the son of a dog had served Attila's interests. Now that he was rid of Teb-Ogatai's malign influence and Ernac's health was returning, Attila thought the affair had turned out well. The Khan was relieved and impatient to press forward with his plans to attack the Acatiri.

Attila was enjoying one of his better humors. He nestled comfortably next to the Khatun. "It was an admirable blow you dealt, Kreki," he said. "I seem to recall that technique. It was given you by my uncle Oebarsius. Clean and neat. I couldn't have aimed the blade better myself."

Kreka knew he was flattering her, but she also knew Attila spoke truth. Hers had been a well-placed thrust and she didn't turn away his praise. The Khatun took pride in her handling of weapons. Her training had been the best and she had taken to it eagerly. She had a talent for the hunt. When she was only Beki's age she had taken down a rare spotted cat from more than one-hundred yards. Once, out on a hunt together, she and Attila had tried for the same stag. Her arrow had made the mark while his fell short. She loved to remind him of the incident, but today she refrained from mentioning it.

"You have a way of putting the compliment that gives the honor to your uncle, my Lord Khan. However, it pleases me that you noticed my poor efforts," she said.

"Some are born mice, some are born leopards. And you Kreki, were born a leopard," Attila said. He grinned. "One cannot travel far from what one is born."

"Ah, such wisdom," she said, falling in with his jesting mood. "Such wisdom. How observant is the Khan."

"No need to mock me," Attila said happily, "when I speak well of you."

He reached affectionately to touch Kreka's arm.

"And you, mighty warlord, who have the gods appointed as your spirit protector? What name are you called in secret?" she said.

"I have many names and none of them are secret," he answered dryly. In a mood to call the names aloud Attila began proclaiming.

"I've heard myself called ravening wolf," he said. "I have been named bloodthirsty demon, pestilential plague, fiend of darkness, savage demon. I am, they say, a rabid rapist, a butcher of pregnant women. I slaughter and devour children. I boil babies and eat their tender flesh. I am the devil incarnate. I am brutish, foul and accursed. And there are worse names than these. The Romans have given me titles designed to curdle the milk of nursing mothers. Do my names horrify you?"

"No," she said. "I've heard more terrible than these. I've heard every epithet applied to you. No need to repeat them all."

"You have thought on these too generous descriptions of me, have you?" he said. "Very well then. Today you will divine the spirit that inhabits me and name my personal protector. What you name will be my spirit sign, Kreki."

Attila tightened his hand on her arm, making his request a demand.

"If you wish it," she said readily.

She made a face, scrunched in her mouth and drew her brows together. "I am thinking," she said, "of the form your spirit takes, asking it to come before me."

Her eyes opened and her features lifted. "I have it!" she proclaimed, "You are the steppe eagle."

"An eagle?" questioned the Khan.

"Yes, you are an eagle," the Khatun declared. "Of all creatures an eagle best loves its freedom. They are wrong who call the eagle bloodthirsty. The eagle kills without passion, it kills as wind blows. It is in the nature of wind to blow and the nature of an eagle to strike. The eagle kills to eat and is serious about each life it takes. That is you, Attila. What more resembles you than a freedom-loving, high-soaring steppe eagle? The eagle acts, but who can claim they know what the eagle thinks."

Kreka's words lost their bantering tones.

What had started as a diversion to erase thoughts of treachery and politics from their minds had taken a different turn. The solemn, unspoken awareness of their common situation rose between them. The spy had not been born who could ferret out the schemes being hatched by Kreka and Attila at this very moment. The beings who war within the heart cannot be seen, nor could they see the Great Tngri who had told Kreka the steppe eagle was Attila's protector. Nevertheless, it struck them that the naming was correct.

"This is a moment to mark," he said.

"It is," Kreka replied. "I will take note of it. When you return from the north the eagle will be embroidered on your battle flags."

Then, taking advantage of Attila's pensive mood Kreka spoke what was in her mind.

"Our people have watched long, and not so patiently, for a war eagle, Attila," she said. "You are what they have sought. No hotheaded fool, no plunder hungry vulture, you are a warlord who can bring Huns together in their own interests. Like the eagle you were born without natural enemies, and like the lord of the skies you have never acquired a normal man's fear."

Placing a hand on his arm and pulling his eyes to hers the Khatun spoke slowly. Confidence in her intuition grew as she spoke, and she found there was much to support her theory.

"You are right about yourself, Attila," she said, nodding. "You are not simply a man of battle, but a man with a larger view. You have watched others and you have learned. The Romans and the traitor Aëtius have been good teachers to you.

"Living in an alien world you glimpsed what is in store for us if we have no common purpose. You know how to keep the affections of your troops. You see what moves them to loyalty and pushes them to desertion. You see, as I do, the coming clash of worlds. The Romans have too many ambitions. They would take over every people, turn every tribe into a Roman tribe whether the people wish to live as Romans or not."

He didn't answer. There was no need. The words his wife spoke were his own thoughts. The Khan knew, had known since long before she spoke, that he must mount a full-scale war against the Empire. That wasn't necessarily bad. Attila did not hate war. Nor, did he, as most imagined, love war. War was his life; he had been born to it as the eagle is born to hunting. He had learned battle technique as an eagle learns the timing of its strike. The Khan was skilled, and he didn't question the rightness of his skills. Had he been born into another situation he might have seen war differently, but Attila was not a man to trouble himself with what might have been.

The problems of life here and now were quite disturbing enough. He had been a mere youngster, chafing under the rule of his Uncle, Ruga Khan, when he first understood the Huns couldn't hope to do more than scratch out a grim existence unless they came together. Each man for himself had been the time-honored way of the Huns. Each took what his strength and cunning could get him and kept what he took for his own tents.

But that way was the past. Once the eastern lands had been in front of them; the pastures and plateaus and all the mountains and oases across the Gobi. Then there had been the western pastures, a land vast as the heavens where the ancients could wander. Storytellers told of these ancients, of the generations who had moved west season by season seeking fresh pastures. Riding and raiding, pushing some tribes ahead of them, assimilating others, the people had moved inexorably toward the edges of the settled world.

Today Hunnic tribes lived head-to-head with the forces of Empire. They touched the hem of Roman territories. How could they fight the Romans at such close quarters? The Gauls? The Persians and the Visigoths? And how to keep the north and the east open for trade and pasturing? This couldn't be accomplished with the old ways. It required a large, powerful, self-sustaining army, an army that could be relied on to come at a call. Attila needed troops who would dedicate their swords to a common warlord.

He knew very well they couldn't continue in the old ways. And they couldn't fight the Romans without taking thought for the fact that they had been changed by their contact with Empire. Attila didn't approve of the changes he'd seen in his lifetime. There were insidious weakenings in the people's thinking, weaknesses that would devitalize them. The ways of Empire spelled death for a free people. Kreka had spoken truly, they might all become Romans whether they wished it or not.

Aloud he said, "One day, Kreki, you must tell me why men make war to get and keep what they need. This is something I ponder and you are a woman of wisdom."

"No need for sarcasm, Attila," she said shortly. "That is not a real question. You know very well why you fight."

"On the contrary, it's a real question," he said affably.

Is he trying to get me to reveal myself or is he serious, she thought briefly. Then, the Khatun laughed with delight, as if it was a huge joke.

"I don't believe you," she said. "If I did I would say the answer isn't as hard to find as you imagine. For every question there's a key. When you find the key it fits so neatly one cannot but wonder why the puzzle seemed difficult. Someday, perhaps, we'll talk of this. Now we deal with the moment. Our lives beg for practical decisions, Attila, and we are both too much creatures of duty to ignore immediate need."

Kreka cut off discussion of the question of men's reasons for making war. She plucked her husband's hand off her arm and rose, slipping off her furs. The day had been long and not without emotion. The Khatun was tired and there were serious matters to discuss before a night of restoring sleep would be hers. She would have to concentrate to keep her attention on the issues. What was important to Attila was important to her.

She turned to face him, noting again the striking difference between his private face and the public face. Before his men, and before the *qara budun*, Attila was every inch the implacable Khan. She wondered how he slipped the public mask so deftly over his private face. This trick was a gift of leadership that he used to great effect. The man of action, the warlord, was also a lover of solitude, a thinking man.

Suddenly, she changed her mind about discussing war. She said, "Tell me, do you wish for a time free of battle?"

He didn't seem surprised by her question, nor did he appear to resent her asking, but according to his way he didn't give a direct answer. Instead he repeated the flattering observations on Kreka's expertise with the sword and told her about the swelling his favorite stallion was having in one of his knees.

This war-horse, Bahgatur, was from the stock of the Khan's grandfather and his father before him. He was not a young horse, the snowy mane and tail were now dull, stone-grey, yellowing at the ends. Still, he remained Attila's favorite in war. Kreka knew Attila would be loathe to lose him in battle. For steadiness, strength and durability Bahgatur was unequaled. He was larger than most Hun horses, and in action he was a horse of undeniable spirit and solid temperament. He had made a unique place for himself in the Khan's affections. Attila had decided Bahgatur was lucky for him.

That's so like my husband, she reflected. He would love a more beautiful stallion for its looks, just as he does a beautiful woman, but he would not value it as he does Bahgatur. He wants Bahgatur, the old and faithful, with him in the north, though a younger mount might serve him better.

Attila is a puzzle, in war and in peace. Untangling the threads he weaves into a world of politics and law, war and battle plans, would take the talents of a god. Imagine him asking my opinion on why men go to war! Someday I may surprise him and tell him what I think. He might even listen to my views. There is such a paradox in his reverence for the old ways and his curiosity about the new. My husband keeps many layers of himself hidden.

Kreka offered polite help for Bahgatur's knee. "For your sake I hope you have Bahgatur with you in the north," she said. "I'll see to a poultice for his knee. My groomsmen will be his faithful nurses until you're ready to ride."

"Tell me," she asked, "when will you leave? What word from Onegesius?"

"The next full moon will see us in the country of the Acatiri," Attila said. "Kuridach expects a show of force and that he will get."

Attila shook his head powerfully, as if affirming the performance of his armies.

"The Acatiri aren't easy to contain, my love," she said. "They have no loyalties. They are like the serpent born with too many heads; chop one head off and another appears, opening its mouth to strike you."

"Many heads, but only one belly," Attila said. "It's the belly we must conquer. If we are lucky — may the Great Tngri ride with us — we'll slit the belly before the season of fat horses ends. Kuridach controls the belly, and the many heads will wither when the intestines of the beast have been destroyed."

Remember," Kreka answered, "it takes only two or three roving bands to form another head; another head, another beast."

He was silent.

"You go at full strength?" she asked finally.

Her question was no more honest than his. She was aware of their habit of keeping political secrets from one another. Kreka had known of the preparations, had seen the comings and goings of Attila's picked men and influential captains from certain factions of the Acatiri. They had been riding in and out of camp for weeks. This was not to be a minor skirmish as Attila would have had the world, or Aëtius, believe.

The Khan planned to take out the main force of Acatiri swiftly and completely. There would be no second chance, no opportunity for Kuridach to change his mind. Attila was staking everything on one crushing assault. When the blow had been dealt he would leave Ellac and Onegesius to keep stray Acatiri bands in line. The Acatiri, and the northern Goths, would be his safeguards. He needed a protective buffer at his rear, needed to be free to spend the coming winter gathering his western forces. He was intent on pushing his campaign against the East Romans. After that, the West.

Attila grunted forcefully.

"In full strength," he said. "I count on more than 50,000 men to start with me, that many are committed to me. We pick up the eastern clans Oebarsius has promised when we reach the west bank of the River Borysthenes. Above the west bank, where the Borysthenes flows into the Pontus Euxinus, we take on another 20,000 men. I'm lucky. Oebarsius and his people know this country; each outcropping, every rise and fall of the land, is familiar to them. There is a level site on the west bank. There I will launch my forces, and we shall see what my plan will do."

The eyes of the steppe eagle flashed; one grey, one green. Many said those eyes were openings to two separate men who lived in the Khan's body. His eyes, they said, were a sign from the Great Tngri. From his babyhood there had been evidence marking Attila as Great Khan.

Attila expanded on his version of how he meant to master the Acatiri.

"Kuridach doesn't know what comes to meet him," he boasted. "He flatters and fawns over me, but imagines he might someday vie with me for the northern territories, and for those bands of brigands he calls warriors. His so-called warriors are undisciplined bandits. He will learn the Khan is unbeatable, and he will learn in one lesson. I have no more than a summer to give to the ratty Acatiri."

Kreka seated herself beside him. "You are confident in this move, I see that. You always have the next battle well-mapped, but there is always another after that. You didn't answer me. Do you ever think of a time without war?"

He grinned broadly. More accurately he extended the grin that already stretched his mouth. "I would rather think of hunting than of war," he said.

"Is that your answer?" she said. "Or is it just your way of turning to other matters?"

Would she ever know what he held in his heart of hearts? Would she ever know what he held most dear?

Attila didn't answer, and Kreka didn't bother to pursue her question.

She looked down at her hands. "You claim I know you so well, Great Khan," she said. "If I do, it surely is a wonder. You offer little help in knowing you."

Shadows slanted over the carpets. They had been talking through the afternoon and Kreka wanted an end to the day. What had been required of her she had done, now she deserved to be alone, free unto herself. Even putting on a fair face before Attila was a strain.

"But I tell you everything, Kreki." Still grinning, Attila slapped her thigh happily.

"Everything you want to tell me, you rascally goat." She brushed his hand aside impatiently.

"Everything you need to know and much you don't need to know," he said. His good humor persisted. "Only a few minutes ago I was a mighty steppe eagle, now I'm reduced to a rascally goat who may become a meal for that haughty bird. How could that happen to me in such a short time?"

"You cannot resist your bad jokes, Attila, but take pity on me. I don't find them amusing."

He glanced at her drawn features. "You are tired, dear one," he said.

The smile he'd kept in place during the afternoon vanished as if he had held it only for her benefit, though surely that was not true.

"I'm sorry," he said. "I should've seen you were too spent for lighthearted foolishness. I leave you to your rest. It is well deserved."

Her mouth formed a tart reply, but before Kreka had the words out she dropped her eyes to her hands again and was astonished to see how they were shaking.

I'm no better than my son, she chided herself. *I tremble from weakness just as Ernac did after his fever.* She wanted to say more, she needed to know more. If not today, another day, she thought. The rest is for another day.

"It's I who should ask forgiveness, my own," she said. "You have the long riding and short rations of war ahead of you. But it's true I'm ready to rest."

Kreka allowed herself a grimace. She had used up her stores of energy today and could no longer hide her emptiness.

As Attila rose, his features became remote. His attention had swerved to the coming days, to gathering himself for the road to war. She rose with him, refusing to allow her control to crumble, refusing also to relinquish these final moments.

The uneasy tension between them lifted. Looking ahead to the months away from one another gave both of them a freshening scent of freedom. Both had an appetite for what was to come, both welcomed the challenge.

Short weeks together and long months apart, this was their pattern, but their bonds were no less strong because of the separations. They had separate duties and separate satisfactions and they relished times independent of one another. Attila and Kreka were united in more than history. Theirs was a union sustained by common goals.

When the Great Tngri takes the spirit from my body, Kreka thought, *the last image before me will be the face of Attila, and perhaps it will be my face that flashes before him at the last.*

"Before you go," she said, "I give you my blessing. May your standard be raised high. May your flag and your sword pierce the heavens. I pray for the Black Banners, that they fly mighty and unbent before you. Go; spill the blood of your enemies as a gift to honor the gods. I call on Dayicin Tngri, the Mounted Warrior, to bless your mission. The luck of the most high will be an invisible shadow riding with you."

She gave him a hasty smile, and found unexpected pride welling in her, a reflection of her own warrior spirit.

"Thank you, Khatun Kreka, for your blessings," he answered graciously. "Your words are generous and beautifully said. They will give me comfort. Be well in my absence."

Attila smiled at her once more and moved to leave.

"Wait Attila!" she cried. "One last blessing. The spirit of Bahgatur, the hero, be with your stallion. May the hero's swiftness and strength dwell in the legs of his namesake, and may he carry you safely."

And to herself she said, "And may your single green eye and your single grey eye come back to me in a head still attached to its body."

The Great Wars

1

"The Khan orders. Shudder and obey!"

The fire storm was ignited. Messengers flowed over the steppes. The order had been expected, and the command rippled outward quickly from the central war camp of the Khan.

The fire storm would be sustained until every creature in its path was driven out or dead. The Khan's armies would leave the land as clean as a vulture-picked bone. No animal scavenger could do better.

In the summer of 445 A.D. Attila was the unparalleled master of swift and thorough decimation. Those clever enough to have thrown themselves on his mercy before this call might live to join him in future battles, and one day might be privileged to share their plunder with the Khan.

On the first day, in the yellow glow of early morning, banners were strung out along the horizon. Felt and silk lifted cheerfully in the cool air off the Danube. Two broad red ribbons sprang up from the crown of each helmet and pointed cap. These ribbons announced that the soldiers rode as horsemen of the Khan. The collars and cuffs edging each man's tunic were bordered with strips of tan for heavy cavalry and strips of blue for light. The gold and silver facings, the officer's colors, cast metallic gleams here and there.

The swarms of men and horses jostling behind their warlord were organized in *toumans*, the time-honored bedrock of the army.

Groups of ten formed squads of one hundred, then regiments of one thousand, until at ten thousand a *touman* was formed. Today forty-thousand bowmen, equipped with lances, body swords and throwing nets, lined the horizon. Attila's army was a merciless war machine, and his enemies had every reason to fear him.

Streaming out across the ground the men forged eagerly ahead, snaking northeastward toward the center of Acatiri country. The skyline was peppered with lines of bouncing ebony dots. The riders formed a ninety-degree arc, a rainbow of undulating horsemen. Their eyes glittered with the twin passions of soldiers. They wanted action, and they wanted plunder. They could feel the iron of their swords piercing the bodies of their enemies, could see the color of his gold. Their craving was tangible, their faces flushed with the prospect ahead of them. They imagined the shining muscles of their arms clutching the fairest Acatiri women, and their saddlebags bulging with plunder.

Before nightfall the initial clash with the Acatiri forward lines was over. The first step of the Khan's order had been carried out. Within the circle of battle the tan scrub grass was glazed with blood. Pieces of men and horses, already beginning to fester, littered the landscape. At first glance the Acatiri dead could not have been distinguished from Attila's men. Then, the Khan's warriors began drifting over the field, sifting through folds of bloody, sodden tunics. They ignored the fixed pupils that stared up at them to pilfer valuables from the fallen Acatiri. Then, they began removing their own dead.

In the next days the bloated Acatiri corpses would grow to bursting on the parched earth, the ground a garden of overripe melons in a blaze of summer sun. Scavengers would approach cautiously, then set to work in earnest. Crows and vultures, hyenas and dun colored dogs, would rip into bellies and squabble over smeary entrails. The stringiest bit of putrefaction would have the attention of the black blowflies.

The Khan's men would not be on the scene. They would not see how neatly the vultures, their glassy-eyed counterparts, erased evidence of the recent carnage. The Khan's murderous forceps, the outspread arms of his flanks, had moved on to the northeast, pushing the furthermost ends of the pincer. Dust would stop the nostrils and fill the throats of the men, women, and children in their path. Mercifully, there would be no survivors.

Attila was using the standard hunting sweep, a staple tactic familiar to every Hun. Years spent on tough, stolid mounts gave Attila's men the stamina and the moves of their animals. They absorbed their horsemanship with the meat that nourished their bowlegs. These men knew, without rule or daily reminder, what they must do. Hunting men, or hunting animals, the job was the same. The only difference between war and hunting lay in the reward. From the hunt they had meat and comradeship, in war, spoils and comradeship.

The movement of the troops began with a sluggish stirring at the outer arms. It gathered momentum as it washed inward. At first, more than a hundred miles separated one end of the army from the other. The far arms would come together only after everything in front of the solid necklace of horsemen had been driven inside their trap. In tandem, as if connected by lengths of rope, the rows of horsemen herded their human game ahead of them, slowly drawing the net tighter.

Occasionally a group of riders was seen to break from the main lines and gallop ahead pell-mell. Within hours they were back in place and another group was off in a similar rush. These forays were not random, though they appeared so to the uninitiated. In the six or eight hours the riders were absent a band of Acatiri had been run to ground and disposed of. Within the seemingly chaotic jumble of horses and men every soldier was in place, the position of every man known.

The troops were professionals, and the strict numbering of the *touman* was more than a convenient counting device. No man would dream of leaving his ten, no man dared to desert a wounded comrade. No soldier who valued his head would turn aside to rape or pillage before his commander signaled permission. The Khan's officers were also careful to hand over the warlord's share to his agents before taking theirs. While the Khan's banners flew over their heads no man would leave the field or ask for quarter. And no man would give it. No foe was spared. When permission to plunder was finally granted a shout would go up and the soldiers would rush for whatever they could grab and carry away.

Messages to and from the Khan's main *ordu* passed easily. Word from the center could reach the outer ends of the flanks in less than a day. Attila's battle design was simple, and mobility was the key. The army foraged off the land. There were no baggage trains, no supply wagons to slow the march. The forward lines were engaged in a continual surge and retreat. The center staged lightning attacks that fell back quickly and allowed the wings to come forward.

This center was made up of elite forces of advisors and lieutenants, picked men who answered directly to the Khan. They were entrusted with cutting out clusters of Acatiri resistance from the main force and destroying them segment by segment. They used a series of swift strokes designed to sever small blood vessels from their arteries. Slivers of Acatiri resistance, confused and cut off from one another, couldn't judge whether or not they met the main Hun force. A few were foolish enough to turn and pursue their attackers. These unfortunates met with the Khan's sharp-eyed, roving units and did not live to tell of their stupidity.

The desultory claw at the Khan's far left began moving faster, keeping pace with the right wing. Soon the center would reach the Borysthenes River, there Oebarsius, and fifteen-thousand of his men would augment the Khan's position on the right. Remnant Scythian tribes gathered along the way would fill any holes that appeared in the left.

The Khan's army continued closing toward the center. Attila was almost ready to regroup and solidify for the final clash with the northern cousins of the Huns.

He had no use for these cousins of his own people. They were unreliable sometime allies. The Acatiri were fierce in combat, otherwise they were an undisciplined lot, lazy and easy to manipulate. Like cattle being herded into a pen, they couldn't comprehend what moved against them.

Attila's army would do its work and slip away. Only the Acatiri dead would remain as testimony. It has been said the movements of an army must be as difficult to track as light over a moonless plain. The Khan's cavalry, and generations of steppe warriors before them, were partial to hit-and-run attacks. His men could spring onto the back of an enemy out of a seemingly empty plain, and they could disappear as quickly as snow melts under a hot sun.

They offered no target to an enemy. There was no force sitting within striking distance of a foe. No intelligence was wily enough to predict where, or when, they would strike. Secrecy, and silence, were Attila's allies. There would be a quick bloodletting, then silence and empty space.

Also, it is said of war ... planning is secret, attack is ruthless....

Under Attila warfare lived up to the saying. He favored an unvarnished form of fighting. What worked was what Attila used. If the Khan had learned no more than this from his father and his uncles, he had learned to be unsparing. Attila took this lesson to heart. No one mastered predatory tactics more thoroughly, or used them to better advantage, than the King of the Huns. His men became veritable centaurs, the shadowy horsemen of bad dreams. Their very name was terror.

On the second day out, before the pincers had closed too tightly, Attila called Ellac from the northern rim. He gave his oldest son the job of rounding up ragtag Scythians and placing them along the edges of his left flank. Like any sensible father, Attila allowed his son to believe he commanded the operation. In fact, Onegesius had been sent behind him. Ellac, the incapable, could scarcely keep a semblance of order. The left flank lagged in spite of his best efforts until Onegesius arrived.

The Khan asked more of himself than he did of his men. He led the longest stretch, a forced march of more than four-hundred miles. He was less than five days in front of the main army. Three weeks after they started moving his central army met the river. There, they joined Oebarsius, and crossed the Borysthenes from west to east according to plan.

With Oebarsius' troops in place on his right flank Attila's armies were complete. Still, he drove the center, not pausing for the benefit of exhausted men and animals. Even the remudas of fresh horses were tiring, but Attila forced them on for another two-hundred miles before allowing a rest. Then he moved the pincers outward until his armies covered a front of one hundred miles once more. When the central army of ten-thousand finished the last hundred miles they were more than eight-hundred miles from their starting point.

The Khan was now in the heart of Acatiri country and anxious to cement his victory. He drove on. From the first, the scattered knots of Acatiri soldiers had presented no coherent opposition. They lacked the supportive presence of their general, Kuridach, who had conveniently positioned himself behind the front lines. The halfhearted forays of the common soldiers and their immediate superiors came to nothing. They were not able to muster even a division under one banner, and what scrap of morale was left to them was squandered in their fumblings. Kuridach's troops fell back, faltering and uncertain.

Attila pressed on, and the day came when his scouts, together with Berichus, his Chief Lieutenant, begged audience. The scouts reported that the core encampment of the Acatiri was just in front of them and could be reached by midday. If Attila wished to take advantage of the swiftness with which he had penetrated Acatiri country he should do so now.

Berichus declared that Attila could have the Acatiri this very day. "Do we attack?" he asked. "What is your wish, my lord?"

Berichus stood before the Khan and waited. His answer was not long in coming.

Attila moved to take his place in the middle of his *optimates*. Here, he was among the picked men closest to him. They were his personal servants and the men of his household. Berichus, his Chief Lieutenant, and Dengezic, the natural warrior of his sons, flanked him. Orestes, Attila's Roman scribe, the Hunnic noble, Edecon, and those of equal rank rode behind him. The burly Scottas, brother of Onegesius, carried the Khan's personal standard.

The steppe eagle, boldly embroidered in red, standing out against a black background, fluttered beside him awaiting the signal. The eagle was a lone, brilliant splotch bristling from the banks of solid black banners that floated above the heads of the men.

Attila moved in front of his companions. He glanced at the bloody splash of his standard, the serrated wings swaying at his side. How

Kreka had managed to embroider the banner and get it to the fast-moving forward lines he couldn't imagine, but he was glad for the sight of it. It lifted his spirits to see this bright omen of victory flying bravely beside him.

The Khan turned his face ahead and raised his sword arm. Scottas hoisted the black and red of the King of the Huns, and the soldiers caught sight of it. Howls rose up. The lines of horsemen swayed and heaved at Attila's back, each vying for a glimpse of the crimson eagle. Then they spied the powerful red wings whipping violently against the cast-iron bowl of sky.

A host of sinewy throats answered the eagle's summons, and the war-horse, Bahgatur, tore ahead of the ranks. Attila gave himself to the frenzy of battle. He was transformed. He now belonged entirely to war, and to his men. The sight of the Khan, his furious torso dashing out before them, his massive bulk covered in fishscale armor, released a fever that had been smoldering in the men. His gilded helmet swept the sky with scarlet ribbons tossing. His lance pierced the very threshold of the heavens, and just as Attila had planned, the sight of him set his troops afire.

The waiting was over. The men had been anointed, and they were pulled shouting into the wake of the Khan. Here was the moment of kindling that waits for every fighting man. Attila was an incendiary flame exploding in their bowels. Doubt and hesitation were consumed, pangs of fear a memory, as the central army of the Khan plunged to clear a path for the juggernaut behind it.

Attila was jubilant. The skill, and spirit, of his men were one, and he could fight with a light heart. He had prepared a rich soil, and today he would plant the seeds of future victories. Today the Acatiri would see the warrior whose leadership was to become legend. Even during the worst days of the eight years of war that were to come Attila's charisma would inspire his men. His unyielding strength would bring them into, and through, many infamous battles.

Attila had found a confederation of loyal clans, with them behind him he would conquer. The confidence, and the lineage of warlords, had been his, but to forge a kingdom he needed a clear victory.

On this day Attila discovered what it was in him to be.

His bravery and personal charm became the Khan's shields. His men began calling Attila "little father", and he lived up to the name. Chastising and encouraging, remonstrating and raging by turns, he treated his men as he did his horses and his falcons. They were his beloved children.

Shortly after midday Attila's army appeared atop the hills above the main Acatiri encampment. The lines sat unmoving, their helmets pricked with sunlight atop the rim surrounding the camp. An unnatural air of tranquility hung over the scene. The manes and tails of the horses floated about the shoulders of the men in cloudy wisps. For some minutes they sat, silhouetted in silence, a heartstopping ghost army. The sight would raise gooseflesh on the bravest men.

The Hun faces loomed somberly over the camp, their dark lines engirdling the horizon, eyes alert for movement below. The sun was angling to the west, casting shadows over a sepia blanket of scrub and burned grasses. Dazzling flecks danced from the lines of weapons, the polished metal of lance and javelin sending skittering showers of light over the heads of the men.

At an unseen signal the lines started moving. The warriors blended into the shadows in front of them as they wound their way through the sprays of foliage. Their bows and lances brushed the sere clusters in a spattering rustle reminiscent of summer raindrops.

Homely camp scenes greeted their insidious approach. The soldiers' ears caught the muted buzzings of flies and the thin-noted bleatings of sheep in the distance. Their nostrils absorbed a pungent odor of cattle, and horse dung, clean smells that were soon mixed with sharp smells of fear, the fetid stench of men sweating into tunics and leggings. The breath of impending death sent icy currents through the close air. Then, came a low sibilance, a ululating vibration rising to fierce crescendo. The howls of the attacking men sliced through the somnolence of the camp.

The Khan's men were upon the Acatiri.

The first zinging thrum brought an agonized shout. The scream of pain signaled a herdsman going down. His death brought the camp to life. After this one lone whang there came a storm of arrows, rattling overhead, spreading the sky with a dark hail.

The cheerless music of pain replaced the snorts and whiffles of grazing herds. Death is a space both longer and shorter than life, and in this hour there was ample space for flesh to meet its mortal end. Hun arrows, swords, and battle axes, moved swiftly. The blade of the Khan's broadsword took more than a dozen men to their final sleep. Attila was given the honor of the first blow. He wielded it decisively, and after that his arm rose and fell without ceasing. The face of the first man the Khan remembered well, those who followed him were but blurs.

A vicious slice from the Khan's blade had found an amazed Acatiri in the act of running for his horse. A single jet of blood slicked Attila's armor as the body of his sword cleaved through the man's waist into his splenic artery. He went down under Bahgatur and his eyes flared for an instant, glaring up into Attila's.

The last face the man beheld was the rough, pockmarked face of an ordinary Hun warrior. There was nothing to distinguish it from any other. The Acatiri lifted his arm, reaching for his sword, but the arm fell back. He dropped his head and bled out on the ground, closing his eyes as if in sleep. He had lost his life to the sword of a noted warlord, but he would not speak of the honor that had come to him.

Attila was aware of the man's eyes. They were a darting flash on his retina in the instant before Bahgatur's legs carried him on to the second kill. Then earth and sky went spinning, and the world exploded in a welter of butchery. The killing was disorderly and dirty, the irreversible handiwork of iron on flesh. The rank, overpowering odor of entrails hung like cooking grease over the camp, but the action was short-lived.

When the fighting was over and his head had cleared, the Khan signaled for meat and drink. Attila was ravenous, his adrenaline flowing. The killing had cast its familiar spell. Bursts of exhilaration, half joy, half pain, streaked through his veins. A pleasing warmth like the satisfying aftershocks of strenuous sex swept over his flesh. He would have food. He would have drink, and women, and, finally, he would have sleep. Exhaustion would creep inside his limbs like a spent animal and settle in his marrow. These last weeks had taxed his strength. Attila had driven himself harder than he had driven any of his men. He could not afford weakness.

The lure of relaxation could be fatal. Attila needed rest, but this was just one day, and one minor battle. There were major campaigns ahead. He must keep himself under tight rein. Before this was finished the Khan's endurance would be severely tested, for the large challenges to his leadership were yet to come. He had scores to settle, and he was not as young as he wished.

One of the bodyguards ran to him with meat and wine. He took the mutton first, lifting a dripping chunk to his cracked lips. His eyes blinked and narrowed, scanning the ground in front of him as he ate. Before him were the lumpen corpses of the Acatiri. Men, women, children, and animals, and here and there the flash of impotent weaponry next to a hapless form. The land was scarcely visible beneath the uncollected bodies and the debris of the surprised camp. Nothing moved. The aftermath of war did not look like the aftermath of the hunt. There were no nobles waiting to plead for the lives of the survivors. Any animal that survived the hunt would be given mercy, not so a man in war.

Attila spat near a spot where the Acatiri corpses sprawled three deep. Acatiri, he thought, are an offence to decency. They will not remove their people from the field. There will be no burial details.

He knew these corpses would remain where they fell. Whatever the indignity that had come to them in death it could not be worse than being abandoned by their own people. Retrieving the dead from the field was a nicety Attila insisted on. A Hun unit that permitted their dead to lie on the field would not have seen the next sun.

And now the blowflies had arrived, swarming so thick over the bodies that they drew blood. Surely, the Khan thought, the Acatiri know I give burial crews safe passage. After the ears are removed for a count of the dead they are free to take out their fallen.

But Attila knew they wouldn't. They were a slovenly lot, a disgrace to the name Hun. He spat once more onto the red earth under Bahgatur's hooves. The ground that sported this accidental harvest of death was of no interest to him. His eyes sought something else. They came to rest on his battle tent bulking serenely above the devastated camp. The multicolored banners flying from the center pole fanned out like fire beacons on the hill above.

That was where he should be, in his tent, drinking, and enjoying women. Attila was ready to relax. The back of the Acatiri resistance was broken. The day had been good to him. The Great Tngri was one with him, and he rode secure.

"The rest of this campaign," he muttered with finality, "will be up to Oebarsius and Onegesius."

He took a wine bowl from the guard and drank deeply. He drained it and leaned over to wipe his beard and mustache on Bahgatur's mane. The bodyguard took Attila's bowl, and the Khan called for his chief groom, Unagan.

First he would deal with the Persian spy, then he would speak with Dengezic. He would have had the Persian's head lopped off before anyone had a chance to speak with him. Dengezic had no subtlety. No one could match him in battle, in all else he was dense. Off the field, the Khan thought ruefully, Dengezic is always trouble.

"Who is the man Edecon told me about?" Attila asked Unagan when he appeared.

"His name is Tadiqin, my Khan," Unagan answered.

Attila grunted, and said, "See that this Tadiqin is in my tent before the sun sets. Bring Edecon and Dengezic with him. After that, see you to nursing Bahgatur. He took an arrow in his right rump today."

The Khan turned and reined off in the direction of his yurt.

2

Attila shed his cumbersome armor and lowered himself onto the carpets. The Great Khan, warlord of a hundred clans, groaned. It was a sound so soft that not even an ear plastered against the felt of the tent could have picked it up. In the comfort of his tent, Attila smiled. He was anticipating a night of surcease, a few hours for sampling the joys of sensuality.

But first Attila had to look at the monster from which no warrior can hide. He acknowledged the lust that the sights and smells of war set loose in him. He asked that the gods forgive an ordinary soldier. For so he thought of himself, as an ordinary soldier who worked hard for his people, a man who deserved his night of comfort. Relaxation was his reward.

The rolled flap of felt lifted at the doorway and Edecon appeared, asking that he might enter.

"Enter, Edecon. Enter and sit," said the Khan simply.

"Thank you, my lord. You sent for me?"

Edecon sat in front of Attila. He cast his eyes down so that the Khan might speak.

Attila answered tonelessly.

"You say there is a Persian spy within the camp?"

"Yes, my lord. His name is Tadiqin."

"Of what importance is one more spy to me? I am weary. The day has tired me."

Edecon raised his eyes to the Khan. His head and arms quivered alarmingly with the choppy, awkward movements that accompanied his affliction.

"I apologize, my lord, for disturbing you," Edecon said, his voice trembling. "I felt you should know of him. I was told of the man by an undergroom, a servant to Unagan."

"Who does this Tadiqin spy for? And why is he more worthy of note than any other spy?" asked the Khan.

"I am told, my lord," Edecon answered, "that Tadiqin communicates with a certain Lord of the Persians. He was taken captive as a child at the time of Bahram. When we were in the grip of famine, we broke through the Caucasus to the Tigris and Euphrates, took much Persian gold, and we carried away many young captives.

"Tadiqin was one of these captives," Edecon went on. "He was a youngster of only eight summers. Since that time he has been diligent in the service of the Persians. Now, he has been rewarded. He has his lord's ear, and he holds a trusted place in his heart. You know, Great Khan, that the Persian nobles still harbor a desire for revenge. They want the gold we took from them."

"I don't need a history lesson, Edecon," Attila broke in impatiently. "What does this paltry person know that could be of use to me."

"There is no man living who doesn't know something the King of the Huns could make use of," said Edecon, grinning wryly.

"It's come to me that, through his satrap, Tadiqin hears of Aëtius' movements. Also, he knows of the Roman's current troubles with the Persians. They keep troops massed along the southern borders, threaten the outposts, and bleed off troops needed for the north. The Empire can't afford to give up a scrap of ground to the east. You have provided safe passage to the merchants along the trade routes, and the Romans need these trade routes open. If we care to use him, we have in Tadiqin a man with an ear next to Persian intentions. He can be of value; a bargaining tool, shall we say."

Attila was quiet, stroking his beard.

In the midst of his silence Dengezic entered with Tadiqin in tow. The slave prostrated himself at Attila's feet. He was stretched to the length of his body, his head buried face down in the carpets. Dengezic stood until given permission to sit.

Attila didn't acknowledge the presence of the slave, and no one moved. At length he said to the body at his feet, "So, slave, your name is Tadiqin. I'm told you have been with us since you were a child. You must remember many wars and many warriors."

Tadiqin didn't respond.

"Sit up! Look at me when I speak," commanded the warlord.

The man curled himself slowly into a sitting position and raised his head. He was not uncomely, and for a man past his prime he appeared to be in good health. The hair on his head was russet, and his skin carried the deep, natural flush of those who spend their days out-of-doors. His eyes, resting on the man who commanded him, were composed and alert.

"You are servant to my personal groom, is that so?"

The man nodded affirmatively. "I serve Unagan, that is so," he said.

"And do you care for my horses?"

"I do, my Lord."

"You have a hand in the care of Bahgatur, then?"

"Yes," he said, "I have had daily care of Bahgatur, since he was but a milk-mouthed foal."

"You have?" Attila said, his eyebrows reaching upward. "You've done extraordinarily well. Why did I not know of you? Others could learn from you. Perhaps you should have your own tent, a few horses of your own to tend and breed? Would you like that?"

"I would consider it a singular honor, Great One," Tadiqin said, choosing his words carefully."

"Then it is done. Dengezic, you will see to giving Unagan his orders for this man's personal stock. He may pick his own horses up to the number of twelve. And he may choose the mares he wishes his horses to use. Also he will receive a certain allowance of gold, which I will name later, with which to purchase what he needs for the maintenance of these horses."

"It's done, father," Dengezic said. But there was doubt in his voice.

"You will report to me personally on the progress of your herd, Tadiqin. As you know, I am very interested in the breeding and care of my horses," Attila said in friendly tones.

"As you wish, Lord Attila. I'm overwhelmed by your generosity." The slave did not so much move as shift the balance of his torso, to indicate his subservience.

"Now I wish to be alone with my son. You may leave with Edecon. My compliments, Tadiqin. It's a pleasure to speak with the man who has had the care of one of my favorite companions in war. We will talk again."

The two men rose and left the yurt. Dengezic stared at his father, disapproval spread over his unimaginative features.

"Well, Dengezic, what do have to say for yourself?" the Khan asked.

"I don't know what you mean, father."

Attila stood and stepped over to his son's side. He grasped Dengezic's arms through his silk undershirt and hauled him to his feet.

"You stupid fool! You don't know what I'm talking about? You don't know what I mean?"

"I don't understand," Dengezic repeated dully.

"You planned to execute this man without asking a question of him. You would have had his head if Edecon hadn't told me of him. Isn't that so?" Attila said scathingly.

"Yes, my lord, yes. But he's a spy," Dengezic said, trying to defend himself.

"Of course he is a spy. Do you imagine I don't know that? By the Great Tngri, are you hopeless?" Attila yelled. In the privacy of his yurt Attila did to his son what he would never have done in the company of another. He spat in the face of his unhappy offspring. In public such insult to a family member could not have been borne. Attila would not have insulted his son publicly. It would have shamed him more than it shamed his son.

Dengezic was silent, unable to think of a retort to the unexpected onslaught. His dignity was bruised, his blood hot and confused.

"How do I manage to get information from so many sources, Dengezic? How do I keep a river of private knowledge coming to me? How is it I know the movements and motives of my enemies. How do I keep track of them? How do I keep the loyalty of a small army of merchants and traders who feed me with information? Is it only gold and killing that get me what I want?"

Attila cursed his son roundly, and Dengezic remained silent.

"Answer me, you cretin. Answer your father."

"I ... I know you have many spies, Great Khan," his son answered haltingly.

"True. But how do I keep spies? By killing a useful possibility, by failing to turn a well-placed man in my camps into my own man. You have just witnessed a spy being turned, Dengezic. You should be grateful for the lesson. This time the lesson was free, next time you may not be so lucky," Attila said.

The Khan's hands let loose their grip on his son.

"Tadiqin is dangerous," Dengezic said, trying to maintain a semblance of dignity. "How do you know he will be loyal. Though you buy him with horses and gold, how do you know you can trust him?"

"I don't know. I'll find out. There are ways. I will test him. In the meantime I'll use him. A man can be killed anytime. Have you no cunning, boy? Did you come from the womb without a brain?"

"I should've come to you, father," Degezic said grudgingly. "I didn't think the man important. You had much on your mind and this was a small matter."

"In my camp there are no matters so small they don't merit my attention. You will let me decide what I need to know. Do you hear me, you ninny?"

"I hear you."

"Then don't let such a thing happen again. Go now, see to your horses. You don't care for them as you should."

Dengezic flushed deeply.

"You are soft on this Tadiqin because he's good with horses. You care more for the welfare of your horses than you do for your men. You see to your precious horses first. Before your soldiers eat the horses have fodder. Their wounds are tended to before the men's. You aren't half so concerned with your men as with your animals. The men deserve more," he blurted furiously.

Attila turned a long, hard eye on his second son. "Horses are a soldier's lifeblood. One superior horse is worth fifty mediocre soldiers, Dengezic. Never forget that. You are a good warrior, but you have much to learn. Now get out. Had you been any other man I would not have forgiven this. Think about what could have happened today, and try to learn from it."

Without another word Dengezic wheeled and was gone.

The Khan's steward entered on Dengezic's vanishing heels. He ushered in the first of the blushing women the Khan would bed this night, and with her enough wine to last until morning.

3

"What is it? What's happened, Edecon?" I said.

My tutor staggered against a support pole as he entered the yurt. He rocked against the heavy felt walls and tripped over my feet, toppling onto the carpets.

"Are you ill, friend Edecon?" I asked solicitously.

"Yes, I'm ill," he answered. "Poisoned, perhaps." Edecon smiled up at me.

I, too, smiled, amused at his reference to my unfortunate experience of several moons past. Even one moon ago I wouldn't have smiled thinking of it.

"Poor Edecon," I said, going along with his attempt at lightheartedness. "Not poisoned by an overdose of wormwood extract, I hope?"

"No, not wormwood. I'm poisoned by my exertions on behalf of your brother," he said weakly.

"How so?"

"Your brother, Dengezic, nearly dug himself into an impossible hole today. Much running back and forth of my skinny legs, and the services of my ready tongue, saved him."

"What happened? Tell me everything!" I begged, hanging on my friend's words. "Every crumb of gossip is welcome to my ears, Edecon. I'm stuck in this yurt like a puling baby. I hear nothing. My father cossets me. He's convinced I'm still too unsteady to sit a horse in battle. I have no useful activity," I grumbled. I knew I revealed bitterness at my enforced idleness, but I didn't care.

"To be brief," Edecon answered, "your elder brother nearly silenced a valuable source of information with his hasty sword. Had I not reached the ears of the Khan before he acted, he would have beheaded the man. It would've been a witless act. Your father's wrath would have fallen hard on his unthinking head had he done this."

"I don't understand. What are you saying?" I asked.

"It seems there's a Persian spy who has been operating from the Khan's stables for years. He carries information to his satrap, who passes it on to Aëtius. I came by the gossip, as you put it, Ernac, from Attila's chief groom, Unagan. The Persian is called Tadiqin. He's an undergroom, servant to Unagan. Unagan only recently discovered that the man is well-connected to a powerful Persian satrap."

"What harm would this spy bring to the armies of the Khan?" I said.

He may have thought I was acting the innocent, but Edecon's answering words were tactful.

"There are always men who wish harm to a successful warlord, Ernac. In this case, as in so many, the situation has its roots in the past."

I was perplexed, but ripe for learning. "What has it to do with? Tell me," I urged him.

"Old enmities," Edecon answered. "Generations ago we broke through the Caucasus mountains, attacked the Persians on their own territory, and bested them. We took gold and many captives. Tadiqin was one of those captives. Not only are Persians worthy warriors, they are a people of intricate sensibilities. They have long memories. And they are sharp-witted travelers with a commercial bent, the sort who happen on useful information wherever they find themselves.

Edecon paused. "Do you understand my meaning, Ernac?" he said.

"I think so. I think you mean Persians are a sly people whose intentions must be ever be watched."

A gratified smile lit Edecon's leathery features.

"That's it," he said. "You can see a person of that sort in our camps, a person without loyalties, could feed Attila with false information on Aëtius' plans. And on much more. Tadiqin has no doubt been funneling information on Attila's plans to Aëtius through his Persian connections. At the same time he is free to spread lies in our camp. A deadly game, for his lies can be used by trusted persons in our camps."

"How? Who would use his lies?" I said.

"Unfortunately there are many who would, Ernac," Edecon said. His words were a warning.

"There are many who are not content, who think they know better than the Khan, and who seek their own ends. Unagan, who is loyal to your father, became suspicious of Tadiqin. Then, he became frightened and, stupidly, confided in Dengezic. Your brother would have had the spy beheaded on the spot."

"But why not? Why shouldn't he have him beheaded?" I said indignantly.

Edecon shook his head disapprovingly. "He should have reported what he knew to the Khan. Attila decides who loses his head and when. Your brother is a good soldier, Ernac. I wouldn't want you to think otherwise. He has the confidence and affection of the men in the ranks. But he's not built for artfulness. He has no talent for guile, he is always in danger of overreaching himself, and his mistakes can be taken advantage of. There are men about with hidden interests, men much cleverer and more adept at scheming than Dengezic."

"My brother would never betray his commander. Never would he go against the Khan," I said vehemently.

"I fear you're wrong, my boy. Dengezic might think he finds something in the affections of the men that works to his benefit. He could fall in with a bit of chicanery, a small deceit that would be seen as outright treachery by Attila. Your father's anger would not be pretty to see if that should happen. Should he get wind of such a perfidy Attila would make Dengezic pay for it. He would never have a son of his executed, but Attila has ways of exacting vengeance. You well know your father cannot abide betrayal."

"You really believe Dengezic would allow himself to be used, Edecon? You think he would try to deceive the Khan in some way?" I said.

"I don't know, boy. I don't know. But if he should try..." Edecon's voice trailed off.

"Yes," I prodded, "if he tried?"

"If he should be so rash," Edecon said, "the consequences would be unfortunate."

I could get him to say no more.

I lay back on my quilts and tried to sleep, but my eyes wouldn't close. I was edgy and out of sorts. In truth, I was outraged, and I no longer cared to stay silent about my feelings. If my mother, the Khatun, had not prevailed I wouldn't be here at all, I thought. I'd be in the home camp with the women and children except that my mother spoke on my behalf to Attila.

A warrior who lets his mother intercede for him is no kind of warrior, I said to myself. The Khan thinks I am a child. I'm scarcely allowed outside my tent alone. Thinking these thoughts I fell into a swamp of self-pity. When I was certain Edecon slept I rose from my quilts and slithered out of the yurt, determined to seek out my brother and find out what had transpired in the matter of the spy.

Dengezic sleeps with the common soldiers and it wasn't easy to find him among so many, but after a short search I made out his face reflected in the starlight. He shared the night sky with countless others. A soldier's war-saddle is his pillow and his quilt is the blanket off his horse, and in summer this is no hardship. These are not men who would notice hardship in any case. They are as impervious as the stones of the Gobi. They do not notice weather in any season.

Hard they may be, but battle weary men stir fitfully in the night. I had to pick my way carefully among them to reach my brother. I brushed my hand lightly across his cheek. His eyes were closed, his face thrown back as if gazing straight up to the heavens.

His eyes didn't open when I touched his cheek.

"Dengezic, my brother," I whispered, "it's Ernac. Are you truly asleep? I need to speak with you."

His eyelids fluttered. My brother opened his eyes but he didn't move.

"Did you hear me, Dengezic?" I whispered urgently.

"I heard you," he said softly. He grabbed my head pressing one hand hard over my mouth and nose. "I heard your approach, oh, stealthy stalker of the night. Now hush."

My brother rose from his blankets, and bundling my gaunt frame like a hunk of meat under one bulging arm he strode out of the circle of sleeping bodies onto clear ground. When he set me down I was breathless.

"How dare you pick me up like a saddle-pouch, Dengezic," I raged. "I would not have disturbed anyone."

"You already have, little brother. You have disturbed the souls of the recently dead with your hubbub," he retorted harshly. "Any ear within a hundred paces has heard every word you uttered. I might have killed you. I would have if your breath had not spoken to me of the shared beds of our childhood."

I hung my head.

"What you did to me is bad enough," my brother said, "but you have disturbed the dreams of other soldiers. A soldiers' dreams should not be violated. What's your excuse for the intrusion?"

"I have no excuse. I simply wished to talk with you, Dengezic."

He sat down beside me and looked into my face.

"That's a lie," he said flatly. "Now tell me why you have come sneaking to my bed in the night like a thief."

I blame my continuing weakness since my illness that at his words I started to cry. I wanted to warn him, to tell him Edecon believes he's capable of an unspeakable disloyalty to our father. But as I was about to open my mouth a cautionary note sounded in my head. I found myself wondering whether Edecon might not be correct. What if Dengezic has a plan he wouldn't wish the Khan to know, I thought?

My tears gave me a chance to reconsider, and I didn't tell Dengezic what I'd planned to tell him. Instead, a waterfall of complaints came spilling out of me. I told my brother I was discontented, that I resented being held prisoner in the yurt of my tutor. I spoke of my growing fear, of my feeling that I would never make a proper soldier, let alone a leader of the people.

My tears, and my whining, must have been convincing, for after I had said these shameful things my brother was silent. We sat together and watched the moon turn the shadows across the plain. The earth, ground that so recently saw awful carnage acted out upon it, was tranquil. At length Dengezic rose. He clasped my shoulder, then he strode quickly away and disappeared to his moonlit bed.

I had said nothing of what I'd come to say. I walked back to camp and crawled into my quilts with my head low. I was still dejected, and none the wiser for my attempt to unburden myself to my brother.

4

"We will have a respite, then," Onegesius said.

"That is the Khan's message," Orestes answered. "From the Khan's *ordu* to the camp of Onegesius, greetings, and congratulations for your contribution to the war against the Acatiri."

"Thank you, Orestes. I am gratified," Onegesius said.

"The Khan has decided not to squander more Hun blood on the Acatiri," Orestes went on. "When you and Oebarsius have finished this job there will be a time of rest. For now, the Khan judges the northern tribes to be contained."

Orestes then addressed tactical questions, future plans that Attila had requested his scribe to transmit to his Prime Minister. Onegesius listened intently.

"My thanks to the Khan's messenger," he said when Orestes had finished his recital.

The scribe nodded. "How do your men fare here?" he questioned.

"We're well, and ready to finish the task. The Khan can rest easy," Onegesius said.

Then Onegesius questioned Orestes. "Who travels with you today?"

"Only Berichus and a few minor nobles," Orestes answered. "They are lucky who didn't come with us. It's been a journey of dust, dust, and more dust. This Acatiri country is not one I would care to call home. I have a perennial cough here. The climate doesn't suit me."

"What word is there from the left flank, from Oebarsius and his troops?"

"You mean the command of Ellac?" said Orestes guilelessly.

"Yes, the command of Ellac," Onegesius said. He didn't respond to the opening Orestes had given him. He let the matter drop.

Onegesius was not a man to fall into a trap. Any words on the well-known incompetence of the Khan's first son could be hazardous. Instead of pursuing his question, the Khan's Chief Advisor launched into a rambling assessment of the summer's campaign against the Acatiri. In the account was a message for Orestes to take back to the Khan. In his oblique way he was telling Attila he understood that this short, successful campaign didn't mean the end of their problems with the northern peoples.

Oebarsius knew, in spite of public pronouncements, that this rabble would always be trouble. No matter how undisciplined they appeared, the Acatiri were fierce and independent warriors. They had been robbed of the ability to nip at the Khan's heels, but only temporarily. They would be quiescent only long enough to free him for his war against Aëtius. The Khan needed above all else to be free of worry about the Acatiri at his rear.

"I imagine you're right, Orestes," Onegesius said idly. "There will be a quiet period. The season of lean horses is almost upon us. The Khan is eager for his chance to go against the Western Empire, but that time is not yet. At least one season of fat horses lies between us and that campaign. First, will be the East. It depends on developments within the Empire, of course, but that is the plan."

"That may be the plan, but the men did not satisfy their need for plunder this summer. There was not much to take off these scruffy people," Orestes said bluntly. "The troops won't wait much longer for their rewards. Full of love for their warlord they may be, but they are children, and children become disgruntled easily. The real gold is in the West, in Rome. The *qara buden* will divide against themselves and their own best interests at any opportunity."

Onegesius sighed. "Yes, we've always been a people prone to divide against ourselves. Most especially the outlying clans. I can pass judgment on these renegade tribes since I count myself a servant of Attila's efforts to unite us. I believe we must fight as one people. And,

I believe in a strict personal code. Attila's men are well disciplined, Orestes. Today they are the only Huns worthy of the name. I would rather be a slave under Attila than a general in the service of the Romans." Onegesius lowered his head in observance of his words.

"You, a slave, Onegesius?" Orestes snorted. "You have a dozen yurts, untold territories, many wives, and countless slaves, of your own. Attila depends on you. Above all other advisors he listens to you. Your future with the Khan is assured. So long as you do not betray him you'll continue to prosper," said Orestes.

"You needn't worry, for you are loyal," the scribe went on. "Those who come to grief with Attila are those who are false with him. To those he loves, and who love him, he is ever generous."

Then, "Will we return to the home pastures when the cold comes, do you think?" Orestes asked suddenly. He was thinking of himself. He wanted to get back to his own wives and herds. Personally, he wasn't comfortable being too long away from his family. Absence bred its own form of unrest at home. He was very conscious of the fact that right now his first wife was agitating for a permanent return to Rome.

"I doubt it," Onegesius said. "The Khan will want to keep the men busy, to keep a keen edge on them. It's easy to lose them when there are no targets for their arrows and no fresh gold for their bags. He may decide on a minor excursion to the west of Acatiri country, then there will likely be a rest of one or two moons before we go against Aëtius."

"To the west of Acatiri country?" said Orestes.

"The country of the Goths. The Goths are a good source of supplies, and a reliable source of food. We may find we need it. If the winter is hard, as the seers predict, the horses can fodder there. The Goths are ready to give of food and pastures when Attila asks. Besides, it's good to remind the servants of the Khan where their allegiance is. They, and Romans like them, are happy to jump at Attila's every request for gold or goods. Isn't that so, Orestes?"

Onegesius was bantering, knowing the Roman-born scribe couldn't contradict him.

"That's so," Orestes agreed. "Perhaps it would also be well to wait for other reasons," he commented. "I've heard stories of recent disasters within the Eastern Empire. There have been riots in the Circus at Constantinople, and plague is visiting itself upon the citizens again. Many hundreds are reported dead, and every breath and every bite of food is taken in fear of the pestilence. Starvation is sure to follow."

"Who brings these tales?"

"Berichus. He's heard of the plague from traders passing east toward the Gobi along the trade routes."

"Berichus is a good man," Onegesius said. "He is one who has, and deserves, the Khan's trust. I'll be pleased to see and talk with him. Give him my best, Orestes. Say we will dine in my tent tonight. Now I must see to my troops. The armies of the Khan may be able to rest easy, but my men have a battle or two to go before we can do the same. Until this evening, then."

"I'll send Berichus to you, Onegesius," Orestes said. He smiled knowingly. "I understand your need to share talk with him on finishing this Acatiri campaign."

"Many thanks for your information, Orestes," Onegesius said. He stood up and clapped the small, neat figure on the back. "I trust, Orestes, that you'll carry the thrust of my thoughts to the Khan."

Attila's Roman scribe affirmed that he would. He gestured acceptance of his dismissal, and bowed himself out of the presence of Attila's second in command.

It had been a summer of rumors. Orestes' smile as he left Onegesius attested to his knowledge of the gossip. The scribe's smile had given it away. It must be a juicy bit that Berichus was longing to drop in the ear of the Khan's Prime Minister.

Loose talk wafted everywhere, carried along with the heat in this baking, forsaken land. While the troops fought and gossiped at the front, people at home engaged in their own work, and their own talk. Most of the gossip wasn't important, but rumors regarding the Khatun were of note. Whispers were now circulating about the Khatun, and they were unsettling. Neither Orestes nor Onegesius would have dared to broach this subject openly.

The poor Khan, Onegesius thought, as he rode from camp seeking his commanders on the lines. He's beset from the rear, and from the front, and his son's are no comfort. They are, in fact, a disappointment. Ellac can never be left to his own judgments. Even Ernac, the son he might have counted on, is more a source of worry than of hope or pride. He's become babyish and petulant since his illness, and who knows if he will ever be capable of command. On top of this, Attila now has reason to fear Dengezic. What a pity. The single natural soldier among his sons may be plotting against him.

Ah, the poor Khan," Onegesius said again.

He shook his head, reflecting on the Khan's bad luck. Disappointment after disappointment had dogged Attila's steps. Riding across the desiccated lowlands, his Prime Minister wondered if anyone other than himself and the Khatun understood the years of dedication, the energy and effort, Attila had poured into molding an army. If no one else did, the two of them understood what the years had exacted from him.

Onegesius considered the past, and he concluded that Attila was born to be the object of envy and hatred. He was a man whose life was littered with the garbage of betrayal. The Khan would never reveal his hurts, but falsity and envy were his constant companions. Disillusionment, and duplicity, had lain with Attila each night of his life. Had he not had Bleda killed, Bleda would have killed him, his Prime Minister thought.

Disloyalty eats at him, how much it has hurt him only he knows. He's not immune from pain. Now there is this nasty talk of Kreka and Adamis. The Khatun, Onegesius admitted with purely male admiration, is a strong and lusty woman, and a willful one. That woman has no fear of the Khan, or of any man. It must also be admitted that Adamis is a splendid specimen. If the gossip is true, they must be quite a pair in bed, he thought. They were certainly a couple to fire the sexual imagination.

Anyone could be tempted, but even if this was temptation and no more it was exasperating. That the Khatun would give even an appearance of unfaithfulness spoke of the restlessness in her. Or, perhaps, of terrible anger. Attila would not do more than speak harshly to her in private. Publicly he'd suffer his humiliation in silence. The Khatun knew this. Even without affection in a marriage, and there was affection in this one, the most lowly Hun wouldn't punish his lawful wife merely for adultery.

But if the tales were true — and here Onegesius found himself amazed at the foolhardiness of Kreka's steward — the affair could end in execution for Adamis. He must realize he had put his beautiful neck on the block. If he was bedding the Khatun his life was worth less than that of a sick dog.

Adamis had found the Khatun attractive, that had long been obvious. Still, being attracted was no crime, and Adamis was open in his symptoms of being smitten. That his eyes were only for the Khatun could be innocent. Yet, where she was, there was Adamis, his focus on her, his handsome face aglow. With Adamis it was different. Brief as he was with others, his attentions languished overlong on Kreka. He fed an unslakeable thirst of the heart, and anyone who caught his looks, saw his attentions to her, must know it.

"By the Great Tngri, it's not fair. Adamis shouldn't be so beautiful!" Onegesius cried aloud. He slapped his horse's neck with the crop, and took the last hillock in a burst of speed.

"The Khan has enough grief without this," he muttered. He let his reins fall and walked out toward the troops seeking his field commanders.

If Adamis was bedding the Khatun, the Khan would be sorely hurt. Not that she was expected to be celibate during his long absences. She had her own life, and as for Attila, his sexual appetites were well known. In any case, wellborn couples commonly took lovers when separated.

But again, he thought, Adamis was different. For all his reclusive ways he had a certain reputation. He was far too attractive to women, a man women looked upon with lust. Onegesius had to admit that any woman might become enamored of him. That was unfortunate. If Kreka was sharing her yurt with this ideal lover who would dare to tell the Khan? It was unthinkable.

The mere prospect made Onegesius quake. Kreka had influence with the Khan. Her every word had impact, and her political opinions carried weight. Attila's peace of mind rested in no small degree in the Khatun's hands. She could weaken his sense of security, and raise destructive monsters of hurt and betrayal in him. She could drive him to recklessness. The Khan could not afford extra strain right now, the next battles were going to be difficult.

How could she do this to him?

He cursed, and made a mental note to run the rumors to ground. At the very least he would find out from what quarter the talk was coming. He would be prepared to offer more than clucking sympathy in case the Khan needed him. Poor man, he thought again, the life of a warlord is not enviable.

His commanders were out to meet him, and Onegesius reproached himself. He shouldn't be caught brooding. He laughed, and called out heartily, hailing the men as they approached.

5

The expansive light of summer has given way to the bittersweet light of fall, and the nights have turned chill. Mist drifts from the earth, and the breath of the horses hangs steaming over the camp.

Messengers have arrived from the war camps. The troops will not return to lie next to their women during the season of frozen ground. The Khan's armies will leave the site of their victories against the Acatiri and march north toward the country of the Goths. They will be quartered there until the next season of fat horses.

"Beki!" Ku's voice carried to the outer edge of the herd.

Ku's voice is not a voice to be ignored. I hurried to her. I left Red Atagha standing, reins trailing the ground beside him.

"I hear you, Ku," I called, running to her. "What's the matter? What is it?"

"Nothing is the matter," she said. "The Khatun requires your presence. A message came for you from the war camp, from your sweetheart, Ernac." She gave out an unholy cackle.

My head was hot but I answered evenly. "A message from Ernac, you say? I hope it's welcome news. Perhaps he's returning home."

"That may be, I wouldn't know. I have work to attend to," Ku said. And she hurried off.

Racing to Red Atagha I dumped his shabrack and bridle off him and rubbed fresh grass over his back and neck to take off the sweat and grime. The grooms will water him, I thought. I sped off, eager to hear the message from Ernac.

At the doorway to the Khatun's yurt I met the startled face of Kursik. He hurried away.

What is Dengezic's paid informant doing here, I thought? I was taken aback.

Kursik, himself, appeared flustered.

"Young girls should look where they're going," he said.

He seemed as much in a rush as I was. What could he be doing here? Did Dengezic send him? This flitted through my head as I plunged through the doorway.

The sight that met me was not unexpected, but I realized I'd been thoughtless. I should have made a noise before I entered.

"You don't bother to announce yourself these days, Bahka Beki?" the Khatun said. Her wide eyes were frosty.

Adamis turned to look at me. His features were veiled as ever, but the flush of recent lovemaking glistened like fresh rendered oil on his skin. His hands were under the loosened waist of Kreka's linen gown, his fingers stroking her skin possessively. They stood with arms laced around one another, and made no attempt to move apart when they saw me.

Kreka's steward caressed her shoulders and breasts as if he was hypnotized. I knew why the snake, Kursik, had been loitering outside. He must have found this quite the titillating scene, the little viper. I knew he would hasten to report to Dengezic. And what a rotten piece of carrion Dengezic is. What kind of man would spy on his mother? Dengezic has not been one to honor Kreka as a son should, but now he's gone too far, I thought.

I'm not fond of gambling, but I'd make bet Dengezic is hatching something. The second son of the Khan is a capable warrior, but he's overly ambitious. I have often suspected Ernac's brother of disloyalty, now I'm certain of his deceitfulness. I won't forget to relate my suspicions to my future husband, I thought.

I dropped my head. I didn't answer the Khatun's icy question, and I bowed as if humbled by my thoughtlessness. Secretly, I was glad I had blundered in and caught Kursik spying.

"I'm sorry, Khatun Kreka," I said. "I didn't think what I was doing. I've been used to this being my yurt. I didn't think. Please forgive me."

I sneaked a glance at the lovers from under my lashes, and I saw Kreka's face had softened. She is as hypnotized as Adamis, I thought. They are like two young lovers enraptured with the first days of their passion. Kreka has had other lovers, but I can't recall having seen her transformed by love.

"What is it you want, child?" she said finally. Extricating herself from Adamis' grasp, she motioned me to sit. She and Adamis reclined on the carpeted sleeping couch in front of me, holding hands and waiting for me to speak.

They didn't seem the least undone by my presence, and I found myself entertaining a stab of pity for the Khan, so far away, and in danger. But why should I feel pity for him, I thought. He doesn't do without the company of women no matter where he is, and war is his chosen life.

"I had word from Ku that you wished to see me, Khatun." I said as I sat down in front of them.

"Of course," Kreka said. She'd temporarily forgotten she'd sent for me.

"I can return later if you wish," I said.

I had happened onto a private scene, but I was the one who was uncomfortable. In spite of my disgust at Dengezic's spying I was not without shameful feelings of my own. It's not my place to judge the Khatun, but I have often been tempted to pass judgment on her. I am very attached to Attila. I tend to make excuses for him where I wouldn't for others.

But who will make excuses for Kreka, I thought. My sentiments wavered. I have love and admiration for both of them. How can I put one above the other? Much of Kreka's life has been spent in loneliness and boredom. Moreover, she carries responsibilities here. When Attila is at war she takes leadership in the home camps. Difficult decisions fall on her, and no one can fault her there. She handles her duties well.

"No, Beki. We will discuss this now," Kreka said, her voice coming up over my guilty thoughts.

"Yes?" I said courteously.

"The Khan and I have made a decision about your future, yours and Ernac's. We've decided there's no reason to delay your marriage. During the next season of fat horses you and Ernac will be married. A wife may be just what my son needs to help him find his manhood. The summer campaign against the Acatiri was apparently not the place for him to find it."

My heart began to flap and lurch, my throat was tight, and my hands damp. This was what I'd waited for, what I had always hoped. For as long as I can remember I have waited for the words that would make my marriage to Ernac a reality. Now the moment was here I was speechless.

"Aren't you pleased at my news?" the Khatun asked, smiling. She was amused that I was tongue-tied.

"Of course, I am," I said quickly. "You know I'm pleased, but there is much to do, much to attend to before a wedding can take place."

Kreka took a long look at me, then turned her eyes to her lover.

"Adamis," she said, "you may leave us." She smiled warmly at him. Adamis smiled back at her. He rose, bowed to us, and left the Khatun's yurt.

"What is it, Beki? What is bothering you?" Kreka said, as soon as her steward had left.

"Dengezic has set his spy, Kursik, to watching you," I blurted. "I ran into him outside."

Her features flickered briefly. "I know," she said.

"You know!" I said, astonished.

"I'm not without a bit of guile myself, Beki."

"Yes, Khatun," I said, "but he…"

Kreka stopped me with a raised hand. She patted the cushion next to her and said, "This is a good time for us to talk together as women. Sit by me."

"I,…" I started to protest, but again she stopped me.

"Please, Beki," she said. "I know this is difficult for you. I wasn't always a middle-aged woman. When I was your age I was as untutored as you are today. We needn't say more."

Kreka was observant. She had caught me in a childish embarrassment. I moved next to her and waited.

"Very well," Kreka said, when I kept my silence. "I will lead off. We haven't talked of men and women, Beki, of their life together as mates. There's not that much to say of the facts, you know what there is to know. The fascinations of sex haven't been hidden from you. No doubt you heard Attila and me, tumbling together on the couches when you were small."

I didn't dare deny it. I'd been witness to their couplings as a child, and she knew very well I had.

"But facts are not what I want to speak of," she went on. "The mere facts are not terribly important. The considerable trouble that sex can cause is inspired by emotions. There are constraints on private conduct, as you know. These rules are unpleasant at times, but they must be observed. Violence, even death, can be precipitated by a foolish indiscretion. Passion is universal, but we are a chaste people. We are not Romans, and we don't approve of sexual frolic in public."

"I would never..." I began.

Once again Kreka cut me off. "I know. I know you have a loyal nature," she said. "Still, after you marry you have to be especially careful. You must set an example. Honoring public modesty, and practicing restraint, keeps relations in the camps orderly and smooth."

Kreka has a level gaze. When she turns her eyes on a person her glance destroys the distance between them. This look inspires people to unburden themselves. When she turned it on me I reacted, though not, I think, as she intended.

"What about you and Adamis, then?" I said boldly. "Is it not wrong of you to take him as your lover? Will your love not hurt the Khan? Will it not cast doubts on your own modesty?"

I imagined my question might make the Khatun uncomfortable in her turn. Perhaps, I wanted it to. If it did she showed no sign.

"There has never been an agreement between Attila and me, Beki, that would deny either of us a normal life when we are apart," she said.

"But with your steward?" I said. "Is that done?"

"Done?" she said, lifting the dark wings of her brows. "I'm not sure what you mean? We don't fornicate in public. I'm trying to tell you that intimacy is private, a thing between two people alone. You needn't concern yourself with that, Beki. How Attila and I handle sex in our lives is not for you to question."

Her defiant answer convinced me Kreka was in no mood to pursue the subject. But before I could find words to continue in another vein she asked me a hard question.

"Are you so upset by the news of your upcoming marriage that you use insolence to mask your feelings, Beki?" she said.

Again she had caught me out. This time I couldn't avoid answering.

"I am upset," I admitted. "I want to be Ernac's wife, you know I do. That I have always wanted. But I'm not sure how well he is, and I don't want children yet. I don't think I'm ready to care for a child."

"Ahh-hhh, how honest of you to say so," Kreka said.

"Of course," she went on. "I wouldn't want you to take on a family before you're ready. Many women have more than one child by the time they're your age, but no one should have children before they're ready."

She smiled.

"But in this, we are in luck," she said. "Women have long since devised ways to prevent life starting in their bellies. There are ways, also, to stop the growth inside you. Measures can be taken so that the child doesn't ripen. If a woman doesn't wish children we have means to prevent it. You needn't discuss these things with Ernac, they are women's lore."

Naturally, I remembered what Kreka had said about preventing a baby from starting in a woman's belly. This was something I wanted to know more about, so I waited to see what she would offer.

"I am concerned for Ernac myself," she said, "but his future health is only one of my concerns. I also have worry for you, little Beki. But you're blessed with a hardy spirit in a hardy body, and I fear my youngest son is blessed with neither."

"He isn't well, then?" I asked anxiously. "I was afraid for him, then Ku told me he was quite recovered."

"Yes," she said, frowning, "he has recovered. But that doesn't mean he's hardy. It will be a long while before Ernac is strong. The confidence of young manhood hasn't yet come to my youngest son. I'm hoping your natural instincts and affections will do that for him, Beki. Your lean, awkward limbs have filled out. You've developed into a delightful woman, an exquisite model of female temptations."

She smiled at me. "Your breasts are lusciously full," she said, "your buttocks smooth and taut as ripe pomegranates, your skin the mirror of spun silk, and your cleft a fragrance…"

At this last my face flamed. Kreka was deliberately trying to bring out awareness of my sexual feelings in me, and she had succeeded. Covering for myself, I moved quickly to ask the question I'd been meaning to put to her.

"I would like to know what these things are, Kreka, these things that women do to prevent babies starting. And how do they stop them once they start?" I said.

She nodded.

"First," she said, "you must know how to block the entrance to your womb with a cap as the Egyptians do. This will protect your womb from the emissions of men. I'll show you how to make a cap scooped from the rind of a lemon. I'll teach you how to take mandrake root, or henbane, and make them into a broth that's safe. Prepared correctly, the broth makes the muscles of your belly contract so that the unborn falls out of your womb before it can survive on its own. This isn't as mystifying as it seems, but these procedures must be done properly to be effective. The lore is surrounded by too much secrecy for my taste, but it won't be secret to you. I'll instruct you carefully, Beki. You shouldn't have children you don't want. I wouldn't wish that."

She placed one hand on my cheek, and looked into my eyes, shaking her head pensively.

"Such troublesome decisions we must make regarding life and death, little one," she said.

"You will make decisions that will bring you grief, Beki. You are a woman. Your choices will stem from experience that differs from the experience of men. But your choices will not be less difficult; no less difficult and no less painful."

Kreka dropped her hand. Her speech was informative but I didn't understand everything she said. As soon as she fell silent, it seemed she forgot I was with her.

"Kreka," I piped, "there's one more thing.

She was back to herself in a flash. "Yes, Beki, what is it?" she said, looking into my eyes.

"I'm afraid for you and Attila," I said. "You're not getting along well. This worries me."

"Oh, my!" she exclaimed. She laughed, showing perfect teeth.

"You are a thoughtful child, aren't you?" she said. "But you have no experience as a wife. Love can be as burdensome as any task. Longtime lovers, husbands and wives, often must find ways to breathe heat back into their life together. Partners may tire of one another, and even a great love may require stern measures to restore it."

She laughed again, and said confidentially, "Have no fear for me and Attila, Beki. You may trust we know our needs as man and wife."

Kreka then said she wished her afternoon rest. She dismissed me with an admonition not to speak of the marriage plans for myself and Ernac until they are officially announced.

I had much to ponder as I left her tent. This woman who has been my mother, though not by birth, is a complex, not to say devious, person. She is like Attila in that she inspires great love and admiration. I do love her, but there's a great deal I don't know about her.

Kreka's complex nature reminded me of Kursik and his spying. He has his counterpart in the war camp of the Khan. Baldin, former servant of the dead shaman, Teb-Ogatai, lives in the tents of Edecon and Ernac. The little cripple is grateful beyond measure to the Khatun for sparing his life. He passes all his information to her. Because of him she knows everything that goes on in the tents of the Khan.

Once more it was brought home to me what a dangerous place the Khan's kingdom is. We live in a realm of intrigue, gossip, and torture-loving eunuchs. The camps are kept busy with treachery and plotting, with the comings and goings of spies from every quarter. A snake sleeps under every pebble, your foot may encounter it at any step. To walk without awareness of malice is to walk like a blind man.

Political plots have always been with us, but they now have a larger dimension. We are facing war on a gigantic scale. The future is not one of raiding parties, that era ended when we engaged the Empire. And war isn't the only threat we face from the Romans. There is an allure in alien thinking. The purposes and sentiments of the Romans invade our heads and take our lives in unwonted directions.

Nevertheless, life holds one or two constants. Out of my need for security in a confusing world I've put much faith in Kreka and Attila. They have been my eternals. I wonder now whether I can be sure even of them.

6

Life is irksome beyond belief since Edecon and I arrived in home camp. Being idle is wearing, more exhausting than the rigors of war. It's no wonder men prefer war to life in the yurts.

Edecon doesn't let me forget the excitement of battle. Indeed, there's so little to occupy us that I hear my teacher's exploits morning and night. He is stuck on tales of his heroic past, he runs on and on and repeats himself. I start to mouth the words along with him I know them so well, and he turns spiteful.

"Ernac, youngest son of the Khan, is an insolent puppy," he growls, and he shuffles away shaking with anger as much as with illness. My teacher would like to be rid of me — but no more than I want to be rid of him.

My only interest lies in waiting for word from the Khan's camps. That doesn't come often, and when it does it's not what I wish to hear. My father intends to remain in the country of the Goths until he mounts his next offensive against the Romans. Edecon says the Khan can't risk losing his troops to idleness. It's important to keep the bulk of the armies together, and far from the easy temptations of the home territories. Of course, he holds out the promise of heavy plunder to carry with them when they do come home.

The cold wears on and on. Yesterday, at daybreak, I went out to check the stores of fodder and to melt snow for my morning gruel. I dug through the frozen crust to get the daily chunks of dried grass for my horses. As I poked through I came upon a poor, dead foal. He was solid ice, his caul unbroken. Neither he, nor the mare who dropped him too early, had had the strength to help him break free. She must have been pawing for food even as she dropped him.

This has been the worst cold I can recall. Even the old men say the bone-cracking bitterness of this winter is the worst they can remember. Snow reaches higher than a horse's head along the tops of the hillocks, mountainous drifts that will cover the ground well into growing season. The grasses should be green, and still there is no pasture. Scores of horses, sheep, and cattle have perished for lack of provender. We have been short on food ourselves.

It's as well for the armies of the Khan that they are wintering off the generosity of the Goths. It is a forced generosity, perhaps, but useful. Edecon is silent on the subject of my joining the Khan's camp. I've almost lost hope that I'll be called, and my spirits slide into a deepening trough. I am lower than a ewe's udder.

There is some news, but not welcome news for me. Formal announcement of my marriage to Beki has been made. Since the Khan is absent in the north I had thought the ceremony would be postponed. In fact, I wished for a delay. I mean no insult to my future wife, who is more lovely each time I see her. She is tempting, but I fear our wedding will serve as one more excuse for my father to keep me from a soldier's life.

Beki is altogether different than the girl I remember from our days of riding out to hunt together. She has turned into a woman any man would desire to bed — or to wed. When I am with her my maleness protrudes alarmingly. I'm sometimes reduced to hiding my bulge with anything that's handy. If her fingers chance to touch mine I am completely undone.

I haven't actually seen my future wife for more than a moon. The Khatun keeps her busy learning the details of a wife's responsibilities. Women have much to keep them busy in camp and the cold hasn't been so tiresome for them. Inside the yurts their fingers move swiftly, sewing quilts and garments, weaving door hangings, horse bags, and tent carpets. The constant need for things fashioned by hand renders women immune to the more boring aspects of life in the camp.

The last time Beki and I met there was no talk of marriage. Instead, we spoke of her suspicions of Dengezic. She says he has set his people to spying on Mother Kreka. She described an intimate scene between Adamis and my mother, and said she'd caught Kursik spying on them. What use he could make of this information I don't know. There is no one in camp who doesn't already know of the liaison between Mother Kreka and her steward.

I have my own uneasiness, but I don't feel free to share it with Beki. I can't bring myself to tell anyone what Edecon said to me about Dengezic. Dengezic, my brother, a traitor to the Khan! I can't face that, and I keep my thoughts to myself. Still, it's a comfort to find that others have disquieting thoughts about my elder brother. Now I know I'm not the only one to doubt his loyalty I must be more than cautious.

The long, terrible winter has finally passed and the grasses are high. With the spring has come the formality of the wedding. Ernac and I are now a married couple.

Almost a full moon since the little ceremonies, and poor celebrations they were. Ernac and I have settled into an awkward kind of life together. He wants to be away with the Khan's armies, that in itself put a pall on the festivities. For me the wedding was lifeless without Attila. He sent most loving greetings, and expressions of regret, saying he wished to be at the marriage of his son, and that he was sure it was one ceremony that wouldn't be a trumpery spectacle. At the word trumpery I knew Attila had composed the message himself and I shed tears.

The Khan's emissaries came to us with gold and silver dishes, coffers full of silks, jeweled ornaments from the east, and perfumes and spices from the south. His grooms brought me a handsome white stallion from the Khan's private stock. No common piebald for the wife of Attila's favorite son! Along with the stallion he sent a dozen or more mares to start my herd.

As a special mark of his favor the Khan has given me a title. By tradition, Ernac, the youngest son, is Keeper of the Homeland. I am to be known as Keeper of the Clan. Kreka has also been generous, even giving Ku over to me to supervise my servants. The Khan has sent Baldin, the Cripple, back to Ernac. He is pathetic in his eagerness to be of service to us. I shall have to devise some useful work for him, something that doesn't require the use of his hands.

Gifts and messages of congratulation aside, there was no denying the lack of fuss made over our marriage. Only the people from our own camp were here to share in the ceremony. It was a disappointing gathering. The cheering when Ernac carried me off to our new home seemed strained. I noticed that the shouts didn't compare with the enthusiastic cheers that sent Attila and Eskayar off on their wedding day. The excitement of other wedding ceremonies seems to me to have been much greater. Ernac comforts me. The important thing, he says, is that we begin our lives together as we had always wished.

Of course, he is right. Now, my husband is grateful to be free of the overweening presence of Edecon, and I'm happy being my own person. When I walk out among the people (I don't think I imagine this) there is new respect in their eyes, and a new desire to be of help.

I don't dwell overmuch on our wedding night. I can't say it was a disappointment. I imagine it to be the same as most. Ernac is not a dashing figure but he is a thoughtful lover, and there's no doubt of his devotion to me. I remind myself that a reliable character can make up for more romantic traits. After all, not every man brings excitement to the marriage couch.

I must say Ernac was more ardent than I expected. He didn't disgrace himself as we fell to rolling in the quilts, and our daily lovemaking has benefitted him. He's not nearly so petulant and discontented as before. I'm grateful that he has regained his wholesome appetites. This renewed vitality is encouraging, and the future looks bright. Each day that I see his strength returning I feel more confident that he'll be the person he was before the poisoning.

7

Late in the season of fat horses, unbelievable as it seemed, Ernac was called to the side of the Khan.

Amid flurries, furbishings of weapons, and pop-eyed excitement, his retinue was readied and hurriedly left us. Ernac was convinced any delay would jeopardize his going. Oddly, I'm not cast down by his departure. Having him in my yurt was pleasant, but he was so anxious to be gone with the troops that I find his absence something of a relief.

I spend the hours on my own needs now, and feel lucky that my time is my own. Marriage, no matter how satisfying, makes you responsible for the well-being of another. I am also lucky in another way. I took Kreka's sound advice. I used the remedies she gave me to prevent a child, and I'm grateful that I haven't yet conceived.

The days are short and soon snow will again lie heavy over the dead grass. We have our food supplies in place and are preparing to work inside the yurts.

Kreka has assembled a ground loom outside her doorway, and one recent morning three untried young weavers examined the contraption. We stared at the warps strung between strong poplar beams, but we had no idea how to attach yarn, no idea, in fact, how to begin.

We squatted in front of the directress, a woman who has memorized and designed more rugs than any of us will in a lifetime. We watched as she traced a complex pattern in the ground. With no further instruction than this she left us to puzzle it out.

Her faith in us was premature. We spent weeks in preparing the wool; turning and swirling the strands in the vats, and more time spinning yarn, rolling the wooden spindles endlessly up and down our thighs, and we were none the wiser as to the actual weaving.

We gathered piles of madder and sage, sorrel and violet, roots, barks, fruits, seeds, and leaves. Then, small containers of charcoal and tea leaves, saffron, pomegranate skins, tiny insects, and odd items obtained from traders. From this assortment has emerged an array of dyes. Gentian, and a deep blue-purple from barberry, also indigo, red from the madder and henna, and crimson from an insect plucked from the undersides of leaves. Yellow from saffron, alder and sage, green from sorrel and violet, browns and greys from bark, charcoal, and tea. Our hands are dark as nuts. I fear I'll never see the natural color of my arms again.

Preparing dyes and spinning the yarn is a long process but we weren't allowed even one row of weaving until we were finished with it. When at last we started, the yarn tangled and turned stubborn in our fingers. I despaired of my wayward hands, but as the days passed I became less awkward, and now I'm fairly nimble. We can all congratulate ourselves; the pattern is working out fairly evenly. I take satisfaction in my lines of knots, which are as even as I could hope.

Laying the cross-lines of weft gave us the most trouble. We were slow, uncertain how to achieve a proper tension. Too little in one spot and a rug becomes slack, too much and it pulls inward. Once we were able to master the tension we began to tighten the weave, pushing backward against the rows of knots. With light wood and bone beaters we moved the lines along. Stroke after stroke we compacted and straightened the rows, and the rug began to grow in front of our eyes.

When the cold settled in, the looms were moved inside a common yurt. There, other women were also busy weaving. We watched, and our fingers began to fly. We discovered the rhythm in tying, affixing, and pulling, so the knots seemed to wind themselves around the warps.

We discovered more in this activity than weaving. Gossip flies here, the tongues moving as fast as fingers. Most of the women are good-humored, but two of them were rather rude in the beginning, laughing at our clumsiness. Our answer was to ask for their help. Being proud of their skills, these two were happy to help beginners and we became friendly. I no longer have to rely on the tales of servants to learn what is going on. The women exchange enormous stores of information amongst themselves.

And, it turns out that exchanging information is a pleasant way to pass the time. In spite of my original dislike I now find myself absorbed in the work. I've been pulled in by the complication and variety of patterns, and by the lovely play of color and light in the wool.

The rugs advance in large forms that flow and swirl, as well as in smaller forms; points, stars, diamonds, fruits, and blossoms. There are designs that speak of clouds and water, of birds, horses, or leopards. There are gardens, profusions of blooming flowers, the branching arms and leaves of broad trees. Along the borders, often eight or more, march rows of slash marks, buds, stars, birds, and intricately hooked forms.

When I was a child I often sat and watched these women, intrigued with their fingers as they moved dexterously between the strands. But I didn't divine any fulfillment in it then. I didn't see the joy in the subtle blendings of pattern, or in the riots of colored yarns. Not until I had engaged in the act myself was I able to understand the attraction of it.

For me, this has been much more than learning an art. I see in their weaving the richness in women's lives. This art has nothing to do with men, nothing to do with hunting, or with war. The closeness that develops between the women shows an appreciation of homely details. The work of their hands is truly the weaving of our lives. Ordinary scenes laid out in color, design, and texture, are like stories the taletellers spin. Stories in words are no more wonderful than stories told in pattern and color.

It dismays me to think how readily I dismissed these arts of our hands. I was right in thinking carpets give pleasure and comfort, but wrong in not realizing how much more they give us. The building of textiles is not a simple thing. It is no easier than making a war bow, or learning the art of the hunt.

In the heart of these dark, short days, which are always depressing, terrifying news has reached our camps from the south. Horrendous earthquakes have crumbled the city of Constantinople.

The first of several quakes apparently came in the middle of the night as people slept. More than fifty-seven towers along the massive walls of the city fell to the ground, and when the earth ceased trembling, rain poured from the sky. It's said the floods swallowed whole villages.

Baldin has been out seeking gossip through his old sources, and he scurried back to tell me the city is in a panic. People are walking the ruined streets of the city semi-clothed, barefoot and bewildered. And the calamities continue. Constantinople has not been spared any disaster. Plague has struck again, and food supplies, failing even before the earthquakes, are now dangerously low. The latest news is more than two moons old, and only the Great Tngri knows what other disasters may have befallen the city in the meantime. It is too dreadful.

There is no affection in our camps for any Roman fortification, of course, but who can say what may be in store for us? Yesterday, I heard Ku, who is painfully superstitious, muttering that the Tngri of the Romans shook the earth as a warning. She says the terrible god they worship will slay them all; man, woman and child.

Ku is right. Many Romans have stopped giving sacrifice to the earth goddess and have completely rejected the old gods. They embrace a strange, new, single god. This god is unparalleled in vengeance. He is so jealous that he threatens to destroy anyone who would worship another god. Ku says this god plans to destroy all rival gods and, thereby, to make himself supreme. But Ku is known to be gullible in these matters. I think she wastes her time repeating crazy talk about a crazy god.

In our own camp Eskam has been directed to cast the haruspices. He will send his reading of the signs straight to the Khan.

8

Spring finally broke through the ice of the long winter.

With warm weather came grass for the horses, and as soon as the herds had recovered some flesh Attila was on the move. He aimed at the provinces of Lower Scythia and Moesia.

Riding with him were the Gepids, led by King Ardaric, and the Goths, led by Valamer. Soon they were joined by smaller clans, and the second full-scale invasion against Eastern Rome was launched.

It was late in the third month of 447 A.D., and Theodosius was expecting the Huns. He was concerned, and with good reason. Summer would lay stifling hands over the shaky borders of the outlying Empire and the northern frontier was already in need of help. More earthquakes, plague, and failing food supplies had followed the onslaught that had visited Constantinople that winter.

After the earthquakes a period of disorganization and panic hit the city. But the praetorian prefect, Flavius Constantinus, quickly directed the fallen walls to be restored. Within sixty days of the first quakes the wall of Anthemius had been rebuilt, and a second wall in front of the original added. New barricades were erected. They were up to 200 feet thick in places. Despite the barricades, when word blew through the city that the Huns were close, the majority of the inhabitants fled. There were reports that the Emperor Theodosius, himself, was preparing to flee.

The Khan, inured to such rumormongering, gave the gossip no credence. Attila did not expect Aëtius to stand idle with the east in danger, yet he was not in evidence. Some muttered he was in hiding, and the defense of the capital was given over to Flavius Zeno, an

Isaurian. The Isaurians were among the most hated foes of the Empire, and Zeno's elevation to position of commander did nothing to bolster the people's confidence. This was the first time, and it would be the last, that Attila would be in a position to engage the undivided forces of the Eastern Empire. Zeno was not a providential choice to lead the city's defense, but as fate would have it no defense was needed. Attila bypassed Constantinople. There were fresh outbreaks of plague within and the Khan had no wish to expose his armies. Instead, he demanded more tribute from Theodosius, and moved on.

This was a summer of superhuman greatness for the Khan. The imaginations of the Romans had worked to transform him into the Antichrist. The Terrible One, they said, had ascended the throne. Attila was widely held to be invincible, and he shrewdly burnished his image. Playfully, but only half in jest, he took the Romans' view of himself as his own and began referring to himself as "The Scourge of God". His men echoed their warlord, and the title stuck. It added another fearful layer to his reputation, and the latest sobriquet did not displease him.

The Khan and his generals fully expected the coming offensive to succeed. Even so, Attila wanted a further sign to bolster the image of his invincibility. When word reached his *ordu* that Eskam's forecasting of the haruspice showed he would gain a mighty victory by launching an attack on Marcianople, Attila's spirits soared. Anticipating success put the Khan in rare good humor.

He remarked happily to Onegesius, "At last reality has caught up with prediction. My reputation is now no larger than fact."

"I have never doubted this day would come," he told his Prime Minister. "When the horses are fat with fresh grass, we move."

Attila was true to his word. Before the Empire could recover from the disasters of the previous winter, his hordes were rushing south through Dacia Rispensis toward Marcianople.

The Imperial army hastened out to meet them. For good, or ill, this was the place they would engage the armies of the Khan. They met at the river Vid with the German, Arnegisclus, commanding the Romans. This was the same Arnegisclus who had murdered the Vandal

John and taken his position as Master of the Soldiers in Thrace. For the past six years Arnegisclus had been in command. Now, feeling secure, he staked everything on one pitched battle.

Arnegisclus himself waded courageously into the midst of the conflict. He went down immediately, his horse struck from under him. He continued on afoot until he was run through. His troops fought on. Obstinately, man by man, they pitted themselves against the frightful force of Huns. Their stubborn resistance was not enough and Marcianople fell with Arnegisclus. More than a hundred years later the city still lay uninhabited and desolate. Victory belonged to the King of the Huns.

Attila had also sustained grave losses. Because of this, or for more mysterious reasons, he called a halt after Marcianople. Incredibly, Aëtius still had not been seen. With no one to goad him into turning his armies toward Constantinople, Attila went marauding. He moved on Greece, devastated Thrace, and reached Thermopylae. There, he took time to flatten the countryside over a wide path before heading home to the heartland.

If avoiding direct confrontation at Constantinople had been part of the Khan's original plan, he didn't share his thinking with his generals. Sound judgment would have discouraged him from sending damaged forces against a freshly fortified city in any case. Even discounting fear of plague, a lengthy, stultifying siege would have been risky. Siege was the least favored tactic of nomadic warriors. It was never an attractive choice, and since Aëtius had chosen to absent himself from the scene, there was no reason to abandon good sense. Dragging a meaningless campaign far into fall had little appeal. Attila didn't make that mistake.

He had already captured more than one hundred cities and more than one witness declared he had ground almost the whole of Europe into dust. When the bloodletting was done no one could number the dead. Attila allowed his warriors to rape, pillage, and burn. They slayed monks and virgins alike. That summer, the Khan's army thoroughly devastated the churches and monasteries, even robbing the

Blessed Alexander, the church of the martyr at Drizipera, and carrying away its treasure.

Ernac had been emboldened by his first battle experience at Marcianople, and afterward he complained to his father of the soldier's brutal behavior. He chided Attila with clucking disapproval.

"You shouldn't let the men indulge their bent for cruelty, father," he said. "It shores up the Roman's view of us. It makes your troops appear undisciplined, and the Romans already think us savage beyond belief."

Attila snorted at his son's words. "We are simple beasts, of course," he retorted, caustically. "That's how Rome sees us, and a good thing too. Fear will cripple the most intrepid foe."

The Khan regaled the young soldier with tales of horrific acts that had been perpetrated by other armies. He recalled that, during his own childhood, Germanic invaders from Gaul had killed hermits, burned priests alive, raped nuns and devastated vineyards, even destroying the olive trees.

Several exchanges between father and son ended with Attila reeling off the brutal transgressions perpetrated by other armies. Finally, Ernac subsided. There was no arguing with events, or with Attila's overwhelming victory. The summer campaign was the Khan's personal achievement. During this summer he became king, commander in chief, and supreme judge, all in one.

The Emperor Theodosius begged for terms and a new annual tribute was set at 2,100 pounds, the current arrears of 6,000 pounds to be paid immediately. Anatolius was again called to negotiate for Rome. He had the prudence not to resist the Khan's terms.

In their circuitous wanderings back to the heartland the armies of the supreme warlord laid waste to a swath of territories south of the Danube. Attila evacuated the countryside and left the Balkans undefended. The peasants fled, and for generations after only the bones of the dead cultivated the land.

The Khan insisted on a strict interpretation of his treaty with Theodosius. For the sake of security, no Roman, not even a local shepherd, was allowed to join his march. In spite of an extraordinarily high price paid in blood, Attila's troops endured. Somehow, the Huns escaped the pestilence that raged among the locals, and the Romans were forced back from the Danube. The Empire was gravely wounded.

The first wave at Marcianople found Ernac placed, by direct order of the Khan, in the front rank of light cavalry. He was chosen to head his unit of ten, placed at the edge of the right flank behind the first two rows of heavy cavalry. He would, therefore, be in the initial charge of light cavalry that would open the battle on the right flank.

Ernac's ten were part of the squad of one-hundred who would ride forward through the heavy cavalry firing an arrow-storm into the enemy. Then, they would turn, race behind the advancing heavy cavalry, and then back once more through the lines.

On the day of his first battle Ernac had been in the *ordu* of the Khan for five full moons. As soon as he had arrived at the front Ernac's strength was tested. He was sent out with seasoned warriors. They ordered him to fit and release, fit and release, fit and release, fit and release. The drill was repeated until the hardened veterans judged him competent with his war bow.

Pulling one-hundred fifty pounds of pressure, the tension of a war bow calls for muscles of iron. Ernac treated his body as a machine. He trained like an athlete, building himself slowly and deliberately. Better to die than fail, he told himself, and he fired hundreds of rounds, pushing himself until he felt secure.

He must be able to wheel, let fly at full gallop, and expect accuracy. He kept at it until the targets of dead animals bristled with his arrows. Only when the targets had to be replaced hourly did he feel himself to be ready. Ernac's war bow had become an extension of his body. The spring of the arc had worked itself into the fibers of his torso.

Ernac had met the standard gauge of a man's fitness for war. This was reported to the Khan. His son was ready for battle and Attila was overjoyed. If his delight was mixed with surprise none saw it. The Khan acted as if his son's success had been expected. Ernac's readiness was evidence that manhood had finally overtaken the Khan's heir, and

Attila was unstinting in his praise. He sent gifts, and messages, of pride-filled congratulation to this son for whom a great future, albeit a future yet to arrive, was ever being predicted.

The son of a warlord would customarily be placed at the center of the Khan's army. Ernac should have been there with the princes, nobles, and others of military rank. His father chose, instead, to separate his son from those who might be tempted to protect him in his first battle experience.

The initiation into the central mystery of a soldier's life carries with it opportunity. If there was every possibility of failure here, it was also possible that an enterprising young soldier would distinguish himself. The world of men destined to wield the sword and the bow is a cauldron of creation. In such a world tragedy can turn to triumph in seconds, and this place of mystery and opportunity would be Ernac's to experience alone. Attila wished his son to succeed or fail without the reassuring presence of retainers and boyhood companions to support him.

The hours before the battle found most men drinking together. Ernac didn't join the men after the rumors of an engagement the following day had been confirmed. He couldn't drown his fear of the coming dawn in drink. His stomach was tight. He was unable to rid his mind of a sick apprehension, and he lay in his tent weak with foreboding.

The Khan's spies had been accurate as usual. When the Huns neared Marcianople it was clear they would be met by a large Roman force. They would be compelled to reply in kind. There would be prolonged hand-to-hand combat. This sent the Khan into a fury. A stationary battle site was not to his liking, the losses would be high. He preferred the feint and retreat, or a surprise engulfment. Ernac knew there was sound reasoning behind his father's thinking. But, obliged to participate in a Roman-style battle, Ernac also knew the Khan would give the Romans a bitter fight.

As Ernac lay in his battle tent, twisting and knotting his quilts around him, he could think of nothing but how he would acquit himself the following morning. The suspicion that he might prove a coward, might run or otherwise disgrace himself, was unbearable. Unbearable as the idea was, it was a possibility.

When his steward roused him Ernac berated him, certain he hadn't closed his eyes for more than a few moments. But the night was gone. Youth and health had asserted themselves, and sleep had overcome him in the hours after midnight.

Rising from his tumbled couch, Ernac donned a heavy silk undershirt, over it the brown tunic bordered in blue, and the quilted cuirass. He drew on his loosely belted trousers and boots. One sip of broth was enough to convince him his gut would tolerate no nonsense, and he left the yurt to seek his groom.

The man was waiting, his gelding, Esla, saddled and ready. Breast padding, and wood-framed war saddle, were in place. The pommel sported the blue ribbons of the Khan's light cavalry. Two quivers of arrows, his lasso, his small sword and javelin, were in holders on Esla's back. His dagger was strapped to his forearm, and Ernac's fingers sought its comforting thickness. The groom handed up his shield and bows. He slung them to his left, opposite the quivers of arrows. He was as ready as any soldier.

Esla, too, was ready, pirouetting on his bunched hind quarters, lathered with excitement. Ernac's chosen gelding was a fortunate piece of horseflesh. Having once been ridden in battle, he would be honored as a comrade in arms. When his usefulness as war-horse was over he would not be eaten, but would be let out to pasture to live out his time in peace.

Esla rolled his neck, his eyes turning back to Ernac in recognition. The young soldier absentmindedly rubbed his horse's neck as he took the reins and placed his boot in the ritually proffered hands of his groom. He swung atop Esla to the blessings, and pronouncements of victory, from the men of his ten. Ten, by ten, by ten, the warriors found their places.

Ernac had never known such loneliness as this. In the company of his fellows, on a fair morning, he felt the cold touch of universal emptiness. An intransigent twitch of his jaw warned him of the rebellious desire to turn and flee. A void opened beneath Ernac. In it he recognized the pit that swallows mortal being. Awakening crashed like live thunder over the head of the novice warrior.

Ernac remembered Edecon's history. In his thirteenth summer he had clothed himself in glory, ambushing a small war party of a dozen men. Alone and unaided, Edecon had attacked them and wiped them out. This had been the start of a great career as a warrior. The numbers of men he had killed had, perhaps, been embellished since the event, still, his history was an inspiring story.

The words of his father came back to Ernac.

— "A leader is no leader who does not ride at the head of his troops. His presence confers dignity on the suffering and death of his men. None dares call himself lord who will not ride in the forefront of battle. The common soldier daily faces death, a lord must risk death with his men."

Ernac could not escape the hours to come. The thought sent a gasp to his lips. Swallowing the intake of breath, Ernac listened, trying to glean what he might from the sounds around him.

His ears brought him no new information. But for the creak of leather, the subdued clink of metal against metal, and the snuffling of horses, there was nothing. No human voice was heard in greeting or complaint. The very air stayed itself.

The massed lines of men awaited the signal from the Khan's standard at the center. The alarm, when it came, was almost an afterthought. After a seemingly eternal wait for a moment which was never in doubt, the signal came. The approaching enemy had been detected and Attila's banner was raised. Each standard bearer raised his flag in turn, and the message was passed along. The outer flanks received the semaphore; still, they waited. Let the enemy make the first move. Let them fall into the gaping center. An amphitheater of horsemen awaited them.

The ranks stiffened attentively. Ernac's mind cleared to a crystalline alertness. When the Khan met the enemy at the center, the order for the flanks would come. Ernac was face to face with the immaculate moment he had so long envisioned for himself. This would be the surpassing test. This was what he had sought, but it was not as he had imagined it. There had been a passionate intensity in his daydream. That intensity had deserted him, leaving detached disinterest in its wake.

My body, he thought, amazed, has nothing to do with what is happening here. Ernac felt he was already dead. As this thought came to him, there was a ripple from the left, the signal flag flipping abruptly up, then down.

The squadron's standard bearers answered, hoisting the brisk banners. The flag bearers pointed their burdens skyward and the lines surged forward as if pulled along by invisible elastic bands. The lurching figures seemed set in motion by a puppetmaster. Their limbs projected an improbable air of pantomime, the perverse jerkiness of life-sized dolls.

An image floated before the eyes of the young warrior. He saw himself cantering across a grassy plain in summer. He was out hunting with Beki, when suddenly a stag leaped from behind a rock. Ernac fitted an arrow, pulled his bow, and the stag became a man. The antlered head became a helmeted head which fell rattling onto the ground.

Before Ernac could comprehend the transformation, their forward movement carried him and Esla into a morass of men and weapons. A welter of sounds floated up behind Ernac's ears but he didn't allow them to seduce him. He didn't turn, instead he plunged ahead. He killed the same stag with the same antlered head again and again. The head became a man's head each time it fell. He heard shouts and cheers, but to him they were indecipherable caterwaulings.

Wheeling, he rushed Esla back through the lines of heavy cavalry. The men who passed him went down in the space of a bare breath. He wheeled again. Ernac could no longer say in which direction he was riding. He simply shot and pulled until his quivers were almost empty. He had one last shot as two more rows of heavy cavalry drove past him. The Romans had punctured the Hun heavy cavalry and were laying in with a will. They hacked at Attila's men, lances thrusting deep, swords and battle-axes swirling about them.

In the years since Adrianople Theodosius' armies had come to understand what was required to go against nomadic horsemen. The

Romans hadn't mastered the mobility of steppe cavalry, but the power of their infantry, learned in the heyday of the legions, was fearsome. When they were engaged straight-out the lances and swords did their deadly work, and rows of kneeling bowmen provided a constant protective hail for the ranks.

Ernac, and Esla, were turning, lazily it seemed, inside the boiling air. Ernac had no sense of time or direction. The slaughter was stupefying. He could not have hazarded a guess as to how long he had been here, within the small grid of his part in the battle. While he had been about the business of fitting and pulling his bow, the field had turned to a charnel grinder. Ernac was familiar with indifferent killing. Son, nephew, and grandson of Khans, Attila's youngest was not horror-struck by death, but at Marcianople there was an extravagance to the killing he had never imagined.

Some went down with scarcely a mark on them, others were opened from groin to throat. Bodies were pierced by lance, carved by scimitar and battle axe. Chests and stomachs, torn hopelessly, went gaping, surrendering themselves to the sky. Globbets of crania, thorax and abdomen, disgorged themselves in front of Ernac's eyes. Skulls exploded, vomiting grey particulate. Arteries pumped, squirting strong elegant jets of scarlet. Lungs fluttered in faltering swells, entrails slithered in curling waves from the warm security of their abdominal walls. Kidneys and livers shuddered in startled convulsion at a sudden rude contact with the air.

Ernac had met war. The reality had not been what he had pictured, but he had been engaged in the thick of battle, and had survived. That was what mattered. He was alive. He had passed the test.

9

For several weeks Ernac remained muscle-sore and bone-weary, but he was grateful that he had not disgraced himself. The army was now nearing home. Riding with the remaining men of his ten, Ernac noted that they did not complain about the brisk pace of the homeward march.

Two days out of the home camps the men had a full moon at the end of the day's ride. It was a great amber globe, so close in the eastern sky it appeared to have settled on the ground. Above, hung a canopy of incandescent stars. Their clarity was observed by the most insensitive. Even for the plains the night was remarkably clear.

The Khan called a halt at a spring bubbling through a jumble of rocks. Here, the water dropped into a natural pool that had welcomed travelers for generations. This was a favored spot for resting, for slaking thirst, and for filling water-skins. The people and animals who traipsed back and forth over the plains on human business had left distinctive furrows around the sides of the pool. The horses fell to drinking while the men emptied skins of wine.

It was early evening, and pleasantly warm, but the season of frozen ground was near, and before morning it would be cold.

Ernac drowsed on his couch. He was startled awake by the Khan's groom who appeared with a request.

The Khan asked that his son ride out with him in the evening air. This was an uncommon request, and Ernac hastened to say yes. He imagined a short ride with informal talk. As usual he had underestimated his father. There was more on Attila's mind than idle talk.

On their way out of camp they cantered silently under the swollen moon. Attila was quiet. The closer they came to the heartland the less he spoke.

His father never engaged in prattle, but he had become inaccessible. The Khan's mood was not ugly. Rather, Ernac thought, it was contemplative, and he understood this. The campaign had exhausted all of them. They had sustained terrible losses. Still, they had avoided the plague, and the home camps were near. There was much to be thankful for.

Ernac didn't believe Attila's silence meant unhappiness, and, certainly, the troops were in fine spirits. They were looking forward to telling tales of war and distributing plunder to wives and families. But Attila was disturbed by something, and Ernac hoped to find out what it was.

Father and son halted at a near landmark, a low hill of dark rocks. Here Attila dismounted, and motioned Ernac to join him. They sat on the hillock of jutting stone and dried plant life, observing the bright display in the night sky. Overhead, an occasional star went shooting through the heavens as if to draw attention to itself, wanting, perhaps, to stand out from its fellows.

Without preamble the Khan said, "Have you spoken with your brother, Dengezic?"

"No," Ernac said, surprised, "I haven't. I thought he was with Oebarsius. Why do you ask?"

"He has returned to us," Attila said. "He has returned imagining himself a hero. He fought well against the Acatiri, I admit, and was courageous at Marcianople. Now he comes asking that land be ceded to him as a reward. I have refused him."

Ernac waited, alert to what his father meant to tell him.

"I want you to do something for me," said Attila. "Find out what Dengezic plans. Behind his request for land is the desire for his own troops. He won't say it openly, but he wants his own army. If his plans go further than that I need to know it. He won't suspect my hand in the inquiries if you're careful."

Ernac was glad no one was nearby to see his face. He wanted time; he needed to figure out how to avoid becoming drawn into a dispute between the suspicions of his father and the ambitions of his brother. Personally, he thought Attila's suspicions justified.

"My brother plays a bad game," he thought. Dengezic couldn't win a contest of wit against Attila. Ernac thanked the gods his brother had known better than to ask him to become involved in his scheming. Ernac was loyal to the Khan; nothing could make him throw his lot in with traitors. Still, he owed Dengezic his good will.

"He has never done anything bad to me," Ernac thought.

It was a dilemma, and Ernac had put off facing it. Since the day Beki had confided that she'd caught Kursik spying on Mother Kreka, Ernac had waited for this moment. He feared the moment, and he had hoped it would pass him by. He was in an awkward position, and he squirmed. Not wishing to commit himself, Ernac tried to sidestep the problem.

"I lost seven of my men at Marcianople," he said.

"You are a soldier, leader of your ten," his father replied, "Your losses were no worse than anyone's. Your men will be replaced."

"I know," Ernac said. "But seven dead. Only three out of my ten survived, and I know these figures were repeated in many tens. These are severe losses."

"Yes. Our losses were heavy. Marcianople was a victory, but it was a rotten affair," the Khan said. "I'm tired of battle, Ernac. I want to hear no more about Marcianople."

"At least Marcianople answered one of my old questions," his son proffered glumly.

The Khan asked him what that was.

"You don't remember," said the newly baptized soldier. "Seasons ago I asked you if you minded losing your men when you went into war. You didn't answer me. You said that was a thing I must decide for myself."

"Mmmmh-hmm," mumbled Attila. "And what did you decide?"

"I do mind. For myself," Ernac said, "I've decided I mind."

Attila hadn't answered the first time Ernac had put the question, and he didn't answer now. The words lay between them like loose cockleburs. They sat together, faces hidden, minds wandering.

When he was a bit younger, Ernac reflected, he would have relieved the pressure of silence with a silly remark. Tonight he was not inclined to break the bleak mood.

"I haven't Attila's ready temper, instead I've learned to relish my fits of melancholy," he thought.

Ernac realized that a distance had inserted itself between himself and his father. Not so long ago he couldn't have separated himself from the Khan's views. His father's frame of mind was one thing, but since Marcianople, Ernac, too, had been in a foul humor. The carnage was not easy to bear, even for battle-hardened soldiers. It turned his stomach. Flesh lying open, slices of bone and brain flung about like so much gravel and cheese curd. It was a raw scene. Seeing seven of his men die before him was not the nicest way to be initiated into a warrior's life.

When he saw that Ernac made no move to rise or speak, Attila mounted, and sat his horse.

"Will you do it?" the Khan said.

The young lieutenant could hardly refuse. "Yes," he said, "but it will not be easy. Dengezic is not stupid."

"Nor are you, son Ernac," his father declared.

Attila favored Ernac with one of his elegant, wicked grins as they faced each other in the moonlight.

At least, Ernac imagined he did.

My father has decided to trust me. After he asked me to spy on Dengezic I had my doubts, but since our return he has given me my own squad to command. Baldin literally scrapes his head on the floor of our yurt when he bows. He addresses me as Lord Ernac, Hero of the People.

My wife laughs at my crimson face. "The commander of the Khan is as great in war as he is in bed," she giggles.

I can't say I disagree. Beki is right on both counts. I'm a blooded soldier, and I revel in the pleasures of my wife's body. No longer do I complain of inactivity or boredom.

Today I'll spend the afternoon at a gathering of the Khan's council. I am called in my capacity as Keeper of the Homeland.

A round of wine awaited the council members, but no one drank. They waited for my father. When the Khan took his seat and lifted his wooden bowl they would stand and drink from the silver and gold bowls. And when he sat they would sit.

Attila looked across the assembly, lifted his bowl, saluted the council, and drained the wine. His nobles stood, drained their bowls, and business began.

The Khan inquired as to the message that had just come from the Acatiri General, Kuridach. Attila had sent an invitation requesting that Kuridach visit the *ordu* of the Khan, and Bigilas now read out his reply.

The Khan's mouth turned down. He demanded Bigilas repeat what he'd just read. He tugged at an earlobe as if he couldn't believe what the ear had heard. Attila turned to his Roman scribe, Orestes, and gave him a questioning look.

Bigilas repeated the message. "The Acatiri General, Kuridach, refuses your invitation, Great Khan. He cannot journey to your camps."

Onegesius averted his eyes, and the council members stirred nervously.

Attila turned away from his scribe and faced Bigilas.

"What reason does he give for his refusal?," my father asked.

Bigilas spread his oily flattery, and after much posturing, got around to an answer. The words he finally mouthed may have come from Kuridach, or, perhaps, from his own head.

"He says, Great Lord, that if it is impossible to look upon the orb of the sun, how can one behold the greatest of the gods without injury?"

I stole a glance at my father's face, but couldn't say how he took the words. Bigilas' pretensions have no effect on Attila, but the words of Kuridach, if truly his, are clearly an attempt to avoid visiting the camp of the Khan.

Granted, an invitation to visit the King of the Huns is not always received with joy, and Kuridach is sly. He knows the invitation could be a trap. He will send a tribute more solid than his physical presence. Gold will placate my father where nothing else serves.

"How much gold comes with his reply?" Attila asked.

"Five-hundred pounds arrived on the heels of his words, and further gifts are being unloaded from the pack-train," Bigilas answered hastily.

"I will inspect these gifts when they are unloaded," was Attila's response. He indicated the council was dismissed, but he signed for me to stay behind.

What he said to me after we were alone I am not free to discuss with anyone, not even with Beki.

10

The season that followed our victory over the Romans has been spent in the home camps. Numbing cold followed the heat of summer, but the time of fat horses is here again.

The quiet of camp life was a welcome rest at first, even for Attila. More than that, of course, there were many matters that required his attention here.

Foremost, was the question of Adamis and Mother Kreka. Officially, and most curiously, this delicate situation seems to have been resolved without spilling anyone's blood. Adamis no longer serves the Khatun. He has his own yurt, and he now serves Onegesius. The former lovers don't speak, even in passing.

Some find it remarkable that Attila took no public vengeance on Adamis, but his decision seems to have been a good one. The Khan and Khatun appear more content together than they have in some time, and this is more than an appearance of happiness, or so Beki tells me.

What took place between my father and mother on the Khan's return from war took place without witnesses. My wife's view, which is trustworthy as any, is that Attila quite simply claimed his prerogative. He ordered Adamis out of the Khatun's service, and that settled the matter.

Any other course might have been humiliating for Attila, but Adamis' head shouldn't ride too comfortably on his neck even now. My mother's former steward may yet meet with an unfortunate accident. That, no one speaks of, which is just as well. Meantime, there is fresh fodder to occupy the minds of the *qara buden*, and the wellborn don't stoop to discussing such peccadillos in public. Most scarcely admit such things go on.

The latest talk is of the Persian spy, Tadiqin, who is being watched by Attila's agents. Also, Kursik, Dengezic's informer, must be dealt with at some point. And, there is Dengezic himself. I don't believe my brother suspects me of subterfuge where he's concerned, but I'm unable to penetrate his mind.

I've kept my word. The information I've been able to glean has been transmitted to Attila. Sad to report, what I found out indicates my father's suspicions were correct. Many riddles remain, and the full range of my brother's intentions remains unclear.

Military plans proceed; the organizing of alliances and tactics for the Khan's war against Aëtius are going ahead. Plans change daily, of course, for the Khan stays ahead of his enemies' knowledge of him.

A delegation to the Romans has been named. The men who are entrusted with this mission will leave for Constantinople within the next few days. Attila is sending Edecon, Bigilas, Orestes, Scottas, and other minor nobles, to meet with the Emperor Theodosius.

Attila's choice of Edecon to lead the delegation was a declaration that my former tutor is back in his good graces. He acquitted himself well in negotiations with the Roman ambassador, Anatolius, now called Master of the Soldiers. I remember this ambassador well. I once saw the blood of a slave water his wine, and saw his hands tremble as the slave was beheaded in front of him. No wonder that he trembled, he was about to offer up his own head to secure an agreement with Attila. This same Anatolius accepted the terms my father laid down after Marcianople. He agreed with my father's demands down to the last detail. The Romans are calling it the Second Peace of Anatolius, but my father credits Edecon with protecting Hun interests in the negotiations. In light of my performance at Marcianople Attila also feels that Edecon proved himself an able mentor to the heir of the Khan. Altogether, Edecon has earned his place in the inner circle.

I learned today in council that the terms of the letter Edecon will deliver to the Emperor are harsh. In it, Attila accuses Theodosius of withholding fugitives, and of failing to evacuate the lands south of the Danube. The lands next to the river were to be given over to us, and the Romans have been tardy in pulling their forces back from them. If they don't comply, my father will renew the war. Furthermore, Attila demands that ambassadors of the highest rank be sent to settle the differences that remain between himself and Theodosius. The Khan does not deign to deal with second-echelon deputies.

Meanwhile, I've been digging out a few crumbs of information on my own. From Baldin I have heard of a eunuch in Constantinople called Chrysaphius. He is currently a most powerful minister to Emperor Theodosius, and he has everywhere acquired an unsavory reputation. Baldin tells me he's the very soul of self-service, a man of overpowering ambition, and an inveterate liar. These reports cause me much concern because our delegation must get past his scheming head in order to make any progress in the discussions.

I have told Beki I don't approve of Bigilas being given a primary role in the delegation. A man such as Chrysaphius can manipulate a man who is not expert in the niceties of diplomacy. Besides, Bigilas is a snake in his own right. Choosing him may have been unavoidable. It had to be someone who spoke our tongue, and not many do. Still, I'm wary of him.

Negotiation after negotiation is being undertaken on either side. There seems no end to talking. Attila maintains that this is the way of diplomacy. Publicly, civil talk proceeds, no matter what deceits may be taking place in private. A Khan's life is complicated, and my own life is no longer simple. The days are filled with diplomatic sessions, tactical reviews, and endless surmisings on future campaigns.

The temporary peace we are now enjoying is welcome to most. For the soldiers these are days of hunting, falconry, drinking, and well-deserved idleness; days without responsibility. I cannot say the same for myself. If I were of a different character I'd be looking with longing to the days before I was married, before my first battle, before I commanded men, before I became official heir to the Khan. The lazy pursuits I indulged in then are no longer possible for me.

There are, however, compensations. Beki and I have settled into married life, and we are as happy as most married people. She doesn't complain of me and I have no inclination to complain of her. There is a harmony between us that's most gratifying. My wife does laugh at the stilted way I express my feelings. She says I was in dire need of a decent sex life, and that having it has at least put me in a decent humor.

She's right in that, but my mood may also have to do with the season. The growing time has descended on us, grasses are high, and animals and people alike are smiling.

Except for my father.

As the days pass and no word of the delegation comes, the Khan becomes disgruntled. I haven't spoken with him, and am in no hurry to. He's not pleasant to be around. One thing only seems good in his life. He and Mother Kreka are everywhere together. Their reunion continues to be a success.

Just when there was open talk of deception, and fear that an outrage had been committed, even that the delegation had been assassinated, word of them has finally arrived.

Edecon has done well. He delivered the Khan's letter to the Emperor and the envoys are on their way back to the home camp with a reply. A man unknown to us, a minor ambassador called Maximinus, leads their group. A person with no title, a friend of Maximinus called Priscus, travels with the delegation. Not one among them claims the highest rank either in Rome or in Constantinople. My father is not pleased about this.

For myself, I am simply curious to hear Edecon's version of what transpired in Constantinople.

"I beg you, Edecon, describe the rooms again. How large were the palace grounds? What manner of man is this Chrysaphius, that he has dominion over the palaces of Theodosius. And why did Chrysaphius ask you to dine with him alone at his palace?" Baldin ran his questions together in a rush.

I had gone to Edecon's yurt to speak of more important matters, but the crippled slave kept yammering about Constantinople.

The little slave crouched on the floor of Edecon's yurt. He hung on his words like a dog begging meat at a banquet. Chin resting in the fistlike stumps of his hands, Baldin's eyes goggled up at Edecon.

The cripple begged earnestly for one more description of the palaces and the riches of Constantinople.

"One question at a time, Baldin. I'll tell you again of the palace. I've already described it a dozen times, but since you cannot get enough I'll give it to you once more," Edecon said happily, and he launched forth.

"I admit it's worth more than one telling. The mansions of the palace were an astonishment."

He shook his head in wonder at the recollection.

"I've never seen anything to rival the Imperial Palaces in splendor. The rooms were crammed; piled high with gold, perfumes and pearls, ivory and indigo, amber, olive oil, salt, and exotic spices. Constantinople has gathered every sort of luxury and lush living unto itself. The coffers of the world have come to rest in these palaces.

"I wandered from cavernous room to cavernous room. Each hall boasted an enormous gilded ceiling, each was held up by columns of exquisitely polished marble. The floors were also of marble, cleverly fitted in colored inlays of intricate design. A forest of statuary stood about the rooms, the figures absolutely lifelike and of consummate workmanship. I couldn't help reaching to touch them. I expected to find the warmth of life in the limbs, and was surprised that I did not. It was an experience to remember I can tell you," Edecon finished, still shaking his head in wonder.

Baldin made a move to urge another telling. He hoped, through repetition, to have a part of Edecon's marvelous experience for himself, but Edecon waved him off.

"Leave us," he said. "I must speak with Ernac, Baldin."

The crooked body skittered out, leaving Edecon and me to our privacy. As soon as his lame form had disappeared through the doorway I turned to my teacher.

"What is this incident I've been hearing about, the odd episode that occurred on the return journey?" I asked.

"It was an unfortunate thing," Edecon said, grimacing at the memory.

"Tell me exactly what happened," I demanded.

"We arrived in Sardica thirteen days out from the capital," he related. "There Maximinus called a halt, and we were entertained at dinner by the Romans. We sat drinking after the meal. Toasts were given all around. Our delegation, of course, toasted the Khan, and Maximinus proposed Theodosius. We had lifted our goblets and were ready to drink when Bigilas spoke. He said a god ought not be mentioned in the same breath as a mere man. Our heads grew hot and we reached for our swords.

"Maximinus spoke up immediately, trying to soothe us. Surely, he said, Bigilas could not have meant that Theodosius was a god, and that Attila was too insignificant to be compared to him. The ambassador called for more wine, bowls were passed, and Bigilas' remark was glossed over."

"That is an unbelievable story, Edecon. Bigilas must have plied the wine cup too freely that night," I answered.

"Perhaps. But there's more," Edecon said. "The next morning as we were riding out I saw Bigilas having words with Maximinus and his friend, Priscus. Bigilas then rode over to my side, and told me of an incident he said Priscus and Maximinus had witnessed. He told of an encounter between Maximinus and Orestes that he purported to find perplexing.

"Bigilas reported the story to me this way," Edecon said. "Several days out from Constantinople Orestes sought to speak with Maximinus. Taking the ambassador aside, Orestes congratulated him. He told him he'd been wise in not inviting me to dine alone with him on this journey. He also told Maximinus he was wise not to have offered me gifts, as Chrysaphius had done in Constantinople."

"What did this mean, that Maximinus was wise not to dine with you or offer you gifts?" I said.

"Apparently Orestes meant to say that speaking to me in private would have placed Maximinus under suspicion from the Khan. That was all Bigilas would tell me."

"What did you say to these odd comments?"

"I said nothing. We rode on, and then Bigilas made a most suspicious proposition. He offered me 50 pounds of gold from his pack-train, saying he knew I had been promised much gold by Chrysaphius. I had only to do as Chrysaphius had asked me, he said, and I would stand to gain. Again, I didn't answer him. Our group rode on ahead to report to Attila. We left Bigilas with the Romans and no more was said of the gold. What do you make of this, friend Ernac? Do you believe this was an attempt to bribe me, or some of our party?"

"The story is perplexing," I said, keeping my face blank. "If such an offer had been made, the Khan's spies would have heard of it. How would Bigilas know of such a plan anyway? I agree with Orestes. If Maximinus offered you, or anyone, a secret bribe, it would be a serious mistake. And Chrysaphius certainly made a mistake if he did so. I don't know how else to answer you, Edecon."

Edecon didn't reply and we parted, each of us hastening toward his own tent.

Edecon is as subtle as his hands are shaky, I thought. His reputation as a mediator is well-deserved. Many a man would have been caught in the net Chrysaphius spread for Edecon, but the Khan's advisor stepped around it easily.

I laughed aloud. My old teacher is still teaching me, I said to myself.

11

The Romans grew increasingly depressed as they penetrated more deeply into Hun territory, and Maximinus confessed his uneasiness to Priscus. Since the strange dinner at Sardica, he said, he'd been tempted to turn back without completing the journey. Priscus confessed he also was uneasy.

The party felt a pall settle over them. They couldn't contain their anxieties, and conversation consisted of litanies of the fearful possibilities ahead. With each step they became more troubled, and on arriving at Naissus they became terror-struck, horrified at the utter ruin that prevailed. Where once a thriving city stood was only silence and rubble. The troubling sight brought home to them the enormous power of the nomadic war machine.

Six years before, the Huns had captured the city, and now, at the birthplace of Constantine, there was only desolation. The buildings were flattened masses of stone, the population was gone, and the river banks outside the city were strewn with the bones of those slain six years earlier. The delegation did not camp within the city.

The next day they reached the banks of the Danube. They were ferried precariously across to the northern side in unstable boats hewn from tree trunks. A number of Huns came to meet them when they landed, and these accompanied the party, watching the Romans' every move. But the warriors were not threatening. Attila was planning a hunt in the newly acquired territories south of the Danube, and these men had been sent to scout the countryside before the Khan's arrival.

Beyond Naissus the Romans approached the encampments of Attila and saw a cloud of Hun tents resting on the plain below. There, they halted and prepared to set up camp. They had scarcely begun unloading baggage when they were stopped by a new contingent of Hun soldiers. Then, a series of bewildering events began unfolding.

The new party of soldiers became excited. They pointed to Attila's camps below, and insisted, in the most insulting language, that the delegation couldn't camp above the tents of the Khan. So the Romans rode below and prepared to pitch camp on the plain. Before they could get set up they were accosted once more. This time Edecon, Orestes, Scottas, and other Hun lieutenants, had ridden out to them. The Khan's lieutenants asked the delegation why they were there, and what they expected to achieve with their mission. The Khan of Khans, they said, demanded immediate answers. They challenged the delegation to explain themselves. Stunned at their open hostility, Maximinus didn't know how to answer, and an angry confrontation followed.

Maximinus tried to tell them he'd been instructed to deal only with Attila. Scottas, in his usual rough way, shouted at him. He said that Attila gave the orders, that they had been told to get answers to the Khan's questions and they would have them.

The Romans feared for their heads, but suddenly the Hun officers turned and tore off toward the tents of the Khan, disappearing as swiftly as they'd come. Priscus, Bigilas, and the others, were left in confusion. Maximinus was still attempting to regain his composure when the Hun deputies came riding back, this time minus Edecon.

Scottas and Orestes proceeded to inform Maximinus of the exact contents of Theodosius' letter. Though they were not supposed to know this, they repeated word for word the text of the emperor's reply to the Khan, and they ordered the delegation back to the Roman frontier.

Maximinus, who had thought he was beyond being flustered further, was struck dumb. He couldn't believe the contents of the Emperor's secret letter had been discovered, and he stood mute. When he finally found his tongue he insisted he was a loyal minion of Rome, and he steadfastly insisted he would speak only to Attila. At Maximinus' stubborn reply, Scottas ordered them out of Hun territory once again, and the party of Huns galloped off.

Now convinced, they had no choice but to turn back the delegation prepared to leave. Before they could get underway a third group of horsemen arrived from the camps of the Khan. They bore an ox, and fish, as gifts from Attila. The new Hun party informed them they would be allowed to stay until the next morning. By now they were too addled to think. They ate the food given them and lay down to a fitful sleep. Morning arrived, and again they were told to leave.

At this juncture Priscus called on Rusticius, asking if he could salvage something from the situation. Rusticius knew the Hun language, and Priscus asked if he would approach Scottas with a proposal to arrange a private interview between Attila and the ambassador. Almost as if he had been waiting for the opportunity, Rusticius departed to seek out Scottas with the proposal. When he found Scottas, Rusticius offered him gifts from the stores of the Romans. Cleverly baiting the Khan's picked man, Rusticius told the Hun noble there was a way to demonstrate the great influence he had with Attila. Scottas had bragged of his close ties to the Khan, and Rusticius said he could prove this by arranging a meeting with Priscus. The implication that Scottas had lied about his influence with Attila infuriated the Hun and he raced off without answering.

The pack-horses went on loading to leave and, at length, they set off for the return. No sooner had they started than they had to be called back. Word had come that Priscus and Maximinus, along with the interpreter, Bigilas, would be admitted to Attila's presence. The three mounted horses, rode to the Hun camp, and passed through a throng of guards outside the warlord's wooden palisades. Inside, after all these days of suspense, they found the king of the Huns sitting in his pavilion on a simple wooden stool. Attila's massive head and chest, the impressiveness of his carriage, and the peculiar intelligence of his deep-set eyes, dominated the space around him.

Priscus noted the sallow face, and the sparse beard sprinkled with grey. He found Attila exceedingly repulsive. Maximinus bowed low, saluted, and handed over the infamous letter.

The other Romans stood at a respectful distance, and Maximinus spoke.

"I bring greetings from your friend, Theodosius, Emperor of Rome. He wishes the Great Khan to know that he prays for his well-being, and the well-being of his kingdom."

"You may tell your Emperor that his deputies might undergo the same fate he wishes for me," Attila replied darkly.

No one in the Roman delegation understood his comment, and before anything further could be said Attila turned on Bigilas, attacking him in the most vile way.

"Shameless beast," he said, confronting Bigilas threateningly. "How do you dare stand here in front of me. You know my terms. I will meet with no ambassadors until every hostage belonging to me has been returned. Explain yourself, you son of an ass."

"I swear to you, Great Khan, I swear on the head of my mother, the hostages have all been surrendered," Bigilas cried in alarm.

"I will have you impaled, you puling wretch. Your leavings will be flung out as food for the birds," Attila yelled. The veins in his neck were bulging with anger.

Bigilas didn't throw himself down but he groveled nonetheless. The blood drained from his face, and his throat convulsed in anguished fear.

"The hostages have not been surrendered. You are a lying dog. There are Hun hostages in the Roman Empire," the Khan screamed, now beside himself with rage. "I know this for a fact. My scribe Orestes will read out the names."

Orestes did as he was commanded, and the list was long. When he had finished reading no one had the courage to speak.

Attila's eyes bored through Bigilas, cutting him to pieces. "Get out," he shouted. "Leave my presence, you filthy piece of carrion. I hereby order you executed. If you were not protected by your rank I'd kill you myself."

Two guards entered the tent and Bigilas was ushered out. It appeared he was being taken into custody, but Edecon, following directly after him, stopped the group as they reached the tents of the Romans.

"The Khan has changed his mind. You are to return immediately to Constantinople, Bigilas," he said. "You will obtain and bring back the 50 pounds of gold you offered me on the way here. Maximinus will stay here until your return."

Edecon turned and left the mystified interpreter.

Bigilas hurriedly prepared to leave, but was interrupted by yet another message. By order of the Khan, the message said, he was forbidden to buy goods in Hun territories. He was to purchase nothing on his way out except food, and nothing on his way back. Further, he was forbidden to trade anything for money until every difference between the Khan and Rome had been settled.

Bigilas did not see the trap in these instructions, and he set off still professing himself unable to understand why Attila had abused him. He arrived in Constantinople unaware that he, one of only three men who knew of the traitorous plot to kill Attila, had himself been betrayed.

He imagined himself safe, for only he and Edecon had been present with Chrysaphius on the occasion of the traitorous dinner. What the eunuch had proposed that night Bigilas interpreted for Edecon, and he then swore the Hun advisor to secrecy.

His proposal would be in Edecon's best interests, the eunuch had said. Many blessings would come to him if he found a way to assassinate the Khan. Chrysaphius proposed that Edecon return to the homeland, murder Attila, make his way back to Constantinople, and live life as a Roman for the rest of his days. In these very palaces, for which he had expressed such admiration, coaxed the eunuch, he could live a life of luxury and power. He then asked Edecon to swear he would carry out the plan.

Edecon agreed, and the pact was made. Attila's advisor gave Chrysaphius his oath as a Hun. From that moment the game was up.

The clever eunuch had not bothered to understand the customs of a people he considered his potential vassals. What he should have known he did not know; no oath is binding on a Hun save that given to another Hun, or to one considered an *anda* brother.

Edecon had sent word back at once of the plot against Attila's life. He also informed Attila of Chrysaphius' attempt to bribe him with 50 pounds of gold, and asked for instructions. The Khan sent word that his advisor was to proceed as if he had fallen in with the plan.

The Hun deputies were also ordered to return, and to act as if they suspected nothing. The Roman delegation would follow, and Attila would handle them.

12

Today the Romans came to Kreka's tents to pay their respects. I was allowed to be there, and it was an enlightening afternoon.

As they traveled about Hun country the Roman deputies have displayed astonishment at what they saw, and when they met with Kreka they were not shy to question her.

They gave the Khatun gifts of gold and silk, and complimented her tents, saying they hadn't imagined life among the Huns was so fine. They noted that Kreka's summer tent was as large as many Roman houses. The women embroidering linen garments at the far end of the tent interested them especially. Kreka invited them to examine the women's work. They looked closely at the stitching and pronounced it of excellent quality.

Maximinus asked Kreka if they might impose on her hospitality to talk at length. She readily agreed and the party seated themselves. They were served bread, tea, and sweetmeats, and since they expressed interest the Khatun gave leave for them to ask whatever they wished, and said she would do her best to answer.

Their first question concerned Bleda's widow, Helche. They had visited her village and had found she was the ruler there.

"How is it," Priscus asked, "that a woman rules over a town?"

Kreka said, "It isn't uncommon for women to rule over a town. Nor is it uncommon for wellborn women to wield authority in the camps."

She told them that women sometimes ruled over whole territories, and that they might take themselves off to war to defend them. She explained that in long campaigns women, and young people, traveled with the troops. The women carried food and supplies, cooked, and nursed the wounded. And, she told them, women wielded weapons when necessary.

"What else," she said, "has surprised you about our country?"

They nudged one another, and the one called Priscus, who seems a thoughtful and curious person, spoke again. He asked about a stone bathhouse they had seen within the palisades of Onegesius. They wondered at the design of the structure, and were quite taken with the deft manner of its construction.

Kreka told them about the architect who had designed it. He had been taken prisoner at Sirmium.

"This man lives happily as a Hun. He wouldn't wish to exchange his life with us for any other," she said. "Many Romans live as Huns, and they prosper," Kreka told them.

Priscus nodded.

"Yes," he said, "I believe a man could live comfortably among the Huns. I came across a man, a Greek, in one of your camps. He appeared well-to-do. He told me he couldn't be induced to leave the villages of the Huns. 'Not for anything, he said, would I leave this place. I have a better life here than I could hope to have in Rome.'"

Priscus said he believed the man was sincere.

"Still," he said, "I find it difficult to believe life is better among the Huns than among Romans."

Kreka asked Priscus why the possibility should astonish him, and he answered plainly.

"I must tell you," he said, "that in Roman territory Huns are considered crude. They are looked upon as less than human."

Kreka shook her head, laughing at his words.

"In fact," he said, "in the civilized world Huns are considered to be no better than beasts."

At this last comment, the Khatun, who might have been angry, laughed even harder.

When she had had her fill of fun she asked Priscus if she might question him in her turn. He answered that, of course, she could.

"Well, then," she said, "what do you think of the banquets you have attended here? Do you not think them civilized entertainments? Are they not lavish enough for you?"

"Most certainly, they are," he said. "They have been well-appointed throughout. Your gold and silver dishes are as lovely as any I've seen, and the hospitality of your houses is beyond criticism. The entertainments were also tasteful. In fact, I thoroughly enjoyed the occasions, Khatun Kreka."

But Priscus looked uncomfortable, as if he wished to say more. The Khatun urged him, and he admitted that he thought the Khan's behavior at one of the dinners was odd.

"Tell me of this dinner. I won't be offended," she said.

"The Khan," Priscus said, "was indifferent to most of the entertainment. He didn't smile, didn't move or speak when the dancers performed. The buffoon, Zercon, now returned to Attila as a gift from Aëtius, acted the fool, and Attila scowled at him. Everyone else laughed at Zercon's antics, but the Khan stared at him sullenly.

"Then, a young man entered the hall and went to stand by the Khan," Priscus went on. "He was an attractive youth, tall and well-proportioned. The cast of his eyes had something of Attila in them, though his features were more those of a Goth. His face was sensitive, even beautiful. Looking on him, the Khan suddenly became all smiles.

"It was the only time that night," Priscus said, "that Attila's face softened. He stroked the lad's cheek and treated him most tenderly. As long as the youth stayed by his side the Khan remained in good humor."

"What was strange about this?" Kreka asked.

"Who was this young man?" Priscus asked, slyly. "Who is he that the Khan treated him, and only him, so kindly?"

I had been quiet while Priscus spoke, but at his last words Kreka and I exchanged looks, and I said to him.

"The man you speak of is called Ernac. He is the youngest son of the Khan," I said, "the heir to his kingdom."

The Khatun extended her hands toward me, then brought them back to her own breast. "Across from me," she said, "sits the wife of that young man, and the woman in front of you is his mother."

"Bahka Beki is Ernac's wife, and I am his mother," she explained. "Ernac is the youngest born to myself and the Khan. He is the chosen of the gods. It's predicted he will recover the kingdom for our people after Attila's death."

The delegation, especially Priscus, reddened. They stammered apologies for their presumption, pleading ignorance. After this exchange the talk faltered, and the group excused themselves from Kreka's tent. The Romans may regard Huns as uncultured, even as Priscus says, but I'm sure they have little notion how they appear to us.

After weeks of negotiation, visiting various nobles, banqueting, and living off the hospitality of Attila, Maximinus, Priscus, and their party, departed our camps. I am not sorry to see them go.

The interpreter, Bigilas, has returned, carrying with him 50 pounds of gold. Ernac was in council to witness Bigilas' arrival and he told me what happened. The interpreter was arrested straightaway and placed in chains, but he was not killed. Ernac says Bigilas returned so unsuspecting that he brought his young son with him.

Attila, of course, called the council to meet, and they had Bigilas brought in front of them. The Khan then asked Bigilas a simple question.

"Why is it, Bigilas," said Attila, "that you carry so large a sum of money?"

"I have money only for necessities, for food, and fodder for the animals," Bigilas retorted confidently. "I have a little extra for fresh horses and pack animals. And certain people gave me money with which to ransom friends. Only if this should please the Khan, of course."

"You are a foul liar," the Khan roared. "This time no quibble will save you. You were to buy nothing in Hun territory until all was settled between me and Theodosius. This pathetic 50 pounds of gold is your undoing. This is bribe money. Do you imagine Edecon didn't tell me of Chrysaphius' plot on my life? I will have justice, and you, Bigilas, will not escape punishment."

Ernac says Attila then turned and ordered one of the guards standing by to kill Bigilas' son. He declared the boy would be slaughtered in front of his father if Bigilas didn't admit the purpose behind the 50 pounds of gold.

"You had my order. You were not to purchase any goods in Hun territory," the Khan yelled at him. "Yet you have brought this gold. Of what use is this 50 pounds of gold if you can purchase nothing? Did you carry a useless weight of gold the whole way from Constantinople?"

Attila motioned, and the guard advanced on the young boy with drawn dagger. In his fear the boy lost control of his functions. He puddled, and shit himself white.

Bigilas broke down. His tears rolled, and he revealed his part in the plot. He begged that the blade aimed at his son should be aimed at himself.

Instead of killing Bigilas, or his son, which he could have done with every justification, Attila ordered the traitor to remain in chains. Orestes, and Bigilas' young son, the Khan said, would now return to Constantinople and obtain an additional 50 pounds of gold with which to ransom Bigilas' life.

"Attila, instructed his scribe before the council.

"Orestes," he said, "take the saddlebag in which Bigilas brought the gold. Show it to Chrysaphius and ask him if he recognizes it. Then, tell Theodosius, who has acted cravenly, that there will be no forgiveness from the Khan of Khans until Chrysaphius has been delivered to me for punishment."

If anyone still required proof, Attila's words were proof that he had been apprised of every detail of the plot Chrysaphius had hatched on his life.

The Khan has made his decision. We will ride out to meet the Roman delegation. As ever, no one can predict my father's actions. It seems that Bigilas' punishment for the plot on my father's life, the worst of betrayals, has been negotiated away.

Within ten days after the young son of Bigilas and Orestes had departed to beg more gold a message came from Chrysaphius. The cowardly eunuch wasted no time in getting a return message to my father. When it's a matter of one's own neck even the mighty are moved to quick action.

Chrysaphius sent 50 pounds of gold in exchange for Bigilas life, and much more than 50 pounds in exchange for his own life. With this golden message came the ambassadors, Anatolius and Nomus. And as my father demanded, they came laden with gold and grain for the Khan's soldiers. To the Khan, himself, they bring an honor. Aëtius has conferred on him the title of Master of the troops in the West. This brought a huge laugh from Attila.

When he heard this he said, "Tribute comes with the title Master of the Troops, and it is tribute that keeps my army with me, Ernac. Aëtius is kinder than he means to be."

We will ride out as far as the river Dreccon to meet the Roman delegation, and there Attila will give his oath to maintain the peace as indicated in his former treaty with the Romans. He will also agree to retire from the territories south of the Danube, and to withdraw his demand for Chrysaphius' life. He will even order Bigilas to be released.

Finally, in a rare display of tact, there has been no mention of the late murder plot at any of the meetings of the council. So end negotiations for what they are calling the Third Peace of Anatolius.

Chrysaphius must imagine he has staged a diplomatic triumph. He doesn't know Attila. He grasps nothing of the Khan's plans to move against Gaul, nor is he aware that my father makes this latest treaty only to safeguard his rear. But, then, Romans have no talent for spying. Their confidence in their own informers is not well-placed. My father feeds their agents lies, and they believe he intends to move next on Italy.

13

It is certain. I am with child.

I have shared the news with no one except Kreka. I'll tell Ernac soon, but for now I want to keep the news to myself.

I would have told no one except for the accident of one recent afternoon. Kreka and I happened on one another, and the circumstance lent itself to exchanges of confidences. We both revealed ourselves that day. Still, I might have said nothing had I not lost my temper.

The loom was humming outside my yurt that afternoon. My weaving companions had left, but I pushed on, eager to finish a section that pictured the head of a lovely bird. I'll take this bird for a border design, I thought. If it works well I'll repeat it in a smaller form along the edges.

I saw the Khatun wandering in my direction. I hailed her, and she stopped to exclaim over my progress. I am proud of my weaving, and I was more than happy to show it off.

"Very well done, Beki," Kreka said. "You've really taken to weaving. I wouldn't have dreamed you'd be so good at it."

I thanked her for her compliment, and she settled to watch me do a row on the head of my long-necked bird. This is a bird I've seen many times in the marshes, a delicate white thing with a small crown of raised feathers.

"What color will you have the beak?" she asked.

"Bright orange-red. I have good dyes for that," I answered.

"Yes," she said approvingly, "that will make the head stand out from the brown background."

"The men are still in council," I commented.

"Still," she said, "and probably will be until late evening. There are difficult issues to be resolved."

"Ernac tells me Bigilas has been freed. He is less than a meal for a dog, that one."

She nodded agreement. "The insignificant one has been freed," Kreka replied. "But that's the least of what Attila has on his mind."

"I know," I said. We sat without speaking as I finished my rows, then we went in to escape the afternoon sun. We sat sipping bowls of tea and goat's milk that Ku had waiting for us.

"I never see Adamis these days," I said boldly, watching Kreka over the rim of my bowl.

The Khatun looked at me. "He's no longer with me," was all she said.

"No," I said, looking at her.

There was an awkward moment. She returned my gaze, and said, "There is much about Adamis, much about the events of these last months, you don't understand, Beki. You had enough to deal with, adjusting to marriage and a new life. I've been reluctant to discuss my problems, though they have weighed on me."

"Your mind must be easy now," I said. "The Khan is very forgiving."

Her mouth tightened. "The Khan forgiving!" she snorted. "It's I who am forgiving."

"How so?" I said. I spoke lightly, although I was seething. I hadn't forgiven her the affair with Adamis, and now I had a chance to let her know it.

"In the matter of Adamis, Beki, the Khan returned a favor, that's all," she said. "I was forced to take a life, and forced to risk another life, for Attila's sake. Sparing Adamis' for my sake was no more than an evenhanded gesture, and Attila knows it."

I passed over what Kreka was trying to tell me.

"You betrayed him in your heart as well as in your bed," I said indignantly.

"I was angry," she said. "I was furious when Attila left for Acatiri country? Don't you know that?"

I shook my head.

"Well," she said, "I was. In a way I still am, but we've come to an accommodation. At least for now."

"An accommodation? You call sparing Adamis' life an accommodation?" I said.

"Yes. It restores a certain balance between Attila and me. This is important between husband and wife."

"I don't know what you mean when you talk of balance," I said. "I would do anything to make my husband happy, I would never hurt him."

Without giving way to childish anger I was determined to have Kreka know how I felt about what she had done.

"Ah," she said dismissively. "so you say now. But this love, for which you would do anything, will give you pain. You are young and brave, Beki, you don't understand how life changes people. Life has only just begun for you."

"It's true, great changes are beginning for me. I'm going to have a child," I blurted.

By then I was too angry to dissemble. Kreka's dismissive attitude, the disdain in her words, were a goad. She seemed to be saying she knew more about life than I would ever know.

The Khatun blanched and closed her eyes for a moment. "I suspected as much," she said.

"Is that all you have to say?" I asked. "Not, congratulations? Not, what good news? Not even, I'm happy for you?"

Kreka put her hand on my arm. "I am glad for you, Beki," she said. "You've fallen in love with Ernac at long last, in love as a woman should be. And he with you. You're right for one another, and I'm happy for both of you. I could wish nothing better for two people I love."

"You're envious, jealous of the love we have for one another," I said.

"By the Great Tngri, Beki, you are even more naive than I thought," she said. Her face was suddenly alive with merriment.

"What's so amusing?" I said.

"I don't mean to make fun of you, Beki," she answered soberly. "I've wanted to talk with you, but not until I felt you were open to hearing what I had to say," Kreka answered.

She threw her arms out, embracing the opportunity to unburden herself.

"Please understand," she said, "that I envy no one their love. I've had everything in a man I could possibly have wanted. And more," she added ruefully.

"You mean Attila," I said.

"Of course, I mean Attila," she said. "He's the great love, and the great problem, of my life."

"He's generous and kind. He's treated you with the highest respect," I cried out. "Yet, I've heard you speak to him with terrible disrespect, and in terrible anger. He should have killed you for the way you spoke to him."

She smiled sweetly.

"I can see it's time we talked as women. There's much you need to hear."

"Perhaps I don't wish to hear," I said stubbornly.

"Perhaps you don't," she said. "Try to listen anyway. When I was young, Beki, as you are now, I believed everything my husband told me. I believed without question. My husband knew best in all things. I wouldn't have dreamed of advising him, most certainly I wouldn't have dreamed of crossing him."

"You learned to cross him," I said acidly.

"Yes, I learned. Just before the war with the Acatiri I did something I couldn't have imagined doing as a young woman, but it was necessary and I don't regret it."

I tried to stop her but she silenced me with a look.

"It was I who poisoned Ernac," she said straight-out. "I poisoned my son, and it was Adamis who gave him the poison. I mixed the goblet myself. Adamis gave it to him on my order."

I gasped, my anger collapsing in a wave of astonishment. Kreka went on as if she didn't see my head was reeling.

"One can't remain an unquestioning young girl for a lifetime, Beki. This, you have yet to discover. When I poisoned Ernac I was acting on Attila's behalf. My husband refused to see how dangerous Teb-Ogatai was to him. Or so I thought then. He is so self-important, this husband of mine."

"How could you do such a thing! How could you poison your own child?" I cried.

I aimed a fist at her chin, grazing it with a savage swipe. "You're a curse to motherhood, you cold-eyed viper. You profane the bonds of affection!"

Kreka jerked her head back, and grinned.

"Sacred motherhood!" she brayed, her generous mouth stretched wide. "Each of us defines motherhood on our own, Beki. Human beings aren't ideas, we're imperfect flesh."

"Flesh and ambition, you mean. You deny your ambition," I said, laboring to master fury with reason. I tried to speak carefully. "You simply couldn't stomach the influence Teb-Ogatai had in your camp, could you?"

"Ah, ambition...," she said, nodding.

"Yes, ambition. You claim no ambitions for yourself, yet you tell me you poisoned your own son on behalf of Attila's ambitions," I shot back. "You defer to the Khan's ambition in every way, and always have, but only because it suits you."

"I defer to no one," Kreka snapped back. "Public power is costly, too costly. After my mother was killed, an insatiable hunger for power consumed my father. That, and a gnawing thirst for revenge, ruined his life. I watched it happen, and I have chosen another road for myself. I may change events, but I will do it in a manner more to my liking. For me, power takes a more benign form."

"So you say," I sneered.

Her eyes turned ugly.

"Don't provoke me, Beki. If I had wanted public power I would have had it," she said with certitude. "That is the measure of my freedom. I decide what actions I take, no one decides for me."

"Tell that to your son," I said, "not to me. He's the one who should hear your lies."

"There's no need. I knew I could save him." Kreka said flatly. "I made up the dose. I knew it wouldn't be fatal if I treated him. And I did. Attila wouldn't listen, Beki. There was no talking to him, so I took the responsibility he should have taken."

"Some say you take too much responsibility," I said, with perverse satisfaction. "I've heard more than one say Attila is too much under the influence of his Khatun, that Kreka, instead of Attila, should be called KhaKhan."

"I know perfectly well what people say, Beki," Kreka said deliberately. "The malcontents and the envious, I know what they think of me."

"And do these malcontents include your son, Dengezic?" I said. "He and his drinking friends are always going on about you, having great jokes at Attila's expense, laughing about his weakness where you're concerned."

"Yes, the malcontents include Dengezic," Kreka said. She chuckled mirthlessly. "Dengezic has become a vainglorious fool. I sometimes wonder if Ku mistakenly placed an orphan at my breast the day my second son emerged from my womb."

"Your son delights in mocking you," I said.

Kreka looked at me and I knew she saw my duplicity. She saw I was trying to lead her away from discussing Attila.

"You'd like me to launch into an attack on Dengezic," she said. "But it's Attila I wish to speak of. Mind you, I shouldn't have to point these things out, Beki. I shouldn't have to explain how calculating Attila can be, or what a hard position he left me in. You should be able to see that for yourself. I had no good choices, child. My husband knows me, he knew I could be pushed into a rash act. What I did exposed Teb-Ogatai. I did what I had to do, but all the while I was full of rage. Attila's conceit had forced me into a terrible place. Surely, you can imagine what it meant. To endanger the life of my son? To risk the orderly life of the camp? Surely you can see?"

"But," I began, "there must have been another way…" Then it struck me. "Baldin," I said. "Of course. Baldin thought it was his poison in the cup."

Kreka held up her hands, spreading her fingers in disgust.

"Baldin was a dupe, both mine and Teb-Ogatai's. His cup of poisoned wine never got to Ernac. The dose in that cup would have killed him, but Adamis intercepted it. Baldin did no wrong, and the pitiful creature doesn't even realize it," Kreka said scornfully.

"But why did you have to poison Ernac?" I said. "You could simply have pretended to poison him."

"Pretend? In this camp? The truth would have swept through the yurts like the grains of a sandstorm. His illness had to be real, there could be no faking. The people had to condemn Teb-Ogatai themselves. They had to see him caught in a treasonous act and give their blessing to his execution."

"You're saying you manipulated the whole thing, that you made it happen. But that's monstrous, you can't..."

"Of course I can. I did. Let me finish, then you can speak," she said quickly. Intercepting my attempt to take the talk in a different direction, she went on with her story of duplicity and death.

"I tried, Beki. I turned over every possible scheme searching for something that would make the people repudiate this shaman. He was gaining a loyal following here in Attila's main camp. We had to be rid of him. The snake that crawls next to your heart must be destroyed. The job had to be done, and it had to be a sure thing."

"The job had to be done," she repeated, firmly.

"You understand, no one else was in a position to act. I wrestled with this, Beki, you did not. You'll have difficult decisions in your own life. May the gods protect you from choices such as this one. Even so, there will be times when you, too, will be forced to take risks. Events have a way of forcing people to act."

"I can't believe it's true, what you tell me. Does Attila know this?" I said, no longer able to hold back my question.

"He does," she nodded. "He knows, believe me. The wretched rascal knew before I acted. He let me do it. He understood the danger, but decided it was the best course. More than that, he knew what it would cost me. My husband owed me a great debt, Beki. When he heard of my affair with Adamis, Attila knew he had, in large measure, brought me to it."

"You blame him! You blame Attila for what you did with Adamis?" I exclaimed.

Once more she lifted a hand to silence me.

"After he returned from the war against the Acatiri Attila confronted me with the affair, with what you call my betrayal. We fought, of course. I lashed out, wanting to hurt him. I told him what I'd done, that I had mixed the dose that poisoned Ernac with my own hands.

"He laughed at me. 'What an earnest confession you give me, Kreki,' he said. Then, I saw what his game was. I exploded. I'd been blind. Attila had used me. I merely saved him a bit of trouble, and made it possible for him to ride off to war with a clear mind. I was beside myself when I realized how stupid I'd been."

"You're sure of this? Attila knew you planned an attempt on Ernac's life and did nothing to stop you?" I said.

"I'm sure," she said. "His spies keep him informed, Beki. He understood what I meant to do. He approved, was even grateful to me. I've loved him too much, this charming husband of mine. He's taken advantage of my love. It's I who will do the forgiving, Beki."

"Taking Adamis as your lover wasn't just payment for his loyalty, it was to hurt Attila," I said.

"Partly," she said. "I wanted to hurt Attila, but I'm a woman and Adamis is a beautiful man. My steward has long been in love with me. I owed him, and I owed myself. I was in danger of becoming a bitter woman."

"Bitterness is a small thing. There is no excuse for doing what you did," I said. "You of all people. You, who so admire control."

"Do you recall the widow, Suvei," Kreka said, "the Goth woman with ten fatherless daughters? She was despondent, she would have killed herself but for Attila's intervention. Suvei was grateful. She was so grateful to the Great Khan," Kreka said sarcastically, "for marrying her out of pity that she dedicated all ten of her daughters to service in his bed. Attila loves women, Adamis loves me. He saved me from my own destructive thoughts. For that alone, I am grateful. I, too, have power, Beki. I know how to show my gratitude."

She stopped. I saw I was free to answer, but I had nothing to say. My body sagged, my anger gone. I had turned into a flattened waterskin, empty of its purpose.

Kreka waited, saw I wasn't going to speak, and said, "There's something else, Beki. This is a thing for you and Ernac to deal with, not me. It involves Dengezic and the rat, Bigilas."

I straightened my back. Kreka knew she had my attention.

"There is no end to scheming, is there?" she said, in good-humored irony. "Dengezic is negotiating secretly with Theodosius. I have reason to think Bigilas has carried a message to him from my son. He wants to strike a deal with Theodosius. Unless I'm mistaken, Dengezic's price for information will be his own army. He'll ask Aëtius for his own troops, and if he's not stopped he'll get them. I'll do nothing to stop him. I won't allow myself to become part of another plot. It's time for younger people to take the risks, to make their own alliances."

I took in every word she said.

"I was afraid this was in the wind," I said. "Ernac's been afraid of it as well."

What I didn't say was that Attila, himself, had asked Ernac to spy on Dengezic for fear of his treachery.

I looked on my foster-mother's face, and found unexpected love for her welling up in me. She has suffered, I thought, and she has endured. She has been hurt, not least by the disloyalty of her offspring. Kreka has been caught in events not of her making, and she has tried to balance love with responsibility. In all she's remained steadfast. Attila has suffered the pain of betrayal, true, but she has suffered the same.

I reached out to touch her hand. "Kreka," I said, "I want to tell you..."

"No," she said. "Better not to say it."

She moved quickly to the door, then stopped. She turned back to me.

"Life is a strange thing," she said. "At one time my heart failed at my husband's every leave-taking. At the start of every expedition my soul fluttered and fell in fear for him. Now, I can't recognize the mind of the girl I was then."

She paused, frowning at me.

"You need for me to say I regret hurting Attila, and that I regret poisoning Ernac. Well, I can't say what you want me to, but I want you to know I still can't bear to see my husband unhappy."

With that she disappeared through the doorway.

Alone, I realized, to my shame, that Kreka understood me better than I understood myself.

It's odd, I thought, that before Kreka's confession I couldn't see her as a woman. I have always admired her, but I saw her as all good, as a child sees a mother. At the same time I depended on her to be tough, to make the strong choice in every situation. Now, I pray for a few crumbs of that strength for myself. I will need strength. I will have my own tragedies, Kreka is surely right in that.

A momentary chill passed through my breast.

14

"That's where it stands," Attila said. "Theodosius is dead, his spine broken in a fall from his horse. Pulcheria has taken Marcian to husband. She bedded him before the body of Theodosius was cold, and a new Emperor of the East, August Marcian, has been proclaimed."

Onegesius and Attila had been out for a day of falconry. It was dusk, and the Khan and his chief advisor were ready for a rest. They were far from prying eyes. There was no safer spot than ground that had been cleared for the hunt.

Onegesius stepped down and lifted a dead bird. He handed Aruvqan's kill up to Attila, who dropped it in his bulging game bag. The Khan took a tiny leather hood with a mini-topknot of black plumes from his tunic and waved it in front of Aruvqan. She perched alertly, talons clutching his glove, head cocked, as he clucked over her. The plump peregrine stared intently at the bulky figure, the man she thought of as her mate. Attila smiled into her eyes, and slipped the little hood gently over Aruvqan's head. He handed her over to his falconer, and watched the grooms ride off.

Onegesius spoke first.

"Where does all this leave us, my lord? There is still the matter of the Princess Honoria and the ring of pledge she sent you before Theodosius' death. Her messenger, the eunuch, Hyacinth, was put to the torture, and before he was beheaded he told Theodosius what he knew. Marcian must now know of Honoria's plans," Onegesius said. He paused, and wiped bloodied bird leavings from his glove onto his horses mane.

The Khan grinned, baring his teeth.

"I can use Honoria's offer. Just as she would use me, I plan to use her. I'll turn her offer to suit myself," he said. "The mighty princess from Ravenna thinks to set me up as her consort in Gaul, but she misjudges my memory. I didn't waste my years as a hostage in Ravenna in mindless games. I learned a little Latin and Greek, and I had Roman politics sitting at the feet of experts. I haven't forgotten those days. Honoria can no longer read my mind, but I can still read the mind of a scheming she-devil. She tried to make her last lover, Eugenius, her puppet. If her plan had not been discovered, and he executed, she would have succeeded.

"Her invitation," the Khan went on, "no matter that it's self-serving, gives me an opening. I'll claim her as my legitimate bride. I'll order the Western government to do no harm to the gentle Princess Honoria, and claim half the Western Empire as my part of her inheritance. I'll swear to avenge her honor if the territory is not delivered up to me. Valentinian would not deliver up any part of his Empire to the King of the Huns, and while he temporizes I'll attack."

"Chrysaphius has also been executed," the Prime Minister said.

"Yes," Attila answered. "Marcian lost no time in announcing that the annual tribute to me be stopped, did he?"

"No," Onegesius answered warily, "he didn't. Old alliances have been overturned, and old friends lost. When Aëtius was hostage in our camps he also learned, my lord. He studied Hun politics, and Hun language, was tutored even by yourself. Now, he forgets what he learned here and seeks allies wherever he can find them. So far, Honoria's brother Valentinian gives no hint that Aëtius could be dropped from favor, but who knows what the future holds. The loyalty of former allies, even including the Franks, is in question, and Marcian declares himself willing to use force against you. Aëtius will certainly use Marcian's threat. Almost overnight, Great Khan, the situation has been turned upside-down."

Attila grunted. "I won't be put off by a change in emperors. As for Aëtius, he's nothing but an opportunist. He was never a friend." With these words Attila denounced the Roman commander, and dismissed him from the company of decent men.

"True, Aëtius was never a man of honorable intentions," Onegesius agreed. "He sees himself as Attila's Roman twin. He would destroy his twin, his equal in ambition and cleverness, though not his equal in courage. Aëtius respects you, Attila, and since Marcianople he's hated you as much as you hate him.

"The battle at Marcianople cleared Aëtius' vision temporarily," Attila said with satisfaction. "But fortunes have shifted once more. We've been in the home camps for two battle seasons, and I've planned well for a campaign against Gaul. This Emperor invites me to smash him but his challenge changes nothing. I'll not take Marcian's bait. I will attack Gaul as planned. The new Emperor's manner is audacious. I won't forget the effrontery, but I've prepared too well for this campaign to drop it now. My forces are at their peak, Onegesius. The young lieutenants smell plunder."

"Young lieutenants always smell plunder. The smell of gold is affixed to the hairs of their nostrils," said Onegesius.

"It would be dangerous to hold them back another season," Attila said decisively. "I can mount two-hundred-thousand seasoned troops against Aëtius. My armies are at their best, I would be a fool to waste them. We cross the Rhine and go against Gaul in the spring."

"That could mean fighting the Franks, as well as Theodoric and his Visigoths," said Onegesius. "Except for the northern Goths, and Ardaric and his Gepids, we'll be going against Gaul without any ally we can trust."

"I welcome a chance at Gaul," the Khan pronounced. "My ambassadors will go to Emperor Marcian, and to Theodoric. They will say — 'Attila, my master and yours, has ordered that your palaces be made ready, for he will soon occupy them.'"

"That is the message you wish to give?" Onegesius asked. He threw a leg over his horse's head and slumped over to rest his spine.

"It is," the Khan replied succinctly.

"But the Visigoths, my lord," Onegesius persisted, "we need them. Theodoric has always been Aëtius' enemy, but your message may force Aëtius to seek alliances with former enemies. When Theodoric understands what your intentions are, he may succumb and back Aëtius."

"He may. If he does, let him. I intend for Aëtius to resist my invasion of Gaul with everything he has. I'll force him to it. He's become soft, but his private estates are in Gaul. He'll want to protect them. These days Aëtius is a politician first. The time when he was a full-time warrior is past. I'm a warrior first, and will be until I die. I'll go against the armies of the Western Empire if I must," the Khan said, "and I'll beat them."

"One more thing before we ride back, Attila," said Onegesius. "I speak, though I hate to, of Dengezic."

"Yes," Attila said heavily, "Dengezic. Well, what have you heard?"

"It seems, my Lord Khan," his Prime Minister said uncomfortably, "that the rumors of Dengezic's offer to Theodosius are true. These rumors have reached the ears of Aëtius. Now Theodosius is dead it wouldn't surprise me if Dengezic took up negotiations with the Emperor Marcian, even with Aëtius."

"Nor would it surprise me," Attila said, without discernible emotion.

"Should I handle this for you, Khan?" The delicacy of the Prime Minister's question was not lost on Attila, and his reaction was immediate.

"No," Attila said, sharply.

Onegesius sat his horse and waited.

Then, "I will handle that myself," the Khan said more quietly.

"Very well. Should you change your mind I am ready."

"Thank you, Onegesius. I appreciate your offer," Attila said, and fell silent.

"You have Ernac, at least," Onegesius said, finally. "He has become a fine young warrior, my lord. You have one son to be proud of."

Attila smiled bleakly. "Ellac should have been my heir, Onegesius. I would have had my eldest son succeed me, but the gods have overruled me. The War God Kundur has deemed Ellac unfit for command. But, yes, I have one son to be proud of. I am grateful for that, at least. One day Ernac will lead the Huns."

"Your grandfather, Khan Balamber, would be pleased with his great-grandson, Attila," Onegesius said.

"My grandfather was a great man," Attila said. "Balamber saw far. He influenced me greatly. Balamber taught me to value the steppelands. He taught me love for the earth. The soil, my grandfather said, remembers. The land has pleasure and pain, he told me. The earth knows what takes place upon its skin. Go where life takes you, and conquer what you will, he said, only keep your *ordu* in the heartland, and you will prosper. He was right. May his bones be at rest in the country he loved so well."

Meditating on Balamber's words, Attila and his Prime Minister rode into the evening hills seeking the comfort of their camp.

Kursik has been murdered by agents of the Khan. He was run through and left for the delectation of the buzzards as he returned to our camps from a meeting with my brother, Dengezic. The little ass thought he could hide his movements from the Khan.

The message is plain. My father knows of my brother's plans, and Kursik's death is his answer. Dengezic had best watch his step. In the confusion of a battle a man may go down under the sword of friend, or foe, and no one will be the wiser.

The home camps are calm, but busy. The days are short. We pray for a mild winter and an early thaw, for the sake of the horses' bellies, as well as for our own.

Beki is plump as a hand-fed bird, and content. She will give birth before the wagons move, and there will be a tiny baby for her to carry into Gaul.

The war-wagons are being repaired. Wheelwrights labor from dawn to dusk fashioning, and exchanging, parts from wheels, and installing spokes and axles where they're needed. One-person carts and family carts also need attention. We will ford rising rivers in the spring and there will be more broken axles, but, at least, we start in decent repair.

The oxen and camels are getting their hooves filed and their harnesses refurbished. The grooms have more than they can handle just checking brands and tending to the health of the horse herds. Each owner's *tamga* must be identified and a count of his horses taken before we start. Cattle and sheep must be checked for injury or illness, and herded into the enclosures at the edge of the camp.

I'm impressed with the endless bags and coffers that are being stuffed with provision and stowed in the women's wagons. Mounds of rugs and quilts, dried foodstuffs, medicines, and cooking utensils are piled outside the yurts waiting to be loaded.

Weapons, of course, are the biggest concern. Commanders are pushing bowyers and arrow makers to exhaustion. I've heard the Khan will employ little heavy cavalry. I fear that's a mistake. We will have only lance and sword to serve as follow-up for arrows and throwing nets. I find myself already wishing battle-axes and heavy cavalry would be there to back us up.

Uzindur and Ebnedzar have been sent on to the north to marshal the Ostrogoths and the Gepids. Neither of them is so experienced as Dengezic, but they'll be useful. Ebnedzar seems able to keep a firm, orderly hand on Ellac without being resented. I hope he can mitigate Ellac's ineptitude. Confusion follows my older brother like the pointing fingers of an evil augury.

Dengezic has been sent as far from the Khan's eyes as possible. He will scout the routes my father plans to take into Roman territory. Cologne, Trier, Metz, Cambrai, Ammiens, Rheims, Beauvais, and Paris all lie along the way. There should be an enormous wealth of plunder in them.

Sending Dengezic ahead could be my father's way of giving him a length of rope to wrap around his neck. The mission may be a trap. I would be sorry if that were the case, but I am not Dengezic's nursemaid. My brother has chosen his own fate. In bad fortune, as in good, each man's fate belongs to himself alone.

The troops spend their days checking personal weapons and horse gear, and their nights drinking and telling tales. I join in occasionally, but I'm not the most convivial companion in drinking. My stomach is weak since my illness.

Yesterday I had a long day in the countryside counting and rounding up horses marked with my *tamga*. My brand is a small circle with a double cross in the center, not an easy mark to spot from a distance. I worked into the evening without finishing the count.

After the evening meal I rode back to camp with the plaintive music of the soldiers for company. The air was cool, and the night unusually quiet. I passed the men's fires, and the spare sounds of tabor and pipe drifted behind me. The music was bittersweet. The sounds of the men piping their timeless songs of war followed me through the dusk and into my tent. I closed my eyes to their mournful songs of bravery and glory, love of family, and longing for the homeland.

Next morning I was roused by loud, happy whoops. The mood had lightened. There were eager cries and the snorting of horses coming from the outskirts of camp. I heard jeers and taunts, good-natured curses, and laughter. The jokes are vulgar. A soldier's humor is not mine, nonetheless, I understand it. They need a brave show. My father doesn't approve of ribald jokes himself — unless he's the one telling them. Attila is strict in everything except his own appetites. His temptations are drink and women. In these he overindulges when, and as, he pleases.

I walked outside following the laughter, and I soon found the source. It wasn't yet daylight, and already men had gathered on dew-freshened ground, engrossed in the starting moves of a wild riding game.

This game is called take-it-away. It is a passion for both men and horses. The carcass of a dead sheep is hoisted into the hands of a single rider, while a host of men attempt to wrestle it away from him. More than a hundred riders were milling about over the field swiping at one another, trying to tussle the trophy from the man who held it.

The players galloped freely, wheeling at will, lunging and chopping at one another with their riding crops in hopes of dislodging the prize dragging at the side of its protector. The riders stop at nothing to secure the coveted carcass, and the game is pursued with a vigor approaching madness. Dust rose around the mass of horsemen in a blinding cloud. Every throat was parched and aching.

This contest is a match for war in its ferocity. Custom demands it not end until the tattered hide has been carried off by a victorious warrior, or until all contenders give way exhausted. I have seen many a man killed in this competition. I once saw a man put his own eye out with his dagger. Another rider had pushed the man's head back onto his arm trying to wrest the carcass from him, and he pierced his eye on his own blade. Better to lose an eye than give up the prize to another! The man was lucky, nonetheless. Should a man fall from his horse he would be crushed under the swarm of pounding hooves. If a man goes down none dare reach to help him.

Take-it-away was my chosen sport until I was forbidden to play it after being knocked to the ground and almost ground under trampling hooves. In the fury of the game, well-trained animals that would normally veer to avoid a man charge over the top of a downed player. Horses seem to catch the madness from their riders.

After my fall my father forbade me the game. I have golden memories, though, and on this particular morning I was caught by the energy of the contest. I admire the skill and muscle that brings a crop slashing down on its target. There is release in rushing over the field, smacking at each other with cruel effect, not caring that your closest comrade takes a cut.

I didn't quit the field until late that afternoon. When I left the last of the bruised and bleeding had limped away to find themselves a well-deserved bowl of wine.

15

My babe made his appearance ten days before the order to set out behind the troops. His birth was not difficult, for which I'm thankful. I'm built for the job, and the work of getting him into this world was only the effort of a morning. I wakened just before dawn with a gush of fluid, and Ku had wiped him off and put him to suckle before the sun came straight overhead.

At first he traveled well. I will say that for his good nature. He cried little, and seemed not to notice the sway and bump of the wagon. Nursing him became a trial for me with the wagons on the move, but he doesn't fuss when I put him aside without a full stomach.

I have given him the name Buqas; little bull.

Buqas is the right name for my gangly boy child. He has little more than his male organs to recommend him. He is of an ungainly length of bone, very unlike a Hun. It makes me suspect that some intrepid Goth, or Gepid, found his way into the yurt of one of my grandmothers and warmed himself under her quilts.

It was Ku who noticed the evidence of future virility dangling from between Buqas' scrawny legs. She lifted him up for me to inspect as she cleaned him off, cackling at how generously he was endowed.

"He will surely be a bull with the women," she said. I took this as a sign and named him Buqas on the spot.

By the time a haruspice could have been done for my son we were on the move. There was no time to have one cast. Any further sign seemed, by then, unnecessary. Buqas' physical attributes were omen enough. The gods have given my son more than enough maleness to satisfy a woman. I can only hope he finds a woman who will see more in him than an oversized penis and testicles.

Ernac saw his son twice before he rode ahead with the troops. He was relieved to know Buqas had arrived safely before the camp wagons set off after the armies. Other than the normal joy in a healthy child, Ernac appeared unsure how to take fatherhood. It's as well my husband will be off at war until Buqas has more to offer him than the mere fact that he's male.

The wagons, and the herds following us, started early during the third moon of the year. Before the ground was fully thawed, we had traversed the small mountains to the west and crossed the Rhine, following rapidly behind the path left by the soldiers. For almost three moons we continued, squeezing the wealth from towns along the way as we traveled. Neither swollen rivers nor unreliable weather slow the progress of the Khan's armies, but the women's carts are slow. We are burdened with plunder, rich layers of fat sliced from the towns of Gaul.

The last town we moved on was Metz. We took it easily, and that ended the towns that held much promise of plunder. The army will, therefore, head straight for Orléans. There was talk of pausing to sack a village called Paris, but the scouts reported it to be poor and insignificant, not worth our time.

A certain Sangibanus, a king of the Alans, has promised Attila easy entry to Orléans. Sangibanus and his Alans are not to be trusted, but they may be of temporary use.

We travel at a frantic pace, and Buqas has taken to putting on screaming spells that I can't seem to quiet. Endless hours spent bouncing in the wagon have bruised my muscle to the bone, and I haven't the stamina I had before Buqas' birth. Often there is no time to eat, and when there is time I have little interest in putting the bowl to my mouth. Lack of nourishment has further weakened me. My milk must curdle as it hits my babe's stomach.

It's time for Buqas to be given over to a wet-nurse, — so Kreka announced at the evening campsite yesterday. He's more active, he sleeps less, and I admit to being irritated by my own lack of rest.

Coming into the first real battle of the campaign I find myself wishing to be free of a constantly seeking mouth at my breast. The truth is I would like to be able to get a close view of the battle when it begins. I may be a mother, but I'm still Beki, the curious. I believe I'll allow the wet-nurse Kreka has suggested.

We're hard-pressed for an hour even to sleep. The Khan hopes to take Orléans before Aëtius and Theodoric, king of the Visigoths, can mount a proper defense. He's right to push, of course. A quick victory would save us heavy losses. There are terrible losses of men and animals in a siege. Though he prepares for siege Attila prefers a swift attack. He will opt for a massive show of force if we have a choice.

Battles don't always conform to what one would wish, and as it happened Attila didn't have a choice.

We arrived at the gates of Orléans to find they were undefended by Aëtius or Theodoric. But the shifty Sangibanus hadn't lived up to his word. Sangibanus, himself, was defending the city, and much more ardently than Attila had expected. Orléans had not been softened by starvation or fear, and the Khan was not inclined to send his army out to unnecessary slaughter inside the walls of the city.

So we are camped outside. We engage in minor skirmishes, and hope to starve the citizens of Orléans into surrender. But an ugly possibility remains. Aëtius may yet bring the legions out to defend his estates in Gaul. If he should decide to do that, the sounds of battle will be heard in the homeland.

We are well into the sixth moon of the year and the heat has settled in. The excitement of days on the move, and the anticipation of plunder, have faded. I think Attila tires of indecision and inactivity.

Tonight, I left my wagon and rode aimlessly out into the evening light. For several hours I circled the camp, going no place, just breaking the monotony and spending nervous energy. I am wild with boredom.

I was right about the Khan. The morning after my ride he moved his main force. The central army has been ordered out to enter the city and take it.

After long days of waiting, our troops have stormed the walls with much pent up energy. Within hours they broke through the barriers and had the spoils of the town in their hands. But before they could secure their position, an order came to quit Orléans. The eagles of the Roman legions, and the banners of the Visigoths, were sighted in the near distance. It appeared Aëtius and Theodoric were coming to the defense of Gaul. Attila would not waste his men defending this city against them no matter how fantastic the pickings.

Our army has withdrawn from Orléans. Now the King of the Huns faces the battle of his career. An encounter with Aëtius is what Attila has waited for. My foster-father has confronted Aëtius in his imagination for as long as I can remember, and he is eager to see the thought become reality.

We are situated on relatively open ground north of Orléans, at a place called the Catalaunian Plains, near Châlons. We sit on low, rolling hills just below the river Marne awaiting the opening of the battle. It's more than half a moon now since we withdrew from Orléans, and still we wait. The summer heat is awful, the air wet and heavy, and keeping spirits up becomes more difficult each day.

Several weeks ago I gave Buqas over to a wet-nurse as Kreka suggested. Now I can ride where I want. Yesterday I did something quite foolhardy I'm afraid. I was anxious to see how far away the main armies of the enemy were quartered. I set out before dawn hoping to circle behind their lines and find them.

I rode all morning in an area of thick trees, and when I came out of the trees I was near the outskirts of a large encampment. Troops from many tribes were gathered there. I saw a group of Alans with them. The Alans are shaky allies, but so far loyal to Attila. It was a shock for me to see them placing themselves with the armies Aëtius will be using against us. I've heard that the troops of Theodoric and Aëtius put together make only half of ours, but to me the Alans looked a huge force.

I turned and rode back to our wagons much sobered by what I'd seen. Armies are massing on both sides. This is not to be a war between Huns and Romans only. At Aëtius side are the Franks, Visigoths,

Burgundians, and Alans, as well as the Roman legions. On our side, of course, are the Gepids and the Ostrogoths. There are also Thuringi, and Bavarian peoples, and a smattering of Sciri and Rugi as well.

I have seen the enemy with my own eyes and the coming battle has become real. It is hard to imagine thousands of healthy, unmarked people, ready to leap for one another's throats when the day of battle dawns. I had no heart to stop by Kreka's wagon when I returned. Instead, I went straight to my own wagon in the encircled laager. I crawled in, took my son from the arms of his nurse, and snuggled close against his warm body.

Still, I couldn't put the men out of my mind. Our wagons are well within sight and sound of our army. We can hear voices, and the clinking of gear, but we don't come together. Attila won't have the troops distracted by women and family concerns. I haven't seen my own husband for many days. Attila is certainly right to keep the men focused on the war they must fight. A formidable force is being readied against us. The nations of the world are gathered here to do battle, and it will be a battle between equals. The losses on both sides will be beyond counting.

I began to understand what Kreka meant when she said she had learned to question. I, too, am questioning. Why are we here? Why are so many nations facing one another in war, I asked myself? Does our human tribe live only for kings, and the wars they decree? Why must this slaughter take place?

I don't see the need for the deaths of countless men and animals. In the space of a few hours thousands of men, women, horses, even children, will be cut to pieces at their leader's command.

I lay next to Buqas feeling my head would burst with anxiety. I tried vainly to keep dire scenes from my head, and I prayed for sleep. Finally, I was rewarded.

16

Someone was shaking me. I turned to throw off my quilts and saw Kreka's face hanging above me.

"There was heavy skirmishing during the night. Already there are losses on both sides," she said. "Bring Buqas and come with me. We'll be safer in the large wagons. It's nearly daylight. With the sun up we'll see the day Attila has been waiting for."

Kreka hustled me out of my small wagon with Buqas and the servants. We hurried to settle ourselves with the other women and children, crouching in the shelter of the wagons. We needn't have hurried — the battle didn't begin until almost the ninth hour of the day when the sun was well up, and the fog had dispersed.

There are no words to describe what took place. Kreka, and I, and the rest of our camp, experienced what cannot be told. I was unable to take in the full meaning of what passed before us. I couldn't digest the scope of the battle, and it was some time before I realized it had started in earnest.

The fighting began directly in front of us. It started a short distance away from the entrenchments around the wagons. We strained to see, then recoiled from what we saw. From then until darkness fell, until our eyes could no longer penetrate the gloom, we witnessed the unbelievable.

Some sought the protection of their wagons, but I couldn't bear to be inside. I found a space between two wagons, and there I squatted, taking in the sights and sounds of those dreadful hours. I felt that watching the carnage would be of help to the men. Why I did, I can't say.

A slender slice of ground, no more than a middling-sized camp, separated our troops from a hill that rose above the plain. Our men, and the Visigoths, both rode out with the idea of taking the hill. A clamor of voices and a scrunch of bodies told us that the enemy had met our lines. The clash of iron laying on armor followed, then the thunk of spear and lance on horseflesh. Each side gained a foothold, but neither could top the hill. The ground shook with the struggle. Both sides were determined to gain the crest.

The Visigoths stood their ground, wielding lances and swords. Then our archers found them, pelting them with a thick hail of arrows. Meantime the Ostrogoths came from behind the Gepids and hacked at Visigoths with body swords and spears.

The Alans and the Franks hurtled headlong into our cavalry, which was massed at the center. They were afoot, their battle axes flying around them in wild paroxysms. If a man lost an axe, stuck in a skull, or knocked from his hands by a Hun broadsword, he battered away with nothing but a shield.

The Visigoths, led by Thorismund, Theodoric's son, labored on. Slowly, they began to push the Ostrogoths down the slopes. We followed their retreat anxiously, fearing for our safety. We were on the verge of fleeing when we saw Attila leading a counterattack. With an upward-sweeping charge he managed to retake much of the ground lost by the Ostrogoths. The treacherous Sangibanus and his Alans, already uncertain, gave way before the Khan. Thorismund was still not dislodged, and with the light fast disappearing, Attila became intent on retaking the lost ground before dark.

Until this point no one had taken command of the summit, and when night fell confusion spread over the hill and onto the plain below. There were no discernible lines. Foe, and friend, exchanged blows, not knowing where, or on whom, their swords were landing. It was truly a massacre. Men leaned on one another, grappling in exhausted couplings until one of them toppled.

Just before the darkness settled for good we saw Attila rush into the thick of the troops on the hill. The Khan rallied the men at the heart of the fighting. He laid right and left, striking at anything that moved.

"All the living, you wounded lying on the ground, up on your feet," he thundered.

"Be up, and killing," he roared. "Be up, and killing!"
"Up, and killing, up, and killing, up, and killing."

For me it is always the same, ever the same. The invisible beat sucking at my loins. The thrill in the vein, and the clutching pulse. Blur of movement, blindness and blood waiting at the edge of the eye. Ever the same and the same. None can see me hesitate. Lift and swing, lift and swing, lay left, lay right, to back and front. The warrior's swords follow me into the slick, black caverns. Gut, and heart, and neck. Strike heart and gut! Strike lung, scrotum, liver, kidney, spleen. Follow me! Follow me! Split the eyes, the mouth!

This fat one, his rosy heart sluicing his blood down the legs of his horse. Now a wizened, wise-eyed veteran; a slice to his throat. Crimson life spattering my sword. This youngster with the velvet hands has poured his marrow out before. The brain that bursts before my eyes has drenched my sight before. Here's another sword arm to part from its body. Scared and skinny, fresh-scrubbed as I at my first slaughtering. I've done for each of them, done for all of them, before. Sever the arm, cleave the thigh, lop the hand from the sword, peel a boot from a foot, rake a testicle from a groin. A mighty swoop, then lean and lop the head. Unleash the artery's thick spurting flood.

What! Wait! Not here, not now! At my back, at my shoulder. Lunge and slide, lay right, muscle to sword. The head leaves the neck, blade a bare shiver in air. Is this my neck, my head? No. I am yet astride! I hear the birthing wail. I live, and breath is sweet. The eyes of death are close, but not for me. Not yet. Not me. Another head — not mine!

Ride! The abyss is ahead! Now leap the void. World, and life, before me! Ride, ride! Life waits beyond the leap!

"Vengeance for the dead," I heard Attila cry.

Again, and again, he shouted his crazed challenge.

I heard his sword meet bone, and again he bellowed, "Vengeance for the dead, vengeance for the dead, vengeance for the dead."

But pain and exhaustion were too heavy, even for men sent amok by a day's spree of killing. The bulk of the armies dispersed, falling back in darkness to search out their units. Kreka had to drag me from the spot where I had hunkered between wagons. My eyes stuck fast to the scene.

I was fearful of what lay on the field, reluctant to face what I must, but the Khatun pushed me, forcing me to my duty. I soon saw what the battle had accomplished. With night, the trickle of wounded making their way back to be tended became a river. Bloodied legs stumbled toward the wagons, walking over the piles of dead and wounded who would not rise again.

Through the night it continued. We bound wounds, and raised water to the lips of the dying, listened to pleadings and groans from men who would soon be unable to ask for help. We watched the lifeblood ooze from organs pierced by lance, and sword, and spear. We bound great, gaping holes ripped out by axes. We struggled in vain to staunch the blood of head wounds, stuffing squares of linen cloth deep in the skulls.

And the wounded kept coming.

The hours passed, and we could still hear sporadic clashes. Angry voices came through the night; ghosts unable to accept the fate that had been dealt them, cries of dead men unable to quit screaming and put down their swords.

I shivered in the damp air. What must that hillside be? Or the plain below? I couldn't envision it.

The news that came just before morning was bad. It set Kreka moving from wagon to wagon, ordering the women to form a pyramid of saddles and other burnables at the center of the laager. Attila sent word that he feared the worst. It was rumored that the Romans planned to storm our encampment. Rather than be taken, the Khan has declared he will set the pile afire and immolate himself on top of it. The women wail, even as they work to make the pyre higher. Many say they will join their men on the fire if the unthinkable comes.

I was working to stem a dark flow of blood from a jagged stomach wound when I glimpsed Kreka coming by with an arm-load of carpets to add to the pyramid. She passed me, her face grim in the light of the torches, and I left the wounded man to grab her arm.

"Kreka," I hissed furiously, "is it true what they're saying? Is that mountainous pyre meant to burn us up? Are we to sacrifice ourselves on it? I'll not do it, I tell you that. I'll not burn Buqas, or sacrifice myself either, if it comes to that."

"The pile is being prepared for burning," she said shortly. "But don't worry, you won't be asked to sacrifice yourself, or your child."

"And you? Will you immolate yourself, Kreka? Would you join Attila on the pyre?" I whispered, feeling it couldn't happen.

"Don't be ridiculous!" Kreka rebuked me. "Not I, not Attila, not anyone. This is for show. It's display; a grandiose gesture designed to make Aëtius believe Attila would sacrifice himself and every man, woman and child with him. The pyramid will rise up dramatically, but it will not be lighted. I'll meet you at my wagon. Wait for me there," she said, and vanished into the dusk.

I returned to the soldier to find no blood flowing through his bandage. I could do nothing for him. I was saddened at the sight of another dead warrior, but weariness blunted my sympathy. I covered his waxen face with a scrap of quilt from the piles I had laid out, and passed to the next victim. I hardened myself to go on with my unpalatable chores. As I turned to the next litter I chanced to look up and saw Ku racing toward me. She was blue-faced, gasping as if each breath would be her last.

"Buqas," she shrieked, "Buqas, Beki! Buqas!"

I raced for Kreka's wagon, my baby's indignant yells coming at me as I ran. I leapt and landed inside to encounter the face of Buqas' wet-nurse squinting up at me, her cheeks streaked by tears.

"I only took him outside to get a skin of water from beneath the cart," she wailed. "I was afraid to leave him inside the wagon, mistress. He was in my arms," she blubbered, "he was in my arms, he was in my arms. Ooo-hh-h, ... ooo-hhh-h, ... in my very arms, in my own arms. Why did the barb enter his body instead of mine?" she cried deliriously.

"Stupid woman," I screeched, and I dealt her a nasty blow to the side of the head.

I snatched my son, and tore his bloody blankets off him. Under the cleft of his little arm I saw where the arrow had entered. It had gone in at the far right of his chest and come out his back. The end of the barb stuck out next to his shoulder blade. I grasped the haft at his chest and gave it a hard shove to the back. Not thinking, I snapped the barb and yanked out the shaft. As the arrow left his body the hole spurted blood. Seeing this red river gushing from Buqas' chest, I closed my eyes and screamed.

Someone wrested him from my arms and shoved me aside. I blinked, saw Kreka's face, and collapsed against her. Wordlessly, I watched her push a dressing against the stream of blood, wind layers of bindings tight around his chest, and make them fast. She stopped long enough to look at me.

"Get up," she said tonelessly, "You have a job to do. Stand up. This is no time for weakness. I'll see to Buqas. He will survive. Get out. Get to your work."

Staggering to my feet I plodded woodenly back to the line of litters. In the next hours I went through the motions of helping those beyond help. I gave each man what aid I could, which was little enough. A few lasted the night, but most did not. The pangs of each death, which I could not ease, melted into a torrent of anguish. One soldier breathed his last, then the next, and then the next. I couldn't separate one face, or one wound, from another. The accumulation of pain was impossible to encompass. Toward morning I walked away, leaving the endless lines of litters lying there with their burdens of suffering. I climbed back in Kreka's wagon, and saw that Buqas slept. When I saw him breathing easily in the crook of Kreka's arms, I dropped like a stone, asleep before my head hit the quilts.

My puffy eyes opened to meet watery daylight. I was groggy, stiff, and unbearably weary. Groaning, I turned to reach for Buqas, and saw Kreka once again. She was lying next to me cradling a gurgling Buqas in her arms. We shared a dimpled smile, and she handed him over. Unable to speak, I rocked him. I pulled his blankets from his wound. There was no blood seeping through the bandages. Kreka was right, he would survive.

"It was a Hun arrow," she said. "You, and your son, were born to the same fate. Both of you have a penchant for Hun arrows."

I smiled.

"His wound will heal," she said. "He'll have less scar to show from this day than you have from that arrow of your childhood."

I looked into my son's face. "We both have the Hun *tamga*," I remarked.

"Yes, you both have the Hun brand," she said. "But thanks to our Great Earth-Mother the wound will heal. Buqas will grow strong and fit just as you have, Beki."

In answer to my unspoken question she said, "The Visigoths decamped before dawn. No one is yet sure why. They left in haste, and barely in time. Theodoric's heavy cavalry took a terrible toll on our troops…"

"And Ernac, and Attila?" I blurted, finding words for my fears.

Kreka covered my hand with hers. "It's all right. They escaped with minor scratches, how I don't know. Dengezic took a wicked sword wound to his chest. I've looked at him, he'll make it back with us. The battlefield in daylight is not a thing you want to see, Beki. The dead and dying are mounded in layers, sealed inside coffins of their own dried blood. Thousands upon thousands were massacred, on both sides. Some are saying that more than one-hundred thousand died. The body of King Theodoric was dug from under his dead men this morning by his sons. He lay crushed under other carcasses, run through by a javelin, and flattened beneath the body of his dead horse," the Khatun said.

"Then, there is a new King of the Visigoths. Thorismund, now leads them," I said. "But who has won the battle? Who has the victory here?"

"No one had a victory here, though both sides no doubt will claim one," Kreka answered. "It's easy to report a victory, not so easy to tell of defeat. So far even Aëtius claims nothing. His own army is too depleted to mount another attack. Both sides look at one another across a land planted deep with their dead. The most bloodthirsty have slaked their appetite for carnage. It was a day of unimaginable slaughter. I've seen nothing to match it. There is no victory for anyone here, Beki."

"What of the Alans, then, and the Gepids?" I asked.

"Also gone," the Khatun said, "and the smaller tribes in their wake. The forces of Attila and Aëtius are all that remain. And while the two of them survive, neither survives victorious."

"Have you seen Attila?" I asked. "What is his mood?"

"Yes, I've seen him. He's unapproachable," Kreka said. "I wouldn't advise anyone to seek him out. We must let him be, let him assess his losses and make his peace with this monstrous happening in his own way. He chose this horror, and he must deal with the consequences."

"Will we be moving the wagons today?" I asked.

"That I did get out of my husband. We will be loaded and ready to start by nightfall, and we can thank the Great Tngri we survived to load up," she said.

There was more irritation than sorrow in her voice.

"I didn't even ask when he planned to move the troops out," she went on. "What took place here in one day demonstrates the high price we pay when demented devils of war are let loose. A sensible man would quit the place as soon as he could get away. But men of war can seldom be credited with good sense."

With this final jab at what the battle of the Catalaunian Plains had cost us, Kreka rose, admonishing me to stay with Buqas as long as I could.

"There will be work aplenty for weeks to come. Take these few minutes with your son, rest while you can," she said kindly.

She left me and my son to comfort one another. I wept with inexpressible exhaustion and relief. I was weeping for my son, but also for the dead. I gave thanks that my husband was alive. I had prayed earnestly for his safety, if not in words, in my caring for those who had fought with him and lost everything. My husband was not among the countless unfortunates, those wretched losers who gave up everything on the Catalaunian Plains. I had watched, and waited, beside the losers. I saw death creep into their eyes, and my heart filled with pity at the emptiness I saw there. Their moment of final passage into sleep was unremarkable.

17

Never had dreams of our own camp been so enticing, never had I looked forward to seeing home, as I did on our return journey from the cursed Catalaunian Plains.

Ten days after the battle Attila gave the army leave to begin the trek home. The vanguard set off, following in the track of the women's carts. After Aëtius had quit the field, and our dead had been buried, the Khan allowed the remainder of our weary, tattered units to begin working their way home behind the wagons.

My father rode alone, wrapped in a black depression. He would have no part of his usual retinue of lieutenants. It was Berichus, Attila's chief lieutenant, who gave me the stark outlines of what transpired in the confusion of that awful day in Gaul.

When his men were moving ahead on their own, Berichus sought a companion. He left his *touman* and hailed me, asking if he could ride with me and those remaining from my ten.

"Welcome, Berichus. Please, join us," I said.

"You're lucky, Ernac," he said. "You have three men from your own ten, twenty or more from your squad."

Berichus' head dropped onto his chest, and his spine sagged until his chin rested on his horse's mane.

"And you, Berichus?" I asked.

"No one, Ernac," he said, "not a single man from my original ten is left. From my squad there are only eight. Out of a regiment of one-thousand, but seventy-two men remain. Never have I experienced a thing like this. I've spent my life as a soldier, and I've never seen losses of this magnitude. This was slaughter beyond comprehension. If I hadn't witnessed it I would have called the man who told me of it a rotten liar."

I agreed with him, and said so. "Châlon made Marcianople seem a practice for young children," I declared fervently.

Berichus was trying to put into words what I myself had seen, and what I'd heard from other commanders. But he was unable, as was I, to come close to the past cataclysm in real terms. Already that day had begun to seem a bad dream.

"What really happened," I asked Berichus, "with Aëtius that night? Why didn't he come after us the next morning, and why did Thorismund scuttle away so quickly? Together, they might have taken out the remainder of our forces. I can't understand why they didn't."

My questions brought a wry smile to Berichus' long face. He nodded, understanding my confusion.

"I must tell you, Lord Ernac, that Aëtius' main force very nearly did overrun our laagers that night. Attila's withdrawal of troops from the hill to deploy them at our camp was all that saved the wagons. The best of our cavalry were helpless, penned within the center of the Visigoth armies. Aëtius, himself, was cut off. He was surrounded by Hun horsemen who had been sent back to defend the laagers. He barely escaped. It was dawn before he joined his main force."

"Why couldn't Aëtius have pursued the battle the following day?" I said. "Had he regrouped and attacked, he could have driven us back. I fully expected he would."

"Aëtius is clever, but not so clever that he saw through the Khan's ruse."

"What ruse? What are you talking about?" I asked.

"Attila's so-called funeral pyre," Berichus answered. "The Khan convinced Aëtius that he would destroy the cream of the Hun armies, that he would die with them if he faced outright defeat. Attila's death is the last thing Aëtius would wish."

"I must be especially thick, Berichus," I said.

"What if Attila was killed, Ernac? What if he was suddenly wiped from the earth? What would happen then?" asked Berichus.

I looked at him.

"Who would fill his place? Attila controls a wall of disciplined warriors, a predictable wall that stands against unpredictable ruffians beyond the borders of Hun influence. Attila is a high mountain between the Empire and the incursions of other unruly peoples. Aëtius, and the Empire, are not so unhappy to deal with your father, Ernac, even though he depletes their treasury annually. Scores of merchants and traders inside the Empire would readily pay out of their own purses to guarantee that Attila remain in power. They need the trade routes safe and moving. Theodosius, and Aëtius, know the value of trade. Attila is a worthy foe, and the Romans can deal with him. In fact, they count on him. They want to check his power. They don't want him dead."

"You mean," I said incredulously, "that Aëtius let us go? He allowed the Khan to retreat with his armies intact?"

"That, and more, lord Ernac. Aëtius counseled the young king of the Visigoths to leave the battle and return to his homeland. He frightened him, saying he'd best return and defend his new crown before the Scourge of God descended on the country of the Franks. Aëtius manipulated the child king. He told him Attila meant to stop on the way back to the heartland and wrest his crown from his head. Thorismund decamped and ran off to defend his kingdom, without questioning the sense of what Aëtius said."

Berichus roared cheerfully. Relating the schemes of these two master machinators, Attila and Aëtius, had restored his good humor.

"Then, we were not defeated at the Catalaunian Plains?" I said.

"We were not defeated, and neither was Aëtius," Berichus replied. "The carnage settled nothing. Be prepared. There will be a massive retaliation from the Khan this next campaign season. I'll guess that your father will go against Italy, as Aëtius expected him to do this season. It's not finished between the two antagonists, Ernac. They are two old bulls, too evenly matched and too stubborn to give in. A match between talented, powerful warlords means a high price in blood."

"I know what you mean," I said.

"You are the only son, Ernac, who could hope to take over after your father," Berichus added. "You have gained his trust. You mustn't do anything to undermine that."

"I have no intention of doing so, Berichus," I said pointedly. I gave Attila's General Commander a measuring look.

"Please don't misunderstand. You are not Dengezic, Ernac, I know that," Berichus answered my look. "But your father needs someone close to him now, someone in whom he has complete confidence. It's not easy for him to find a man he can unburden himself to. He's much alone, as every warlord is in the end, and suspicious of everyone."

Berichus then changed the subject.

"I was sorry to hear about the injury to your son, Ernac. I'm glad the incident didn't end in his death. He'll have a tale to tell his grandsons, won't he? The first wound he took in war was at the battle of the Catalaunian Plains, before he could even sit a horse. This battle will be a favorite for generations of taletellers. I'm sure of very little, but I'm sure of that."

Berichus sighed. "I'm looking forward to being home," he said. "My own son is eager to hunt with me, and I'm more than ready to oblige him."

"Thank you, Berichus," I said. "I appreciate your concern for my son, and I agree it will be good to get home. I'm anxious to get to know Buqas, and to reacquaint myself with my wife."

I didn't question the Khan's Chief Lieutenant further. I knew why he'd left his squad to ride with me, but his warning was unnecessary. I intend to steer clear of my father and his temper.

I, too, would like to forget there is such a thing as war, but I am well aware what Berichus says is true. There will be no end to the enmity between the two warlords until one of them actually is dead. Roman Aëtius may be, but he's every bit as much the ambitious warlord as my father is. His thinking is closer to Attila's than it is to his Roman countrymen.

I had grasped what Berichus had come to tell me. Now, I wished to put war, and warlords, out of my mind. I wanted to see Beki, and my son. My firstborn, in the recent frenzy, nearly deprived his father of the chance to see him grow up. I intend to spend some time enjoying him in his childhood.

18

My hopes for a season of quiet were in vain. We enjoyed little of what should have been a well-earned rest before another campaign was announced.

Late in the season after our return from Gaul my father ordered a foray into Italy. To my relief the raid was small and brief. Attila merely wanted to give Aëtius a reminder of what was to come.

Short as the raid was, Onegesius didn't survive it. He had sustained a terrible wound to his back in Gaul. It never healed properly, and on the march back from Italy he succumbed to a fever that had been lurking inside him. He died one night alone in his tent, and we carried his body home. Mourning ceremonies were brief. The cold was threatening to settle in, the ground already partially frozen. The long campaign in Gaul, and the late raid into Italy, had left the gathering of supplies for winter undone. Necessity takes priority over observance, and Onegesius was buried without fanfare. It didn't seem right to me that the passing of the Khan's Prime Minister, and great friend, was not marked with proper formalities.

Attila misses Onegesius. He keeps to himself, more hermit-like than ever. Onegesius' death has made it plain how few men the Khan feels close to. Few have his confidence.

Another blow came in an unwelcome announcement from Orestes, the Khan's Roman scribe. He is returning to Rome to stay. Attila will miss him. Orestes brought laughter to his dealings with my father. He performed his duties nobly, and he stuffed the Khan with timely nuggets of information. He leaves for purely personal reasons, or so he says. Attila did not try to change his mind. As soon as the troops returned from Italy the scribe left us, and there is one more hole in the handful of my father's intimates.

Attila hasn't been a merry presence in camp. Only Edecon, Kreka, or his grandson, Buqas, can make my father smile. He never had much interest in the children of Ellac, or Dengezic, but he harbors a soft spot for my wife, Beki, and my son, Buqas.

Yesterday I came upon these three outside camp. It was a rare sight. Buqas, Beki, and Attila, were trying to wrestle a sheep to a standstill, and I decided to see what they were up to. They had the animal saddled. Attila was giggling, mimicking Beki's fumbling efforts to tie Buqas onto the saddle. The toddler was intent on staying upright, his back straight as a sword, his short legs spraddled over the sheep's back. Attila's teasing, and her fruitless efforts to keep Buqas on top of the ewe, had made Beki crimson with frustration.

When Buqas fell for the fourth time Beki lost her temper, and Attila announced that an expert would show how it was done. He produced a piece of leather thong and encased my son in the cording. He lashed the thongs around Buqas' torso, then around the underbelly of the ewe, as one would secure a bellyband on a horse. Once again the crazy pair placed Buqas on the sheep's back. They went pelting along behind the galloping animal, shouting encouragement above her baa-ing protests. The bucking of the sheep soon slipped the thongs from Buqas' waist and turned him upside down. His head went bumpity-bumping along the ground as the angry ewe twisted in an effort to dislodge her tormentor. Attila hastened to cut his grandson free, and, finally, my wife and my father admitted failure.

They started to walk away, but the child refused to be defeated. He scrambled after the ewe, grabbing at strands hanging from her wooly neck. He clutched the neck of the sheep, repeatedly heaving himself up one side only to slide off the other. His antics sent the three of us into spasms of helpless laughter. Beki and I were bent double, and

Attila's eyes were running a stream. My father's laughter was a welcome tonic.

In the fifth month of the following year we marched on Italy. We crossed directly over the easy passes of the Julian Alps along the path that many invading armies had carved out before us.

The Khan knows that less than half the force he took against Gaul will suffice for this campaign, and he has elected to go with a force of only one-hundred thousand. There will be only a small contingent of wagons and carts behind us. Beki, and the Khatun, will not be coming. A wise decision, as Buqas is now running everyplace and is impossible to keep track of.

We passed directly down from the mountains onto the plains of Lombardy, there to besiege Aquileia, the most heavily fortified bastion standing in the way of those who would attack Ravenna or Rome.

The cowardly Valentinian hastened to sequester himself in Rome, and Aëtius reportedly watches the campaign unfold from the safety of his estates in Gaul. Italy, to all appearances, has been abandoned. Lucky Aëtius, lucky Valentinian, for though the town of Aquileia has been attacked numerous times, it has never been stormed. The Khan intends to take it, and the fighting will be fierce.

Before we reached the plains Attila sent instructions for new siege-engines to be built and brought forward by Roman prisoners and deserters. Until they arrive we will occupy ourselves with dealing crude blows aimed at the walls of the city.

Last evening I spoke with Edecon, and he complained of weariness. New responsibilities have fallen on my teacher's shoulders since the death of Onegesius. None of us realized, until after he was gone, how much the Khan depended on his Prime Minister for companionship. Edecon is aging rapidly. He is feeling the brunt of my father's bouts of ill-temper. His shaking disease is worse, and at times he falls and stays there not caring to rise. I think he is taxed beyond his strength.

"This damp air, Ernac, is not agreeable to me," he said, petulantly. "My bones ache constantly. Pestilence hangs about the land like a rotten mist. In spite of the infernal heat I'm chilled through. So much rain in summer isn't natural. It dampens the soul as well as the bones. Snow, in its season, is healthier."

"Take heart, Edecon," I said. "The siege-engines will soon arrive, and we'll be finished with this place."

"It can't be soon enough for me. Perhaps, not soon enough to save the campaign," Edecon exclaimed. "The Khan has lingered here too long trying to crush the walls of Aquileia. We should have been on to Milan before this. There is plunder in Milan to keep the greediest young lieutenants sated. Attila has made a mistake. It's too late in the season. Our momentum has been lost."

"Patience, Edecon, patience," I said. "We'll be on our way to Milan before the next moon. You lose hope too easily these days."

"I know it. I know I do," he said. "I'm a tired old man, Ernac. Maybe it's time for me to kill myself."

"Dear friend, you mustn't talk this way. You worry me. You have many good years left," I said soothingly. "This is an uncomfortable time, but like all discomforts it will pass."

I wasn't sure I spoke the truth, but it seemed the only thing I could offer my dismally depressed teacher.

He's right in one thing, we've delayed here too long. If Attila still intends to reach Rome this summer this was a mistake. The troops may soon be complaining as Edecon is now.

Two days after my talk with Edecon the first wooden siege-engines arrived and were set up. Their towers in place, the Roman and Avar prisoners, and the mercenaries, were ordered to begin the bombardment. The mercenaries are an assortment of infantrymen and spearmen. They are scraggly types, hardly worthy of being called warriors, but they're good with siege-engines. Manned by these footmen, the engines started throwing up rock, pelting at the walls.

A storm of stones was soon tearing at the fortifications of Aquileia. Within hours even the thickest sections of wall showed the effects. The seals between stones began breaking apart, small breaches became genuine openings, and then the Roman-style torsion engines were put to work. The bastions were quickly leveled to crushed rubble. In less time than it takes to tell of it our men were inside raging through the streets.

The city was razed, and no one was spared. In our hurry to be done with this frustrating campaign I admit there were acts of brutality, but by the next season my memory of the day had dimmed. I can now barely recall what took place, can't remember how many I killed, or how they fell.

We hurried, then, pushing deep into Italy. At our approach most cities opened their gates without question, for tales of the fall of Aquileia had raced ahead of us. A few towns, however, refused to open to us. These were destroyed and their people put to the sword.

Northern Italy fell with scarcely a murmur, and Milan has accepted the Khan's terms for peace. The Roman treasury will pay the tribute he asks, and so we enter Milan, the richest city of Northern Italy. Attila is the more elated with his conquests because his victories have plunged Aëtius into despair. It's said he's virtually in hiding, not knowing which way he might turn to thwart my father. The Khan has bested his old enemy this time, though still without the face-to-face battle he yearns for.

"I've decided I will inhabit this palace," Attila announced, looking about at the expanse of the great hall.

"This palace," Edecon replied, shuddering, "this dank, filthy edifice, will be the death of me."

The Khan gave his advisor a blank stare.

"I will have my own sleeping couch, my carpets and quilts," he said. "You may bring yours in as well, Edecon. You will inhabit the palace with me. Scottas and Ernac, also. I will sit on the throne of Milan, and sleep in the Imperial Chambers beginning tonight. Prepare for a celebration on that account."

With that the Khan turned and walked away, leaving Edecon to the arrangements, and to his grumbling.

"We could be on our way to Rome," he muttered. "We should be. But, no, now that the men have their plunder the mighty Khan must stop to see how it feels to perch his behind on the throne of this ugly palace. He must have glory and turn decadent, drink civilized wine and sample city women. He must mingle with the simpering fools of the court and idle away another campaign season. He struts like a preening peacock. All this to tickle his vanity. Attila is ridiculous."

Edecon rambled on.

"You're extraordinarily critical of the Khan today, Edecon. More than usual I would say," I said, at his back.

My words echoed, ringing hollow through the stone hall. Edecon jumped to hear my voice.

"Excuse me, Lord Ernac," he said lamely. "I didn't know there was anyone but myself in this draughty, nasty cave."

"Clearly," I said, amused, "you did not."

"It's what I feel. I'm sorry to say it, Ernac," Edecon said, "but I'm astonished at Attila. This delay has ruined the only real opportunity to take Rome that I will see in my lifetime."

"That may be so," I replied, "but if it is, my father has his reasons. You know him as well as any man, and you know he doesn't take a step, or fail to take one, without a reason. His purpose may be one he shares with others, or more likely, one he keeps to himself. If I know nothing else regarding my esteemed father, I know that his acts are reasoned out beyond what most men would imagine."

"You haven't always spoken of your father so adoringly, Ernac," Edecon dared to say to me.

"No, I haven't," I agreed. "But I happen to agree with his decision not to march on Rome this summer. I'm not sure that would be wise. Stories of plague and famine have been coming through the Khan's spies in the south. Tadiqin has become a rich source of information. The little Persian spy my brother would have beheaded is an accurate and useful informant. He says there would be no fodder for our animals, no drinkable water for the men, in the south. That's the situation."

"Perhaps you're right," Edecon began doubtfully.

He was interrupted by an onslaught of slaves who had to be dealt with. They were given their orders for the banqueting, and sent out to haul the Khan's personal belongings into the palace.

The evening started well enough. The rosy flush of our easy march through the north was still visible on Attila's cheeks, and the mellow wines of Italy loosened tongues and eased frayed tempers.

But, then, came a dreadful moment.

Dusk was settling, and we moved inside to inspect the great hall. Torches were being lighted along the walls, the slaves putting fire to them in the vast gallery while merrymakers seated themselves at the far end. We followed the lighting with interest, watching each torch as it blazed up, eager to see what would emerge from the gloom.

Being a small company, we chose to gather in a cozy corner, and so, sat peering curiously toward the other end of the cavernous hall. The sconces along the sides were arranged so that the walls leaped out at us as soon as there was light on them. An enormous mural appeared at the far end, the colors popping out to reveal a court scene.

At the center of the thing were two golden thrones, and on them, robed in gilt and jeweled garments, sat two figures wearing fancy crowns. The crowns were of an impossibly ornate design, heavy with gold and gems laced through the fretwork. Directly in front of the two elaborately garbed figures lay the bloodied bodies of their enemies, obviously prisoners who had been brought before them and killed. The faces of the kings smiled benignly down on the evidence of their vindictiveness.

It was plain that the two figures on the thrones were the Emperor Valentinian III and Aëtius, the Magister Militum of the Western Empire. The vanquished, lying dead in front of them, were Huns. Our company grew deathly quiet, stunned by what the mural insinuated.

Attila rose from his banqueting couch. He walked deliberately down the length of the long hall, and halted in front of the mural. He stared up at it, examining the details. He absorbed the depiction of the triumphant kings, Aëtius and Valentinian, presiding over the execution of dozens of Hun prisoners. When he turned away his face was pale as the marble on the floor, but he said nothing. He moved back to his seat, and picked up his goblet of wine. He drained it down, and then he spoke.

"Where do the court artists live?" he demanded of the slaves.

"At the edge of the city in the artists' compound, Lord Attila," one of them answered.

"Fetch them to me," said the Khan.

"Perhaps they are abed, Great Khan," one said.

My father's eyes ran over the heads of the slaves as if measuring their necks for his sword.

"Nevertheless, we will summon them, Great Khan," one sensible slave put in quickly.

"Good," he said. "They will come and receive my instructions," Attila said. He glared at each man in turn, certain they had no choice but to obey.

The slaves ran to do his bidding, and whatever the artists may have been doing, they were soon prostrating themselves before the Khan.

"Which of you is chief artisan here?" asked my father, when their heads were on the floor in front of him.

One of the men spoke up, saying he was the person honored with that title.

"The figures in the mural," my father said, pointing to the intolerable wall, "will be painted out and replaced with the figures of myself, and my Magister Militum, Berichus. The bodies of the dead prisoners will likewise be painted out and replaced with bodies of dead Romans. This will be done within the space of one moon or less," my father said.

He turned to Edecon, and said, "I will move back to my tents tomorrow morning. I will return to the palace when the changes have been completed."

Attila dismissed the court artists and went on eating and drinking as if nothing had happened. As far as I know he said nothing further about the incident, and the work was completed within the time he mentioned.

My father's reaction to an affront is never the same. We thought he would behead every one of the Milanese slaves who witnessed the events of that evening, and the artisans with them. But when the painting had been transformed, he ignored both artists painting, as if the incident was the sort of thing he dealt with frequently.

It's possible more might have been made of the episode of the offensive mural, but shortly after we were ensconced in the palace again a messenger arrived from Valentinian. It happened that I was walking with my father in the gardens of the palace when he arrived. Attila asked the interpreter to read the message straight out.

The interpreter read from his parchment.

"From the Glorious Emperor, Valentinian III, and the Honorable Commander Aëtius, greetings to the King of the Huns. It is our pleasure to request that the Khan consider a meeting with an official of the Holy Roman Empire, Pope Leo I. Should the Khan agree to our proposal, the meeting will take place at a site of the Khan's choosing, and at the Khan's convenience. His Holiness, Pope Leo I, ardently wishes to discuss matters of benefit to the Great Khan, Lord of the Huns."

"Should I wait for your answer, Lord Attila?" the messenger asked.

"Yes, wait," said Attila. He winked at me, and motioned me out of range of the hearing of the others.

"Aëtius has decided he is beaten; he is suing for peace," my father said in a low voice. "Do you think, Ernac," he said, "that I should meet with this chief shaman of the Romans?"

Attila didn't try to hide the satisfaction he took in the request. "We have some experience with shamans, you and I," he said smiling. "We know they can be good or bad. Still, sending the most powerful shaman of the empire to negotiate with us is significant. What do you say, shall we see what this person has to offer in sound judgment, or, perhaps, in tribute?"

Attila's eyes twinkled. I could see he wanted this meeting.

I answered as I thought my father wished me to, and the messenger left with the Khan's reply. The summer season being well advanced, fodder is in short supply, and Attila doesn't want the negotiation delayed. He has sent word he will meet with this shaman two suns from now in the Ambuleian district of the Veneti at a certain well-traveled ford of the River Mincius.

Word came back the following day that this Pope, Leo, accepts the time and place of the meeting as proposed by Attila. He will bring as attendants an ex-consul, Avienus, and an ex-prefect called Trygetius. The Khan has asked me, Edecon, and Berichus to attend him in the encounter, and we have gladly agreed.

I doubt the wisdom of negotiating with a shaman rather than with an ambassador, though I wouldn't say that to my father. I've no trust in men of religion. Too often they are not what they seem. I've been stung personally by the tail of one such scorpion, and my experience has bred profound suspicions in me. There are evil and ambitious shamans, just as there are evil, ambitious soldiers.

Still, I suppose we should see what this Pope Leo has to offer, and of what he is made. His reputation is that of an unbending man, an ardent pusher of his faith. I hear he is quite the influential personage in the Empire, part of a group calling themselves Christians. These Christians are strict in their belief that there is but one god. This god rules through fear, no other god being allowed space in the domains he lays claim to. A very strange god, indeed, if this be true. If this shaman is the chief worshipper of such a god he may be stiff-spined like his god, and not a man of common sense.

It strikes me that such men are not trustworthy. They deal not in practicality, but in fears and figments of the mind. Meantime, however, I will take the example of my father and the wisest of our people. I will not pass judgment on the gods of others.

We arrived at the appointed place first, and the man who calls himself Pope Leo followed quickly on our heels.

He came on a horse glistening with gold harness and bridle, caparisoned with heavy silk and gold hangings, and embellished with jewels. The regalia of his horse would have put a Persian satrap to shame. The priest wore a king's crown, the garments of a king, and conducted himself as a king.

In addition to two formal attendants, the shaman brought with him an interpreter and six retainers packing a large meal. It was a heavy repast, complete with fine wines. He ordered it spread on the ground on linen cloths. When the meal had been laid the chief shaman dismounted, requesting that the Khan and our group dismount and partake of the feast.

I looked at my father, Edecon looked at me, and Berichus glared at Leo.

To my great surprise Attila got off his horse, sat with the man Leo, and ate from the dishes laid out on the cloth. Berichus and I shook our heads and remained on our horses, but Edecon also dismounted and ate with my father. After his appetite was satisfied the Khan asked the retainers to hand up portions of the food to Berichus and myself. They did as he asked, and we ate while Attila and Pope Leo had a second goblet of wine.

Preliminary formalities done, my father and Edecon again mounted their horses and sat waiting. This, for some reason, made the shaman flush. His skin, which is thin and rather pink, seemed set afire. He is a man no older than my father, I would say, but his hair is white as the coat of a stoat in winter.

Finally, the chief shaman mounted his own horse and began the negotiations. Speaking to the Khan's interpreter, he said, "We thank you for your generosity in meeting with us, and we offer our heartfelt good wishes to the Khan, Lord of the Huns."

His words were relayed, and my father sat his horse saying nothing. After an awkward pause Leo spoke again.

"Firstly, Lord Attila," he went on, "I wish to plead for the lives of Roman prisoners. I would ask they be returned to us. Our hearts are sore, and we grieve for them, for their sad state as slaves of the Huns, and for their absence from the world of Christendom."

"The life of a slave in any country is not a good one," my father said. "The Romans have slaves aplenty to feed. As for myself I also have more slaves than I care to feed."

"Then, Lord Attila, you will consider my proposal," said Leo.

"Perhaps," Attila said. "What do you offer in return for the prisoners?"

"We are prepared to offer gold. The amount, if reasonable, may be named by yourself," the priest answered.

Attila quickly set an amount. He asked for the usual twelve solidi per head for common soldiers and, because he was in a generous mood, said he would ask only five-hundred solidi for civilians of high station.

"I recall that Theodosius once paid me three-thousand, six-hundred solidi to ransom a certain Bigilas. But Bigilas was a special case," my father said, not disguising his smile.

The priest didn't respond to Attila regarding the ransom of Bigilas, but he agreed promptly to the amounts mentioned.

Then, "Those captives who wish to leave our country will be given back to you on delivery of the amount named here. You have my oath on it," my father said.

Pope Leo gave his own oath as to the amount of solidi to be exchanged for the captives, and told one of his attendants to write this on two parchments. One he kept for himself, and the other was handed to the Khan's interpreter to be passed on to his scribe.

My father spoke up, saying, "Not all these prisoners will wish to leave us, priest. Many have become Hun in their ways and they like our life. These, you may not take. I deem it their choice whether to leave or stay."

Again the priest agreed, but said he hoped the prisoners would be allowed to carry out the rituals of the Christian faith which were as important to them as their lives.

Attila shrugged. "I care not which of the gods people worship, or what rituals they do to honor them," Attila said. "What difference does this make to me? There are many gods. All gods have some power in them."

My father's words brought a sour look from the Pope, Leo. He protested, and gave a lengthy speech on his god and exactly how he was to be worshipped.

"There is but one God," the chief shaman pronounced firmly. "He is the one, the true, the only God, whose son was Christ. In the holy body of Christ, the divine, life and spirit did meet and become one. That is the Christian belief and it allows of no other. Any other belief is heresy."

One of the Pope Leo's attendants, the man they called Avienus, tried to interrupt the priest's flow of talk, but he would have none of it. Brushing the man's hands aside, the priest hushed the ex-consul, reprimanding him severely in rough tones. Leo went on until he had finished his cant.

"There is one God," the priest barked at us. "There has been, and will be, but one divine nature on this earth, the spirit of God in the living body of Christ."

Attila looked at the shaman strangely, but said nothing in response to this outburst. Instead, he asked what other business Leo had to transact with the Lord of the Huns.

The priest straightened on his horse and said, "The gracious Valentinian III, Emperor of Rome, wishes peace in Italy."

"We are empowered here today," said the chief shaman of the Romans, "to beseech the Khan, Lord of the Huns, that he retire from the city of Milan, and from Italy, and that he return to his own borders beyond the Alps."

Attila nodded. "And what is the price of this peace? What do Valentinian and Aëtius offer me for peace in Italy?" he said.

"I am empowered by my Emperor," said the Pope, Leo, ignoring my father's reference to Aëtius, "to affirm that the annual tribute once given by Theodosius be resumed immediately on the departure of your armies. I am further empowered to offer recompense for the tribute which has not been paid since the death of Theodosius. For this the Emperor will give the Lord of the Huns the sum of one-thousand pounds of gold in one payment. One payment only."

"That will be agreeable," my father said. "Then there is the matter of the Princess Honoria, who is betrothed to me. I demand she be sent to me so that our mutual pledges may be finalized and she become my wife. It is Honoria's wish, and mine, that this ceremony should take place."

"I have no authority to speak to the question of Honoria's pledge to you, Lord Attila," the priest said with a severe face, "but I am honor-bound to relay your demand to Valentinian. And that I will do."

"I expect this to be done as I ask," said my father confidently.

The Pope Leo, then, and for a second time, conferred the title Master of the Troops on the Khan. The first conferring of this title was done by Aëtius, and as all present were aware the title means nothing beyond the amount of tribute due from it. This time the conferring of the title is but a seal put on the peace agreement, a way of insuring that tribute will continue to flow to Attila as promised.

With this, the business to be transacted seemed finished, but instead of saying the words that would have ended the meeting, my father gave the priest a hard look and spoke straight to the priest's face, not as if he was speaking through an interpreter, but as if he was talking in the same language.

"What is this thing you mention called a heresy?" Attila said. "For this you have had many executed outright, and have burned and tortured many others? Since before the time of my grandfather Khan Balamber we have been hearing references to this new Roman Tngri. These are things we don't understand."

The Pope Leo's head jerked upright on his neck and his pink skin again turned an odd bright-red.

"It is heresy not to believe as a Christian. To believe in any God but the one true God is an evil thing. Heresies must be punished," he said.

"But what is that," said Attila, "to believe as a Christian? What does it mean?"

"It means you must bow down in submission to the will of the one and only God," said the shaman Leo. "You must accept that Christ, God's son, is your savior. You must accept the Holy Church as his one and only instrument. And you must swear to accept the Holy Mother Church as representative of God on this earth. What the church says is correct. Belief in the divine nature of Christ and in his Church is the sole path to salvation."

"And what is this salvation?" said my father. "If I would swear as you say, would this save me from death? Would I then have impregnable powers? If I gave my oath to this god, that I would believe in him and no other, would I have his promise that I could not fail? Would this god insure that I prevail over other men in battle?"

"You would not be saved from death," said the chief shaman of the Romans.

He spoke as of something abnormally serious, and he said, "Even the Son of God was not saved from death. Spiritual powers can be increased only if God chooses to grant them. That is between you and God. The one, the true God, has no time for temporal powers, no time for armies or kings."

"Then what can this Tngri do for me?" said my father. "My Prime Minister, Onegesius, now dead from his wounds in Gaul, didn't trust shamans who follow only one god. We Huns believe in many Tngri. We see that power comes from many sources. Among us are counted ninety-nine Tngri. We see no harm in many gods, no disrespect in the numbers or kinds of Tngri a people may choose to honor. Onegesius and I often spoke of these matters. He was a very wise man, my Prime Minister, a very thoughtful man. I miss his good counsel."

Attila sat looking into the face of this Pope Leo, measuring how he was taking the things said to him. I could see he did not like what was being said.

Also," said my father, "my wife, Khatun Kreka, who is much revered in our country, believes Christians are crazy. She says those who believe in a Tngri intent on destroying all other gods are not right in their heads."

By this time the interpreter was too flustered to translate my father's words without stumbling. I'm not sure exactly what he said to this chief shaman, but for the only time that afternoon the man Leo openly lost his composure.

Whatever the words the interpreter relayed, they must have been accurate enough, for the Pope Leo abruptly signaled his attendants to mount up. With scarce an attempt at the proper display of manners, and with a few terse words of good-bye, they gathered up their gear and prepared to leave.

The chief shaman of the Romans hastily drew a sign, a four-cornered symbol, in front of his face with his fingers. And with that the whole party lit off in a flurry of black looks, as children will when they suspect they've been bested in argument.

We, too, turned to ride away, and I asked our interpreter, "What was the four-cornered sign this Pope, Leo, gave us as he left?"

The man told me it was called the sign of the cross, that it was a sign among Christians meant to ward off the evil-eye.

The eccentric priest of the Romans must think we Huns have an evil nature and that he had to protect himself against us.

I heard my father, riding ahead with Berichus, make a remark to his old comrade in arms. He leaned over to Berichus and said quietly, "What we have seen in the person of this priest is the pomp of idiots. It's a bad game he plays."

Berichus smiled, and replied, "The pomp of idiots is a game not to be compared with the prudence of kings, my Lord."

I thought this a peculiar ending for a diplomatic negotiation. This Pope, Leo, may be an influential man in Rome, but he has not the skills of a diplomat. He is as I imagined he would be, stiff-necked, and bristling easily when baited. My father was able to prick his thin, pink skin without half trying.

I was now certain I'd interpreted the twinkle in his eye correctly as we walked in the gardens of the palace. Attila was curious about this shaman, and he wanted a chance to match wits with him. He has had his chance and has seen in person what the man lacks. He doesn't have the smoothness and tact of a professional ambassador.

All this is of no matter, the Khan got what he wanted at the River Mincius. His tribute from the Western Empire is assured, his pride has been stroked, and we can leave this country of epidemic and famine. Our departure can't come soon enough for me.

19

"You were hard on the shaman," Edecon said.

"He's a fanatic," Attila replied. "I had suspected as much, now I'm certain."

"A shaman's duty is to defend his faith," Edecon said placatingly.

"This display was more than duty," the Khan replied acidly. "Kreka is right, Christians have crazy notions."

Attila glowered at Edecon. His jolly mood had disappeared. Even the widening horizons that signaled the edge of the homeland didn't rouse him. He was sunk in an impenetrable gloom. *On the return he has been surly and quarrelsome. He's touchy with everyone, and his ill-temper grows as we travel.*

Nevertheless, Edecon decided to try again. There was something he very much wanted to know.

"You never did intend to go for Rome did you, my lord?" he said.

"You are perceptive," Attila answered shortly.

"But why? I can't see why? Rome was within your grasp. If we had not stopped in Milan you could have had Rome, Great Khan," Edecon said, returning to the subject that had puzzled and irritated him for weeks.

"I didn't want Rome," Attila said.

"But why not?" his advisor's voice rose along with his vision of the city. "The palaces of the Empire could have been the palaces of the Huns. I don't understand." He shook his head.

Edecon liked to imagine himself wandering the streets of Rome, passing at will through the rooms of fabled buildings, with his Khan as Italy's ruler.

"I'm not stupid, Edecon," Attila said.

The Khan opened a crack in the armor that protected the secrets of his mind.

"In spite of what people are saying, I never wanted Rome," he said. "Gaul, yes. The whole of Gaul I could have used, could still use, but Rome is too far and too foreign. And it would cost too much to keep it. It would drain my resources. I've watched Roman Emperors make that mistake. Valentinian, and Theodosius, and how many before them, have not been able to grasp what the Empire has cost them. From Aëtius to Galla Placidia, not one has been able to see it. No, old friend, I'll not be pulled into that quicksand. Extending reach beyond ability to control is not for me. What I take I want to use before it rots."

"What are your plans for the coming season, then?" Edecon asked.

"To go against Constantinople," the Khan answered readily. "Marcian has refused me the tribute Theodosius promised. He will have my ultimatum as soon as we arrive home. The tribute comes, or I take it. I don't really even want Constantinople. I want secure grazing lands for the animals, gold, and goods for our people. Let the Romans have their cities. I have to keep Marcian believing I would have the cities if I could, that's all."

Attila had said what he intended to say. He motioned his standard bearer and a signal was passed. The company would halt here for the night.

The vanguard had hopes of reaching Hun country by the following sunrise. They had ridden without rest since before dawn. The group riding with the Khan dismounted, grooms and stewards running to set up tents and light fires.

It had taken them several days to dismantle the trappings the Khan and his party had set up in the palace, and when it was done he was away in a rush. The result was a jumble. Slaves couldn't find their utensils or rugs, and they went from animal to animal searching for the boxes and bags that held what they needed. Angry that his evening meal was late, and in a foul temper generally, Attila lashed out at everyone.

"Kreka should be here," Edecon whispered to me. "She'd straighten him out soon enough."

"Why don't you see if you can straighten him out, Edecon," I said blandly.

My teacher looked at me and wandered over to the Khan's tent.

"May I enter, my lord?" Edecon asked with perfect courtesy.

Attila motioned him inside.

The aging warrior squatted on the carpets in front of the Khan and sighed loudly.

"You feel your years, old friend," Attila growled, and he signaled a servant for bowls of wine.

"I do, my lord. Never more than during this season. I am keenly aware of my aching joints and failing limbs."

Attila offered Edecon the first bowl.

"Ah, thank you, my lord. This will help," he said, taking a long drink.

"You need someone to comfort you, a young wife to wait on you and warm your bones in the night," the Khan said.

Edecon smiled.

"A new wife may be what I need, but the woman would be a sorceress who could bring my manhood back. My loins are not even lukewarm. I don't believe a woman could cure me."

Attila threw his advisor a bleak look. "We are both getting old, Edecon. I, too, could use a young wife. Italy sapped my strength, as well as the strength of my armies. We avoided the worst of famine and pestilence, yes, but the men have suffered. We left too many men in Italy. Too many were lost to plague and flux. It is better to die in battle."

Silence descended on the two soldiers. In the stillness a shadow fell over the doorway.

"Take heart, father. Your food will be here shortly," Ernac said.

"Join us, Ernac," Attila said. "Have a bowl of wine. We've earned an evening's relaxation."

I was pleased to have the invitation, and after one bowl of wine found to my amazement I wanted another. It doesn't happen often, but that evening I entered that brief, blessed state wherein one is both brave and brilliant. The reins on my mouth slackened. Generally, I keep my thoughts to myself and I feared I might say more than I intended.

"Edecon and I were saying," my father said, "that what we need are young wives. How about you, Ernac? Are you ready for a second wife? You've been wed long enough to produce a son, and your son is old enough to be on his horse. Maybe it's time you took a new bride."

The Khan gave Edecon a devilish glance and they grinned at me.

I smiled back foolishly. In another mood I wouldn't have taken so kindly to their banter, but at that moment I thought it was funny.

"Where shall we look? What sort of girl would you like?" my father persisted.

"Burgundian women are fair," Edecon offered. "Were I a few seasons younger I would have one myself."

"Come, Ernac, speak up," Attila said. "How do you take to Edecon's suggestion. Would you have a Burgundian girl?"

"I'm sure," I said truthfully, "any girl I married would not be safe in her quilts at night. Beki would have her killed. She's jealous, and not shy to wield her power as first wife. We haven't been married long enough for Beki to approve of another wife, and she would have to approve. She might kill me as well as my bride. I tremble to think of the pummeling I'd get if I mentioned another wife."

"My son is afraid of his wife. It is a bad thing for a husband to be afraid of his wife. We must do something to correct this, Edecon. What shall we do?" Attila said, slyly.

"If you have the answer to bad-tempered wives, Attila," Edecon answered, "you are the wisest man in several kingdoms. No man I ever heard of can keep a jealous woman from her revenge."

My confession had been meant in seriousness. Apparently it was comical. The Khan guffawed and Edecon began to titter. They fell into fits of merriment.

At this point the Khan's meal arrived, and being, by now, in a better mood, he insisted I stay and share it. As soon as I ate my flapping tongue became still. With sobriety my new-found openness left me. I begged permission to leave, saying I had to see to the health of my men.

That, at least, was the truth. Many men are still recovering from the sickness they contracted in Italy. It keeps their insides running like a foamy river, and some have been laid so low they forget themselves, pissing in their tents from weakness. I should make them pay the mandatory fine in gold for their lapse of behavior. Instead, I give them a tongue-lashing. I would insist on the fine except that this sickness weakens a man so that he can scarcely sit up. So many have suffered from this illness that the return home has been delayed.

After I left the Khan's tent I found I was refreshed. Wine can raise the spirits, but the Khan is more fond of it than he should be. Two or three bowls is one thing, drinking until you can't get up is another. That, I don't approve of. When my father reaches a certain stage of imbibing he fancies himself a jokester. Some men have a natural talent for jokes, but Attila does not. His humor is coarse, yet those around him must pretend his distasteful witticisms are amusing.

When Ernac had left the tent Edecon and the Khan smiled at one another. The young man's observations struck them as the prudishness of youth.

They were alone, and Edecon spoke freely.

"Ernac has become a fine man, Attila. Your last son is the one who should have been your first." Edecon pronounced with satisfaction. "I nearly despaired of him after his poisoning, but he recovered to become a real warrior. He's handsome, a man the women like. Beki won't be able to keep him happy without help. In spite of his fears of reprisal he will take a second wife before long. I will begin to look for a suitable..."

Edecon stopped, leaving the thought in midair. He frowned in dismay. This was the first time he had broached the subject of Ernac's poisoning with Attila. He was afraid he'd said too much, but Attila didn't seem to notice.

"You're right, Edecon. Ernac is a son to be proud of. Onegesius remarked on it after he saw him fight at Marcianople. Much of the credit can be given to you," the Khan said. "You did a fine job with him. You have my thanks."

"It was my pleasure," the Khan's advisor said, and he adroitly shifted the focus of conversation. "Truly, my lord, perhaps it is time for you to take another bride. There will be a break in the spring. You could devote that time to a new wife. I do think a Burgundian woman would be a good move. Who knows, you might want stronger ties with that part of the frontier. Burgundy lies in a strategic place. That small patch of territory at the southern end of Gaul could be very useful. It wouldn't be a bad idea to seek a bride from that country."

Attila grunted. He was ready for sleep. As far as he was concerned the conversation was finished.

Edecon bowed himself out of Attila's presence. He thought the Khan was warm to the idea of a Burgundian bride. A new wife would, indeed, be good for him. He could use a fresh lease on life, and he would benefit from a season without battle. He hadn't noticed, Edecon reflected, how easily Attila tired these days. The weight of years was bearing down on the Khan.

Attila, almost single-handedly, had been responsible for the burgeoning of Hun influence. He had planned, and labored, and fought, for his people. Over and again he had proven himself worthy of his title, worthy of the trust of his people.

We older ones deserve a rest, and most assuredly he does, Edecon thought.

"We've come to depend on Attila too much," the old warrior muttered drunkenly as he went reeling back to his yurt.

"He hasn't been Khan nearly as long as his Uncle Ruga. He hasn't ruled as long as many another Khan, yet I can't imagine any other man as Khan. What would we be without him? Still, we must face it. Attila is no longer young."

Edecon dropped onto his couch with a grateful groan.

Our losses were severe in Italy, he thought, and Attila must be ready for another campaign by spring. It cannot be otherwise and he knows it, for many still ask why he didn't attack Rome. The rank and file are always looking for new sources of plunder, always restive. They hear rumors, and they think the worst. The Khan has his promise of tribute from Valentinian, but Marcian has not yet acceded to demands for tribute. And Dengezic is fomenting discontent among the battalions under his command. Attila cannot afford a delay. It would make him appear weak.

This next season will be the final push for the Khan, Attila's advisor told himself. It will be his greatest effort. Then, he can give over responsibility to younger men.

"I'm glad he has Ernac," Edecon muttered. "Every man is entitled to one son he can rely on."

20

Tadiqin slept and ate next to Bahgatur for the better part of one moon. He plied the great horse with every potion he knew, but no nostrum, no amount of massaging his belly or urging him to his feet could help him. Time had run out for the Khan's favorite. Bahgatur's heart was tired, and with the wisdom of acceptance he wanted to meet his final hours in comfort.

Kreka offered to spell the obstinate little groom, but the Persian refused to leave the side of his charge. Horse and man had been together for years. The time spent caring for Bahgatur, grooming, and fussing over every change in his coat, every slight dullness in his eyes, had altered Tadiqin. Though he could not have said it, Tadiqin loved Bahgatur. He was aware the Khan's anger would be great should harm come to him, but his concern for Bahgatur's welfare was genuine. The groom was trying to deny the truth of the horses' illness.

Finally, Kreka insisted Tadiqin accept help, and together they pled with Bahgatur. They whispered to him of the turbulent battles of his past, recalled to him the hours of his pride. They rubbed him with oil, and tempted him with grain and his favorite sweets.

The morning came when he would not rise, and Tadiqin sat on the ground stroking him. Bahgatur's head rested in his lap. Tadiqin rested his head on Bahgatur's forelock, and his tears formed a salty stream that flowed into the yellowing mane. Bahgatur's coat had been pure, fresh snow, his eyes bright as polished flint. He had had carriage, endurance, and unfaltering courage, and his good sense under fire, had been a joy to watch. Warriors had looked on Bahgatur with pleasure and envy. All those who saw him fell under the spell of the magnificent animal.

No soldier who had seen him carry Attila into battle could forget him. His head would turn, he would catch a whiff of the enemy, his muscles would gather in barely containable energy. The raise of his neck, the lift of his head, the roll of his eye, signaled as surely as the raising of a standard when the battle was about to commence.

He had given many an aspiring young lieutenant an extra reason to distinguish himself in hopes of being rewarded with a foal from his lineage. When he was gelded there was mourning among the men who had hoped to have a colt from him and hadn't had the luck to get one.

That evening it was clear Bahgatur would not stand again. Tadiqin was overcome by a sense of loss. A soughing groan escaped the horse's throat, a tremor possessed his chest, and then there was no more. The film of death slid over his eyes and the flies swarmed, springing, it seemed, from his very pores. They pulsed in matted clots along the line of his ears and eyes. The buzzards gathered to wait their turn, and still Tadiqin couldn't bring himself to leave Bahgatur's body.

When it was fully dark Kreka lifted Bahgatur's head from the groom's lap. She helped him up, and signaled for slaves to hoist the dead horse onto a litter. Heaving, and grunting with the weight of him, the men set to work. They managed, finally, to lift him, and they lashed his carcass onto the bed of the drag.

The Khatun had already chosen a burial site for Attila's war-horse and the party set out. The site had been chosen because Attila was fond of the place. It was located at the bend of a river, and this late in the season the water would be low, and the ground there soft and easy to dig.

The sounds of night creatures accompanied the small group as they walked. At dawn they reached the river's bend, and by mid-morning Bahgatur was in his grave, safe from the crowds of carrion eaters perching hopefully nearby. A cairn of stones was erected at his burial site. Later, if Attila wished it, a marker could be placed high on the bank.

Two suns after the exhausted burial party returned to camp the first of Attila's advance scouts rode into camp. The Khan, the messenger reported, was anxious to reach the home camp. He was only half a day behind them.

"I wish you'd been here, but there was nothing to be done. He was ready to die," Kreka told her husband.

The evening meal was over, and the Khan was drinking hard. When Attila was told of Bahgatur's death he called for wine. He listened, heard Kreka out, and said nothing. He lifted one wine bowl after the other. Before he had downed the bowl he held he was reaching for another.

"Don't take your grief out on the groom," she said. "This is a great loss for Tadiqin. In a way his loss is greater than yours. The little Persian's care of your war-horse was a daily devotion, as well as a daily duty. He will be lost without Bahgatur. No horse will replace Bahgatur in his affections. He was only a boy when he began caring for him. They were youngsters together."

Attila no longer listened to Kreka. An empty bowl dropped from his hand and he toppled onto the carpets. Kreka threw a quilt over her husband and left him where he fell.

"I should not have told him. I should have waited. He deserved a night's rest," she thought. But then, she thought, someone would have let it out, a person eager to express sympathy would have told him. His favorite was gone. What did one night matter?

The Khatun stripped to her thin, linen underdress and let her hair fall. She pulled a mirror from the top of a high trunk and surveyed herself, swinging her plaits free in the last rays of sun that streamed through the doorway. When the light hit her head she was startled at the grey hair that drifted among the dark. Attila has no grey in his head, she thought ruefully.

She turned to look at him, studied his sleeping face, and saw that his beard was grey. He'd carried a scattering of white for years, but now his beard was more white than dark. In the evening light she saw how puffy his face had become. There were sickly yellow pouches beneath his eyes. He looks bad, she thought. The Italian summer has taken the life out of him. The Khatun resolved to let her husband sleep until he woke of his own accord.

Kreka stepped to the door of the tent to catch the breeze. She looked toward the west where a roseate glow lingered. The late season evenings were still warm, but soon cold would overcome the heat. Kreka dreaded the cold. She didn't tolerate the season of frozen earth well these days.

This was the sort of night she loved. A fluid sweetness filled the air, and no wind masked the music of evening bird sound. She felt the relaxation of earth and growing things, the hush that penetrated the smallest spaces. These things were much to her taste. Normally, this tranquil evening would have put her at peace. Tonight she was not at peace.

Kreka turned back inside, finished inspecting her face, and carefully tucked away her mirror. This mirror was the only personal object she had that had belonged to her mother. The mirror had reflected the face of her grandmother, and her mother as a young woman.

Kreka moved to her husband's sleeping body and lay down in the crook of his arm, curling herself into the shape of his inert form. She did not fall asleep immediately. She'd been hearing gossip. Were the rumors true, she wondered, or had her spies failed her. If the gossip was true, Attila planned to take the Princess Ildico to wife in the spring. Kreka had heard that Ildico was beautiful. Political it might be, to marry a Burgundian Princess, but the Khan did not wed ugly women.

Kreka had seldom been jealous of Attila's other women, his secondary wives and concubines. Only once or twice had she had twinges. Uzindur, and Ebnedzar's mother, Elminyar, for example, had given her a few pangs. Elminyar had been a woman of warmth and intelligence, and in the early days of Attila's marriage to her Kreka had plotted many an ugly deed against her. Once, when he had spent several nights running in Elminyar's tents, she had very nearly given way to spite and had her killed. Elminyar, poor woman, had died young, and without Kreka's help. She died giving birth to Uzindur, and any threat from her had not materialized. The Khan's newest wife, the moon-faced Eskayar, was beautiful, but she was of a bovine nature. Attila liked fire in his women as well as beauty.

Was she capable of sexual jealousy even now? Did she still feel a woman's need for Attila? It struck her that she wasn't sure. The brief tug in her loins could be jealousy, or it could be the involuntary jerk of tired muscle. What difference did it make if he had another wife? What difference where he spent his time, who he confided in, whose counsel he listened to? Did these things matter as they once had?

Kreka explored the peculiar notion that she was no longer in love with Attila. Searching through layers of memory, she looked for the answer. It occurred to her that this focus on her husband was a lingering habit she hadn't thought to let go of.

What she had felt for him was still with her, Kreka decided, but like the memory of pain that lives beneath a scar, the ache of wounded love fades. A sense of release came over her and she fell asleep beside her husband.

"The ground is hard, the forage is gone," the Khan exclaimed. He squatted, scooped up a small handful of bone dry earth, and let it sift through his open palm.

"Yes, the grass burned up early this year," his wife answered. "The rain is late, and so far there's no sign of a break."

Attila swung back on his mount. The Khan and the Khatun, with stewards and two dozen servants, were riding out on the following dawn to Bahgatur's grave. Attila was bent on paying his respects before the weather changed and rain raised the water to cover the resting place of his companion.

The Khan had wakened early and summoned the servants. No one except the Khatun would ride out with him. He would not have Edecon, Ernac, or Berichus; no advisor or lieutenant was called.

They approached the gravesite at midday. Sun fingered the landscape, splashing over the horses flanks and brushing their manes with bronze flecks. The light lacked intensity, however, and there was hesitation in the air. The season itself seemed unwilling to move on. The Khatun watched for autumn and made sure this tender slice of felicity didn't pass unnoticed. Kreka, herself, had grown ripe. She was sensible to small pleasures.

She gave him directions, and Attila left the group to find the spot where Bahgatur's memorial stones clustered at the foot of a ravine. The cairn sat next to a steep bank around a sharp curve of hill. From where the small party sat waiting it could not be seen.

The Khatun remained where she was, watching Attila disappear down the bank.

Kreka ordered the rugs put down and a light meal to be laid on the grass, but she continued to sit her horse. She had made no offer to walk with Attila. It was proper that he say good-bye to his war-horse alone.

Attila stood in front of Bahgatur's burial cairn for some time, his face impassive, his mouth unmoving. At length he turned away, but before climbing back up the bank the Khan studied the contour of this bend of river. He stared fixedly around him, storing the details, putting each rock and curve in place inside his head.

Kreka's eyes followed his return. When his head appeared above the bank, she smiled, and as his familiar bowlegs rolled toward her she saw that he was preoccupied. She knew his moods, especially after a campaign. The tilt of his head, and the hunch of his shoulders, told her he was wrestling with a problem.

"Let's stay a bit. I'm tired, I need to eat before we start back," she said when he reached her.

After a summer apart there were matters Kreka wished to pursue with Attila. This excursion gave her a chance to catch him alone. The Khan wouldn't have admitted he needed rest, but he would take it if she asked for herself.

"Could they see the spot?" he asked, staring at the servants.

"No," she said. "I kept them back. You weren't in sight. No one except Tadiqin has seen the spot. The slaves who carried Bahgatur to his rest are now in the land of eternal seasons."

"That's as well," he said.

She slid off and they arranged themselves on the pillowed stools to eat.

"Tell me, why didn't you go for Ravenna? Or for Rome?"

Kreka asked her question as soon as they sat down.

"Ravenna," the Khan snorted.

He speared a piece of lamb. "I had quite enough of Ravenna when I was a hostage there. Why would I want to go back?" he said, talking through a mouthful of meat.

"There might be memories there for you," Kreka answered. She had heard tales of women in Ravenna, and of his escapades as a young hostage. She was curious, but she left the topic. "As for Rome," she went on, "people still wonder why you didn't move on the Western Empire. They see weakness in the fact that you turned for home instead."

"I have no need of Rome," he said. It was the answer he gave anyone who asked. "Pestilence and famine were raging in southern Italy. The men have suffered enough."

"The suffering of your men never bothered you before. Why should it bother you now?" she asked.

Kreka chided herself for speaking so harshly. She knew Attila was not uncaring. She knew that beneath the tough casing was a man who bled like all men. Yet, the Khatun also knew he wasn't inclined to reveal himself without a prod and she had a strong need to hear Attila's thoughts.

"You think me totally ruthless," he said. His eyes would not meet hers, and Kreka saw she had miscalculated. Her words had hurt him.

"Not totally," she said.

"My skin has become thin and my wife enjoys scratching it," he said.

"I see you aren't in a talking mood," Kreka said, squinting into the sun. "But then you seldom are."

"Life becomes tedious," Attila said. "I have little to say."

"Tedious, is it?" Kreka said.

His words had set her teeth on edge.

"You've just returned from a punishing war, and your losses were enormous, even for such an ambitious campaign. You occupied the Palace at Milan, sat on its throne, and met with the chief shaman of the Western Romans. Right now you're planning another major campaign against the Eastern Empire, and you tell me life is tedious. By the Great Tngri! What would it take for you to feel excitement?"

She knew Attila hadn't fully recovered from the trek home, still she was impatient with his indifferent pose and his terse responses.

She decided she wanted to smoke her husband out.

Kreka jumped up and spun around, setting her turqoise and silver earrings tossing about her head.

"You plan to wed the Princess Ildico when the cold season ends," she said. "Why did you not tell me?"

"I don't choose to quarrel with you, Kreki," Attila said. A troubled shadow crossed his face.

"You mean you choose not to answer my question," she replied acidly. "Very well, I'll answer for you. You think a new wife will bring back your youth."

"I can have women without taking them to wife, Kreki," he answered simply.

"A whore isn't the same thing as a lovely young wife," Kreka said. "You want a beautiful woman who will flatter you, an adoring, innocent girl who will take you back to the days of your youth."

"Perhaps," he said. "Perhaps I do."

His mouth set in a flat line.

"You're a pathetic, lecherous, old goat," she flared. "The heat in your loins is gone. You're an old man pining for his lost potency."

"I'm aware of my weakness," he said. "You don't have to point it out."

"If you know, then, why not speak? Why must you be drawn out? Is it so dreadful to say what you already know?"

"I don't have your gifts of speech," Attila said. "What I might wish to say flits in and out, and when I would put it in words the image escapes before I can speak."

"You haven't had to put things in words," she came back at him. "Your orders are obeyed, your slightest whim catered to. With fear, and with gold, you have created armies of warriors and slaves who want nothing so much as to please you. No effort is too great if it pleases the Khan. Everyone counts on your benevolence. You have life on your terms. Why should you trouble to explain yourself."

"I've done my duty. I don't take advantage of the people. I am fair. What more would you have me be?" he asked.

"Ah-hhh!" she exclaimed. "It's Attila, pillar of rectitude. You're besotted with your own nobility."

The Khatun was exasperated. "I suppose you never won a woman's body in a gamble. You never allowed the bandits among us freedom to molest and maraud where they chose, never bought and sold free men. You do what you please, when you please, you old fraud."

"I'm not worse than any man, Kreki. Don't make me out a scoundrel. I'm not corrupt. I'm faithful to my duty."

"Your duty," Kreka scoffed. "How is it warlords always call up noble aims when they're challenged? How is it that anything a warlord happens to want becomes transformed into love of his people when a question arises about his actions?"

Attila stared at his wife. His eyes flickered.

"Duty has always come first for me," he declared. "You know this. You ask me to take pity on Tadiqin, whose duty is so important to him, and I will honor your request. Tadiqin's life is safe. I, too, take comfort in duty. Don't chastise me, Kreki. A momentary fit of jealousy has had the better of you. You're being unreasonable."

"Unreasonable!" she echoed. "As if you were reasonable. Of course, you are Khan, you don't have to be reasonable. You needn't have a reason to do what you do. You needn't feel anything about what you do."

"That's not so. This is ugly talk," he said. "You make me out an ogre. Have I the face of a demon? Is that how you see me? Am I incapable of love, of human feeling? Do you see me as the Romans see me, then? Do you hate me as the Romans hate me? Is that what we've come to?"

"You aren't an ogre," she said, a bit more calmly.

He had deflected her anger, still, she would speak the truth as she saw it. "I love you, Attila, but you baffle me. And yes, I've hated you at times. With good cause."

"You have had cause to hate me," he nodded. "You aren't an easy person either, Kreki. You can be very hard. We aren't so different, you and I, but we have different lives."

"I know I can be hard," she said, "but you set yourself up to be beyond question."

"I learned that from the Romans. Emperors must be above question," he said, his voice stiff with irony. "For Rome," he continued, "war against Attila is more than war against a dangerous invader. The Empire's view of me goes beyond hatred of an enemy."

"I don't excuse the Romans, Attila, but you had little to learn from Rome. Rome learned from you. You have taught others how to succeed in war, and you carry your skills far beyond the simple needs of your people. You need to curb your excesses in battle. You can't justify slaughtering so many without a good reason."

"I kill no one without reason," he said, with pompous formality. "I protect, and provide, for my people. Leadership was expected of me, and I have given it. I've lived by tradition, and honored custom. It's because I've succeeded where others have failed that I am hated."

"How long must you go on with this warring life? Must you destroy everyone who begrudges you your success before you quit?" his wife asked. "That would take many years. The list has become long."

"My friends are gone," Attila said, wistfully. "Only enemies remain to me. A man must have something to live for. If not friends, then enemies. I've lost Onegesius; a very painful loss. My Roman scribe Orestes is leaving me for Rome, and my son plots with Marcian against me. Bahgatur is gone. My loyal Uncle, Oebarsius, grows old. Edecon is feeble. Who do I have around me? Who can I trust? And you, do you think of leaving me as well, Kreki?"

Attila's lower lip went slack.

Kreka saw that he was genuinely distressed, and in spite of her resolve she softened. What he said was true. From the large group of strong, talented men who had marched to victory with the Khan, most were dead. And most of those who still lived were beyond caring. Of the few he trusted only Edecon and Berichus remained. Now, when he should have been able to share his satisfactions with comrades, he was alone. It's no wonder he grows morose, and no wonder he feels sorry for himself, she thought.

The Khan interrupted Kreka's sympathetic broodings.

"I have picked this place for my burial site," Attila said. "I will be buried here with Bahgatur, just as you suspected. I make you witness to my choice."

His words fell on the Khatun's ears like a thunderclap.

"Buried? Why do you think of death today? Are you ill?" Kreka asked. She turned to peer at Attila, considering the significance of his words. A furrow appeared between her brows.

"I'm not ill," he said, "only bored with the sameness of life. Will you witness my choice?"

"Of course, I will. Everything will be done as you wish." She sat gazing at her husband with open concern. When she regained her composure, she added, "That is, it will if I'm still alive myself."

"You will be alive long after I am dead," Attila said. "I'm confident of that." He shot her a glance. "Maybe you would wish to rule after my death," he added.

"Be serious," Kreka said. "This can only be one of your nasty jokes, or an attempt to pry information from me. Either way, it's not funny."

"I am serious, never more so," he replied. "Better you than Dengezic, or Ellac."

"If you're sounding me out, I'll repeat my position. You know I won't take public responsibility. I don't care for the role," she said firmly. "I'd never do it."

He looked at her thoughtfully, but let the question drop.

Attila snapped his fingers, "A goblet for the Khatun," he told his steward. "Pour for the Khatun."

"You want to get me cockeyed," she said, smiling.

He smiled back at her.

"All right, I do," he said. "We've never been drunk together, not even when we were young." His eyes sparkled.

"Pour," she said, decisively, reaching for the wine.

They lifted their goblets and grew nostalgic. Wine and kindly feeling flowed between them. They reached the place where murky issues become clear, and from there they went on to that risky spot where reason disappears, and the impossible becomes possible.

At this verge, Attila became talkative.

"Tell me, Kreki," he asked, "what is a necessary war? Is it a war fought for territory? For plunder? You are eloquent, you should be able to tell me."

"You asked me something like that long ago," she said, glancing at him suspiciously. "Don't you remember?"

"What was that?" he asked. He didn't recall ever having asked such a question.

"You asked me why men had to go to war to get what they needed. Those were not your exact words but that's what you meant."

"And you have an answer?"

"I have no answer, but I've thought about it. I think you asked the wrong question."

"What should my question have been?"

"You should have asked why men choose war to get what they need, then act as if there was no other way to get it."

"Well, what other choices are there?" he said.

The Khatun looked into her wine cup as if it might give her the answer.

"What choices are there?" he said, again.

"You're good at mediating," she said, "and you like to match wits. Why not trade wits, instead of lives? Eskam believes the time is coming when you must learn to bargain."

Attila's laugh was unpleasant. "Eskam is a wise man, and a powerful shaman, but he should keep to his haruspice reading. If I tried matching wits without risking lives what would an enemy think? They would think Attila was afraid to go to war. I would be flayed alive, our people along with me."

"You won't change," she said.

"No," he said, "I won't change. I can only be myself. I am a warrior. Don't try to mold me, Kreki," he said, suddenly angry.

"Is there no way to end this life of war?" she said. She sat back on her stool and stared drunkenly into her husband's eyes.

"Of course. Every warlord will pledge not to be the first to attack and it will all be finished," he said.

"You aren't serious," she said.

"I am," he said foolishly, nearly as sodden as his wife.

"Tell the truth, Attila," Kreka said. "You're drunk and so am I. There's no one to hear us. Tell me what you think."

"The truth," he said. "We've seen the truth in our lifetime. An uneasy truce makes a temporary end to war. A truce is better than war, but vows of peace don't hold, no matter how sincere. Two warlords pledge peace, then one dishonors his pledge. Another plots how he can steal the march on the other two, and the battles begin again."

"Then I am right," Kreka said thickly.

"How so?"

"There is no end to strife for those who rule," Kreka said. "No answer for men like you. For many people life holds pleasure as well as duty, but not for you."

"I rule in war," he said, "but the hungers of herds and flocks, the appetites of the people, rule me, Kreki. Staying ahead of hungry, restless tribes is no easy thing."

"You are hostage to the people's needs, but you are a leader, you have impact," the Khatun replied. "This goes deeper."

Attila grunted. "I will tell you, Kreki, the thorn that sticks in me is Rome. It's an empire without sense of proportion. Rome would gobble the earth. The Empire wishes to continue grabbing territory until the earth is nothing but desiccated battlefield. Rome would make true believers of us all. The shaman, Leo, made that clear. We have many gods. We take any who are loyal, treat them as Huns, and let them believe as they wish. With us, a person can keep his private views. The god of this Pope, Leo, is unnatural. He would enslave men in every aspect of their lives. If we desert the old gods our self-respect will shrivel and turn to dust."

"I agree," Kreka said, decidedly. "Nevertheless, I wouldn't devote my life to stopping Rome. You give your life to duty and you believe others can do the same. There is a sad accounting for that kind of life. It drains the joy out of men."

"I have enjoyed my life," Attila said, bridling defensively.

"You have taken your joy in excesses," she retorted. "You've snatched what you could between wars. Too many wars, too many women, and too much wine; these have been your so-called joys."

"Pleasure is hard to find, joy difficult to hang onto," the Khan said, offended. "You shouldn't look down on me, Kreki. Or have you forgotten Adamis?"

"I haven't forgotten," the Khatun said quickly. And after a pause, she said, "I have forgotten nothing."

"Let's not hurt one another," Attila said. "I don't want that. Have I not been a good husband to you? And a good father to your sons? Have I not taken your wishes to heart?"

"You have," she murmured. "You haven't been at fault where I'm concerned."

"You've known of my plans to wed Ildico for some time haven't you?" he said after a short silence.

She nodded.

"Your spies are a match for mine," the Khan said, wishing to compliment her. "We are a match, are we not?"

"We're a match in most things," she admitted. "But my head is spinning. I can't hold my wine as well as you, but then no one drinks like Attila."

He gave Kreka a smile, and went to stand in front of her.

"Why not make peace between us? It would be a step toward these solutions you speak of, eh, Kreki?"

He lifted her up off her stool, and they held to one another, swaying gently over the dry autumn ground in a spirit of resolution.

How curious, she thought, as she stood closed in his arms, she had taken Attila to task over his unending love of war and he had answered by making peace with her.

Kreka was grateful to him, but even drunk she couldn't bring herself to say it.

21

The cold has disappeared and it was a comfortable winter. There was little snow, we had ample fodder for the animals, and no one froze fingers feeding starving creatures.

Suddenly, the grass has sprouted and the foaling is upon us. The women, myself included, have been on the run, but the men have little to occupy them. Ernac is giving signs of restlessness. Though he won't admit it, his time in Italy gave him a taste for war and the excitement of foreign places. His constant need for sex is beginning to irritate me. I suspect he's been listening to Attila's counsel and is considering taking a second wife.

Another wife will end the special closeness Ernac and I have had since childhood, but I'm not uneasy at the thought of other women in Ernac's life. He's been absent a great deal since our marriage, and I have interests of my own.

Before the lambing I was busy with Buqas, and with the repair and building of new looms. Now, of course, the camp is worked-up over the Khan's coming marriage to a Burgundian Princess. The Khatun, and the people of her tents, are determined the celebration will be lavish, and faultless in hospitality. We hear that the whole of the princess' court, several hundred in all, will be in attendance.

The Burgundian's name is Ildico, a woman of incomparable beauty, it's said. Her disposition is said to be as charming as her person and the camp is anxious for a glimpse of her.

One early morning Ernac was at loose ends. He fell eagerly on Beki's suggestion that Buqas should visit the Khatun's tent. Hers was a hasty suggestion, designed to get Buqas out of the way. Beki and Ku were turning out the tents, taking the trappings apart piece by piece, shaking out rugs, and inspecting everything for the smallest flaw.

Ernac and his son left the women to their chores and headed for Kreka's yurt. There, they found the Khan idling away the morning. Attila greeted his grandson with a pleasure born of boredom. Casting about for something amusing to do, Attila decided to be a difficult horse Buqas was breaking to rein. He hitched the child up on his back and ran with him. The game was a success, but after much zealous plunging and bucking the Khan was breathless and he dumped his grandson unceremoniously.

"More Tila," Buqas shrieked at his grandfather. "More Tila. Tila, — Tila, Tila, Tila!"

The child threw himself on the ground and rolled, yelling fiercely. Ernac and Attila were bemused by his display of temper.

Kreka came outside to see what the screaming was about. When she saw it was her grandson, she frowned, hauled Buqas abruptly to his feet, and gave him a smart rap on his bottom.

"Buqas, do not call your grandfather Attila. You must call him the Khan," she said.

The boy looked into his grandmother's eyes uncertainly. He decided the reprimand was serious, and repeated after her, "the Khan."

"That's right, the Khan," the Khatun said, sternly.

"Khan," Buqas said solemnly, staring at Attila from dirty, tear-stained eyes. His grandfather swung Buqas back onto his shoulders and jumped up and down while his grandson beat on his head.

"You indulge this child, Attila," his wife said peevishly. "You'll make an ill-mannered tough out of him. His mother won't appreciate it," she admonished her husband. "Beki won't tolerate such behavior."

"A rowdy game won't hurt him, mother," Ernac said. "He needs rough play. I was too much in the women's tents as a youngster I don't want that for my son."

"It may be that he needs male games, Ernac," Kreka said, "but he needs discipline as well. Your father and I didn't spoil you. No, nor or any of our sons. Attila's gone soft."

"I didn't have time to spoil my sons," Attila said, grinning good-naturedly.

At length, even the Khan tired of the blows that rained on him from Buqas' flailing arms, and he set the boy down. This time he meant it, and there was more wailing, throwing of arms and legs, and rolling in the dirt.

Kreka turned away angrily and retreated into the yurt leaving the men to deal with the unruly child. Beki's timely arrival rescued Attila and Ernac from their shamefaced inability to control Buqas. He was wallowing on the ground, gasping and red-faced, when Beki appeared. She brushed past the men, jerked her son unceremoniously to his feet, and marched him off.

"Find something useful to do with your day," she called back at them.

The Burgundians have arrived. Ildico's court rode into camp late yesterday, and her retinue is impressive. They carry every luxury with them, even private musicians and tutors to teach the princess the Hun tongue! The transporting of her wardrobe required more than twenty horses and mules. They have chosen to set up their tents at the northernmost edge of camp where they can have a degree of privacy. Her people will need what privacy they can get. Little time is left before the ceremonies begin.

"You're not dressed, lady Beki?" came a voice from outside. "Hurry, the others are leaving."

My enthusiastic steward, Taqua, was impatient. He was fussing, pecking at me like an energetic little hen. "Are you not going with the others to see the Princess Ildico?" he cried. He darted inside the yurt, fairly hopping, hoping to infect me with his eagerness. He wanted to be the first to glimpse the princess.

"Not right now, Taqua. I'd rather wait until she's caught her breath," I said firmly.

I could see Taqua's restiveness was not to be contained so I sent him off with a mission. "You go on, Taqua. Observe everything, and report to me what you see. I want to know if her court is as grand as they say. I've been told that even the necks of her maidservants are weighed down with jewels."

I watched as Taqua scurried importantly away. Ildico must certainly be tired, I thought, and no doubt confused as well. I didn't blame her for wanting a bit of privacy. I later learned from Taqua that before she could gain the inside of her tent Ildico was surrounded by curious Huns. The well-meaning crowd couldn't wait to see her, and they pressed close. The Princess was not used to the open ways of Huns, and, not knowing what to make of this throng of grinning faces she shrank back from them.

Taqua said he had a glimpse of her small, white face as the mob pressed in, pushing and shoving. The single glimpse told him that Ildico was young and inexperienced, and also that her beauty has been in no way exaggerated. Ildico's skin, he says, is white as mare's milk, her eyes blue as lake water. But her hair, he told me, really catches the eye. It is red, and falls like a shining ripple of flame down her back to the tops of her thighs. She is long-legged, as tall, perhaps, as Kreka, and slender, altogether an exotic, foreign looking woman, he said.

Before Ildico arrived the Khatun had sought me out to ask if I would be a companion to her while she is with us.

"I can count on you can't I, Beki?" she said. "You will talk to her, make her comfortable. I have to settle all the details of the celebrations. I'll need Ku if you can spare her. No one has been through these wedding routines more often than Ku."

"I'll be happy to do whatever I can," I said. "And you can have Ku. You needn't have asked, you know that."

"I knew you wouldn't let me down, Beki. You're my mainstay," she said. The Khatun hugged me warmly, and scurried off. She was a picture of distraction. I haven't seen her since.

So my job is that of informally welcoming Ildico. The formal welcome will be given at a banquet in her honor the night before her marriage. The ceremony is now only four days away. There will be no time for her to see much beyond camp as she, and her people, will need at least two days for their own preparations.

I found myself a bit unsettled as the time neared for me to approach Ildico's tents. The morning after the court arrived, however, I gathered my entourage and we set off to greet her. I took my personal servants, my excellent steward, Taqua, Laudaricus, the youngest son of Edecon, and, of course, Eskayar, whose beaming face gave me much encouragement.

We found Ildico easy to talk to. She was sweet of nature, but very agitated. She asked many questions about the protocols expected of her and we told her what she needed to know. She was most eager, and naturally so, to learn what sort of person Attila is. She has been preyed on by the usual court gossips, treated to lurid descriptions of Attila, especially that his body is malformed.

Ildico knew Eskayar was one of the Khan's minor wives, and addressed her first halting questions in that direction. She got no answer that satisfied her. Eskayar merely blushed and looked to me for help. Eskayar tries hard. She is genial by nature, but she's not good with words. Ildico then looked to me as the most likely source of information, and thrust question upon question at me. She's not fluent in our tongue, but she expresses herself well.

"Do you know the Khan? Are you close to him?" Ildico shrilled. Her voice is high and reed-like. It's the only unattractive quality she has.

"I believe I am," I said.

"Please, speak truthfully, then," she said with childlike seriousness. "Does he have the torso and head of a horse, and the legs of a goat?"

There were gusts of laughter in the tent. I didn't wish Ildico to think we were impolite, and I quickly hushed the servants.

"What you heard is not true, Ildico," I said. "You needn't fear. But you'll see for yourself soon enough. There would be no point in lying, would there?"

"But," she said, in her nasal voice, "I heard it from the mouths of people who have seen him."

"I don't know who these informants are, or why they would describe Attila this way. I can't think why anyone would tell you such things. In any case they are mistaken," I reassured her.

"He looks like any Hun warrior," I went on. "He's short of stature, heavy of chest and shoulder, his hair is black, and pulled into a topknot according to a warrior's custom. I must tell you, Ildico, that Attila is my adopted father. To me, he seems the handsomest of men. I've had nothing from him but kindness. I don't deny he's terrible in war, but he's known to indulge his wives and family. In our camps wellborn women have a great deal of freedom and, within reason, your wishes will be respected. You will not be ill-treated, I promise you."

Ildico touched my hand. "Thank you," she said simply. Her pale, soft eyes shone. They spoke as loudly as if she'd shouted her thanks.

"It's generous of you to share your views of Attila with me. I can't thank you enough. I've been unbearably afraid. The stories I heard about the Khan so unsettled my nerves I thought of bolting and running for home on the trip here. You've set my mind at ease. I'm grateful to you."

"I'm more than pleased to be able to correct the gossip," I said, smiling. I congratulated Ildico on her coming marriage, and we dropped the question of Attila's supposed malformations.

The Princess seemed genuinely relieved, apparently accepting of my version of her future husband. She became bubbly, and chattered brightly of the differences she'd noticed between Hun dress and that of her own people. We passed the morning pleasantly, comparing customs and manners. Early in the afternoon Ildico grew tired, and we excused ourselves; we to our daily tasks, and she to her wedding preparations. She may be featherbrained, but Ildico is affable. Once the formalities are over she'll relax and it should be refreshing to have her here.

The day following the wedding had been extraordinarily quiet. Everyone was exhausted from the ceremonies and the merrymaking. No one in camp stirred before midday, and even then the waking was painful. It was late in the afternoon when I heard the first disconcerting waves of sound. There was a hubbub emanating from the direction of Idico's tents.

I rolled from my couch and peered out. I saw Ku billowing toward my tent like a pale cyclone. The blood had drained from her florid face. Her mouth worked, but no sound came from her throat. It was as if the power of speech had been snatched out of her.

I grabbed her and shook her until her teeth rattled. Still Ku didn't speak. I was so alarmed by the look of her that I finally gave her a ringing blow to the head. Instead of recovering her senses Ku collapsed. Her eyes rolled in her head, and she fell to the floor sobbing.

A black tide began to well in my chest.

"What's the matter with you?" I screeched. "What is it? Is it Ernac? Has something happened to my husband?"

She moaned. "Oh, no, oh, no, it's the Khan. It's the Khan."

This was how I learned of the death of Attila.

22

Berichus rolled over and sat up. His head was buzzing. He heard frantic voices. What was going on?

"Lord Berichus! Lord Berichus!"

The guard at the door was shouting at him.

"What is this? Why do you disturb me?" Berichus yelled out.

"Please, get up! You're needed in Princess Ildico's tent, my lord. It's the Khan," the guard managed, his voice shaking.

Berichus' muddled head didn't take in the sense of his words, but the panic in the man's voice was unmistakable. Something dreadful had happened. Berichus, himself, was suddenly struck with terror. He grabbed up his sword and ran straight for the northern end of camp.

The Khan's Chief Commander charged furiously into Ildico's tent. He was stopped by an unbelievable sight.

The new bride was lying outstretched atop Attila's inert body, her flaming hair spread wildly across his chest. It was matted with drying blood, and she was wailing piteously. Her head dangled and twisted to the side. Her face was hidden by a scrap of embroidered linen pulled over her like a mourning veil.

The Khan lay face up, his head fallen back onto the pillows of the wedding couch. Smears of dark blood were crusted on his throat, and trickles had seeped into his tunic, staining his mouth and beard.

Berichus moved with pure instinct. He lunged forward, and lifted his sword to decapitate the woman. He would have had her head off in the instant, but for a swift, powerful arm that reached from behind and stayed him.

"No, Berichus," Ernac commanded, restraining the officer with difficulty. "Listen to me! Ildico did nothing. Attila passed out from too much wine. He had a nosebleed and strangled in the stream of his own blood."

"Surely, he can be saved. He can't be dead," Berichus exclaimed, unbelieving. "We must get him up."

Ernac shook his head.

"He's been dead for some time. When there was no sound from the bridal chamber by midday, the guards broke in. This is what they found. We can do nothing," Ernac replied.

The shock of it hit Berichus and he fell silent.

"We must get his body out and into his own tent. I'll inform the Khatun," Ernac went on, his voice hard.

There was a rustle from the doorway. Edecon rushed in and saw Attila's colorless face resting among the pillows. He gasped and fell to his knees. Like Ku, the breath seemed to have been sucked out of him. He turned to Ernac, grasping for something to steady himself. Ernac reached out and took Edecon's clammy, trembling hand.

His eyes pleaded with Ernac, asking that the scene be erased, that it should not be true.

"I'm sorry, Edecon," Ernac said. "You see how it is.

Edecon nodded weakly.

"We cannot linger," Ernac continued urgently. "We have work to do, my friend. We must be about it. We can't appear indecisive."

Again Edecon nodded.

"There can be no rumors of foul play," Ernac said. "We can't have any harm come to Ildico. We will say Ildico's father is gravely ill, and that her presence is required at home. As soon as the Khan is safe in his tomb, she leaves. You, and my father, have taught me well, Edecon. Now my lessons must be put to use."

Ernac turned and left without looking again on his father's face.

For me, the days following Attila's death are a blur.

Ku took over Buqas' care. I helped with the arrangements wherever possible. Had the situation been left to me things would have moved at the pace of an inchworm. I couldn't grasp it. I couldn't believe Attila was truly gone, and I wasn't the only one. People moved about the camp as in a dream.

It was the Khatun who held us together. Kreka made the decisions. She gave orders for the burial preparations, and my husband was beside her in everything. Ernac's staunch nature has been a tremendous comfort to all of us, most especially to Edecon, who has turned overnight from an aging soldier into a doddering old man.

Ildico is scarcely in her right mind. Ernac says that after a decent period of mourning she'll be sent back to her own people. Indeed, that will be best. Here, she has no one except her serving people, and without the protection of the Khan she would be prey for any man looking to gain from a political marriage with the widow.

I witnessed the preparations. I saw Attila lying on his burial platform, and, still, it was not real. To see Attila laid out for burial, to see him sleeping beneath the black and red of his tents, was not something I thought I would ever witness. It was a spectral scene. But, inevitably, the *strava* began and the Khan was carried to his grave. The people of his household went on foot, straggling behind the warriors.

The voices of the men lifted in the Khan's funeral dirge, and the echoing sounds gave a sad dignity to their words. They slashed their faces and let the blood run, as they circled ever closer to the catafalque to surround the body of their lord. A deep chorus of grief welled up through the dirges.

Over the men's chants, the women's voices came keening. Their high, ululating notes pierced the clear air, and pierced our hearts as well.

A lonely wind swept over the funeral cortege.

> Attila, the great king of the Huns,
> the son of Mundzucus,
> the ruler of the most courageous tribes;
> enjoying such power as had been unheard of before him,
> he possessed the Scythian and Germanic kingdoms alone
> and terrorized both empires of the Roman world
> after conquering their cities, and

> placated by their entreaties
> that the rest might not be laid open to plunder
> he accepted an annual tribute.
> After he had achieved all this with great success
> he died, not of an enemy's wound, not betrayed by friends,
> in the midst of his unscathed people, happy and gay,
> without any feeling of pain.
> Who therefore would think that this was death
> which nobody considers to demand revenge?

The last lines of this dirge have stayed with me.

'Who therefore would think that this was death which nobody considers to demand revenge?'

In grief and joy, we celebrated, and we mourned. With reveling and lamentation we said good-bye. The shamans had washed and dressed their lord, and three coffins surrounded him. His favorite weapons, and regalia of imperial stamp were beside him. The Khan's *tamga* was embroidered on the silks, and when they saw his sign the warriors slashed their flesh with renewed fervor.

The Khan's personal insignia was flown for the last time. The ranks of banners emblazoned with his emblem were raised, and a thousand red eagle's wings gave salute as the men circled the moving catafalque.

The Great Khan was placed inside his tomb after nightfall. Only Kreka and Berichus returned. His advisors chose to stay with him. Edecon, naturally, joined him. Without the Khan he would have been a lost soul. Eskam, in spite of his fierce loyalty to the Khatun, declared his fate tied to the Khan, and he too followed Attila into the land of eternal seasons.

Eskayar mourns doubly. She has lost both husband and father. It falls to Ernac to take her as second wife when her mourning is over. All of Attila's wives will eventually be Ernac's responsibility. Thank the Great Tngri I get along with Eskayar. A second wife must come soon, and I couldn't choose one more to my liking. I wish my only worry was a second wife for my husband. I might have been upset by Ernac taking a second wife so soon, now, that is insignificant.

During this period of mourning we exist inside a thick forest of bewilderment and uncertainty. Nothing can be settled officially. The real decisions are still to be made. Even after the mourning period is over I see confusion and uncertainty ahead of us.

Who will be named Khan? This is the question everyone is asking.

Ernac is concerned. He's afraid Dengezic may move to call a *quiriltai* and have himself declared Khan. So far only vague talk comes to us about his plans. Ernac is the official heir, and the Khan's personal choice, though loyalties are divided. Already, there are factions supporting the claims of Ellac and Dengezic that are openly active. Uzindur and Ebnedzar hover impatiently, waiting to pick at the leavings. They will divide what remains after the large territories have been parceled out.

Attila's death has flattened us. It's as if a black night fell over us in the middle of a sunny day. His death has taken the heart out of us. In one impossible stroke of ill-fortune our security has been ripped away. I still imagine I will see him ride into camp in a flurry of activity, or come upon him striding out of his yurt, a cheerful laugh of greeting trailing behind him.

Less than ten suns ago our lives were normal, now we are children without a father. Attila was our stability. Life cannot be the same without him. The camp is gripped in a paralysis of disbelief.

In the days after Attila's death Kreka hadn't been able to weep. The enormity of the loss froze the tears inside her. The Khatun kept to her yurt and spurned offers of company. After Attila's burial Beki sent Ku around to her, begging that her daughter-in-law, her adopted daughter, might pay her respects. The Khatun couldn't refuse.

As she waited for Beki the tears came, and she greeted her with a countenance swollen by grief. Beki barely recognized her. Waving her to a seat, Kreka contrived a cracked smile.

The Khatun's attempt at courtesy was painful. I wasn't sure what to say to her and I jumped in awkwardly.

"You've been unbelievably strong," I said. "It's you who kept us from crumbling. I'd like to comfort you, but I don't know how."

"Don't try," the Khatun said gruffly. "Just sit with me."

I managed, for what seemed an age, to hold my tongue. Tears were coursing down the Khatun's cheeks, soaking her waist, running down onto her hands. Her strong fingers were nestled in her lap, exhausted.

"How did you imagine this? How did you think he would die?" I finally said.

My question was a selfish one. I have imagined Ernac's death more often and more vividly than most young wives would. I had seen Ernac so ill that he had died in my head many times over.

Kreka laughed. It was a sound more shocking than her shattered smile.

"I pictured more than one scene," she said, "but not, I must admit, the scene that happened."

"You imagined he would die in war," I said.

The Khatun tried to focus on Beki's question, and her tears began to dry.

"I suppose," she said at length, "that war was first on my list. But the Khan was a man of more than one weakness, and his weaknesses were all dangerous."

I said nothing. I waited, my face a careful mask, hoping she would go on, and eventually she did.

"He was a great warrior, but he was not a great man," she said. Then, she added, "He was a tough man to deal with."

I wanted, as I had so many times in the past, to defend Attila from Kreka's criticism, but I swallowed the impulse. Instead, I said, "You were devoted to him, I know that."

This brought a ragged sigh from the Khatun.

"Oh, yes, I was devoted to him, that much is certain. But devotion can be a burden. I was weighed down by it. My devotion nearly did me in. Don't misunderstand me, Beki, Attila wasn't a vicious man. I've known vicious men, and the Khan wasn't one of them."

Kreka looked at me. She met my gaze for the first time since I entered the yurt, and I saw a mix of grief and melancholy in her eyes. It's hard on her, but she's dealing with it, I thought.

"War, wine, and women," she said. "Common failings of men. Amusing, really."

"What do you mean?" I said, frowning heavily. "I don't see the humor."

"War, wine, and women," she repeated. "Such ordinary, unattractive weaknesses, such folly in a man who revered discipline and duty if he revered anything."

She lowered her eyes. After a moment she raised them, and there was anger in them. "His excesses were stupid. I told him so more than once," she exclaimed passionately.

"It was the least dangerous of his weaknesses that killed him," I said.

Her eyes flew open. "That is arguable," was her quick retort.

I hid my smile. Kreka would recover. Her ability to view events without blinking, even what affects her most personally, is one of her strongest assets.

"And what are your weaknesses, Khatun Kreka?" I asked.

She nodded, as if the answer was plain.

"My greatest weakness has just been carried off to rest forever in his tomb," Kreka said, matter-of-factly.

"Attila was my soft spot. I forgave him too much. I forgave things that shouldn't be forgiven. But I do not forget them," she said.

"What of the good?" I asked. "Do you forget there was good in him?"

"Yes," she said, "there was good in him. You're right, of course. I tend to forget the good in him. Now that he's dead maybe it will come back to me. When we were very young..." she began, then she stopped.

"When you were young?" I prompted.

"Never mind," she said, dismissing my question. "When people get older, Beki, their minds go to their youth. They become garrulous. But the youth of others is a bore. Only those who lived it find it interesting. The past is foolish prattle, meaningless, unless it belongs to you."

"You never bore me, Kreka," I said honestly.

"Someday, then," she said. "Someday I'll speak of these things. Not now. Now, I need sleep. I sleep a great deal these days."

"And you deserve it," I said, automatically.

"Perhaps I do, perhaps I don't," she said. "I have much to settle within myself, too much to be without sleep."

"Can I ask something?" I said. "Would you answer one question for me?"

"What is it?" she said wearily.

"I wouldn't ask, but it's important to Ernac."

"Well, then, ask."

"In Italy," I said, "did Attila have the victory he claimed, or was his proclamation hollow? His armies took great losses, and he didn't get to Rome. He didn't even try to take Rome, and Marcian still refuses to pay tribute. It seems to me the Khan came out of that campaign less than the powerful warlord he wished the soldiers to believe."

"I was right about you," the Khatun said, looking past, instead of, at me. "You are the perfect wife for Ernac. You'll be a great help and support to him. And he will need it."

"What do you mean, he'll need it?" I said.

"My own life hasn't been easy, Beki, but I don't envy you yours. I have lived mine, you must live yours," she said enigmatically.

"But my question. You haven't answered me," I persisted.

"I can't," she said. "I don't know. The last time my husband and I talked alone we spoke of war only in general terms. We spoke mostly of private things that day."

The Khatun smiled. Splendid memories of a wine-soaked afternoon near Bahgatur's grave filled her head. That place was a sacred spot, the resting place of her beloved.

"Well," I said, "it's a pity he died before his final victory. He would have conquered Rome. He would have gone on. There would have been another victory, and another, until he was Khan of Rome."

"Or he would have gone on to final defeat. At least he was spared that," Kreka said.

Some habitual perversity in her nature, I thought, insists that she disparage him even after he's dead.

"I don't believe that. He would not have been defeated," I said stoutly.

My antipathy broke through. "He would have conquered, or died trying," I said. "Attila was invincible. He would have saved us from Rome."

Kreka looked at me, transfixed. Her thoughts were directed not to me, but to her husband.

"He couldn't have saved us, Beki. He couldn't save himself. No matter now," she said.

"Attila once told me death would be his saviour, Beki. Death, he said, was the only saviour he believed in."

"That doesn't sound like Attila!" I exclaimed.

"Attila loved life, it's true," she said. "But he was a realist. He saw more clearly than most men."

Kreka stood and began to pace, as she does when she's thinking.

As if she'd discovered some unnamed source of decay in life itself, she said, "His life was as bitter as it was sweet. Whatever he did, whatever he may have been, he was lovable. I cared nothing about the wars. I cared about him. He would have life completely on his own terms. He couldn't have it, and that caused suffering for those close to him. Do you see?"

I did see, but I knew there was more. Kreka makes a fuss about Attila living on his own terms because she does the same. She, also, is both good and bad. The Khatun has taken up sword and bow in more than one war. She's had moments of glorying in war. This woman poisoned her own son in order to destroy an enemy, yet she manages to make it seem she was merely protecting the Khan's interests.

Kreka is no stranger to violence, or to politics, I thought. In spite of her protests she is political. She may not wish to rule, but she's not averse to wielding power when it suits her. Kreka and Attila knew how to wield power; now that power passes to others.

Kreka stopped pacing and looked at me.

"Don't seek Attila in other men, Beki," she said. "You won't find him in Ernac, or in anyone else. Attila is dead."

I flushed. The Khatun had caught me out once more.

Kreka sat down, placed her head next to mine in comradely fashion, and thwacked me on the knee.

"Ah!" she exclaimed. "It's lucky you weren't of an age to vie with me for Attila."

The Khatun's eyes flashed cold and dark, and her voice crackled with energy.

"I would have won Attila," she said, with satisfaction, "but I would have lost a friend."

I left her tent as befuddled as when I entered. I didn't get anything from her that could alleviate my fears. The future remains as murky as ever.

Kreka might have been speaking of Ernac's future, and of mine. I admit her advice is sound, but ours will be a different time. Who knows what storms will swoop down on us, or how we will deal with them.

Not, perhaps, as well as the Khan and the Khatun dealt with theirs. It would be no exaggeration to say they succeeded. I'll follow Kreka's advice in one thing at least, I'll not go looking for Attila in other men.

And that will not be easy, I thought.

The Khan was too large a presence, he spoiled us for other leaders. With him, goes the confidence he inspired. Tremendous energy flowed from him. He filled people with his spirit. The foundation of our belief in ourselves is gone. A man such as Attila is a security for his people while he lives, but when he dies he leaves the survivors crippled.

No one is equipped to take the place of the Khan. Much as I admire my husband, and I do have every confidence in him, I know he's no Attila. The omens, and the haruspice, lied. Ernac will not recover the kingdom of the Khan, nor will any of his sons. My future lies with Ernac, not with the kingdom. Until the day Attila died that simple fact hadn't dawned on me.

I felt a sudden, uneasy urgency. I wanted my child. I wanted to gather Buqas in my arms, to huddle with him inside my own tent. The light seemed unnaturally dim and a film started to cloud my eyes.

When I reached my yurt Buqas ran to me. His fat arms wound happily around my neck, his smooth face pressed against mine. I held him close, and my eyes cleared.

After Our Story Ends

Ellac was the first of the brothers to die. I can't say I mourned him, he was much older than Ernac and I didn't really know him. I saw him only on state occasions, and didn't care much for what I saw then.

At the battle of Nedao, one year after Attila's death, the eldest of Attila's sons fell to Ardaric and his Gepids. Ellac was but one more casualty of Attila's death, a casualty, really, of his own ineptitude. Except for the tribes under the leadership of Dengezic and Ernac, our warriors have remained leaderless since the Khan's death. They are broken men, acting from confusion, rushing hither and thither in ill-formed raiding parties that end predictably. They've become as they were before Attila, swords up for hire to the Empire. Even before the battle of Nedao, the core of the Khan's armies had disintegrated.

There is much irony in the fact that Attila did not live to see what happened to his enemies. Two of them had well-deserved reckonings. Only a year after the Khan died Aëtius was assassinated by order of Valentinian, and six moons after Aëtius' death Valentinian, himself, fell victim to a palace conspiracy. He was run through by his own palace guards. It would have been extremely satisfying for Attila had he known what happened to them. I wish he had lived to see their ill-fated end.

But there are more recent deaths. Last year, seventeen years after Attila died, Dengezic was killed. His head was carried on a pole through the main thoroughfares of Constantinople and fixed on a post in the Circus for viewing. We were told the whole city turned out to see the head of the Khan's son stuck up on a post. The brothers,

Uzindur and Ebnedzar, the only other heirs of Attila, also fell in battle. All are gone except Ernac.

Soon after the Khan's death Dengezic dropped his negotiations with the Emperor Marcian, and moved his own armies to the north above the Pontus Euxinus toward the River Don. Dengezic was smart to take that course. Perhaps his spies found out what was in store for him if he stayed in the homeland. My husband has told me what he could not have while Attila lived. The Khan, long ago, instructed Ernac to have Dengezic killed should he make any move to take over in the homeland.

After Dengezic moved to the north he and Ernac managed to get along fairly well for a time. Together, they attempted to have the market at Naissus reopened for trade as in former times. But without Attila here to keep the pressure on, Rome would not agree. Dengezic also tried to mount several campaigns against the Goths, but they failed. He was harsh and impolitic in his dealings with his fellows. He had neither the skill nor the charm of his father.

Before they died, Uzindur and Ebnedzar operated for a time farther west, nearer to Gaul. I was sorry to hear of Ebnedzar's death. I wasn't close to him, but I admired him. He carried himself a bit like the Khan. Had he been one of Kreka's sons, and a legitimate heir, he might have been a notable leader.

We — that is, the Huns under my husband's command — are still headquartered in the Dobrogea, southeast of Attila's home camps. After the Khan's death Ernac brought us here, and here we remain. It has been a fertile pasture. It has fed and nourished our animals well these past seventeen years.

As I look around today so many faces are gone from us that I feel old myself. The men and women I grew up with have grown children, and those of Attila's and Kreka's time are dying off. The cripple, Baldin, is still alive, but he sits staring. No longer does he cut capers of excitement at the latest morsels of gossip. And Ku is gone from us, dead these five years. I sometimes long to see her.

Strangely, though, I miss Kreka more than anyone.

When I list the dead, I should mention my first son, Buqas. My firstborn was taken by a fall from his horse just before his fifth year, a bare three years after the Khan's death.

My other children, three living sons and two living daughters, are grown. Their lives no longer concern me directly. My daughters have their own husbands, their own tents and flocks, and have had for several seasons. My sons have been given into the care of Ernac's chief steward for their training. I am free of caring for others, and I'm glad of it. Being constantly answerable for the safety and well-being of others is a heavy burden.

Since my children are gone a new world has opened for me. It's something I had no thought of taking on, and no notion I was destined for. I've become a keeper of our history. Kreka was right in this, as in so much else. My curiosity, and my habit of reflecting on what I see, have been useful.

To be the bearer of history is a position of honor. Though, in some measure, all stories are a devising of the teller, I hope I have the wit not to overdo my own views. I want to deal fairly with events as I know them, but I also want to be able to call up something of the flavor of Attila's time.

It was on the occasion of Kreka's death two full seasons ago that I understood I was to become a carrier of our history.

Adamis had called me out in the middle of the night, begging me come to the Khatun's tent.

"She'll let no one near her. She's weak, Beki," he told me. His handsome face was pinched with worry. One of the Khatun's first official acts following the Khan's funeral was to call her former steward back into her service. Now, he never leaves her side.

I had offered my help when she first fell ill, but Kreka would allow no one but Adamis to tend her. He was in attendance day and night, and he was exhausted.

"The sickness now attacks her lungs," he said dispiritedly. "The coughing came on suddenly, so savagely I'm unable to contain it. She takes no nourishment. These last two days she's been unable to rise, and barely able to sit up."

I couldn't refuse the pleading in Adamis's eyes and I went with him.

A small, wasted figure greeted me from the quilts. I tried to hide my shock at the sight of her. The Khatun was flushed, and coughing violently. I could see Adamis' report of her condition hadn't been overstated.

Surprisingly, she appeared glad to see me.

"Beki, I'm pleased you came," she said between spasms.

"What can I do for you, Khatun? I'm sorry to see you so ill," I said, without hesitation.

"I appreciate your candor," she answered. "I'm dying, Beki. There's nothing you can do. Adamis will see to my comfort. He knows what to do."

"Do you want to talk?" I said.

"Yes," she whispered. "But you must bear with me. I will be tedious."

I inclined my head, indicating my willingness to be patient.

"I know you don't approve of me, Beki," Kreka said, fixing me with her eyes. Her gaze, at least, was as strong as ever.

I wriggled uncomfortably, waving my hands in a poor attempt at disagreement.

"Please, don't make me laugh. I'll die coughing before I can speak," the Khatun joked.

I waited quietly for her to go on at her own pace.

"You tried not to judge me, Beki, but you did," she said quietly.

She patted my hand. "It's all right. I judged in my time. You haven't allowed, though, that tragedy comes to everyone."

"I don't know what you mean," I said.

"Don't blame Ernac for Buqas' death, Beki," the Khatun said. "No one is to blame. His father didn't take Buqas off on a hunt planning to kill him. His death was an accident. You know Ernac is not a harsh man. He was crushed by his son's death."

"Buqas was too young to go on a hunt," I said, stung by this abrupt reopening of a wound I had thought healed. "He hadn't even five summers. It was Ernac's fault. He shouldn't have taken him."

"Don't continue to hold this against him. Your disapproval hurts him," she said.

Kreka was short of breath, speaking slowly. "Ernac loves you, Beki. He's hurt by your withdrawal from him. It's a dozen years since Buqas was killed. Let it go."

"You didn't lose your firstborn," I said heatedly. "You don't know how it feels. You, of all people, have no right to counsel me to forgive my husband. You never forgave the Khan in the slightest thing."

Adamis gave me a warning glance and lifted a bowl of broth to the Khatun's mouth. She sipped the liquid and gained the strength to go on.

"No, I didn't lose my firstborn, but I lost others," the Khatun declared. She raised herself on one elbow and said vehemently, "I have the same feelings you have. You've never given me credit for ordinary feeling. Give me credit now."

Fleetingly, I was reminded that I, too, am willful, and I tried to quell my hostility.

"I'm a selfish woman, I know that," Kreka said.

I raised a weak hand to disagree, but she slapped it down. She was sick in body, but Kreka's spirit was as dominant as ever.

"Compared to Attila," she said, "I'm a cold-blooded person. I've seen unselfishness, and I am selfish."

I couldn't control my mouth. I interrupted her.

"Once, after the Khan died you wanted to tell me something, something about the two of you when you were young," I said. "Will you tell me now?"

Adamis began wringing his hands, hovering protectively. She waved him off. "Let me talk," she commanded. "I've little time left. I'll say what I want."

"Ahhhh," she said, falling back on her couch. "That's better. My mind wanders. What was I saying?"

"You were talking about Attila, about the two of you when you were young," I pressed her.

Kreka's mouth widened, and she produced one of her glorious smiles.

"Of course," she said. "I was telling you about that cold night. Ellac was a tiny thing, born at the beginning of the season of frozen grass. I was exhausted from lack of sleep and from nursing. Attila had to drag me outside. He came for me, in a cold so deep that the wood creaked and complained with it. The ice snapped the center pole in the yurt. Attila roused me from the warmth of a bottomless sleep, and I heartily resisted going. Nevertheless he would take me.

"'You must see something,' he said."

She stopped, breathless, and Adamis appeared from the shadows to hold her. After a silence she continued, her words slurred and stuporous. Adamis has drugged her broth, I thought, he means to save her strength.

He propped the dying woman in his arms so she could continue her story. It was a tender scene.

When she took up the tale it had fallen in pieces, and I had difficulty making sense of it.

"We sat with him in the numbing cold of that night," she said.

"Sat with who?" I said.

"The newborn, the foal whose dam had died," she said, impatiently.

"He was a lovely babe, Beki. Attila found a mare for him, but she was troublesome, and he ended by cuddling the gangly creature himself. He held him close, coaxing the mare to nurse him. I wasn't much help. I could think of nothing but warming myself back in my yurt. The morning sun had cracked the sky when at last he got the mare to take him. You would have thought Attila, himself, had given birth to that foal," she said.

"He watched him guzzling at her tits, and he yelled in triumph," she went on. 'Is he not beautiful. Is he not beautiful?' he whooped."

The Khatun chuckled.

"The hideously cruel Khan, the fearful demon Khan," she said, "reveling in the life he'd saved."

Kreka's head swayed in Adamis' arms. She sagged, yet memory forced her awake.

"What exuberance he had then," she said. "The blood ran so full in him. He roared, hoisted me over his shoulder, and ran with me, shouting like a madman. He dumped me on the sleeping couch inside our tent. And, then, what lovemaking!"

Her eyes widened at the memory.

"That foal," she said, finally, "was the sire to Bahgatur."

The Khatun was exhausted, but she had another confidence to share.

"I discovered what it was to trust. I gave myself over to Attila's steadfast nature. I loved him for what he didn't know he'd done. He had answered a need of the moment. He felt neither cold, nor pain. He forgot himself completely."

She rambled on, floating.

"We love, we hate, we act. One round, then another, and another. He lost hope, that's what killed him," she gasped.

"You mean Attila," I said.

She smiled tremulously. "You see, I've become garrulous," she said.

Then, "You must tell this after me," she said. "Else why did I bother to recount it?"

She leaned toward me and her burning face touched mine. "He found no forgiveness in his life, Beki," she said. "No one forgave him anything. Certainly, I did not. I pray he has found forgiveness in the land of eternal seasons."

Kreka was becoming agitated. I tried to soothe her, but her hands grabbed at mine in a nameless questioning.

"Who knew him?" she said.

"You did. You knew him," I said.

I found I could answer her with assurance.

"Yes," she said. Death rumbled in her voice.

"We battled one another; we stood together against everyone else. It was a grand partnership, but we were fated to be hard on one another. We lived in troubled days."

Her throat constricted, strangling her.

"Did I say it? Did I say it?" she whispered.

"What?" I asked. "Did you say what?"

"How I treasured him, how precious his very being was to me, the joy I had in his presence. Did I say it?" she said. A savage stab of distress dilated her pupils. Her agony appeared fathomless.

Finally, I felt compassion. I pitied her, lying helpless, facing death, and tortured by regret. I caught my breath and unwonted tears spilled down my cheeks.

She tried once more, but speech failed her. In spite of Adamis' strong arms under her the Khatun's head gave way. Her body lolled awkwardly, insensible to the coughing spell that rattled her bones.

Adamis signed that he wanted me to leave. I gave no argument. That was the last time I saw her. Kreka died the following day.

Ernac came to tell me of his mother's death.

"The Khatun is dead," he said, simply.

I did take him in my arms, then, and if I didn't entirely forgive him for the death of my firstborn we are friends once more, as well as man and wife. It's no use to say what might have happened. Buqas died. We go on.

Yet nothing shines as it did. There is no way to explain what Kreka and Attila were. Simply put, no woman is the Khatun, no man is the Khan — nor will be. The fortunes of the time, and the stuff of the men, didn't favor Attila's sons. If any of them had had Attila's substance the story of the Huns following his death would be a happy one, and it is not.

All is not gone, of course. We have our flocks, our herds, the freedom of our camps. We have no real cause for complaint, but it is not the world we knew under the Great Khan. The truth of that day is not ours, and our children's truth will be different still. Those days had clarity and bright promise.

The intervening seasons have given me independence, and confidence in my opinions. I'm used to having my own way these days. Last night, talking to my husband, I was open in my disapproval of Kreka's unsparing attitude toward Attila. I did feel for her at the time of her death, but as I thought back on it I remembered how roughly she treated him. After more than seventeen years that still upsets me.

"She let nothing pass," I said to Ernac. "She called him on everything, took him to task on every issue. She never let up on him."

I raved on, criticizing Kreka and her implacable nature. Ernac put up with my tirade for awhile, but finally, in his firm, quiet way he stopped me.

"What would you have done, Beki?" he challenged me sternly. "You are as unforgiving and unsparing of Mother Kreka as she was of Attila. Tell me, had you been Khatun, first wife of the great and formidable Khan, how would you have handled him?"

I stared blank-faced at my husband. The best I could offer was a frustrated shake of my head.

In shadowless nights when the moon hides herself from the earth I lie in darkness picturing the vitality on Attila's face. I feel once more the bitter taste of loss, and, as I did the day he died, I grieve for him.

But it was Kreka, not me, who posed the final question. Who knew Attila? Who knew what he was?

Who knew Kreka, for that matter? She was a healer, a seer. More truly even than Eskam she saw the future. She knew the kingdom would follow the Khan into his tomb, the pieces falling, like bone, into blowing dust. What Attila fought to unite, his sons could not hold together.

The Khan and the Khatun were born to ride the currents. No matter what untested wind touched their lives they found the strength and resilience to ride it to the ground until the final storm took them to the skies. I am a heavier seed. I labor to illuminate what they were and pass along what I can of their essence.

I would say, to those who wish to hear, that Kreka and Attila lived honest lives. Attila did not tolerate dishonesty, and we learned to honor his way. Those who were willing to work, those who respected the rights of others, were safe under Attila's rule. Even the little Persian groom, Tadiqin, who informed for Attila during his last years, became a person of property. Being trustworthy, he prospered.

My father and mother were uncompromising. They didn't turn away from what was meted out to them and they mastered their lives as well as anyone can hope to do.

But as Kreka said, the past is boring to those who took no part in making it. When I reach a garrulous old age I'll be lucky to find any sympathetic ear. When the time comes I hope someone will witness what I wish to say as I once listened to the Khatun.

Stories go on in a kinship that grows even after death. My adopted mother and father live inside me, though I am but a small part of what they planted. I don't know whether they were as large as we saw them. That is for others to decide. I have tried to understand what it was in them that was indelible. I've come to believe their mark was passion. They had intense feeling, for one another, indeed, for everything they touched. They cared mightily for the people, and for the land.

They reminded us how rich we are, blessed by the bounty given to us by Etugen Eke, our Earth-Mother. Her gifts, just as the gifts Attila and Kreka gave us, cannot be measured. The lessons of their lives is an awareness not for words.

The Khan, and the Khatun, had exceptional vigor and nerve. They pulled us along with them into a place of heightened awareness. Now, raiding and war go on as ever, but there is no one to stir the imagination. We live on a tasteless ground of daily scratchings and purposeless concerns.

I sometimes walk out at dusk as Kreka did when she was pondering a problem. On such evenings the land speaks to me. She must also have heard these everlasting whispers. Yet I cannot say what filled her head as she wandered here.

That may be just as well. And, perhaps, it's just as well there are few beings such as Kreka and Attila, beings so forceful they seem to challenge the timeless ways of earth.

Days like ours, a time filled with prosaic concerns, would not have suited them. Attila liked to say he was a common soldier, and Kreka called herself an ordinary woman. In trying not to boast, they lied about themselves.

Attila was an uncommon man; Kreka was an uncommon woman. They were a perfect fit to the bold world of their time.

21-75